3/''

WASHOE COUNTY LIBRARY

3 1235 03516 606

D0437112

IV

A FRIEND OF THE FAMILY

Also by LAUREN GRODSTEIN

The Best of Animals
Reproduction Is the Flaw of Love

A
FRIEND
OF
THE
FAMILY

a novel by
LAUREN GRODSTEIN

ALGONQUIN BOOKS
OF CHAPEL HILL
2009

Published by

ALGONQUIN BOOKS OF CHAPEL HILL

Post Office Box 2225

Chapel Hill, North Carolina 27515-2225

a division of

WORKMAN PUBLISHING

225 Varick Street

New York, New York 10014

© 2009 by Lauren Grodstein.

All rights reserved.

Printed in the United States of America.

Published simultaneously in Canada by Thomas Allen & Son Limited.

Design by Laura Williams.

This is a work of fiction. While, as in all fiction, the literary perceptions and insights are based on experience, all names, characters, places, and incidents either are products of the author's imagination or are used fictitiously.

LIBRARY OF CONGRESS CATALOGING-IN-PUBLICATION DATA

Grodstein, Lauren.

A friend of the family : a novel / by Lauren Grodstein.—1st ed.

p. cm.

ISBN 978-1-56512-916-0

1. Suburban life—New Jersey—Fiction.   2. Fathers and sons—Fiction.

3. Psychological fiction.   I. Title.

PS3607.R63F75 2009

813'.6—dc22   2009024476

10 9 8 7 6 5 4 3 2 1

First Edition

For Nathaniel
and in memory of his great-grandparents

A FRIEND OF THE FAMILY

CHAPTER ONE

THESE DAYS, WHEN people ask how I'm doing—some of them still ask, you'd be surprised—I shrug and say, as manfully as I can, "Much better than you'd think." And this is true. I am fed, I am clothed, I still have a few patients, the Nets are winning, and my mother, thank God, has finally agreed to the assisted-living place in Rockland. And I have a home, of sorts—the room we built for Alec above the garage so that he could pursue his oil painting with the firm scaffold of our love and money under his feet. God forbid that Alec should ever have felt unsupported—that we should show dismay at his dropping out of Hampshire after three semesters and almost sixty thousand dollars of tuition, books, board, and other proofs of parental esteem. Sixty thousand dollars vanished—puff—like smoke; our son fails out of a college that *doesn't even give grades,* and in response we build him an art studio above our garage. And here's the kicker: we were happy to do it. This was one of many lessons we took from the plight of our friends Joe and Iris Stern, whose daughter Laura was lost to them once, and is again, now.

My new home, the studio, is floored in gray, paint-speckled linoleum. Alec's old drawing table sits in the corner, next to a double-sized futon buried under a pile of airplane blankets. On the opposite wall rests a slightly corny oak dresser covered in scrollwork and brass, which Elaine's parents gave us for our wedding and we dutifully kept in our bedroom for twenty-plus years. An armchair from the same era. By the armchair there's a stack of books, some Alec's, some mine: Bukowski and Burroughs, a small selection of graphic novels, and thrillers I no longer have the taste for.

I read in this studio. I sleep. Sometimes, on weekends or late into the evening, I listen to the Kriegers fighting next door. Our garage is situated along the property line; the Kriegers recently finished an addition, and now, without even trying, I can peer right into their granite-and-stainless kitchen and watch them go at it. Jill Krieger is a harridan, it turns out, and Mark likes to throw things. I wonder when this started. Elaine and I always liked them, always thought they had a very nice marriage, nice young kids; sure, their addition took forever, but at least they had the courtesy to keep the exterior tasteful. I wonder if Elaine can hear them. She and I never fought, you know, never like that.

If people keep asking me, look deep into my eyes to see if there are any secrets left in my stubbly soul, I tell them, "Listen, life goes on." And I'm not just feeding them formula, pap. Life really does go on. That's what I've learned. It goes. You'd be surprised.

BUT THERE HAVE been moments. Today, for example: A Saturday, too warm for April, I eat lunch with my mother in Yonkers and stay in her asbestos-ceilinged apartment for as long as she'll let me. We have egg salad, watch *Law and Order,* four in a row, until finally it's time for her nap—Peter, she says to me, her breath heavy with mayo, I love you, but if you don't leave soon I'll have a fit. So I leave, although it takes another two slices of coffee cake; I kiss her on her soft cheek, get into the rusty white Escort I'm driving these days, cross the Tappan Zee, and drive slowly south along the Hudson toward the Palisades. Last month I discovered this small park down there, a little paved area jutting into the river, where a few fishermen and lost sailors were gathered to catch toxic bluefish and use the dented Portosans.

It's three o'clock when I park, and muggy. I take a spot on a peeling bench, roll up my sleeves. The new-money types eat sandwiches on their decks, and the immigrant fishermen fill up buckets with poisoned blues. I watch them, and the minutes turn into an hour and a half. I've become so good, these days, at just sitting. The city hums across the water, Harlem, Washington Heights. Light filters underneath the George Washington Bridge. I study the pools of oil on the surface of the Hudson and smell the dying fish.

I've always liked being near water, although I've never been especially handy around it; I don't boat, I don't fish, and when I used to frequent the JCC, I'd find myself on the basketball courts twelve times as often as in the pool. But still: a decade and a half ago, we took regular vacations to the beach, we and the Sterns, down to Delaware because the area seemed a little more wholesome than the Jersey shore, or maybe just farther away. Every morning the kids would pick the perfect sandy spot twenty feet from the Atlantic, and we'd spend two weeks freckling ourselves under the August glare, then eating dinner at crab barns out on Route 1, platters of steamed Maryland blues. The Stern children (first two, then three, then four of them, redheads like Iris, her fecundity a marvel) sucking on crab legs with joy, my own persnickety son daintily peeling a shrimp because he didn't like food with claws. Neal Stern, seven months younger than Alec, shoving a crab carapace in his face. Iris Stern wiping Old Bay seasoning off each long finger.

It was a summer ritual for years until Laura Stern, their oldest, started high school and had no more patience for family vacations and five-hour late-summer drives. The same house every time: a ramshackle clapboard on Brooklyn Avenue, a washing machine but no dryer, a dishwasher that was constantly humming, three blocks from the main drag, a block from the beach. Nautical gewgaws in the bathrooms, sand and salt everywhere. The kids ran around half-naked all day while Elaine stayed demure in her black terry cloth cover-up and Iris gallivanted in a white bikini that Joe teased her about when he thought nobody was listening. "Would that thing turn see-through if I got you wet?" I did my best not to listen.

I liked to spend time by myself at the water's edge even then, watch the old-timers scoop up clams an hour before evening's low tide. Kids would skate around their grandfathers' knees, duck down with their plastic sieves to shovel up empty handfuls of sand, while the old men would carefully tread over the same patches of clamming ground. I'd daydream about getting a clam and crab license, giving up my practice, moving the family down to a rickety house by the Delaware shore, where it was always warm and sunset and Iris Stern was always making coffee in the kitchen in her white bikini and my son would laugh and run around for days at a time. Then the tide would sink and I'd go back to the house, take a shower, remember who I was and where I came from. An internist in New Jersey, educated on scholarships, raised in Yonkers, married more than a decade. Husband, father, basketball enthusiast.

I was never as grateful as I should have been for everything I had.

Here on my bench beneath the Palisades, the mosquitoes start to come in, and the fishermen start to pack up. I watch a red and white cigarette boat circle the park slowly, wag itself back and forth, causing waves to ripple up against the log pilings that defend the park from the grime of the Hudson. There's a young man behind the wheel all by himself, and it strikes me as unusual to see just one guy in a sport boat on a Saturday. He steers with a single hand and drinks a beer. He needs a crew of semiclad blonds around him, I decide. He needs a blasting stereo.

Across the river, the sun angles down behind Riverside Church, making the building glow.

"You know that kid in the boat?" the last remaining fisherman says to me after the cigarette boat makes another slow turn around the pilings.

"Should I?"

The fisherman shrugs. "He looks like he knows you."

I give him a quizzical look.

"The way he's circling," the man says, rubbing his chin with a fishy old hand.

"Nobody knows me," I say, grand and melodramatic. This, by the way, isn't exactly true, but it is how I would prefer things.

The cigarette boat circles again, slowly, and then once more.

NINETEEN NINETY-ONE, AUGUST, the summer of the Russian coup and the end of the Soviet Union, Joe Stern left the beach house early and came back with a bag of boardwalk cinnamon rolls and six newspapers: the *Times,* the *Post,* the *Baltimore Sun,* the *Philadelphia Inquirer,* both the Rehoboth and Wilmington dailies. Wake up the kids, he said to me. It was maybe eight in the morning; back then, all five of the kids and also my wife used to sleep till at least half past nine. Iris tended to get up at six to jog.

"It's their vacation," I said. "They'll wake up on their own."

"History, Pete," my old chum, college lab partner, best friend, said, spreading the different front pages across the picnic table on the deck. "The coup failed. It's the collapse of the Soviet Union. The cold war is over."

Above me, I remember, seagulls circled and cawed, putting me in mind of vultures, although really they were just after dropped bits of cinnamon roll. "If the cold war is over," I said, "which I happen to doubt, then it will still be over when the kids wake up."

"You doubt it?"

"You don't?"

"All the news that's fit to print, my friend," Joe said, smacking the front page of the *Times*.

I picked up the *Sun* and read a few sentences under the screeching headline, but nothing to convince me that it was time to salute a new world order. "It'll take more than this to end the cold war. We're in Delaware. History doesn't happen while we're vacationing in Delaware."

"Who cares where we are?" Joe said. He laughed, rubbed his hand over his bald spot, his gesture when he was nervous, happy, or amused. "What does that have to do with the news?"

A change in the way things have always been, and I'm reading the Baltimore paper? "I just think, I think it'll be louder when the cold war is over. We'll all hear it."

"You can't hear it?"

"Not really."

I grew up crouching under desks at PS 145 and knew that if the Soviet Union was really going to collapse, it would be a slow-motion, lumbering thing, the felling of a grand oak, bringing down everything in its path. It wouldn't be a failed coup launched by a bunch of grumpy, bald dodderers while I sat on a deck in Delaware. I put down the *Sun*, picked up the *Philadelphia Inquirer*—the same information, the same tone. "They just want to sell papers," I said. "There was a coup. It didn't work. This isn't the end of the cold war."

"Not everything is propaganda, Pete."

"Look," I said, "you can dismiss me if you'd like, but you've got to admit that something as enormous and . . . and indestructible . . . and evil—"

"Evil?" Joe chuckled. "You sound like Reagan. The Baltic States already split months ago. The Soviet Union is done." Joe rubbed again at his bald spot, said laconically, "We're number one."

"I don't believe it."

"Pete," Joe said, "get with the program."

I couldn't have told even Joe, and wouldn't have tried, but I remember feeling a chill at that moment, looking over the papers, the pictures of the different Soviet conspirators lined up like mug shots on the various front pages. I wiped my hands on my knees, stepped off the back deck, gazed up at the seagulls, still circling. There had never not been the Soviet Union in my life. There had never not been this particular enemy. I remember feeling bizarrely afraid. I walked out to the back fence of the weed-pocked yard in Delaware and looked out at the backs of all the other houses, still sleeping. I thought about everything I couldn't keep safe, or even keep the same.

"So what do you think of this, Pete?" my wife asked me when she had finally absorbed the papers. I poured us some coffee from the thermos on the table. She was looking at me with a flatteringly grave expression, as though I were holding the world's only crystal ball.

"If it's true," I said, "if it's happening the way they say, then I think it's very dangerous."

"Really?"

"The cold war was stasis, Elaine. Us versus them, good versus bad. Instability, especially in that part of the world, is dangerous. This makes me concerned. Not panicked, but concerned."

She nodded, turned back to the paper. "I see your point."

"Again, not panicked."

"No," she said. "Of course not."

Usually I liked responsibility: my wife generally trusted my judgment on matters of international consequence the same way she trusted me with the paying of bills, the hiring of plumbers. I think it's because I always spoke with authority and because I always had a clear sense of what was right and what was wrong. Elaine used to appreciate that about me. Until my recent troubles, I'd always had a pretty good idea of what good would come of things, and what bad, and I knew how to prepare.

"Well," Elaine said. "Well, I guess I won't worry too much either, then." And then she squeezed my hand.

A few minutes later, Iris emerged from the kitchen, her two younger children filing behind her like ducklings, the baby, Pauline, in her arms. "It looks crappy out today," she said. "Maybe we should rent some movies?"

"Movies!" seconded Adam, her younger son. There was a rental place right near the boardwalk, stocked with lots of fare for children and a surprisingly comprehensive adult section behind a black curtain, which Elaine and I had checked out the previous summer, feeling giddy and brave.

"Pete says instability in Russia is dangerous." Elaine folded her newspaper. "I guess we could go get a movie."

"Well, of course that's what Pete says." Iris grinned as Neal, her older boy, gave me a shrewd look. "Pete likes things the way they've always been."

"Not really," I said. "I'm just not sure that a haphazard breakup of the Soviet Union is necessarily in our strategic interests."

Iris laughed her heavy, infuriating laugh, and her kids started pulling through the mess of papers on the picnic table to find the comics.

She let Pauline out of her arms, and the little girl skittered back into the house. "Strategic interests, Pete?"

"What's the matter with that?"

"This is good news," she said.

"We don't know what kind of news it is," I said.

"It's a relaxing day, we're on vacation, our kids are happy, the world turns out to be an interesting place." She was in her bikini, one of Joe's flannel shirts on top as a nod to the darkening weather. Her red hair was pulled up in a clip on top of her head, and she'd suspended sunglasses in the cleft of her bikini.

"Pete usually knows which way the wind blows," my wife said, and I loved her for it.

"Remember our sophomore year?" Iris asked. "He didn't want to go down to DC to protest because he was afraid it would reflect badly on his medical school apps?"

"What does that have to do with anything?" I said. "Anyway, I had to study."

"I know you did, sweetheart," Iris said. She tousled my hair — unlike her husband, I still had a thick head of it — then plopped herself at the picnic table next to me. "I'm just teasing."

"Well, stop."

She laughed again. I wondered if Iris teased me because she knew I'd never really hold it against her. She folded a paper hat out of newspaper for Neal. Elaine gave me a smile over her paper, and Adam stole Neal's hat, and the seagulls, which had subsided, began to caw again. I knew my face was red — I was never very good at being teased — so I dug up the sports page, checked on the Yankees, since my Nets had yet to start their season. Eventually, Elaine got up to pour more coffee, and Joe brought out a fresh plate of cinnamon rolls, and Alec woke up and shuffled onto the porch to see if I wanted to go to the driving range, which I did. The rest of that day's schedule is lost to me. I'm certain that by dinner we were talking about other things besides the Soviet Union.

And that was 1991. A long time ago.

But I ask you today, have events not borne me out? Rogue nuclear weapons, a breakdown in command of the Russian army, a frightening centralization in the world oil market? An autocratic KGB man at the country's head? Rising AIDS rates, a widening wealth gap, the largest land mass on the planet—I ask you, Iris, have events not borne me out? Is it so hard to imagine that I might have been right?

At night, in that beach house, Iris and Joe slept in the bedroom on the second floor, and Elaine and I slept one floor down from them, and we could hear them together, always past midnight, although we tried not to. We heard them almost every night, and rolled our eyes at each other, and usually woke up in unrumpled sheets ourselves.

I have not seen the Sterns in almost a year now; I no longer sleep next to my wife. The four of us stayed together for all those years, from the University of Pittsburgh to beyond, moved to the same New Jersey town, rented shore houses, ate countless dinners, signed on to care for one another's children should the unimaginable happen to us. I happen to have a brother, a biological brother, whom I don't like very much. I have a best friend whom I miss like a brother, but whom I may never speak to again.

The Soviet Union collapsed and misery ensued, but that was not the worst thing that could have happened.

Now, AT MY little paved park by the Hudson, the last old fisherman starts packing up his gear slowly, arthritically. As he turns to bring his cooler from the car, I notice the tiniest shuffle in his gait, probably something not even his wife has yet paid much attention to. Parkinson's, in all likelihood, although a neurologist would be better equipped to make that evaluation. Still, I've sent a handful of suspected Parkinson's cases to specialists in the past several months, including a heartbreaker, a thirty-seven-year-old single dad; I've started seeing the disease everywhere.

"Hey, asshole!"

The fisherman and I both turn. The red and white cigarette boat is stalling in the water about fifteen feet from where I sit, and its young captain has perched himself up on the deck, a pair of binoculars around his neck.

"You know who I am?" the kid shouts.

I stand to get a better look. It takes me a minute, but I do in fact know who he is: Roseanne Craig's brother. A nasty piece of work; he used to torture his sister, my patient, Roseanne. They worked together on the floor of Craig Motors. He's been bumping into me every so often these past few months, on line at the Grand Union, buying beer at Hopwood Liquors. He even slashed two of my Audi's tires last September, before I traded in the Audi for the Escort, which I don't think he recognizes as mine. An elderly patient saw him do it and called the cops, but I didn't press charges.

"We're gonna fucking have your ass, Dizinoff!"

Slowly I put my hands on my knees; slowly I stand up. "Are you stalking me, Craig?"

"We're gonna fucking have your ass! I'm just telling you now! Get ready!" His voice is strained across the water.

"Have you really been stalking me?"

"I'm not stalking you, Dizinoff. I'm warning you."

"Very kind of you," I say. How did he know I would be at this park? Why does he have a cigarette boat? I look up and down the river, not sure who or what I expect to find, but I expect to find something: a camera crew, the long arm of the law.

"I'll get you!" the kid on the boat screams.

"You should get out of here," the fisherman mumbles in my direction. He's slitting open the side of a bluefish, the blade of his knife sliding neatly through the pearl gray skin. With a bare hand he slides out the fish's entrails and throws them back into the river, where they roil for a moment before disappearing. I don't want to get out of here. This is my park. This is a place that's still mine.

"Kids like that . . . ," the fisherman warns.

"He doesn't know me," I say, absurdly.

"You never know what they're gonna do." He puts the bluefish fillets in his cooler, picks up the next wriggling fish, knocks its brain loose against the piling, and lets it rest on the bench to be gutted.

"Dizinoff, you listening to me? We're going to have your ass! Decision comes fucking Monday. You listening, motherfucker?" The kid bends down into the cockpit of his boat, and despite myself, I shiver. From the interior, the kid removes something small, silver, shiny. Aims it at me. I take a deep breath. Squint, try to figure out what he's holding.

A can of beer. For Christ's sake.

Today is Saturday. On Monday, the judge will let us know whether she'll take the Craig family's case. On Tuesday, my wife will finally go see the lawyer about the divorce. And then I will know what's what, and I can plan for the rest of my life.

"We're gonna destroy you," the kid says. Then he pitches the can of beer at me, unopened, surprisingly hard and fast. It hits my shin before I can move, stings like a bitch, falls to the pavement, and explodes, sending up a geyser of beer against my legs.

"You should get out of here, man," the fisherman mutters, almost as if he's talking to his fish.

A few feet away, the beer-can bomb rolls to a stop, foams, and hisses. I cross my arms against my chest. My pants are drenched, my heart is thrumming, the kid in the boat sneers but does not laugh. "Are you crazy?" I shout.

The Soviet Union. Good and evil. Once upon a time I knew what was right and what was wrong.

"Fuck you, Dizinoff," the kid calls, pulling out another can of beer, aiming it at me.

And I buck like the coward I am. Heart racing, I turn, run, trip, fall, rip my pants, stand up again. I make it to the car, reach into my pocket for my keys, try to ignore the blood matting the hair on my shins and my heart pulsing in my ears. I hear the cigarette boat turn and start slapping away along the river. He's done with me, but my heart won't quit—I am shaking when I sit down behind the wheel of the Escort. I lock every door. I feel parking-lot gravel buried in the cut in my leg.

By the water, the fisherman is still cutting up his catch. Waves from the wake of the cigarette boat splash up against the piling, but the fisherman doesn't seem to notice them, or else he doesn't mind. I see the boat slip down the Hudson like a pleasure cruiser, and I feel the blood trickle toward my shoe.

WHEN I FIRST met Roseanne Craig, the girl was twenty-two, a Cal graduate, the daughter of an acquaintance from the JCC whose hypertension I had diagnosed maybe three years before. I didn't know her dad particularly well, only enough to nod at him in the locker room, but he had a network of auto dealerships in Teaneck and Paramus where Joe, among others, bought and serviced his Lincolns, Jeeps, and Cadillacs. Roseanne, just back from Berkeley, had been suffering from weight loss and mild depression, and her father, not knowing where else to go, had sent her to my office in Round Hill. I had a reputation, after all, for figuring things out.

Eyes clear, chest good, heart thwop-thwop-thwopping. No fluid in the lungs, no swelling in the hands or feet, no distended veins in the neck, no nodules on the thyroid or masses in the abdomen. No patient complaints besides the aforementioned weight loss—although she still cleared a solid 150—and perhaps a generalized malaise.

"You're sure you don't want to see a psychiatrist?"

"Oh, I have a therapist," she said. "She does reflexology, too." Months later, when I told that to my lawyer, he snickered and made frantic notes.

Roseanne Craig was a pretty girl, tough-looking, with dark brown eyes and black hair. She had skeleton tattoos on her upper arms and another large one, I noticed, on her left breast. A frog. "It's this whole story," she told me, though I didn't ask. The frog was surprisingly well done, one of those black-spotted jungle frogs, and it kept its lifelike eyes on me as I palpated.

"We used to call my ex-boyfriend Frogger." She closed her eyes as I pressed my fingers on her breast, standard procedure in my office for several years now.

"Frogger, huh?"

"Hence the tattoo." She didn't seem the least bit depressed to me, but her skin was maybe a little yellow, and with the tattoos—I decided to order a hep test and kept her talking. "He dumped me three months ago"—aha! the malaise—"for a dude. He said it was accidental, like he hadn't planned it or anything, but . . ." She sighed heavily as she buttoned up her shirt. "It was some grad student from

Stanford. He told me like a month after I got this fucking tattoo. We were going to move to SF together. Open up a Marxist bookstore. And I was going to bake brownies—like a Marxist bookstore-café. And now I'm living with my fucking parents. Sorry," she said, wagging an eyebrow at me like a dare. "I shouldn't curse around doctors."

"Curse away." We returned to my office, her combat boots clomping on the floor; Mina, my rather conservative Lithuanian office manager, took note of the boots and rolled her eyes.

"And so," I asked, once we were back in my office, "with all this stress in your life, you haven't been able to eat?"

"I don't know." She shrugged. "I guess. I've definitely lost weight. My clothes are loose."

"How much weight, would you estimate?"

"Maybe eight, ten pounds? I don't know," she said. "This is all really my dad's idea. Seeing you, I mean."

"Okay," I said. "Well, I think you're probably fine, but I'm going to order some blood work just to make sure, and if you're feeling depressed and you don't like your therapist, come back to me and I can refer you to a"—I couldn't help myself—"a real doctor."

"Oh." She sighed dramatically. "You're part of *that* medical establishment, then."

"I'm not sure which particular medical establishment you mean."

"The one that disrespects alternative therapies. The one that would rather feed me antibiotics than send me to acupuncture."

"Actually," I said, leaning back in my chair, "I think antibiotics are overprescribed. I have no problem with acupuncture. And if your reflexologist is doing the job for you, that's terrific. But I'd still like you to see a shrink."

"I just never really liked shrinks much."

"Some of them are nice."

"Some of them are full of crap."

"I'm recommending one to you who isn't."

"Promise?" she asked, smiling. She really wasn't as tough as she first made out.

"Promise," I said.

She tucked a piece of black hair behind her ear, smiled demurely, took the sheet I'd ripped from the prescription pad with the name and number of Round Hill Psychiatric.

When Roseanne Craig left my office, I never thought I'd see her again.

THE DRIVE FROM the park back to Round Hill takes about fifteen minutes, although today I take the long way up to Route 9W, through the back roads of Rockleigh and Alpine. Up here, in winter, the trees are bare and you can see straight across the Hudson; in spring and fall, wild turkeys and deer congregate on the shoulder. Today somehow I miss my exit and have to double back to Maycrest Avenue, Round Hill's main drag. Down a long, steep hill to the heart of town, punctuated with speed traps, stoplights, and DRUG FREE SCHOOL ZONE signs. This is a town that likes to play it safe. My fingers are tight on the steering wheel.

Our prosperous little hill is divided into three parts, east to west: the School District, the Manor, and Downtown. The School District is geographic, not administrative, and named for the three square miles surrounding Round Hill Country Day—lush two-acre plots bearing Tudor palaces, Spanish-style haciendas, Georgian piles with helicopter pads and infinity pools. We've got celebrities up there, two or three well-known rap stars, the CEO of the hospital, and a handful of dermatologists, plastic surgeons, and orthopedists.

In the Manor, where Elaine and I live, the plots are more manageable, three-quarters of an acre at most. The houses are mostly Victorians and colonials, sometimes a shingle-sided renovation, and a few 1980 "contemporaries" with birch siding set on a slant and trapezoidal windows. Downtown is literal, at the base of Maycrest Avenue; it's where we keep our hospital, our businesses, our blacks, and the public school where nobody we know sends their children.

Still stinking of beer, with blood crusted on my jeans, I pull into the driveway of the pale green Victorian house on Pearl Street where Elaine and I have lived since 1982. We bought it for $125,000, fingers crossed and breaths held; Bert Birch had offered me a partnership with privileges at Round Hill Medical Center, and even though Elaine and I both thought, privately, No, not here, we don't know anyone, how will we afford this? we kept our doubts entirely to ourselves and moved in. As soon as Joe was finished with his ob-gyn fellowship in Baltimore, we persuaded him and Iris to move to town, and they did, and we let out our breaths a little. But we'd been isolated and nervous that whole first year, and for some reason trying to get pregnant, too.

I put the Escort in park and look up at our house. Elaine's Jeep is in the driveway, and so is Alec's Civic. I wonder if they're spending the afternoon together, maybe sharing last weekend's crossword, a simple pleasure for them both. I know how happy Elaine is to have our son back. To be honest, he's a better housemate than I've ever been, neater, more considerate, and, unlike me, he enjoys most of the things his mother does. At night, from the studio, I can hear them play their favorite music: that Cuban band from the movie, some African chanting Alec picked up from a friend who went in for the Peace Corps. It all sounds like high-end restaurant music to me, but who cares what I think? Not these two. No reason to.

Does Roseanne's brother come here? I wonder. Does he know

where my wife and child sleep? Does he care about them, or is his rage only directed toward me? I reach down and wipe my bloody leg, pull out a tiny piece of gravel. I was a coward, but so was the kid. Throwing beer cans. Screaming obscenities.

I roll down the window but the house is quiet, although I see lamplight burning from behind the living room shades. Reproduction Tiffany lamps that we bought in Bedford during our marital renaissance, six years ago now. She's done the crossword by them ever since. If Craig has come to the house, if he's stood outside, maybe he's watched her complete the Sunday. If he touches her, even thinks of touching her, I swear to God I'll kill him without a blink.

Elaine and I have known each other for more than half our lives. She's watched over me. She still watches over me, despite the doubts about me that she regrettably holds. As I watch, the Tiffany lamps go dark, and a minute later, after she's fetched her jacket, her purse, and her keys, my wife stands at our front door, looking out at me in my little white Escort. I wave at her. She blinks, smiles sadly, and waves back. She's kept her hair short in recent years, and she's put on forty pounds, but I can remember her clinging to my side back in college, eating cinnamon rolls in Rehoboth, and if I could only scroll back time and do it again, every day would be a renaissance.

"You coming in?" she calls from the top step of our porch.

"You going out?" I ask.

She pulls her jacket around her shoulders and nods.

"I think I'll sit here for a while," I say.

Elaine has grown used to what could kindly be called my eccentricities. She shrugs, descends from the porch, and steps lightly to her car. She swings her purse at her side. It breaks my heart to see her go.

CHAPTER TWO

LOOKING BACK, AS my circumstances often suggest that I do, I
see my thirties and forties as a vast steppe; only occasionally did the
landscape bulge or dip. Bert Birch had brought me in because he
was heading into his midfifties and his wife had been warning him
for twenty years that she'd leave him if he didn't find a partner and
take a vacation with her once a year. In 1982, Bert was fifty-five, an
old-fashioned kind of doctor in an old-fashioned kind of office with
one nurse, one secretary, and half a day off on Wednesdays. He kept
Popular Mechanics in the waiting room; occasionally, quietly, he made
house calls. He ran a comfortable, neighborly practice, and although
he was based at Round Hill Medical Center, most of his patients
came from the less swanky communities down the valley: Bergentown, Hopwood, Maycrest Village. They were teachers, postal clerks,
cops, hairdressers. Bert took care of generations of the same family,
celebrating their births, mourning their deaths, bringing home, at
Christmastime, fruit baskets or homemade sheet cakes or bottles of
lambrusco. He'd been at it for twenty-seven years, had taken over the
practice from his own father, who remembered when cows used to
graze where the Sunoco now stood.

During the decade we worked together, we got along very nicely; I
know for sure Bert felt fatherly toward me despite his sometimes gruff

demeanor. He made bad jokes. He threatened to take me golfing. His wife, MaryJo, often invited Elaine and me over for operatic Italian dinners; she was from four generations of North Jersey Sicilians and referred to her impeccable tomato sauce as "gravy." In the warm light of the Birches' rambling center-hall colonial, Elaine and I would scarf down platters of scungilli marinara, *trippa fra diavolo*, rigatoni, meatballs in gravy. There were five Birch children and six Birch grandchildren and often they'd cram in at the table right next to us. Elaine and I never wanted children quite as badly as we did during our drives down Maycrest Avenue, full of MaryJo's decadent cooking, arms still aching from the warmth of one Birch grandbaby or another.

As I grew more comfortable in Round Hill, I began branching out, joined the JCC, started making connections with the other local docs. I was interested in developing a good reputation, and although I had no problem with your everyday checkup, your diabetic accountant or petit mal secretary, what I longed for were the specialty cases, the sleuthy diagnoses nobody else had been able to figure. I'd caught the Sherlock Holmes bug during a medical school rotation, when I intuited a case of Goodpasture syndrome in a twenty-four-year-old graduate student who thought he was having a mind-blowing asthma attack and a hangover. I had just finished a unit on nephrology, so my mind was in the right place, but still, because I was paying excellent attention, I probably spared the kid a lifetime of dialysis. I'll never forget him—his name was Paul Chung, he was studying to be an architect, and we shared the same exact birthday. For maybe four years after, he sent me Christmas cards.

Anyway, during those first few seasons, I'd stay late at the office, taking patients long after Bert had packed it in, then go home to curl up in the downstairs study and pore over *JAMA*, the *New England*

Journal, journals for specialties I hadn't pursued. I'd become an internist because I liked the diversity of cases, because I liked primary care, and because I didn't feel like spending any more time in training. My brother, Phil, was already making fifty thousand dollars right out of NYU Law; I wanted to start earning, too. As an internist—a sort of jack-of-all-trades—I could peruse articles on subjects from gastritis to hemodialysis, learn how to tell Crohn's colitis from ulcerative. I would refer the exotic patients to the specialists, but the specialists would make their diagnoses with my hunches in hand.

Still, it wasn't just ambition keeping me in the study; I guess it rarely is. Elaine and I had been trying to have a baby for four years, and her inability to hold the embryo—or our inability to discuss the matter with anything like honesty—made me feel increasingly lost and insecure in our bedroom. We'd been to the fertility doctors, who told us that there was nothing physiologically wrong with her and advised us to just, you know, relax. Just relax? I can hardly imagine a doctor with the cojones to make that suggestion today—but back then, in 1983, it seemed like fair enough advice. Relax, do what nature tells you, and Elaine, take it easy those first three months, not so much running around, okay? And oh, how she took those doctors seriously, as though they were headmasters, prison wardens. Lying on her back eighteen hours a day, rising only to eat, take a shower. But it didn't matter—by eight weeks in, the bleeding would start, and it wouldn't end until we were in the emergency room, waiting for an ultrasound to confirm what we already knew. Those years were the first period of several during our marriage when I took to sleeping on the couch. Sex in the evening, just to get it over with, and then me in the study with my quilt and my *JAMA.* If it bothered her—and it must have bothered her—she never said a word.

This is something about himself that Alec still doesn't know: how much he was wanted, how difficult it was to have him. And during some moments of adolescent rebellion, and again during the wars over his dropping out of Hampshire, when he would scream that he wished he'd never been born, Elaine would grab his flailing arms, hold him still, and say, You can never say that. That's the one thing you are never allowed to say.

He was born at Round Hill Medical Center on July 4, 1985, nine fifteen at night. As we held Alec for the first time, the town fireworks began to whiz and bloom, celebrating 209 years of democracy in America and also, Elaine and I were certain, our son's long-awaited arrival.

AND SO THE steppe unfolded. Our boy reached a height of six foot four by his fifteenth birthday but, almost certainly to spite his old man, showed little to no interest in basketball. Instead, he began studying art, both at Round Hill Country Day and in private lessons with a local sculptor three evenings a week. Our living room filled with pieces of cherrywood or palm carved into abstracted parts of the female form: almost always gigantic breasts. Alec assured us this was serious Art, so what if our living quarters looked like a Dada bordello? He began painting, too, still lifes of flowers, lemons, and his iPod, or the contents of our bathroom garbage can. Once, he drew a picture of me dozing on the couch, just sketched it while I was sleeping there, completely vulnerable. He showed it to me the second I woke up, and the picture both embarrassed and moved me—how invasive, how impudent, to draw for posterity the way your father drools in his sleep, but then there was something loving, too, about the attention to detail, the way he caught the plaid of my collar, the uneven bump of my chin. I brought the picture to my office to hang up, but then got embarrassed and brought it back home.

Thus Alec prospered in an entirely different direction than the one I would have expected, but prospered nonetheless, and so, happily, did my wife. Elaine had completed her PhD in English literature at the City University Grad Center a year after we moved to New Jersey, but she'd never plunged into the quicksand of the academic job market. She wasn't much for competition, and also we'd been trying so hard to start a family—so she kept her PhD to herself, and not once did any invitations arrive at our house addressed to Dr. and Dr. Dizinoff.

But when Alec began his sixth-grade year, Elaine suddenly felt the urge to go back to school herself. A few calls to former professors landed her an adjunct spot at Bergen State, where she was assigned the perpetually unpopular *Beowulf*-to-Chaucer survey. It was a position for which she would be criminally underpaid, but she threw herself into the course with gusto, and eventually the chair agreed to give her a per-course raise of five hundred dollars, which fanned her usually unfannable ego. Sometimes, in bed, we'd play variations of games wherein she was the sexy professor and I was the naughty student. I think she liked these assignations more than she would have initially guessed.

And so this was how I galloped across my steppe, healthy and oblivious, even though people dear to me were strapped into their own hellish roller coasters and couldn't find the escape latch. Or, to be less preposterous about it, almost fifteen years ago, my best friend, Joe Stern, had a problem with his daughter Laura, a terrifying problem—the kind of thing impossible to imagine when parenthood is new, the baby is six months old and drooling into her rice cereal, and your wife looks like the Madonna, long hair and clear skin, spooning Gerbers into the kid's peachy face.

The year Laura turned seventeen, there was a rash of neonaticides across New Jersey. Cheerleaders delivering at their proms, abandoning their babies in Dumpsters, that kind of thing. Iris said to Laura one morning, as the girl was heading out for school, Honey, can you even imagine? and Laura shook her head. Later that same afternoon she was admitted to Round Hill with major blood loss, and her baby, at twenty-five weeks' gestation, was found dead in a trash can not too far from the Round Hill Municipal Library. Laura had delivered in the second-floor bathroom. The baby's skull was crushed in like an egg.

Was the baby alive when Laura smashed its skull? That was the crux of the legal battle, and also, secondarily, whether or not Laura had been in her right mind. Joe and Iris, who'd been thinking of moving to the School District, immediately took their house off the market, probably with some relief. Iris was friendly with a wonderful big-firm litigator, and together they found Laura the very best representation to face off against the State of New Jersey, which was battling in the name of Baby Girl Stern. Joe took care of the psychiatric angle, and forget about Round Hill, they went to Columbia, the chief of adolescent psychiatry. Four days a week. Joe and Iris both began seeing therapists themselves and in their spare time tried to fend off the press.

Where was I during that time? Looking back, all those years ago, it's hard to remember exactly. Absorbed in my work, I guess, making money, worrying over some stocks and daydreaming about renovating the kitchen. I was captain of the JCC men's basketball league, thirty-five-and-older division. So maybe that—and then of course there was parenthood, and work, and my own marriage, which was suffering from predictable twelfth-anniversary doldrums (Elaine wanted to try for more children; I refused to even talk about it). But I suppose, in the end, my absence was due to what it was for all of us: discomfort, the general impossibility of knowing what to say, a vague disgust at what Joe's daughter had done, and the self-satisfaction of not having had it happen to us.

But one morning, just after six, I was at the JCC shooting the ball around; Elaine's snoring had woken me up. And who should walk in but Joe, whose calls I hadn't answered in the past week and a half. "Jesus, Joe," I said. He was gaunt; he'd lost at least ten pounds while I wasn't paying attention. His Eagles T-shirt hung loose over his shoulders, and his shorts sagged.

"Pete." He nodded and threw his ball at me. "Twenty-one?"

"Twenty-one," I agreed, dropping my own basketball. Six in the morning was still early at the JCC, and we had the court to ourselves. I thought to myself, The nice guy would let him win, poor bastard, and then I thought, Joe would know if I was letting him win. So I brought up my game, played him hard, our sneakers squeaking on the polished wood. In sixteen minutes we were tied at twelve, and although Joe had elbowed me to the floor twice, I'd hung him up twice myself. In another ten minutes I'd won the game.

"What are you doing now?" he asked as we toweled the sweat off our necks.

"What am I doing?" All my days started the same way back then: the JCC, ten minutes in the sauna, then a shower, a stop at the Dunkin' Donuts for a cinnamon cruller and a large coffee, in the office by 7:45. I'd always toss the doughnut bag in the lobby garbage to hide the evidence from Mina—she disapproved of sugar in the morning, or, frankly, ever.

"You want to get breakfast?"

I'd known him at that point for twenty years—I'd been the best man at his wedding, he was my only child's godfather, I'd eaten a thousand meals with him. What made me feel so strange about eating one more?

"Or if you've got to get going—"

"Breakfast sounds great," I said. "I was just thinking about eggs."

He had a nine thirty appointment, he said, on the Upper East Side—a Cornell psychiatrist nobody we knew had any ties to. His partners were taking on more than their share in the office so that he could attend to his family problems, his psychiatric needs and those of his daughter, his legal meetings, his lunch breaks with his wife. Joe was now only seeing his high-risk patients three afternoons a week. But still, he said, he liked to make time for breakfast.

In the car, Imus blared from the radio. I moved to turn it off, but Joe said no, leave it, and we drove to the Old Lantern in silence except for Imus's yammerings about Janet Reno's decision to fire ninety-three federal attorneys. In the parking lot, I wedged my Lexus into a corner spot, and Joe and I dashed to the diner with our jackets over our heads. It had just started to rain.

"So how's Iris holding up?" I asked after we had sat down and chitchatted the waitress into bringing us some coffee.

"Iris?" Joe blinked. "You know," he said. "She's got everything all figured out. Spreadsheets." It was an old joke between us that our wives were the brains of our respective operations, and we were just the appendages.

"I'm not surprised."

"Budgets, strategy plans, doctors' appointments, lawyers. The trial's set for December." Today was the last day of June. "This lawyer we hired, I called your brother about him. Phil and I talked the other night. He said he's very good."

"Well, Phil knows the field," I said, guilt-stabbed. My brother had managed to return Joe Stern's calls, and I hadn't.

"He offered me Knicks tickets."

"He what?"

Joe laughed, rubbed his hand on his bald head. It was the first smile I'd seen from him that morning.

"Your fucking brother. He said, Joe, I know you're going through a difficult time right now, and I'd like to offer you something to help. I have Knicks tickets, next week, right on the floor. I want you and Iris to have them."

"You've got to be kidding me."

"I took 'em, too," Joe said. "What the hell? It'll be good to take Iris out to a game. You know how she ogles the players." This was another joke between us, that our wives liked to fantasize about musclebound yahoos whenever circumstances allowed. As far as we knew, this wasn't true about either one of them.

The waitress came back for our order, a western omelet for me, oatmeal and a poached egg for Joe, and as she disappeared we lapsed again into silence. I wanted to ask about Laura—how she was doing, of course, and what her shrink thought, but also all the questions everyone else at Round Hill asked when we passed one another in hospital hallways, at the Grand Union, at the Garland Chophouse, where we took our Saturday dinners: How did they not know? He's an ob-gyn, for Christ's sake! A high-risk ob-gyn! Their own daughter!

And then, in quieter whispers: Did she really bash in the skull? Just bash it in like a Wiffle ball? And then, quietest of all: So who was the father, anyway?

"She'd stopped talking to us, that's what it was," Joe said after a few minutes. He'd been fingering the table-side jukebox, just like our kids did when we brought them here for milkshakes. The songs were throwbacks, they'd never really been popular—B sides by Donovan, Freddy Fender, Gary Puckett and the Union Gap.

"But everyone says that about teenagers—they just go silent one day—and what the hell did we know? Although now, looking back, Iris says she wouldn't even let us touch her. That should have been a clue. She'd go to give her a hug, fix a button or something, and Laura would just shrink."

"Well, kids can—"

"No, no. The psychiatrist said it's one of the signs—one of the signs, a classic. They don't want to be touched. They're sure you're going to be able to feel it. The baby."

"Joe, I don't—"

"She started wearing really baggy clothes—I don't know. She always wore baggy clothes. She's been stealing my old sweatshirts since she was twelve. She's always been shy about her body." He looked up at me as if for my approval. "Other girls in her class dressing up like Madonna, and there's Laura in her huge flannel shirts and old jeans, her head in a book."

"She's a modest kid."

Joe grunted. "So she's not showing, of course she's not showing. The end of her second trimester, she's got the abdomen muscles of a seventeen-year-old, she's hiding everything in flannel shirts. We're supposed to chart her menstrual cycle or something? Count tampon wrappers in the bathroom?"

"Of course not."

He waved me off. "That's what New Jersey says. We should have known."

"Fuck New Jersey."

Joe shook his head. I paid closer attention than I should have to my coffee. Laura Stern—what did I know of her? It had been a couple of years since we'd spent time together down in Delaware, and even then she was so much older than the other kids, it had been easy not to see her at all. A heavy crust of teenage acne, flannel shirts, sure, and a precocious taste in literature, head always bent in something absurd, *Middlemarch*, *The Mill on the Floss*. Even at the beach. Who was she having sex with? Back when I was in high school, nobody had sex with the Laura Sterns.

"The thing is," Joe said, "we always felt close to her. Or I did, I guess. The other three were the kids, but Laura, she was like our lieutenant. Second in charge. We were so young when we had her, and she always had that grown-up thing about her. A serious kid. So smart."

"I know, Joe."

"So then what did she think we would have done to her, exactly? If we'd found out? What would we have done?"

"She was just scared."

"But why? Why would she be scared of us? Doesn't she know us?" It was this, I knew, that was really breaking his heart more than anything, even more than the library delivery and the dead baby in the garbage. His own daughter felt she couldn't tell him the truth.

"Listen, you can't—"

"Why didn't she trust us?" His voice cracked and broke.

Back to my coffee. I heard morning regulars shuttle in, the local dentists, the cops, Tim, who managed the Chophouse. Joe was still waiting for an answer.

"She wouldn't want you to know that she had a boyfriend," I said. "Or that she was, you know, sexually active."

Joe didn't say anything until the waitress brought our food to the table. "A boyfriend," he said. "As far as I knew, she didn't even have any *friends*." I looked down at the burnt edges of my toast.

"She could get life in prison," Joe said. "They're going to have a hearing, see if she should be tried as an adult."

"Oh God," I said. "Ah, Joe . . . I don't—"

"That's what New Jersey wants, since she's only ten months shy of eighteen. So they try her as an adult, and they win, she gets life in an adult prison. No possibility of parole for thirty years."

He closed his eyes, then opened them and looked straight at me with his bleak, bloodshot gaze. "Can you believe that, Pete? My little girl, in jail for the rest of her life?"

"That won't happen." Although why wouldn't it?

"But what do we do? What can we do?" His eyes trapped me. "Pete, we'll bankrupt ourselves before that happens. We'll spirit her to Mexico. We'll figure it out. I'm not kidding."

"Joe, that won't happen."

"Thirty years in medium-security prison. Do you know what those places are *like*? Do you know what can happen to a girl like Laura in a place like that?"

"Listen—"

"She'll be in confinement, no community, no visits except behind bars, plate glass, no future, her company is murderers and gang members, she's alone, she grows old, we die, and she's still behind bars."

"Come on—"

But he waved me off.

"Come on," I said again. I don't know why.

Laura was born our first year out of college, when we were all just twenty-three. Joe and Iris were in Philly together, Iris for an MBA at Wharton, and Joe at Temple for medical school; they'd spent the summer before they started school trying to figure out if they should get engaged or move on to less familiar horizons, since they'd been dating for three years already, after all. Then, during her first week of school and Joe's third, Iris found herself throwing up between classes, exhausted in the afternoons. Joe proposed, they were married over winter break, Laura was born in early spring. A redhead, just like Iris.

I remember those days with fondness, although of course I wasn't the one trying to juggle an MBA course load with a newborn, or living with my parents and sisters and brand-new wife in the one-bathroom North Philly row house where I'd grown up. In those days, I was comfortably stationed in a dorm at Mount Sinai, and Elaine shared a big two-bedroom on Columbus with two roommates; what did we know about cramped and broke? What did we know about mastitis, no privacy, kid sisters taking forty-five-minute baths and the baby needing to be changed and the diapers in the bathroom vanity and everyone in the house screaming? Elaine and I knew nothing—in fact, the cheeriness of home-cooked meals and little babies appealed to us, so we took weekend drives to see Joe and Iris whenever we could tear ourselves away from New York. We liked to walk Laura, in her little stroller, to the zoo or Fairmount Park, let Joe and Iris take in a movie by themselves. Elaine and I were engaged but planned to marry only after I finished medical school. When we visited Joe and Iris for the weekend, Mrs. Stern made us sleep in separate rooms.

After their graduate degrees, the Sterns moved to Baltimore; Joe did his training at Hopkins, and Iris took a job in the corporate services division at First Mariner Bank. They put Laura in nursery school and day care and worked long hours, but despite their benign neglect, the girl seemed to be growing into a well-behaved and intelligent little person. She was fond of finger painting—well, all children are—but Iris treated Laura's finger paintings as if they were real masterpieces, getting them nicely framed and hanging them above the mantel. And you know, all dressed up like that, the paintings sort of looked like modern art. Elaine cooed about them; we all did.

"And I'm not surprised they're blaming us, you know?" Joe said, putting down the salt shaker he'd been fiddling with. "If it were someone else's kid, I'd blame the parents, too."

"You wouldn't—"

"I mean, I think I *want* to be blamed. I want it to be my fault. I don't want it to be hers. It was us, we were shitty parents, we deserve this."

"But you've been wonderful parents, Joe," I said. What would Elaine say here? I tried to channel my wife. "To all four of your kids, you've been wonderful parents."

"*I'm an obstetrician, Pete, and I didn't even see my own daughter's pregnancy.*"

"She wore baggy clothes—you said it yourself."

"I would have sworn on my life she was a virgin."

"Come on."

He pinched the bridge of his nose. If he cried—well, that made sense. Had it been me, maybe I would have cried, too. Alec was eight years old back then and the idea that my own child could be a stranger to me while he lived in my house, that while I worked to keep him warm and clothed and fed, he could harbor terrified secrets—I thought of Alec's fragile shoulders, his bowl of silky brown hair. I thought of the way he murmured in his sleep, fragments of television commercials, Top 40 songs.

"We'll spirit her to Mexico. You'll help us, Pete. You'll help us get her out."

I nodded. There was nothing to say but, "Of course."

"We've got her on antidepressants. Now Iris is taking them, too. Maybe I'll start. They don't seem to be helping that much, but I like the idea of medicating my way out of this."

"Do you think you're depressed, Joe?"

"I'm not depressed." He rolled up his napkin in his hand. "I'm just sad."

My omelet, flecked with red and pink and green, looked garish, ridiculous, barely like food. I picked up my fork, poked at it.

"At least the kids don't know what's going on. I mean, Neal knows something's up, and we've tried to ask around it, to see how much he's figured out. But he just thinks Laura's sick, and he doesn't want to know more than that, thank God."

"Thank God."

"Something like this, it's so beyond them. It's so beyond us—how couldn't it be beyond them? How could they even understand it? How could we explain it to them?"

"Of course you're not going to talk to a second-grader about what happened."

He looked at me sharply. "You don't talk to your kids, that's how they get in trouble, Pete."

"Yeah, but—"

"You gotta talk to them. You've got to know what's going on."

"In the second grade?"

"You underestimate your kids, they'll crush you. They'll crush you with what you never could have expected."

As for me, I thought there was a big space between underestimating your kids and terrifying them, and Joe's sweet-faced little babies— let them be the last people in Round Hill not to know what Laura had done. When Pauline was born, four years earlier, we'd delighted that there was another baby girl; we slicked Alec's hair and put him in a button-down shirt for Pauline's naming at Temple Beth Shalom. I remember watching him watch the newborn little girl and jealously eyeing Neal, who was protective about his new sister. "How come Neal gets one?" He tugged at my sleeve. "How come Neal gets a sister and I don't?"

I shook my head. So many times in this life I've had no idea what to say. But then I had an inspiration. "You know, if you ask nicely, maybe Neal will share his."

Kids hate to share. "Why can't I have my own?"

"Because you're our one and only." This was lame, I knew, but he seemed to take it okay, plugged his thumb in his mouth, and I was hugely grateful for this odd moment of complacency.

I wanted to find Laura Stern and shake her, hard. Her parents would have taken the baby in. *We* would have taken her in.

"She wasn't viable." Joe took a bite of his oatmeal, put the spoon down still half-full. "That's the thing of it. She wasn't viable. The autopsy proved it."

"Conclusively?" I said. "Well, that's good, right?"

"I've seen babies like that, Pete, underweight, underdeveloped lungs," he said. "Even if you stick 'em in a NICU for fifteen weeks, there's no guarantee they'll survive. They're blind, you know, more than half the time. Brain-damaged. And sometimes they just die no matter what. But if they live, it's no kind of life."

"So that's good, then, for your case."

"We have to prove it, though. It's very tough to prove whether a baby was alive when it was born."

"Can't an autopsy look for oxygen in her lungs, something?" This was something we never discussed in medical school.

"They could still get her for mutilating a corpse."

I nodded. "Sure." Mutilating a corpse.

"She could get eighteen months just for that."

"Well, that's . . . better than the alternative."

Look, I'd been in the restrooms in the Round Hill Municipal Library. Mint-colored tiles rimmed with black. Old-fashioned pedestal sinks. Lots of mirrors. So I couldn't help thinking, the stalls—did she use the handicapped stall?—even so, it would have been no larger than a walk-in closet. She probably birthed crouching over the toilet. And then she took the nearest heavy object (or had she come prepared? a hammer? her little brother's baseball bat?) and cracked in the wailing newborn's skull. Took it to the Dumpster behind the library. She used a sweatshirt to clean up the blood from the bathroom floor; the sweatshirt was now official property of the state. And although I didn't want to think about it, I couldn't stop myself: Where was the baby when she cleaned up the blood? On the floor? In a sink? Was the skull cracked yet? Was it alive? Crying? Twenty-five weeks: The baby was blind, almost certainly in respiratory distress. Lying on a bathroom floor. Its skull as thin as parchment.

"What are you thinking?" Joe, my oldest friend, asked me.

"Nothing." I forked tasteless, ridiculous food into my mouth. I wondered if he'd ever asked her: Was the child alive? I wondered what she'd said, if she'd even known.

Laura was bleeding profusely: uterine atony, postpartum hemorrhage. She must have been terrified, but she had her wits about her enough to take a cab to the hospital. The cab driver was going to testify for the state that the girl seemed calm, reasonable. The only thing out of the ordinary was the blood. He didn't ask questions, and Laura didn't tell anyone the baby's whereabouts until the next morning. The police waited until the Ativan wore off and the family's lawyers arrived.

"We buried her in Iris's family plot," Joe said. "Next to Iris's mother."

I swallowed.

"We had Rabbi Ross come, give a blessing. Iris and I went by ourselves. Laura didn't want to come. That was fine. My mother stayed with her. Rabbi Ross came out, said a few words. Maybe we'll put up a headstone some day. I don't know."

"Well," I said, while secretly I was thinking, But won't they need the body for evidence? I was thinking, Is that even legal? To bury the victim before the verdict? But isn't the baby in New Jersey's protection now? What I knew about the law you could fit in a teaspoon.

Lying in the sink of the Round Hill Municipal Library. Waiting for its skull to be crushed in like a can.

"We gave her a name."

I blinked stupidly.

"The rabbi asked if we wanted to. I didn't know what to say, but Iris said yes, we did. She said it was the right thing to do."

He was whispering again, in that fluorescent-lit diner. Our big-bosomed waitress dipped by with her coffeepot, Gary Puckett and the Union Gap crooned on someone else's jukebox, eggs cooled in front of us, New Jersey rush hour traffic whizzed outside. But in our booth, all was still.

"We couldn't let her go to heaven as Baby Girl Stern," Joe whispered. "We just couldn't let that happen. She needed a name. Iris was right."

"Heaven, Joe?"

"We named her Sara," he said. "That was Iris's mother's name."

"Well," I said. "Well, that's a nice name."

Although I desperately wanted to, I couldn't look away, so I watched a tear leak from his eyes and trace a spidery path down his cheek.

"Ah, Joe."

But then, thank God, he blew his nose, rubbed his bald spot again, and apologized that he really had to go, he was sorry, he had a psychiatric appointment to make, and this goddamn doctor charged too much for him to risk being late.

"I'll call you, Joe," I said as I dropped him back at his car in the JCC lot.

"That would be great, Pete," he said. "We're busy with everything, but—"

"I'll call you," I said. But for some reason I kept imagining Sara

Stern in a Dumpster behind the library, her skull caved in like a soft piece of fruit, and it took me many weeks to pick up the phone.

I'M A LUCKY MAN, I know that. I was lucky that morning, listening to someone else's terrible news, and I'm even lucky now, warm in my studio, an unpredictable shower awaiting me in the tiny bathroom, and then a lumpy futon, the squall of the Kriegers outside. The lingering scent of my son's oil paints in the air in this large-enough room. My son, my wife, my job, my mother, my brother. I have done enough damage to lose them all, but something tells me that no matter how much I deserve to, I won't lose them entirely. This doesn't necessarily feel right, but I am chained to my good fortune.

And then the cell phone rings. My wife? No, it's my old friend Joe, who must have sensed I was thinking about him. What does he want with me now? What's there for us to talk about? Joe has my future balanced on his fingertips and he knows it. This whole malpractice case—one soft exhale, and he could blow my whole life and livelihood away. It's an uncomfortable position for old friends to be in, but there it is. My cell phone stops ringing, catches its breath, starts up again. I watch it go, lights and vibrations and an electronic version of Vivaldi's *Four Seasons*. Joe doesn't leave a message. I turn my cell phone off.

I miss talking to Joe sometimes, I really do.

Two neighborhood tomcats are fighting outside; they've both got the springtime joneses, but most of the female cats around here have been spayed. The pickings are slim. I like April, never mind Eliot; I like the tomcats, the optimism in the magnolias, the secretaries taking off their stockings, outdoor cups of coffee, smokers clustering again by the front entrance to the hospital. Joe and I used to take long bike rides up the Palisades the first warm Sunday of the month, snow sometimes still receding into the hawthorns along the highway.

Roseanne Craig said to me once that in Northern California it was always springtime, until suddenly, for reasons she still didn't quite understand, she woke up and it was winter.

AFTER MY BREAKFAST with Joe that morning, I went to the office, unsettled. My patients didn't notice, but Mina did, and she made decaf in the afternoon instead of regular. I took off by six, no rounds, and back at home Elaine and I made spaghetti while Alec was at soccer practice. I poured us each a big glass of dolcetto before we even got started.

Although we both enjoyed it when it happened, Elaine and I rarely cooked together. She was content to do the lifting in the kitchen in exchange for my dish washing and coffee brewing afterward. Still, every once in a while the urge struck, and she and I would make something simple and happy together: fried chicken, spaghetti and meatballs. That night, still hopped up on guilt and shivers, I thought cooking with my wife would settle me. I downed my wine quickly, and she put NPR on the little kitchen transistor, the market report.

Elaine and I had been married long enough to feel as though the exchange of a few sentences was a momentous conversation, which was all right; what I mean is that we were as comfortably quiet together as most couples we knew, and relied on oldies-but-goodies (Alec, vacation plans, bills) to keep the engine of our marital discourse lubed. Now, of course, we had an enormous thing to talk about in the form of our oldest friends' daughter, and I was glad not only to have Elaine to talk to, but also, perversely, to have something new to talk about with Elaine.

"They gave the baby a name," I said as casually as I could, chopping oregano while she scraped carrots into the sink.

"Sara," she said.

"You knew that?"

"Iris asked me if I knew what the rules were for naming the dead. We talked a couple days ago."

"What did you tell her?" Elaine and I had been lapsed Jews for many years, but she'd been raised in a semi-Orthodox home in Squirrel Hill, the Jewish part of Pittsburgh; her father had been a cantor, and her mother the longtime president of the Temple Sisterhood. My wife had a religious streak she didn't try to hide, and a certain depth of Judaic knowledge.

"I told her that whatever she wanted to name the baby was fine, as far as I knew. I was surprised, though. First of all, she never really liked her mother. Remember how she used to bitch? Second, you'd think the name would be up to Laura."

I was surprised enough to put down my knife. "Why would Laura get to name the baby?"

"She's the mother," Elaine said. It was ten of seven, and the light in the kitchen was just starting to slant. I took a bulb of garlic from the basket hanging near the window and started peeling its papery skin.

"She also murdered the child."

"Murdered? That's what you think happened?"

"Elaine—"

"You don't know that. We're all so quick to condemn, all of us. But we have no idea if the baby was alive, we have no idea what was in that poor girl's head—"

"She crushed its skull."

"You don't know why she did it."

"So you're pleading insanity?"

"I'm not pleading anything," Elaine said. She threw the carrots into the salad bowl and wiped her hands on her jeans. "I just think we should show our friends a little loyalty, and Laura, too. We've known her all her life."

I was honestly surprised at Elaine's reasoning. Rarely did she disagree with me so staunchly. "I'm being disloyal?" I said.

"You're not the judge here."

"Who said I was?"

"Listen, I know how you think. You're a moralist, you know? You live in black and white. Gray is beyond you."

"What's so gray about delivering a baby in a public restroom and smashing in its skull either shortly before or after it took its first breath?" Her whole line was making me feel unreasonable.

"You don't know the entire story, Pete."

"But those are the facts, Elaine."

She looked at me, her hazel eyes colder than I would have preferred. I remember having the strange urge to rub her hair between my fingers, to feel its softness.

"You should know better, is what I mean. You have the moral code of a teenager, that level of sophistication. Right is not always right, and wrong is not always wrong."

"What are you talking about?"

"Pete," she said, "the world is not always as easy as you'd like." Her face turned mottled, then pink. "And just because a teenager delivers a baby in a bathroom and disposes of it . . ." She paused. "You of all people should know the world is not as easy as you'd like. You're a doctor, Pete. Come on."

In all our years together, I'd grown to rely on Elaine's support — to

lean on it like a post. She so rarely contested me or took serious issue with my interpretations of the challenges that buffeted our lives.
So why now? What was different about now? If anything, I'd have
expected her to take my line *more* seriously than usual, since this was
a more-serious-than-usual event in our lives. In everyone's lives. In
the hospital, at dinner parties, wherever Round Hillers found one
another, it was tough to talk about anything else.

"The poor girl, hemorrhaging, panicking, disposed of her baby in
a Dumpster, which is, of course, outrageous, but"—Elaine gripped
her wineglass—"but because of those very reasons, because of the
outrageousness of it, and because we know Laura, we know she's a
good, moral person—don't you think there *has* to be another reason
this happened?" She put a hand on her hip, all earnestness. Maybe
this was simply maternal of her—we had, after all, pushed the girl's
stroller around Fairmount Park all those years ago. "Don't you think
something else had to be going on? In her head?"

"How should I know what was in her head?"

"I'm just asking you to show a little sympathy, Pete."

"Sympathy." The market report was preaching the gospel of Berk-
shire Hathaway. Up five points: dispassionately, I listened to myself
grow richer for a minute or two. In the morning, Kenny, my stock-
broker, would call to congratulate himself on how he'd handled my
money.

"Elaine, in my day, baby killers were baby killers. Or to rephrase,
when I was growing up, if a girl got pregnant and had the baby and
murdered that baby, the reasons *why* she did it would not overrule the
fact that she did it in the first place. Perhaps it was a more black-and-
white time, I don't know."

"In your day, girls had abortions in back alleys."

"An abortion would have been a fine alternative. As opposed to murder."

"You really think she's a murderer?"

"I don't know what else you'd call it."

"It's happened throughout history, Pete," she said, using the voice she had used to explain human reproduction to Alec the previous fall. "Iris has talked to sociologists, psychologists. I put her in touch with people at Bergen. Girls who give birth alone, or who cannot support their children, or who consider themselves outcasts from their society—"

"Laura Stern's an outcast?"

"Pregnant at seventeen? Of course she is."

"Being pregnant doesn't make her an *outcast*. She could have told Joe and Iris. What would they have done to her but been the loving and supportive and wonderful people they are?"

"Presumably she thought they would have punished her. Ostracized her."

"Joe and Iris?"

"Of course it's not what they *would* have done, but it's what she thought they would have done. She probably felt she couldn't disappoint them. They've always had very high standards for their kids, you know."

"So it's their fault?"

"That's not what I said. It's just that they expect certain things from all four of them. And pregnancy certainly isn't one of those things."

"I can't believe you're blaming Joe and Iris for this."

"I'm not blaming Joe and Iris!"

"Listen to yourself."

"Pete, why are you so angry about this?"

"Why aren't you?"

"Pete," she said, and nothing else. Which is where we ended it. Elaine made salad dressing. I set out the plates, still at a loss. How many years had it been since we'd suffered this sort of philosophical difference? And over something like this. A dead baby in a Dumpster.

But soon enough it was easy to focus on other things: We had dinner on the table. Alec got dropped off from soccer and sprawled himself across the wooden bench that served as our fourth, fifth, and sixth seats and wolfed down half his spaghetti in the time it took Elaine and me to finish our salads, but we were happy enough to have him home that we didn't pick on him about anything. He was not yet allowed to watch television unsupervised, just to give you a sense of the innocence we tried to impose on the kid.

But later, after sliced-up pineapple in front of the second half of *The Adventures of Milo and Otis* and a shower and homework check and a lazy round of dishes in the stillness of the late-night kitchen, I washed my face and brushed my teeth and climbed into bed next to Elaine, who I thought was sleeping. I touched her shiny hair, then pulled the quilt over my shoulder; when we were newlyweds, I used to coerce her, every night, to cuddle against me and sleep with her head on my shoulder and her hand on my chest, but that was years ago. Sometimes I used to sandwich her between my legs, and if she tried to move in the night, I'd wake up, grab her, pull her to me, squeeze her like an anaconda.

"Peter?" Her voice, scratchy in the dark.

"I thought you were sleeping."

"I was."

In the winter, she slept in long flannel gowns; in June, she slept in my old T-shirts. I reached down to touch her leg.

"Do you believe in heaven, Pete?"

"What?" I kept my hand on her solid thigh.

"I'm just curious," she said. "I really don't know what you'll say. We never talk about these things."

In our dark bedroom, I thought of a million things at once: A thirty-year-old patient dead last week of septicemia; Alec running into the kitchen, shin guards smudged with dirt and grass; Elaine's shoulders moving to the tiniest rhythm as she chopped carrots. Her soft blond hair. Joe's face flashing, that spidery tear down his cheek.

"Sometimes heaven," I said. "Sometimes hell."

"I believe in heaven," Elaine said, and maybe that was why I pulled her close to me. I held her tight. "And I believe in the untarnished soul," she murmured into my chest. "That we all have one, no matter what we've done in our lives. I've been thinking a lot about it these days, ever since what happened. And that's what I believe."

But the untarnished soul, as far as I knew, did not apply to Jews.

"Look, the baby probably wasn't viable," I said, my mouth near her hair. "If that's what you're thinking about, you shouldn't worry. It doesn't matter what Laura did to the baby. It was doomed when it was born. It would have been brain-damaged and blind."

Elaine was quiet for a while, but I knew she wasn't falling asleep. "I've known Laura Stern her entire life, since she was just a baby herself. Don't you remember? What a beautiful baby she was? She did what she did for a reason. She deserves our sympathy, too."

"Okay," I said. I'd give in tonight.

"She deserves our love, just like any human being. If there's a heaven, let's not deny it to her."

I didn't ask Elaine what her reckoning was, why our local baby-skull smasher belonged in heaven. I only kissed her head and wondered at the way she saw the world, and at the largeness of her mercy.

THAT PATIENT WHO died of septicemia, by the way, was one of the very few patients I lost that year. To be fair, I was an internist, so most of the really sick ones I sent on to specialists; my deaths were almost always the hypertensives and the diabetics with early expiration dates in their charts. But the septic was a different story altogether, and an awful one. Louis Sherman was an associate at Goldman Sachs, himself the father of a newborn, and the ten-month owner of a gorgeously restored Victorian not too far from our own. A wife as blond and lovely and gentile as they come, and this Louis, five seven in thick soles, frizzy hair circling a bald spot, grease on his tie, a triple-jointed nose—who could blame him for selecting as a life partner the slightly insubstantial but beyond charming Christina Sherman, née Connell? The kid knew luck when he stumbled on it. He'd been my patient since he was a teenager and, both a mensch and a generous spirit, apologized for not inviting me to the wedding, but because of his parents' objections to the match, the two had decided to elope.

Now Goldman Sachs types are usually a lot more slick than Louis was, but the kid was a Harvard-certified genius, the kind of Renaissance whiz who beat an old Russian at chess in the park at dawn, made a client ten million by lunch, took a fifteen-minute break to make all the right picks in a rotisserie baseball league, and relaxed after dinner by fiddling a Haydn number on his cello. He was a big donor to Israel, the Fresh Air Fund, the Museum of Modern Art. He spent his Sundays with his baby at his mother's house to give Christina time to catch up with her girlfriends (the baby, by the way, made everything okay again with his parents, as it usually does—she was a twinkling little girl they named Ashley). In short, he was beloved, and on his chart the only oddity was the absence of a spleen, removed after a brutal hockey injury when he was nine.

Christina called me at home on a Sunday night, a privilege I re-served for favored patients. "Louis has a fever, bad pain on the right side of his belly. He's nauseous. Appendicitis, right?"

She really wasn't as dumb as her in-laws made her out. "Sounds like a reasonable assumption. Take him to the ER. I'll meet you there."

The inflamed appendix was removed laparoscopically by a surgeon I liked a lot, and I saw the whole family during rounds the next day. I'd taken care of each of them: Steve Sherman, a math teacher who looked just like his son, down to the thick, owlish glasses; Shelly, a yenta of the first order; and Louis's brother, Joel, a poet, the in-dulged family gadabout. The lovely Christina; the lovelier Ashley, now perched on her daddy's tender lap. "That was a close one, huh, Doc?"

"Not particularly," I said. "Your wife knew what she was doing." The chart proved we'd taken the right precautions for a guy without a spleen; he'd been vaccinated against pneumococcus and other nasty bugs, and we were going to keep an even closer eye on his tempera-ture than we usually did for postsurgical patients. But his spirits were good, his color was fine, the appendix hadn't ruptured—Christina had convinced him to go to the hospital even though he was certain it was indigestion, and had saved him a world of trouble—and I expected nothing but the most positive outcome. I shot the shit with the family for a little while, some good-natured teasing about the Knicks' terrible fortunes (the Shermans were all devoted fans who knew I pledged allegiance to the grungier Nets), and Joel announced, shyly, that he'd just placed a poem in the *Paris Review*. I told him I'd subscribe. I held the baby.

Louis left the hospital the next morning and returned, comatose and dying of septic shock, the evening of the following day. A nicked bowel. Peritonitis.

"It was just so fast," Christina said, as pale and cold as frost. "He said he felt a little hot, and the next thing I knew—it was just so fast."

Louis died three mornings later, six months shy of his daughter's first birthday and his own thirty-first. I was there when he passed, in the back corner of the hospital room, the family standing around the bedside, murmuring their wrenched, dreadful good-byes. His daughter even at six months was quiet and still, as if she understood the lifelong enormity of losing her father. She gripped his finger the way babies do as he slipped away.

What can be done for a case like this? What can I say to the family? What can I do for these breaking hearts? I am as powerless as a child. I can prescribe Xanax for anyone who wants it. I can listen. But I cannot explain why this would happen, beyond hideous fortune and gruesome bacteria, and of course, I cannot bring back the dead.

The shivah, at Louis and Christina's house, was hell. I stood in one of the darkened guest bedrooms and held Steve's hands for a good twenty minutes. We were standing by the window, looking out on a beautiful April evening. The magnolia in the yard was cloaked in blossoms, and the rabbits that lived under the purple hydrangeas were foraging in the fading daylight. The air in the room smelled heavy with food and sweat and burning wax and Lysol and clean linen. Steve didn't cry, didn't speak, just held both my hands in his own. His grief was stark and monstrous behind his thick, gentle glasses. The room was silent.

Jews love life. Doctors love life. It is entrusted to us to preserve it, to do whatever must be done to preserve it; I had failed as a doctor and a Jew, although the Shermans would not think to blame me.

As the room darkened, Shelly knocked on the door and then came in. I let go of Steve's soft hands, he took his wife in his arms, and together they rocked back and forth, her head buried in his neck, a slow, pathetic, inconsolable waltz.

This is what parents who lose their children should look like. Twenty-five weeks or thirty years. Doesn't matter to me. This horrible waltz is what it looks like to be the parents of the dead.

I sat in the Shermans' lovely kitchen that evening and watched the yahrzeit burn. I was the last person to leave.

LAURA STERN'S TRIAL loomed. Alec would soon turn nine. One steamy July night, walking to Carvel to pick up his Fudgie the Whale birthday cake, I saw Laura Stern, by herself, slowly picking at a bowl of chocolate soft-serve on a bench outside. *They let her out by herself? Should she be left alone like that?* She was wearing an enormous blue T-shirt, smudged glasses, dirty sandals. She took the smallest possible bites of ice cream, mouse bites, a defiant breath before she opened her mouth. Her hair was greasy. Her fingers were small. Without quite realizing what I was doing, I hurried Alec into the shop, my hands on his shoulders, awkwardly guarding my son's eyes so that he wouldn't have to look.

CHAPTER THREE

EVENING IN THE garden of good and suburban, I find myself reading a dusty copy of a book by an author I've never heard of before, which I found wedged between the futon and the studio wall. I've enjoyed digging up the detritus Alec has left in this room, not that there's been too much of it, and not that any of it has been particularly informative. Acne gel: so my son worries about zits. Hair gel: he worries, too, about his hair. The books, the Colgate toothpaste, the minifridge full of soy milk and Kashi, the iPod shuffle someone gave him for his high school graduation, not knowing he already had the iPod with the video capabilities. In the bottom drawer of his drawing table, a short stack of *Heavy Metal* magazines, which turn out to be not about music at all but rather an odd hybrid of sci-fi and tits. And this book I'm currently skipping through, moody and poorly written short stories about men who reject society to live in the woods. *Gauguin's Brotherhood.* Inscribed to Alec from someone named Haley, whom I've never heard of, urging him to be well and live according to his strengths.

It occurs to me that if Alec were a wilier kid, he'd have realized that I would try to excavate him from the ruins he'd left behind, and maybe have left a few messages among his garbage to throw me off. A couple of unsent letters—although who sends letters anymore?—or a journal half-full of entries. He was so intent on letting me know I was a total bastard, but it was easier than I wanted it to be to drown out his indictments with the hum of my own guilt. I don't need Alec to tell me I was a bastard when I know it so well myself and when I believe, in my heart, that I never acted without his best interests in mind.

My son looks just like me, physically speaking. Have I mentioned that? He always has. Were it not for the obvious difference in the period in which they were taken, his baby photos would have been indistinguishable from mine. After he was born, Elaine took great pleasure in showing off the baby pictures of me and Alec that she kept side by side in her wallet and having friends bubble about the uncanny resemblance. We were both chubby, Buddha-bellied kids; now we're both tall and lanky, although there's every reason to suspect that he, too, will soften in the gut sometime around fifty, that his hair will thin in the middle of his scalp, and that his eyes will become increasingly nearsighted (although right now he's irritatingly well built, with a thick head of sandy hair and perfect vision).

Throughout his boyhood, Alec was curious about other people, polite, diligent about schoolwork, compliant about chores. He was reflexively kind to strangers. On myriad trips to New York City, God forbid you pass a homeless person and not flip him a quarter—Alec wouldn't speak to you for an hour. I cannot number how many times I've looked at him and been almost knock-kneed with pride and thought, Yes, yes, that's my son. This, I've been told, is a condition peculiar to baby boomer parents, but it doesn't bother me.

If Alec would listen to me now, I would tell him that I've always had his best interests at heart. But I would say it more convincingly than that; I'd try to get around the clichés. Other fathers, I know, they get over their sons—they experience some profound moment

of disappointment, catch the kid whacking off in a bathroom, realize he's a shit to his mother, or just slowly lose the romance they
once had with him, let it curdle the way all romances can. But that
had never happened to me. Sure, I'd had plenty of opportunities to
fall out of love with my son: he'd dropped out of school, he'd run
away a few times, he or some of his friends had stolen two of Elaine's
opal brooches for reasons that he never quite made clear. His senior
year in high school, he got busted at a high school kegger with five
ecstasy tablets on his person, and another time loitering by the town
elementary school in the vicinity of two known marijuana dealers,
Dan Herkel and Shmuley Gold, whom I remembered carpooling
home from Hebrew school ten years earlier. Drug-free school zone,
kids! Pay attention to the signs! Dan and Shmuley both got proba-
tion, but my lawyer brother, Phil, did some maneuvering for us, and
Alec got released with a (skin-tingling) slap on the wrist. He went to
Hampshire scared straight.

And then, three semesters later, he dropped out.

Yet is it too ludicrous to say that of all the people in my life—mother,
father, brother, even my wife—is it too ludicrous to admit that Alec
is my one and only? Others have been better to me, and others have
tried harder, but there's nobody I've ever loved more.

He has said to Elaine quite seriously that as long as I'm here, he
won't even look in the studio's direction. He has said to her that he
doesn't know how she still lives in the same square acreage as me. She
told me she feels as if she has to defend herself against him, defend
herself for taking so long to make up her mind. I tell her she shouldn't
take that from him, that she is, after all, his mother, but she just
shrugs. She says maybe he's right.

Across the darkened lawn, I see the lights in the master bedroom
flicker on. We've always had these flimsy shades in there, always

cocooned in this idea that nobody would want to bother looking in. But it's so easy to look in. The Craig boy could do it. Anyone could do it. Alec—I see him in profile—is standing by the window, talking on his cell phone. I have no idea who he talks to anymore. I hope maybe he's dating someone, although I doubt it. There haven't been any strange cars in our drive, and his car's been parked here too many nights. He gesticulates, shakes his head, snaps off the phone. Leaves the room.

A fight? I'll never know.

True to his word, he doesn't once look in the studio's direction.

LAST YEAR, OBVIOUSLY, it was different.

January 1, 2006, marked the eleventh annual Stern New Year's brunch open house, a tradition ever since Joe finished building an elevated deck with only the help of a rented circular saw and the *Time-Life Complete Home Improvement and Renovation Manual*. Seven hundred dollars' worth of oak four-by-fours and a nail in his thumb that required an early morning trip to the emergency room. I happened to be in the ER when they brought him in, teased him while a resident put in the stitches. "All this, Joe, just to prove a Jew can do manual labor?"

"You goddamn Yid," Joe said, squeezing his eyes shut against the pain. "I'll show you manual labor right in the face just as soon as I can move my hand again."

The deck turned out to be a beauty: Iris stained it dark walnut and the Stern family took to eating every weekend meal out there from March through October under a big pink umbrella on the cheap patio furniture Joe bought from Sears. Sometimes Elaine and I would stop by during walks around the neighborhood and dig into Stern leftovers or drink scotch and maybe share a cigar with Joe and Iris, the four of us passing it around like a joint. The kids—Neal, Adam, Pauline—would scramble to the rec room to play video games; if Alec was around, he'd join them. Suburbs, man. I don't care what anybody says. It's the only civilized way to live.

The New Year's brunch ritual mandated that cocktails be served on the beloved deck, no matter how frigid the temperature. Joe liked it that way, but Iris kept a Dutch oven full of hot cocoa bubbling in the kitchen for those too sane to brave the weather. Usually the men would stand out on the deck, blowing on their hands and talking about football, and the women would huddle around the hot chocolate, nibbling guiltily on doughnuts and bitching about their husbands.

January 1, 2006, Elaine woke up first—a rarity—and put on a yoga tape in the den. Alec woke up next, dry-mouthed from too much partying the previous night, tiptoed into our bedroom, and plugged through our drawers of drug samples until he found a hidden stash of naproxen. His jostling and slamming woke me up.

"What are you doing?"

"Headache."

"What time is it?"

"Almost ten."

"You're kidding." When was the last time I'd slept this late? We'd had dinner the night before with my office mate Janene and her husband, Bill, at the Garland Chophouse, $160 per couple with a bottle of domestic champagne thrown in, and I remembered, in the panicky delirium of the last day of the year, deciding to splurge on three bottles of 2003 Dominus to wash down our T-bones.

"Where's your mother?"

"Downstairs ashtanga. The incense is going."

"I see."

I found my robe and tiptoed down the stairs, for some reason delighted to find my wife on the rug, in her green Hampshire sweatsuit, in full downward dog.

"Trying to start off the New Year with some good karma, huh?"

She looked up at me and sighed. "Don't make fun."

"I'm not," I said, and I wasn't. "Want me to make coffee? Or would herbal tea better suit the occasion? Maybe we have some chai?"

She lowered herself into plank position and then into cobra (I'd taken a few ashtanga classes myself when the JCC offered them), and then she collapsed on the floor. "Coffee would be terrific," she said. "We really drank way too much last night, didn't we?"

"We certainly did," I agreed, heading into the kitchen. "What time does Joe want us over?"

"Twelve, twelve thirty," she said. "There's a babka in the fridge. It's for them—don't touch it."

"Babka, huh?"

"I got it at the Rockland Bakery yesterday. I mean it, Pete, don't touch."

Slowly we drank our coffee, showered, and dressed: I wore my jeans-and-tweed-blazer usual, and Elaine spent some time on her makeup and hair. Twenty-five years of marriage, and perhaps more than our share of connubial ups and downs, and yet, at least that morning, neither one of us looked much the worse for wear. She dressed in a pretty turquoise blouse and black pants and I helped her adjust the heavy straps of the compression bra she still liked to wear so that they didn't peek out from her shirt.

"You look great, Lainie," I said, kissing her neck.

She patted her hips. "This year, I swear, I'm losing twenty pounds."

"You don't need to do a thing." She actually looked rather fetching to me—I had a soft spot for *zaftig*—so I patted her ass, but she slapped me away.

"Get real," she said. "I'm not even eating any of the babka. No eggnog either." Elaine loved eggnog. "I mean it, Pete. Twenty pounds by December thirty-first."

As we fussed with our coats by the back door, Alec looked up at us from his perch at the kitchen counter, where he was devouring a New Year's breakfast of cherry vanilla Häagen-Dazs and picking idly at the crossword. "Where are you two going all dressed up like debutants?"

"It's the Sterns' brunch," Elaine said, touching up her lipstick in the mirror by the door.

"You weren't going to invite me?"

I thought he was kidding.

"Dude, what the hell? Just let me get dressed. I'll be ready in five minutes."

"You want to come?"

"Why wouldn't I want to come?"

"Why would you?"

He gave us a confused look, stuck the ice cream back in the freezer, and jogged up the stairs. "The Sterns throw a great party," he called, which was, I guess, the best and only reason to go to any party at all.

Since he'd been home from college, Alec had been either recalcitrant or put-upon, and only since we'd finished renovating the studio above the garage had he shown any interest at all in civilized behavior. I was never entirely sure what our exact crime was, or why he was so bent on returning to live with us, its perpetrators, but Alec had a list of accusations a yard long that he often rattled off, unprompted. It seemed one big problem was that by insisting he attend a four-year college, we were forcing him to live according to the bourgeois mandates (I kid you not) of our choosing, not his. Also it proved that we didn't really believe in him as an artist, because if we *did* believe in him, we'd have used the money we were otherwise spending on tuition on a grand tour of European galleries and museums. According to Alec, four years of gazing at the fabled canvases in the Louvre, the Tate, the Reina Sofia, and the Uffizi would be a far better use of his time and our money than "bullshit figure drawing" at Hampshire. And for all I knew, he was right, but that didn't make him any less of a shit to be around, nor did it mean that Elaine and I were about to let him screw around Europe for four years on our dime.

The studio above the garage appeased him somewhat, and he got a job working nights at Utrecht art supply in the city and made friends with a few of his co-workers and taught after-school painting at the Red Barn Cultural Center. He'd started to become an almost-benign presence in the house, and we liked having someone to talk to besides each other. He conceded to the occasional Nets game with me, and over beers and veggie burgers after the games (he had the exact feelings you'd expect about eating meat) we talked, man to man, about nothing in particular.

"Is Neal home from Boston for the break?" he asked as we drove over to Freeman Court.

Neal Stern was almost the same age as Alec, but to my and Joe's disappointment they'd never really gotten along, not even as kids. Totally different spirits; Neal studious and snarky, Alec earnestly bohemian, petulant, but sometimes, despite himself, charming.

Elaine turned to the backseat. "I suppose he is."

"That kid's probably made a million bucks already, huh?" Alec said. "Biomedical engineering?"

"You've been keeping up with Neal Stern?"

"Come on." Alec laughed. "Like you guys haven't mentioned him enough? I have his whole biography memorized."

"We've mentioned him?" I honestly had no idea that we brought up Neal Stern, and I immediately felt defensive both for myself and for my son.

"I don't remember having said his name more than twice in the past six months."

"Hah!" Alec barked, and then, just to make sure we got the point, he did it again. "Hah."

"Really?"

"Neal Stern is graduating Phi Beta Kappa from MIT. Neal Stern has co-published eleven papers in leading biomedical journals. Neal Stern won a summer NIS fellowship to study protons in Germany." But Alec sounded more amused than bitter.

"Protons, that's right," Elaine said. "That was last summer, wasn't it?"

"Hah," Alec muttered again.

"You know, if it matters at all, not only do I not remember mentioning Neal Stern in such admiring tones, but if I did, it wasn't because I wanted you to act more Nealish," I said. We were already almost at the Sterns' house. The day was sunny; we could have walked. "I'm just as surprised at that kind of ridiculous achievement as you are. I was mentioning it only as a sort of Ripley's Believe It or Not. Not as an object lesson."

"Yeah, well, for your information, Neal Stern has always been a total asshole."

"Hmmm . . . ," Elaine murmured. "Is that true? An asshole? But don't outrageously smart people often have rather poor social skills?"

"That's a stereotype," Alec said.

"Or maybe he's just a little inept?"

"Mom, he's an asshole. Not to break your heart or anything."

"Pete, is that true?" Elaine was incapable of thinking the worst of people, especially kids. She looked over at me, and I shrugged.

I knew that Joe, too, often thought his oldest son was something of an asshole, although he rarely let on. But throughout the kid's childhood, I'd seen Joe offer him some fatherly trifle—a game of catch, a bowl of salami and eggs, a trip to Great Adventure with me and Alec and a few other neighbors—only to watch him get rebuffed without so much as an apology. "Dad, I don't have *time* for that"—redheaded Neal typing vigorously on his expensive laptop, and Joe retreating in wonder and sadness.

"You know who's going to be there, actually," said Elaine as we found a parking spot a block away from the Sterns' already-crowded street. "Laura. She's home from California. She moved back into the house last week. Iris set her up in the basement. I think she's planning on staying for a while."

"You're kidding." I hadn't seen Laura Stern in at least a decade, if not longer. Joe and Iris kept us apprised of her peregrinations, but rarely in great detail. "I thought she was raising high-end goats or something."

"She was," Elaine said. "But then she decided enough was enough and she wanted to come home."

"High-end *goats?*" said the incredulous boy who wanted to spend four years backpacking from Belgrade to Barcelona. "Who *are* these people?"

"Iris's sister has some kind of farm in Sonoma," Elaine said. "She was making goat cheese for restaurants. You can buy the stuff at Zabar's."

"Goat cheese," Alec said dismissively as we walked up the Stern's cobbled path. "Kills a baby and goes off to Sonoma to make *goat cheese.*"

"Alec."

"Smashes in the skull of a—"

"That's enough," Elaine said sharply. Alec sighed heavily but kept his mouth shut.

The party was already in full swing and the Sterns' house was crowded with the spicy holiday odors of perfume, eggnog, French toast, and a wood fire. Someone's children chased someone else's children up and down the staircase. I heard Vince Dirks, my office mate, chortling in the living room. Bill Rothman found me as we tossed our coats in the guest bedroom. He placed a heavy hand across my shoulder.

"I'm a wreck."

"You drank too much last night, Bill. I tried to stop you."

"Three bottles of Dominus. Three bottles! You can't waste that. What could I do?"

"You have a point."

"Janene's still passed out at home. The kids think it's hysterical. They've never seen their mother with a hangover before."

"She'll be okay?"

"I left some aspirin and Pepto by her bed."

"That's nice of you."

"The least I could do."

"Happy New Year, Bill."

"Happy New Year, Pete." And then he hugged me, because he was a pediatrician and that kind of guy.

Downstairs, I wove my way through the New Year's revelers and traded auld lang synes with my familiars. You live in a suburban town for twenty-three years, you can't help knowing every local. Through the French doors to the kitchen I saw an elderly man I didn't know talking to Christina Sherman, recently engaged to a Manhattan lawyer, Shelly told me, and as gorgeous and lithe as ever. She would always be recovering from Louis's death, but she was too wise to let herself rot in grief. She'd taken a teaching job at Round Hill Country Day, and I often saw her early at the JCC, her in her spandex running clothes, me sweating, embarrassed, in baggy shorts. The old guy was standing very close to her, practically breathing down her neck, but Christina was too polite to back away. I thought about going to say hello to her. I hoped she wouldn't leave our little town for the big city.

"Pete!"

"MaryJo." I turned. Bert had died eight years ago, but MaryJo still made the rounds. So did her kids, and her grandkids, now old enough to bring their own tubs of rigatoni to a neighborhood potluck. I kissed all the Birches on the cheek and helped myself to a steaming ladleful of pasta and ricotta before anyone else could get a spoon in.

Out on the deck, Joe was wearing a beat-up parka and a Santa Claus hat, whipping up his special New Year's peppermint martinis (schnapps, vodka, a candy cane for a stirrer) for all comers. "Dr. D.!" he said when he saw me. "Happy New Year!"

"Happy New Year yourself, old man," I said, slurping down my rigatoni, wishing for some reason I had a Santa hat of my own. "You got any grown-up drinks back there?"

"Bloody Mary?"

"I said grown up." I was a firm believer in the hair of the dog.

"Attaboy." Joe grinned and poured me a scotch. There was a hearty minyan milling on the deck, all men except for a fierce, feline-looking Asian girl in enormous pants, a camouflage jacket, and steel-tipped combat boots. Soon Neal Stern emerged from the kitchen with a mug of hot chocolate in his hand and put a possessive arm around the girl, whose frown softened into a gentle sneer. Neal was balding, just like his dad at his age, but he'd had the questionable inclination to shave his head, making him look both dorky and felonious. He was freckled, skinny, with a bulbous Adam's apple and dark eyes set a bit too close together; I had no idea what he'd done to win the girl, but I imagined it had something to do with the very profitable future he seemed assured of.

"Dr. Pete," Neal said—Dr. Pete was what all the Stern kids called me—and removed his arm from around his girlfriend to shake my hand. "This is Amy."

"Nice to meet you, Amy. Happy New Year."

Amy blinked at me. "Well, yes," she said like a sphinx. Then she turned her wintry gaze to Neal. "I'm totally frozen out here. I'm going inside."

"Broads," Neal said to me after she'd removed herself from our company. "Can't live with 'em, can't live without 'em, right?" He chortled in a mirthless way, and I knew that if Alec were outside with us he quite possibly would have socked Neal right in the freckles. But I was an adult, so I made conversation.

"I hear your sister's back in town, huh?"

Neal circled a finger around his ear to signify "crazy," then took a fat sip of hot chocolate. "She showed up with her backpack last week, looks like she hasn't showered in days. Almost ten o'clock at night. I'd just gotten home from school. Amy was in the guest bedroom, you know? 'Cause Amy's from Hong Kong and she wasn't going to go all the way home for break. So she was just going to stay here, with me, but of course my parents are like, No way is she staying in your room." Neal made the crazy gesture again, and I thought of old Mrs. Stern, keeping me and Elaine separate on our trips to Philadelphia.

"So I ask her, What are you doing here? And she says, Is this my house or isn't it? I'm here because I'm here. Let me in. And what could

I say?" He laughed. "She hasn't lived here for thirteen years, though, you know? So how could this be her house?"

"I guess it's been a while since you two spent much time together."

"Since I was a kid," Neal said. "I mean, it's not like I really know her—it's more like I just know *about* her."

Joe, I could tell, was listening in, even though he was faking interest in a conversation with Stu Hurdy about the koi pond Stu was installing. Joe kept his eyes on Stu, nodded intermittently, but tilted his Santa's hat in our direction and sucked on the vodka end of his peppermint stick. Joe almost never mentioned Laura anymore; he was too protective. I suddenly felt like a prick for bringing her up with a shmo like Neal.

"What I mean is, Laura's been gone ever since I was, I don't know, seven years old, so it's not like we're great friends or anything. I've only seen her once a year, if that."

"Anyway," I said, trying to divert the conversation.

"And you know, the way she lives, it's just laughable. Like she's some sort of renegade. Remember how she was living on that island down near Puerto Rico, dreadlocks down to her ass, making jewelry for a 'living'?" Neal put the quotes in with his hands. "Met us in Florida so she could ask my parents for ten grand. Which they gave her, of course, no problem. Because God forbid she should lose her mind and do something stupid and they have to pay for more lawyers."

Joe was still listening over Stu's deadpan description of koi hibernation; he turned and glared at Neal. I remembered the Florida extortion, more than seven years ago—a family trip to Miami to celebrate some cousin's bar mitzvah, Laura appearing out of nowhere, like a winsome rag doll in handmade clothes. She'd been living in a trailer on Vieques with a girlfriend who spoke no English, working to rid the island of its U.S. military presence and, yes, making jewelry out of cowrie shells. She needed money for an operation for her roommate. She'd been out of the psych ward for eighteen months. Joe and Laura wrote her a check, on the condition that she get a haircut, buy a dress, and come to the bar mitzvah. She vanished from the Marriott lobby while they were at the reception desk, checking her in.

"So now we're supposed to welcome her back with open arms even though she's treated us alternately like a bank and a group of strangers for ten years."

"Neal, stop it," Joe said, cutting Stu right off. "You've said enough." Joe's voice was mild, but his expression was fierce in a way I rarely saw it.

"Whatever, Dad. You might be in her little cult, but that doesn't mean—"

"Neal," Joe said, and that was all, but his tone now matched his expression, and Neal was smart enough to shut up. There was something about the subject of Laura that made all us parents prickly. Joe turned back to Stu. Neal looked at me and rolled his eyes.

"So anyway . . . ," he said.

"Anyway."

"I guess I'll go inside and find Amy." Marginally louder: "And don't worry, Stalin, I'll mind the censors." Did Neal really just compare his father to Stalin? I watched as he loped back into the kitchen, an ironic tilt to his shaved head.

"That kid," Joe said, his expression softening but that fierceness still in his eyes. He forced a little laugh. "Never fails to say what's on his mind, you know?"

"A strong personality," I said.

Joe sighed heavily. "That's one way to describe it."

"Anyway, Joe, the thing about it is you've got to watch for raccoons." Stu Hurdy was unstoppable. "Raccoons can fish just like bears. You've seen those nature movies? They stick their paws into the pond and scoop them out like it's nothing. It's really quite remarkable to watch. But evidently there are certain plants that are naturally raccoon-repellent, you install them around the pond and it saves the fish from . . ."

Joe gave me a bleak look. I tipped an imaginary Santa's cap in his direction and went into the kitchen to find my wife or kid. I was hit with the woodsmoke and eggnog but also something else — the vague but persistent smell of striving, of other people's koi ponds. Round Hill isn't New Canaan or even Bernardsville; for the most part it's a new-money kind of place, more Jewish than those other chimneyed suburbs, more Korean and Italian, too. We've got more doctors here than socialites, more lawyers than casual investors, and many more outer-borough accents. Our children, who attend fancy colleges and decide to become oil painters (or set designers, animal behaviorists, poets) are not like we are, we who went to City College or Queens College or Pitt on scholarship. They take things for granted that we never will, talk casually about tennis and the Tate Modern in ways that give us secret, overweening pleasure. As for us, we like it here in Round Hill because we're twenty-five minutes from the Old Country, because as Jews we're always afraid of being run out — but at least from here it's easy to get back home: the Bronx, Brooklyn, my own little Yonkers.

"Dr. Dizinoff! We were just talking about you!" Shelly Sherman and the beauteous Christina were standing over the Crock-Pot of hot chocolate, and Ashley Sherman, now almost fourteen years old, was leaning shyly against her mother's flank. Ashley, after a promising start as a toddler, had turned out to favor her father's phenotype almost exactly: the same frizzy brown hair, the same owlish eyes, the same hooked Ashkenazi nose. I assumed, however, that she was as smart as her dad had been; she was our town's reigning junior-level chess champion and had been written up several times in the *Round Hill Robin.*

"What were you saying about me?" If I were the type, I would have muttered, Aw shucks. "Only good things?"

"It's the Nets you like, right? That's the team?"

"It is," I confirmed, kissing Shelly and then Christina New Year's hellos.

"Oh, good," Christina said, extending her cheek, "because my friend Harvey has some season tickets he's just too darn busy to ever use. I thought you might want some."

"Why not?"

"And not to brag," she whispered, "but I think those tickets are very good."

After a decade and a half in the Northeast, Christina still had her loose-voweled Atlanta drawl, and for a minute I feared I was reddening under her close attention.

"I don't know the least thing about basketball, and this one here"— she tousled Ashley's rough curls—"she's too busy with her school-work to want to go all the way to the Meadowlands for a game."

"Well, that's very nice of you. I'll buy them from you." Sports tickets were favored currency in Round Hill: tickets, time-shares, late-night medical advice.

"Oh, don't be silly, Pete. We wouldn't do anything with them otherwise. You'll take 'em for free." She lay a beautiful hand on my arm for a minute, and I'll admit it, I tingled right through my jacket. "Ashley, aren't you going to say hi to Dr. Dizinoff?"

"Hi," the girl said, burying her mouth in her mother's side.

"Hi, sweetheart."

"Well, we should get going soon, but I wanted to ask you about the tickets. I'll come by the office and drop them off."

"Or I'll bring them," Shelly said. "I have an appointment two weeks from now, a checkup." Louis's death had turned the two ladies into fast friends. I still saw all the Shermans regularly except Ashley. They still trusted me completely, despite the loss they had suffered under my watch, a loss that still caused me such shame.

"Well, looking forward to it," I said.

And as the Shermans disappeared, my wife, whose presence I'd been completely unaware of, came up to me with a wry smile and powdered sugar on her sweater. She stuffed half a doughnut into my mouth and said, "Happy New Year, baby."

"Happy New Year to you," I said, trying not to choke on the doughnut. Elaine laughed. She was in a good mood and, I think, judging from her breath, had spiked her hot chocolate. She kissed me on the cheek. The kitchen had cleared out — open-house guests were like a tide, with their own hourly ebb and flow — and so it was just Iris, Elaine, and me in the room, each of us a little bleary from the night before and the frenzy of the party.

"Happy New Year, Pete," Iris said.

"Happy New Year, Iris." She was curled up in the breakfast nook, letting the mess in the kitchen build around her. She had a dusky voice — it was one of her innumerable charms — and a perfectly wonderful way of adjusting to chaos. Glasses and mugs piled up in the sink, stray pastries lined the counter, and the Crock-Pot of hot chocolate had spilled over and dribbled pools of chocolate on the floor, but Iris just sat back under the window, her grayish red hair pulled back in a ponytail, her cool green eyes half-closed. Once upon a time, I had loved her beyond reason.

"This is a wonderful party," I said, and I slid next to her in the breakfast nook.

"Are you enjoying yourself?"

"How could I not?"

"Doughnuts and shots of scotch and people who admire him," Elaine hummed. "These are a few of Pete's favorite things."

Iris laughed. "I didn't know we were serving scotch." She leaned her head against the frosty window behind the breakfast nook. She was wearing a black turtleneck and bronze hoop earrings and looked as much like a graying bohemian as she did a commercial banker. There had been an article in the *Wall Street Journal* about her a few years ago, some dilemma she had had with unethical clients, a pixelated picture on the front page, her hair pulled back, severe glasses. The story had claimed her income was somewhere just north of a million dollars. According to my brother, the *Journal* underestimated it by at least half a million.

"That much money? Come on, Phil. These are people who buy their sneakers at Target."

"Congenitally cheap," Phil explained to me. "The quirks of the truly wealthy."

In half a lifetime of talking about everything, Joe and I never talked about the article. I was ashamed of my jealousy, and Joe, I think, was ashamed of how much money his wife made. He was ostentatious about frugality, liked to complain about his daughter Pauline's J.Crew habit. But that year, when we went to the City Opera for a modernist staging of *Bohème*, Elaine poked me in the side. She was holding open the program, fingernail pointing at the tiny type in the back: the Sterns were in the Director's Circle, one hundred thousand dollars plus. And when we needed a new lobby at Round Hill Medical Center, were looking for named sponsor opportunities, Joe quietly arranged for the thing to be built by some hip Manhattan architects and named for his dead father.

"There's scotch out on the deck, I believe," I said. "Joe was keeping it for his closest comrades. Want me to get you some?"

She shook her head. "Unlike some people, I can't drink scotch in the afternoon."

"Who are you kidding, Iris?"

"Oh, come on, Pete." She winked at me. "Them days are long gone."

"Them days," Elaine echoed. She sounded wistful. Them days, them days, them boozy, steely, wintry, pot-fueled Route 80 West days. Iris used to sit next to me in statistics. She wore short skirts, huge earrings, go-go boots, and low-cut peasant blouses in the dead of winter. She was from Allentown, where her parents ran a struggling butcher shop. She and I were both funded by the same scholarships. She walked me to organic chemistry and warned me about my future.

"You better do well here, Pete. Med school exemptions are harder and harder to come by."

"So I've heard," I said, and boy, had I heard: classmates were going to medical school in Mexico, Belgium, New South Wales. "But there won't be another draft."

"There won't be another draft?" She laughed. "Don't be an idiot. Only an idiot would believe a goddamn thing Nixon says."

"There's no way anyone's going to send me to Vietnam," I said. "I don't care what it takes." I didn't even know what Nixon had said on the matter. I was only sure I loved Iris Berg with every filmy corpuscle in my body.

"You're an idiot," she said. And I was.

From the deck outside, Stu Hurdy, red-cheeked from the winter and the booze and the pleasures of his emerging koi pond, banged loudly on the window. Iris turned and banged back.

"What a bunch of fucking drunks. I'm too old for this kind of thing. Remind me why we keep doing this every year?"

"Your husband enjoys playing Santa," I said.

"Playing Santa." She sighed. "Of course he does. My husband, Kriss Kringle." Iris often spoke this way about her husband, in tones of charmed exasperation or grim tolerance. They'd been married for longer than Elaine and me by four years, had four children, and had built a (very) prosperous life and suffered both normal and unique sufferings, yet still Iris often made it sound as if Joe was the little brother she'd allowed to tag along. At Pitt, after I'd introduced them, Iris would often shake her head at me and ask me how I'd let her get talked into this, "this" meaning a long-standing love affair with Joe Stern.

"You should ask him," I'd say, because I never had the courage to say, Well, Iris, because you wouldn't have me.

"So is everyone behaving themselves out there?" she asked me, raising a languid arm above her head. "Do I have to go outside and take charge?"

"You don't have to do a thing," I said, patting her narrow knee. "I met Neal's girlfriend, by the way. He seems quite enamored."

"Amy?" Iris smiled. "She's a hoot, isn't she? Straight from Kowloon to Cambridge, her father's big in Red Party politics, supposedly. Her mother was raised in Singapore. She's full of disdain for the American way of life but drags Pauline to the mall every chance she can get."

"She seems like she's good at taking charge."

"Oh, she's got a pair of brass balls on her." Iris grinned. "Bosses my son around like a foreman. I've never seen Neal kowtow like this, not even when he was trying to sucker teachers into writing his college recommendations. I get an enormous kick out of it, to tell you the truth."

"I didn't even know Neal was dating," Elaine said.

"They've been together for almost six months. Neal thinks he's gonna marry her, I can tell. He's probably right. Brace yourselves for a Jewish-Buddhist ceremony on some lucky-number date this fall."

"Really?" Elaine said. "That's so exciting!"

"Please," Iris scoffed. "She's only in it for the citizenship."

"Are we talking about Amy again?"

I looked up. The voice was an echo of Iris's, sardonic, grumbly, but still it took me a second to put it together.

"Dr. Pete," Laura Stern said. "It's been a while."

My goodness.

"Hello," I said. "It certainly has."

I hadn't seen her since the week they took her to Gateway House thirteen years ago, and Christ, the girl had changed in a million beautiful ways. Back then she'd been hollow-eyed, eviscerated by the trial and the confinement and everything that preceded it. A criminal, a teenager, depressed and hidden in oversized shirts. But now—now she was like Iris twenty years ago, only more so, or better, or right here in the soft pink flesh.

"You remember Laura, don't you, Pete?"

"How could I forget?"

But she was nobody I'd met before. Thick reddish hair falling over her shoulders, white skin, green brown eyes, a pale smattering of freckles, thin shoulders, white blouse. Benign smile, demure twinkle in her eyes. She'd spent the past three years tending goats. I stood.

"Laura," I said. "How are you?"

"I'm well," she said, and she leaned in to press her cheek to mine. She smelled like clean laundry. The girl who'd made cowrie-shell jewelry on a godforsaken island, washed her dirty clothing in a creek for three years.

"Hey, Elaine."

"Hi, sweetheart," Elaine said, her voice soft with familiarity. Elaine knew Laura almost better than anyone did. They'd corresponded while the girl was at Gateway House and even after: Elaine had sent her her Bergen lecture notes on Chaucer, the Angles and Celts, the Norse influence on the English language; Laura sent back long letters about the terrible food at Gateway, taking up smoking, trying to quit, missing her siblings. I frowned whenever the letters arrived, and often thought about tossing them before Elaine came home, sure that Laura was bad, bloodstained, and that Elaine shouldn't spend her time on charity cases, even the daughter of our closest friends.

Elaine and Laura hugged. "You look beautiful, Laura. Just beautiful."

"So do you."

"Oh God, no," Elaine said reflexively. "I got so fat."

"Stop it, Elaine. She's right—you look great."

Laura smiled at me, and did I note something complicit there? I felt instantly guilty—although at that moment I had less than nothing to be guilty about—and sat back down next to Iris. Laura scooched in on the other side of the breakfast nook. Elaine pulled up a chair. "So," she said. "Tell me everything."

"Mmm . . . let's see." Laura pulled a crumb from the babka sitting on the kitchen table. "I was in California, as you guys probably know. Learning cheese making with my aunt Enid, which is an experience I only recommend for the truly dedicated or the truly insane. We managed a flock of fifty-two floppy-eared Nubians and seventy white-spotted Alpines on one hundred acres of Sonoma pasturage. We had two thousand-yard sheds full of sixty-four-gallon bulk stainless tanks, milking equipment, pens, everything. Enid and I had to oversee the milking, the aging, the caves, the packaging. I was supposed to help with the distribution. Marketing. Thank God I spoke Spanish. Enid's a nut, you know."

"Be fair," Iris said. "She's built a million-dollar business out of a flock of goats."

"She's a nut," Laura said, more definitively, and I thought, Takes one to . . . "And then I was in France for a month after that with my cousin Harris—remember him? Steve's son? He got an internship at a vineyard and asked me to come along."

"A vineyard?" Elaine said. "How lovely. I didn't know."

"Neither did we," Iris said. "We never know where she is half the time. We just assume she's somewhere in the world living the life of Riley."

"Oh, come on, Mom," Laura said, rubbing her mother's shoulder as though Iris were a recalcitrant child. "I was picking grapes in Alsace," she explained. *"Le vendange.* Late harvest. Part of the whole riesling process." Elaine and I must have looked perplexed. "I've been trying to learn about traditional foodways, putting together this body of knowledge that's really being lost. Wine making, cheese making. I'm thinking of taking some bread classes next."

"Ah," Elaine said. Iris smirked.

"So what brings you home?" I asked. "Bread classes?"

"Oh, you know," Laura said, waving her hand in the air. She had small hands, freshly painted fingernails, light beige, a small pearl ring on her right index finger. There was something almost costumey, though, about her decorous getup.

"She needs money," Iris said blandly.

"I'm sorry?"

"She needs money," Iris repeated. "She came back home because she's broke."

"Thanks, Mom."

"I'm sorry." Iris sighed. "What I meant to say was that my sister is selling the goat farm to an Austrian dairy conglomerate, and after a brief vinicultural tour of eastern France, Laura came home to reassess her prospects for a while. And learn how to bake bread."

"My mother has a way of making it sound as though I've been frittering away my life instead of educating myself for the past eight years," Laura said.

"That's not what I said—"

"She also likes to make it sound as though I didn't have the right to return to my own family. As though I were somehow unwelcome."

Elaine and I both reached for the babka at the same time.

"You could have called first," Iris said, her voice flat.

"My mother," Laura said, "seems to like it when I call first."

Were they really going to fight like this, right in front of us? Elaine plucked more cake. "Well, let's see what you've missed here in Round Hill—"

"I've missed something?" Laura asked, flaring her attention at my wife. "Isn't the whole point of Round Hill that you can be gone for ten years and not miss a thing?"

"They busted a school board member for kiddie porn a few years ago," Elaine blurted.

"Ah," Laura said after a few seconds. "Well, I guess that's something."

The sullen teenager clutching *Daniel Deronda*. The girl in the news stories, in the big flannel shirt. The toddler clutching roses at our wedding. The day they took her to Gateway, leaving before dawn, stealing away like thieves in Joe's Volvo. She twirled her pearl ring on her finger and smiled benignly at me, then Elaine, then her mother. (The Sterns weren't cheap, by the way. They kept their money in trusts for Laura to use in perpetuity.)

"You know," she said, "I was just thinking it would be nice to get to know my siblings a little better. It's been a long time since we all lived under the same roof. And Neal's home for winter break for maybe the last time, so I thought I'd, you know, interact with him a little bit before he goes off to the world of high-profile bioengineering. And before he marries the Red Menace."

"Well," Elaine said, "I think that's lovely."

Malva, the Jamaican housekeeper who'd worked for the Sterns for eighteen years, emerged to interrupt our reunion. Malva was tall, chesty, and chronically impatient. She wore a cross the size of a fist around her neck. "You're out of tonic in the living room, Iris."

"There's more in the basement," Iris said. "We've got a couple of cases. Grab Neal and Adam to give you a hand."

"Neal's upstairs making out with his girlfriend."

"Well, for Christ's sake, Malva," Iris said. "Stop them."

"That's not my business," Malva said, her eyes narrowing. She had a daughter in nursing school in Ohio, a son in prison in Kingston. "That's your business," she said. "You're the mother."

"I don't feel like being the mother," Iris said. "I'm sick of being the mother. Would someone else please be the mother for me? Malva, could you please do that? I'll give you a raise."

Malva crossed her arms. "Iris, you pay me and I will do my job and get more tonic, but I do not, will not, stop your son from doing whatever nasty business he do with his girlfriend upstairs. It makes me uncomfortable."

"Oh, fine, Malva. Be that way."

Just then, Alec poked his head in the kitchen, looking a little flushed from spiked eggnog. "Alec, go help Malva get the tonic from the basement," Elaine ordered.

"Sure," he said, surprisingly amenable, and he followed the housekeeper down the stairs.

"That's not Alec," Laura said.

"You haven't seen him in a while," Elaine said. "He's really grown up."

"The last time I saw him, I think I was babysitting," Laura said, which was a lie; we never asked her to babysit. "How old is he now?"

"Neal's age," Iris said. "He's twenty."

"Jesus Christ," Laura laughed, slapping her hand against her forehead. Everything about her felt more and more theatrical. Iris was still leaning back against the window with her eyes closed. "He's finishing college!"

"Not exactly," I said. I stood to pour myself some coffee. In a moment, Malva and Alec appeared at the top of the stairs, each loaded down with a pallet of tonic, and Laura leaped up to help. She took the weight of half of Alec's pallet in her own hands. "Alec Dizinoff," she said, "I'm Laura Stern."

It was a cartoonish, ludicrous transformation that came over my son. His eyes got big, his mouth opened slightly, he breathed heavily through his nostrils as though he'd just spied the Holy Virgin in a pat of butter. The two of them gently set the pallet on the kitchen counter. I put down my coffee to help Malva.

"Hello," Alec whispered. He cleared his throat.

"How are you doing?"

"Good." He still looked like a cartoon. "How are you?"

"I'm well," she said. "Just back in town. I don't think I've seen you since you were in grade school."

"I guess," he said.

"What are you giving me that look for?"

"A look?"

"Like you've just seen a ghost." This grown woman was teasing my twenty-year-old son.

"It's, you know . . . ," Alec started. "I just . . . it's been a long time."

"I know it has," she said. "What have I missed?"

"Missed?"

She tried again. "What have you been up to since we last saw each other?"

"Oh. A lot of things, I guess."

"Like puberty?" Oh, I couldn't believe this. My poor boy turned scarlet; Laura noticed and tried to soften up. "And high school and college and everything else . . ."

"Actually, lately I've been, um, making art."

"Really? What kind? Where are you working?"

"Oil paintings, mostly. I have a . . . I have, like, a studio in the garage at my parents' house, I've been working there for the past six months, so . . ."

"You're kidding. That's so great."

"I'm not. Um, kidding." They were still standing by the counter. I watched them, forcing myself not to interrupt. "And also I've been teaching oils at the Red Barn Cultural Center and, you know, trying to find a gallery to represent me. Maybe somewhere in the city. I don't know, it's not that easy to find good representation, but there are a couple of artists' co-ops in Piermont . . ."

"That's amazing, Alec," Laura said, and she touched his arm for the tiniest of seconds. "That really is."

"Oh, it's not, really," he said, but he was blushing. Laura leaned her arms on the counter, and Alec followed suit. They were cordoning themselves off in this way, but I could still hear them. Iris and Elaine shimmied out of the breakfast nook to go pester Joe for some New Year's martinis.

"You know," Laura said, "one of the things I like best about coming home is catching up with people I never would have expected to. In the past three days I've seen so many people. Kids I went to school with, my sixth-grade teacher, Mrs. Hammel—"

"You had her?" Alec said. "Mrs. Camel?"

"Mrs. Camel, oh God, totally." Moira Hammel had an unfortunate humpback; I'd seen her for her osteoporosis a dozen times over the years, but unfortunately her spine was deteriorating, leaving dozens of small compression fractures.

"She was the worst, right?"

"Once I actually did it by mistake in class, was like, Mrs. Camel, I have a question—"

"You didn't—"

"And the whole class got very quiet, and she turned those weird eyes on me—she had eyes like a lizard, remember?—and said, What did you say, little girl?"

I doubted sincerely that Moira Hammel turned into the Wicked Witch of the West, or that her gentle blue eyes could put anyone in mind of a lizard.

"And the whole class was silent, and I said, Nothing, Mrs. Hammel, and she just stared at me for, like, five whole minutes and I almost had a seizure I was so scared."

"Jesus." Alec was giving the story more laughter than it warranted.

"I was so racked with guilt, I went up to her after class and apologized. But then she didn't accept my apology."

"Really?"

"Just shook her head and said, One day, Laura, you'll understand. One day. And then she turned her hump on me and I cried the whole way home. It was like I understood right then. Whatever it was she wanted me to understand."

"Wow," Alec said. "And then you bumped into her?"

"Two days ago at the Grand Union. I introduced myself and we had a very pleasant conversation and I could tell she had no idea who I was." Moira Hammel has a bit of dementia, true—but trust me when I tell you that *everyone* in Round Hill knew who Laura Stern was.

"And I almost cried on the way back home this time, too. She looked so terrible. And she was all alone."

"Wow," Alec said again, all eloquence.

"I know." Laura returned her hand to my son's arm. "She was all by herself, you know?" She let her voice go small and fragile, and I could see Alec's posture change; she was getting him to protect her, reassure her. "All those single servings in her grocery cart. A single chicken breast. A single pint of ice cream."

Oh, please. Moira Hammel was champion of her bridge club, still managed to do water aerobics every day, and had three granddaughters who doted on her.

"It's really sensitive of you," Alec said. "To even notice."

"Well," Laura said. Her hand was still on his arm, stroking it just the tiniest bit, and the rising bubble of panic in my gut, so small I could have ignored it, should have probably ignored it, burst acid inside me. Laura curled a wisp of hair over her ear and sighed. Alec toed the ground like an idiot. He looked up at her, blushed, looked back down. Their mothers toddled back in with glasses full of peppermint schnapps.

"Elaine," Laura called, "why didn't you tell me Alec had grown up to be so handsome?"

"I know." She giggled and collapsed back down into the chair next to me. "Isn't he gorgeous?"

"Just gorgeous," Laura said, and Alec shook his head bashfully and grinned like a fool, and her hand was on his arm the entire time. I wanted to jump up and say something. I wanted to pull him away. She was thirty years old, way too old, way too. Well. New Jersey had prosecuted her for murder, let me remind everyone. Murder! Alec was blushing like an idiot. His mother was drunk.

"So maybe we can see each other again?" Laura whispered.

"Maybe we can," Alec whispered back.

There were several grown-ups in the room at this point, but it was only apparent to me that the child among us was in big trouble.

ON THE WAY home from the party, my son was full of questions. How long would she be in town? What was she doing here? Was she seriously just going to crash at her parents' house?

"I really have no idea," Elaine said from the backseat. "Why don't you ask her?"

"I guess I will," Alec said as we turned onto Pearl Street.

"You got her number?"

He gave me a look as if I were the dumbest person in New Jersey. "I know how to find her, Dad. Freeman Court is ten blocks away."

But later that afternoon, he came down from his studio to the big house, our house, to forage in our refrigerator. I could hear him rattling in there like a chipmunk. I was lying on the couch in the study with my journals, my laptop perched on my chest, aimlessly scoping out a few wine auctions and debating whether to nap. Alec came into the study with a handful of potato chips; he smelled vaguely like pot, which he sometimes did and which Elaine and I had decided, with the patient help of a psychotherapist, not to get too worked up about. Either it was a phase or it wasn't, but either way it wouldn't kill him, unlike many other things he could do in his spare time. Still, it annoyed me.

"Got the munchies?"

He rolled his eyes at me. "I just wanted a snack."

"I see."

"Is there a problem?" Were we going to bristle into a fight? No, Alec licked his palm of potato chip crumbs and sat down in the old leather chair in the corner of the study. He was half smiling.

I rubbed my eyes, scratched my chin, rolled my ankles around in their sockets. When I turned my head again, he was still sitting there, licking his palm. "So to what do I owe this privilege?"

"Nothing," he said.

"Just a social call?"

"Can't I visit?" He frowned, offended. "Do you always have to sound like such a shmuck?"

"Alec," I said. "Cool it."

He shrugged, then nodded distractedly. He had an anxiety-making habit of bouncing his knee up and down at a split-second pace. He sat in the study chair and bounced, bounced, bounced like a jackhammer.

"Well, Son, not to be a shmuck, but if you're going to sit there, please stop doing that thing with your leg."

"Did Laura Stern really kill her baby?"

"What?"

"Did Laura Stern really—"

"No." I sighed, put the computer on the coffee table, rubbed my eyes again, and sat up. "At least not according to the State of New Jersey."

"I know," he said. "But I was wondering what you thought."

"I'm content to have faith in the judicial system's verdict."

Alec looked around the room. His expression was alert, his hands wouldn't be still—maybe he wasn't stoned after all? He was freshly showered, his head still damp, and he'd shaved. A baby face, his light brown hair curling in the steam heat from the corner radiator.

"I have these vague memories of it, you know?" he said. "I remember the trial was in all the newspapers. And on the local news, too. And the way you and Mom were always whispering about it."

"You were very young."

"Not really," he said. "I was old enough to figure out what's going on, more or less."

I sighed. "We tried to protect you."

"Well, the story was all over the place, front page in the *Record* every day," he said. "You couldn't have protected me no matter how much you wanted to."

"I suppose."

"What did you guys think of it?" he asked.

"We thought it was a tragedy, obviously." I could see where he had hurt himself shaving, nicked his Adam's apple and sutured the wound with toilet paper. "Your mother took a rather . . . anthropological view of the whole thing, if I remember correctly."

"Anthropological?"

"She read some article by Stephen Jay Gould."

The light in the room was dim, and I could hear Elaine outside, doing endless laps on the treadmill while she watched *Sex and the City* reruns on the living room TV. I used to love to watch that show with her, a guilty pleasure.

"What about you?"

"I honestly don't remember."

Alec raised an eyebrow but let me get away with it. "Laura used to scare me," he said.

"Really?"

"It was the part about crushing in the baby's skull. I don't know, I don't even remember what she looked like back then, but I remember imagining her late at night, having nightmares that the baby killer

was going to come get me. That's what we called her in school," he
said. "The Baby Killer."

I felt my heart sink. "We should have talked to you about it."

"But?"

"But . . ." I said, "but we were scared of what she did, too. Scared
of what had happened to our friends."

"Really?"

"Sure. And we were scared of how close this kind of violence came
to breaking through our own little fortress. Round Hill had always
felt like the sort of place where violence couldn't . . . where it just
didn't happen. And then, one day, it did."

"Even though violence happens everywhere."

"We pay a lot of property taxes to pretend it doesn't," I said, and
Alec rolled his eyes. I coughed.

"Well, anyway, I suppose it all turned out . . ." And without warning, a feeling I hadn't felt in years clogged me. It was the desperate, nauseating feeling of revulsion. A blind, suffocating newborn
in a sink, waiting to die. I could see the faint lanugo on her head
and limbs, her mottled pink chest, her face crumpling in pain. Legs
skinny and frantic. A thumb the size of a pea. Struggling to collect
oxygen. No mother's breast, no warmth, the cold porcelain sink.

"Dad?"

I hadn't believed the State of New Jersey's verdict for a single
second.

"It all turned out . . ." I took a deep breath. Began again. "For the
best."

Alec nodded. His leg relaxed. I forced the old revulsion to seep out
of me slowly; I revised all the images in my head one by one. I cleaned
up the library bathroom, wiped up the blood, wiped up the toilet seat,
took the baby out of the sink, placed her in Laura's arms (but Laura

now looked like thirty-year-old Laura, lustrous red hair, pearl ring). I kept revising, as effortfully as I could. No more Laura, no more baby. After a bit more effort, in my imagination the Round Hill Municipal Library was just a library again, the bathroom was just a bathroom, and we were all going to be all right.

"It did, I guess," Alec said. "Turn out for the best."

Laura had seemed so graceful in the kitchen, and so clever, not at all the blank, nervous girl I remembered. What had happened in the past thirteen years? Gateway House, first, a psychiatric facility in Morris County that specialized in the mentally ill but not the criminally insane, a crucial victory for the Sterns, as the distinction meant they could legally monitor her treatment and she could leave the place once the doctors pronounced her cured, instead of when New Jersey pronounced her baby avenged. This the doctors did when she was nineteen, deciding that the fog had lifted, the paralyzing depression had been vanquished, and the odd combination of factors (guilt, anguish, serotonin imbalance) that had led to Laura's infanticidal rage in the Round Hill Municipal Library bathroom would never again conflate. She was released on her parents' recognizance. Iris picked her up, drove to Newark Airport, and flew with her to her brother Lee's exotic-animal rescue center on Oahu for a six-month mother-and-daughter sabbatical. Iris, who was already a few steps behind at the bank, who would never become quite the commercial finance powerhouse she could have been, owing to the extraordinary demand on her attention her daughter necessitated, never once blinked about the assignment, even though she was slightly phobic as far as large animals were concerned.

Tending to the macaws and the emus, the ferrets and the circus orangutans, Laura took another step in the long process that had begun at Gateway House. She stayed in Oahu for two years, then moved to her aunt Susie's in Blue Bell, Pennsylvania, where she worked as a nanny despite Susie's husband's timid objections. From there, the debacle in Vieques, but soon enough onward to her aunt Annie's welfare-to-work nonprofit, and then her aunt Enid's goat farm. A gracious network of family members helping Eliza-Doolittle her from the sullen baby killer of her youth into the polished, flirtatious young lady who had frightened me so that morning.

"Why are you frowning like that?" my son asked, serious in his corner chair. "Do you not want to talk about Laura?"

"Listen." I decided to attempt my best paternal insight. "The Sterns have spent a lot of time and energy trying to get past what happened to Laura. I think they've finally succeeded as much as they ever will. I think that's why she came back. She's going to be part of their family again."

"Did they ever find out why she did it?"

"No," I said.

"Do you think they ever will?"

"Does it really matter?" I had asked Joe the same question, and he had given me the very same answer.

"She was probably terrified," Alec said.

"That's what I always thought."

We were quiet again.

"So did seeing Laura upset you?" I asked. "You haven't laid eyes on her since she went to Gateway."

"Upset me?" Alec looked confused. "Why would it upset me?"

"You said it yourself—she used to scare you."

"When I was eight."

"Well—"

"No, Dad," Alec said, folding his hands together. He was smiling beatifically now in the darkening corner. "She didn't upset me. That's not the word I'd use."

"So then what?"

"You *know*," he said. He was still smiling. The shadows separating our house from the Kriegers' lengthened.

"I do?" I asked, although I knew what he was going to say. I braced myself. One time, when I was just a few years younger than my son, I'd felt the same way about a girl.

"She made me feel good."

"Oh."

"She made me feel better than anyone ever has."

What was odd was that even as we sat there, I could feel everything changing and knew I was powerless to stop it and powerless to predict what would happen next. If I could go back in time, I would—but no, I've got to stop thinking that way. There's nothing else I would have done, anyway.

"Dad?"

"Alec?"

"You're spacing out."

"I'm not. We're talking about Laura Stern. This morning you were making fun of her goat cheese aspirations."

"I didn't know what I was talking about."

"I see."

In the living room, Elaine got off her treadmill, snapped off the television, and headed for the kitchen. I could hear her plodding footsteps. "Alec!" she called. "Alec, did you spill these potato chips all over the floor?" Every so often she could let out a high maternal squawk.

Alec leaned in, dropped his voice to a half whisper. "Like, you know, Dad—like, did you ever just see someone and that moment think to yourself"—he took a breath—"I could marry a girl like that?"

"Excuse me?"

"Alec, get in here and clean this crap up!"

He was starting to blush. "Forget it—"

I looked at my intoxicated son for a long minute. There were a million things I could have said. I went with, "I suppose I know what you mean."

"You do?"

I paused for a minute. "Sure."

Alec smiled gauzily. As far as he knew, his parents' marriage was a long stroll on a beach at sunset.

"So what happened?"

"Alec! Get your butt in here now!"

It was the fiction that I stuck to. "I married her."

CHAPTER FOUR

AFTER NOT HAVING laid an eye on Laura Stern for more than a decade, I saw her again three days later. Alec, who in general only came near the big house for food or sleep or a soak in the upstairs Jacuzzi, was sitting on the porch, drinking from a steaming cup of Starbucks; Laura Stern was puffing away on a Marlboro at his side. I guess he'd neglected to tell her that ours was a nonsmoking house.

It was one of those anomalous January evenings — more and more frequent, I guess, since America finally won its war on the ozone layer. Fifty-eight degrees, starless, breezy. Confused crocuses had already started to push through the earth, and the town geese had never even bothered to migrate. I'd come home early, having finished up rounds that afternoon, and thought about maybe shooting some baskets in the driveway under the motion-detecting lights.

"How was your day, Dad?" How was my day? I was disgusted to see them there. Alec looked as happy as a fistful of balloons.

"It was fine. How was yours, kids?" I said, immediately feeling stupid. Laura Stern was no kid. "You two just, um, hanging out?"

"Alec wanted to show me his paintings," Laura said. "He's really so talented. I've never seen anything like that deer series he's painting. The representation of life just squashed away, the trail of the car or whatever it was. God, there was so much color on that canvas, I couldn't believe how intense it was." She paused to smile at him, and he hid his face behind the Starbucks cup. "He's really going to make a name for himself in the arts, don't you think, Dr. Pete?"

"You can just call him Pete," Alec mumbled.

"I like saying Dr. Pete," Laura said. "It makes me feel like a little girl again."

"He is very talented." For some reason I was stuck on the walkway in front of the porch; I didn't want to walk past them, nor did I want to skirt them entirely and head in through the side door.

"So what are you and Elaine up to this fine evening?" Laura asked. "It's a nice night for a walk, isn't it? Practically spring." Was she trying to get rid of us?

"I haven't really thought about it yet."

"The Red Menace is making dinner tonight. I was hoping she'd do something sort of authentically Chinese, but it turns out all she eats is steamed carrots and eggplant."

"Isn't that authentically Chinese?"

She laughed. "Only if you eat a fortune cookie afterward."

Alec laughed, too, which was a sound I didn't hear all too often. Laura was wearing a puffy green jacket, a fuzzy yellow hat, and absurdly tight jeans. Why such tight jeans? Why couldn't I move? "Anyway, I really can't think of a nicer January than this. For New Jersey, I mean."

"In California," Alec ventured, "it was probably like this all year round, right?"

"Yeah, almost always sixty, seventy degrees. And at night the goats would horn around in their sheds—you could hear them—and Enid had a couple of sheep that would bleat in their pens, and there were dogs and some cows. It was really nice."

"Were you sorry to leave?" Alec asked.

"No," she said. "It was time."

"You know," I said, eager to end this jaunt through memory lane and thinking maybe it'd get them off the porch, "I was thinking about shooting some hoops. Taking advantage of the weather."

"Dad, we're kind of hanging out."

"You shoot hoops right here? On the driveway?" Laura said. "That's so great! Could I join in?"

"You want to shoot?" I asked. "I, um . . ." Alec looked panic-stricken; I imagine I did, too. "That would be—do you know how to play basketball?"

"I have no idea." She laughed and ground the cigarette end onto the bottom of her shoe. "But I bet you can show me."

"Actually, maybe I'll just go inside and start on dinner."

"Oh, come on, Dr. Pete," she said. "Let me just try. I promise I won't get hurt. And if I do, I won't sue."

Alec still looked panic-stricken. But what did he want me to do? "Okay," I said. "Let me go upstairs and change."

The kitchen smelled like Crock-Pot stew, and Elaine was in the bathtub with a book when I got upstairs.

"You're home early," she said. She had a towel wrapped around her head swami-style, and a glass of wine perched on the soap ledge.

"What is this, a Calgon commercial?"

"One of the few privileges of the middle-aged housewife," she said, "is the early evening soak. Don't worry, dinner's on downstairs. You'll get fed."

"It smells good."

"So then what's that frown for?" She put her book to the side of the bathtub and stepped out of the tub. Her body was rosy from the steam, and her nipples—one pink, the other, a tattooed construction, Nubian brown—were pert and hard. Well, the fake nipple was always hard, but nevertheless the effect of my wife rising out of the steam ordinarily might have given me an inclination or two — but not with Laura Stern downstairs, manhandling our son.

"Pass me your wineglass?"

"What's the matter with you?" She wrapped herself in a towel and drained the tub, then handed me her glass of half-spoiled something. She kept all our unfinished bottles on the counter for cooking and had zero appreciation for when one of them turned bad.

"Jesus, you should toss this."

She shrugged. "The rest of it's in your stew."

I collapsed backward on the bed, loosened my tie, kicked off my cruddy loafers. "Laura Stern wants to shoot hoops with me."

"Say that again?"

"Laura Stern wants me to go downstairs and shoot some hoops."

"Hmmm . . ." She tugged on her underwear, her thick white bra.

"She's downstairs with Alec, sitting on the porch. She's smoking." Elaine detested smoking.

"And?"

"And I thought I'd get rid of them if I told them I was planning on shooting around outside for a little while, but instead Laura Stern announces that she'd like to play with me. She's never played basketball, but if she gets hurt she won't sue."

"Is that a joke? That she won't sue?"

"I assume."

"So then go play with her."

I pulled a pillow over my eyes. "Elaine, what is Laura Stern doing on our porch?"

"It sounds like she's smoking and waiting for you to go play some basketball with her."

"Please tell me you think it's a little odd that a grown woman wants to spend her free time hanging out with a twenty-year-old boy."

"No," she said, pulling on a faded black turtleneck. "But I do think it's a little odd that you're so upset about it. Go downstairs and shoot around for fifteen minutes. I'm going to make a salad."

"That's it?"

"What else do you want?"

"You really don't think this is weird?"

"Pete, relax, okay? Go shoot some hoops or you're going to make yourself crazy and me along with you."

I spend all day telling other people what to eat, what to drink, what to do if they see blood in their stool; sometimes it's a relief to just follow orders. I traded my khakis for shorts, laced up my sneakers, and took a breath. Laura Stern was home for the first time in years, clearly distanced from her family, looking for someone to treat her kindly. She found our son. She wanted to shoot some hoops. Innocent as a lamb.

Downstairs the two were sitting and talking like old friends; Alec was moving his hands expansively, and Laura had her head tilted almost all the way to her shoulder. From her profile, I could see the purse of her lips as she concentrated on whatever he was saying, nodding along as he spoke. She had a wrist cocked, a cigarette burning between her fingertips, her chin wrinkled. And as I looked at her like this, she reminded me not so much of Iris but of old Mr. Stern, Joe's dad, who died twenty years ago.

I rolled my shoulders, flexed my knees. Jesus, what is it about being fifty-three that turns your head so easily to the past? Memories seemed to corner me more and more frequently that January: I'd be driving to work and see an old lady in a bright pink dress and almost have to pull over because suddenly Aunt Iz was calling to me over the banister in the building I grew up in in Yonkers, asking how I'd done on my chemistry test; I could hear her as if she were in the backseat right behind me, and feel the hair on my arms prick to attention. This sort of hallucination was due, I'm sure, to the very fact of being my age, to the knowledge that the better part of my life was behind me, that no matter what medical science came up with in the next few decades, I wouldn't live to see as many new years as the old, dusty ones I'd already seen. You are who you are at fifty-three, and even if the person you are is lucky and happy, the crush of it — the kneecapping crush of it — is that anyway it's too late. My fifty-three-year-old overweight diabetics would die of stroke in fifteen years; my fifty-three-year-old hypertensive, sedentary middle managers would die of kidney failure. They would not lose weight, they would not start to exercise, they might not even remember to take their meds. They were fifty-three; they were who they were. And as so many doctors before me have noted, it's often easier to die than to change.

Old Mr. Stern — he told me to call him Niels, but I never could — ran a dry-cleaning establishment for thirty years in Center City Philadelphia, near Rittenhouse Square. Sometimes he'd find turquoise necklaces, pearl earrings, in the pockets of his customer's coats; he was so nervous about holding on to those semiprecious baubles that he'd drive them to their owners' houses right after he closed up shop. Once, he found a small bag of cocaine in the pocket of a three-piece suit (he wasn't certain what he'd found, but Joe's sister Annie put a little on her gums and confirmed it). So distraught he could barely finish his sentences, and half-convinced, I'm sure, that some Colombian drug lords were about to bust into his little shop and rape his seamstress, Mr. Stern drove across the Ben Franklin Bridge to Camden and dumped the whole bag into the Delaware River along its grimier shores.

Mr. Stern was sixty-five when he was diagnosed with colon cancer; it was a death sentence, and Joe asked if I'd like to go with him for a visit, since the old man had always liked me and I think he was nervous about facing his dying dad alone.

"He wants to live to meet the baby," Joe said, rolling down the windows a fraction so we could feel the exhaust rise off the turnpike as we drove down to Joe's childhood home. Iris was six months pregnant with Neal, and they knew it was going to be a boy.

"What do you think?"

"I've talked to his doctors," Joe said. "It's unlikely. It's metastasized to his liver. He's got tumors the size of lemons. They give him six weeks, maybe two months. He's on some codeine now to manage the pain, since nobody sees much point in surgery."

For some reason, Joe's dad had always thought I was an intellectual, and he treated me as if I was a man of reason and literature while his son was nothing but a science geek. This wasn't fair, of course, nor was it true, but I relished the old man's quiet approval. The first time we met I was midstream in a course on Melville that, if I remember correctly, fulfilled some crucial writing requirement. My hardcover *Moby Dick* spilled out of my backpack (we were at the student union, drinking coffee—the Sterns had stopped by on their way back from a weekend in Ohio) and Mr. Stern was entranced.

"At last the anchor was up, the sails were set, and off we glided," he murmured in his fairy-tale German accent. "It was a short, cold Christmas; and as the short northern day merged into night, we found ourselves almost broad upon the wintry ocean, whose freezing spray cased us in ice, as in polished armor."

"I'm sorry?"

"Your book," he said, picking the tome off the floor. I'd been carrying it around for weeks, hoping that somehow the novel's pages would penetrate the fibers of my backpack and insert themselves into my nervous system without my having to do any of the miserable work of reading.

"People keep waiting for the great American novel. They don't seem to realize it was written one hundred years ago by a customs inspector from New York." The dry cleaner tilted his head at that thoughtful angle. "Few other novels have the majesty, the *bravery,* of *Moby Dick.* Melville does things on that boat, switches perspectives, spends wonderful moments in a church, a boardinghouse, the belly of the ship . . ." He trailed off. "What would you say is the great American novel if not this one?"

"I, uh . . . I really don't . . ."

"Niels, leave him alone," said Mrs. Stern, but smiling.

"It's a good, um, story," I said falteringly.

"I should say so."

My own father had neither the time nor the inclination—when would he read a novel? On the grimy train to Midtown, standing up, jostled by a hundred other gray-suited commuters? On the exhausted ride back home, still standing room only? After dinner? Most nights he'd fall asleep with the *Forward* on his lap, a glass of ginger ale in his left hand. Weekends were for working, or for taking the occasional drive to the beach at City Island. Sometimes, if the mood was right, he'd take us to a Sunday movie at the Yonkers Triplex, then dinner at Peking Palace. If he had advice for us, it was not about which books to read, but rather about why General Motors was a fail-safe stock, or how to find the nearest shelter in case the Russians started meaning business. Two Fridays a month he stopped at the grocery on Central Avenue to add to our stockpile of canned beans.

"So now what?" I asked Joe as we dodged the awkward southbound merge of 80 and 46 and 95. Joe, a Philly-style driver, glared at the on-coming cars but couldn't bring himself to give them the finger.

"I think—," he said, "I think the idea is to put him in hospice, see what we can do about his pain, help him get his affairs in order. He can still eat a little, sleep. He's on codeine. And of course he won't complain."

"Of course."

"It's just such a bitch, though, especially for my mother." Joe tapped his fingers on the steering wheel, then rubbed them anxiously on his bald spot. He wanted to be anywhere else. "They're too young for this."

"How's she holding up?"

"Alternates between denial and rage," he said. "Either she acts like it's all going to be perfectly fine or she starts railing against doctors, as though it's our fault somehow that my father got cancer."

"You know how people are when they're starting to grieve."

"I told him for years to get a colonoscopy. He wouldn't. We'd fight, you know? Just getting him to stop smoking a half pack a day . . ."

"He was a stubborn guy."

Joe shrugged, checked his rearview mirror. "They're all stubborn, that's the thing," he said. "That's how they were raised. That's how they raised us, how they got through the daily business of their lives. They worked like animals. My dad at the store, your dad with the insurance. They wore out their shoes, you know? All that shuffling every day. Worked harder than I ever will in my entire life. But never buckled his seatbelt, never put out the cigarette, never got a goddamn colonoscopy."

"They invented seatbelts too late."

"No excuse," Joe said.

Both our dads had spent the bulk of their best years doing things they didn't feel like doing: Joe's dad at the shop, my dad pounding Ninth Avenue, soft leather briefcase in hand. People never stopped needing insurance, he reminded us, and he never stopped trying to sell it to them.

But then again, every so often my dad would take off an entire weekend, and we'd drive deep into Westchester, me in the front seat and Phil in the back. We'd go scout properties in White Plains or even up in Chappaqua, Yorktown. "What do you think, guys?" my dad would ask, slowing down in front of a FOR SALE sign, a shiny new ranch with a one-car garage and dogwoods dripping on the front yard. "Good schools, safe neighborhoods, low taxes." A caress in his voice.

Sometimes my dad would stop across the street — keeping the motor running — and we'd all imagine it, the bicycles in the driveway, the fort in the backyard, our very own bedrooms. We'd seen television; we knew how it was supposed to be. We'd roll down our windows and stare. Board games stacked neatly on the shelves above my desk, Davy Crockett wallpaper, pennants from the local high school team. And then, blinking awake, we'd understand the impossibility of leaving Yonkers for greener pastures. My dad would pull a K-turn. We'd be home in time for supper.

"What do you remember, Joe?"

"What do I remember?"

"When you were a kid," I said. "What stands out?"

"Ah, you know — there was so much. Phillies games at Connie Mack, April right through September." His voice wistful. "Ocean City in the summer. Grilling hamburgers on Sundays. My dad really liked to do that American stuff. The Liberty Bell every Fourth of July, then fireworks."

"Sure," I said.

"It's those baseball games I miss, I'll tell you. I should have made the time to go. It's been at least a decade. I never go to games anymore. I should have taken him to see the Phillies."

"Don't do that to yourself."

"Indulge me," he said. "My father's dying."

I patted his shoulder once, trying to be supportive in as masculine a fashion as I could manage, then turned to gaze out at the highway again. Our fathers. I had just spoken to mine the day before; I'd been calling him every day since Joe found out about his dad, and he was delighted at the attention, although he tried to be gruff about it. We talked about maybe seeing a Nets game together; I told him I'd see about seats.

When we pulled up to the row house on Rawle Street where Joe had grown up, where Laura had lived as a baby, where Elaine and I had spent so many chaste youthful weekends, I felt unexpectedly relieved to see that the place looked exactly the same. Three stories of dark red brick, white shutters, gleaming black iron railing along the stoop, gingham shades behind the windows.

"Boys, boys, Peter, I'm so glad you could come. How was the drive? Are you two hungry?" Mrs. Stern bustled to mask her nerves, barked at us, took our coats and sat us down and yelled upstairs at her husband to come down, the kids were here. The house looked great, but Mrs. Stern looked terrible: wan, so skinny her collarbones stood out sharp as files. I remembered her as bright-eyed, jowly, with a full European bosom and thick brown curls. Now her hair was lank and completely gray.

"Niels, *Nissim,* the boys have come to see you. Come on down," she called upstairs again before backing into the kitchen. The pictures of FDR and JFK were on the wall where they'd always been, but they had neighbors: Jimmy Carter, Ronald Reagan, Al Gore, innumerable shots of Stern grandchildren in all manner of sports uniforms and Halloween costumes.

"*Nissim! Unten gekommen,* come on, let's go."

"Ma, it's okay. I'll go upstairs in a minute."

"He's not dead yet, Joseph," Mrs. Stern said, and she sat down at the table. She was fierce in a way I knew Joe could be, too, tougher than me like steel to cotton. She came to the States with her little brother when she was still just a girl, sponsored by some cousins in Philadelphia, who put her to work immediately in their shoe factory. In Frankfurt, where she was born, she would have learned the classics, French and Latin, would have studied math and science in the private school where her father served as headmaster. In Philadelphia, she pushed grommets into calves' leather until pebble-hard calluses burned on her hands. Her father and mother both died in the Holocaust.

"So, how's the baby?" she asked, putting a plate of dry biscuits on the table. I felt a brisk chill on my neck, touched beyond reason that she'd remembered our five-month-old in the midst of what was happening to her husband.

"He's doing great, Mrs. Stern. Thanks for asking."

"You have pictures?"

"Does he have pictures," Joe snorted, and I dutifully pulled my wallet from my pocket. There was an entire foldout section dedicated to my son, from hospital-tagged newborn to drooling, half-falling-over chubster. Alec asleep on my chest on the couch, Alec and Elaine by the JCC kiddie pool, Alec with a full beard of homemade pea mush, waving a spoon in the air.

"Gorgeous." She sighed. "That's a gorgeous kid. He has your chin, doesn't he?"

"To be honest, I can't find much of a chin yet."

"No, I can see," she said, taking my wallet and holding it close to her face. "There it is, your little tricky chin. And Elaine's smile."

How could she remember Elaine's smile? It had been years. "You're right," I said. "The smile is pure Elaine."

"He didn't come easy, did he?"

"I'm sorry?"

"I was always asking Joe when you were going to have a baby. He told me to mind my own business. And I know no news is bad news as far as babies are concerned. Especially because I could remember you two with our Laura, how good you were. You were meant to be parents, I always thought."

"Thank you, Mrs. Stern. It feels—it feels good. We're really enjoying it." She nodded: of course we were enjoying it. "And you're right, it wasn't so easy. But the wait was worth it."

Mrs. Stern waved her hand in front of her eyes. I remember a whole group at our Pitt graduation; she was the only one of a half-dozen mothers who refused to cry, and now here she was tearing up over my fertility problems.

"Soon we'll have six grandchildren, you know that?"

"I know."

"Susie's two, Annie's two, and soon Joe's two. Iris is having a boy."

"I know."

"They'll name him for Niels."

I looked down at the billfold, my fat, cherubic son. "Maybe Niels will get to meet him—they'll get to name him for someone else."

"Maybe." Mrs. Stern coughed, pushed the plate of biscuits at me. "Where did Joe go? He just gets here and then he disappears. I think he's very upset with what's happening. He's too sensitive, don't you think?"

"Joe?"

"That's why he's an obstetrician. He only likes happy medicine."

Who told her obstetrics was happy medicine? "It's got to be hard for everyone."

"Susie's here every day," Mrs. Stern said. "She's been bringing the twins, shows up in the afternoon, lets me take a break. She's very good at handling all this. I always think she's the one who should have been a doctor, you know? She's tougher than Joseph."

"Joe's pretty tough, actually—"

She shook her head. "Nah, he's a cotton ball. He's like a puff of air. Not like his father. Sometimes all I can think of is the pain he's in, and watching him trying not to let on that he's in so much pain."

I wanted to say something useful. "The medicine," I fumbled, "should be taking the edge off."

"How could medicine help you forget, forgive me for saying, that you're dying?"

A grunt, a hacking cough, and next to the table stood Mr. Stern. Haggard, yes, and much too thin, but dressed neatly in a soft cotton button-down and striped trousers. I had expected a bathrobe and a grizzly beard. Joe was holding his arm.

"Mr. Stern." I stood up, wasn't sure what to do, and decided to go for a handshake, but the old man gave me a hug. He wasn't so old, actually. He just smelled that way—menthol and mothballs—and felt that way through the loose cotton of his shirt.

"You look good, Pete. Fatherhood becomes you." Niels Stern had a much softer accent than his wife, even though he was older when he arrived in this country, twelve to her nine. He'd lost four older half brothers himself in the Holocaust, plus a half-dozen nieces and nephews, all four grandparents, a trembling quantity of aunts, uncles, and cousins, and who knows how many friends. His father had been the assistant rabbi in a middle-class suburb of Berlin; he got out of the country even after the immigration quotas started to seize up, owing to some little-known clergy exception. Mr. Stern used to tell the story all the time, how his family headed first to Memphis and then soon enough to San Francisco, Newark, and finally Philly, where they spent the rest of their lives—his father, his sisters, and a mother so homesick that when she died three years after they settled in Tacony, everyone said it was from heartbreak, even though it was probably colon cancer, just like her son's.

"You don't have to look at me that way, Pete," Mr. Stern said. "Between you and my son, a man could get a complex. Nettie, you got any soup for these boys?"

"Who said anything about soup?"

"I thought you were going to make me some soup."

"I made blintzes."

"Ma, you didn't have to do that." But I could tell Joe was thrilled that she did. Mrs. Stern's blintzes were heavenly, ethereal things: linen-pale crepes filled with sweet cheese and fried in butter. Joe used to come home from Pitt on spare weekends just to eat his fill.

"Shush," his mother said. "I didn't do it for you. It's the only thing your father can stand to eat."

"I wanted soup."

"I'll make you soup tonight," Mrs. Stern said to the dying man. "Stop complaining."

That afternoon, despite ourselves, Joe and I ate six blintzes apiece, drowning in sour cream, cherry preserves on the side. We ate hard biscuits and drank hot tea in glasses and watched Mr. Stern pretend with all of it, funneling some food in a napkin and then retreating to the couch to lie in pain. He ushered us over to talk to him.

"It's the drugs, you know. They take it all out of me. But on the other hand it feels nice to finally relax."

"They strong enough, Dad? You want me to get you something stronger?"

"Why stronger? I'm feeling fine."

"You don't have to say that if you're not," Joe said.

"You think I'm lying to you?"

"You just don't have to be Superman, Dad. If you want stronger pills, just let me know."

"Let me be," his father said. "My doctors here are doing a fine job. Be my son, not my oncologist, huh? Pass me that blanket over there?"

Joe tugged the blanket over his father's bony shoulders. The old man sighed, sank himself into the couch. Joe stood to draw the drapes, then snuck out the double doors into the kitchen. Maybe his mother was right, that Joe was, despite his years of medical training, a cotton ball.

"So what are you reading these days, Peter?"

"Good question," I stalled. The last book I'd finished even a chapter of was *What to Expect When You're Expecting,* a copy of which we'd had in our bedroom for four years, tempting us, tempting fate.

"It's hard, I suppose, with a new baby on your hands. No time to really dive into a book."

"I was thinking of picking up *Moby Dick* again," I said, which was true—I'd been thinking about that book ever since Joe told me about his father's diagnosis. I'd never managed more than seventy pages the first time around, even after Mr. Stern's endorsement.

"Ah, *Moby Dick.*" The old man smiled, and his chapped gray lips turned rosy. "Our old favorite, right?"

"Absolutely," I said.

He turned his gaze to the wall, turned to oratory. "All are born with halters round their necks; but it is only when caught in the swift, sudden turn of death, that mortals realize the silent, subtle, ever-present perils of life."

"You're just showing off now."

"That's right." Mr. Stern chuckled. "It's my privilege."

We listened, then, to the noises of his disease—intestinal gurgles, the soft whoosh of his labored breath—all alongside the sounds that had accompanied Mr. Stern's home life for almost forty years, the creaks of gravity buffeting the old row house, his wife's footsteps and the faucet in the kitchen, his son in the hallway, pacing. Mr. Stern sighed with wistful pleasure. The things we'll miss aren't the Caribbean islands we'll never see, the bosomy blond we'll never share a shower with, the million dollars we'll never spend on the shopping spree of our lives. Instead—and maybe everyone else already knew this, but it felt, on that couch, like a revelation to me—what we'll miss is our wife's callused hands. The worn porcelain in the upstairs bath. The couch we read five hundred books on late at night, the perchloroethylene stink on our pants, the luxury of our shoulders sinking into these good, soft cushions.

He turned his head from the wall, and it was possible his face had a little more color. "So when I'm gone, you and Joe will watch out for each other?"

"Oh, come on, Mr. Stern," I said, sounding more than I would have wished like an abashed teenager.

"You'll watch out for each other," he said. "Like you've always done."

"We will."

"It's a nice thing to have friends, Peter," Mr. Stern said. He closed his eyes. "You boys are very lucky."

"I know," I said, and I did.

Then Mrs. Stern came in, fed him some pills; soon he was asleep on the couch, and he lay there all afternoon as still as night while Joe and I watched college basketball in the kitchen and Mrs. Stern cleaned the clean house. Late in the afternoon, Susie showed up with her girls, and after a half hour of tickling the kids, Joe and I took our leave. Niels roused, barely, smiled at me, tried to shake my hand. He was dead ten weeks later to the day. Iris went into labor during the fourth night of shivah, and her son, like his older sister, spent his first week on earth at his grandparents' small row house in Philadelphia. He was, as Mrs. Stern had predicted, named for his grandfather.

ALL THIS FROM a cigarette burning in Laura's hand, the angle of her chin, the purse of her lips. Then Elaine snapped me out of it. "Don't worry, you don't have to go out there," she said. She had crept up behind me while I was gazing out the window. Mosquitoes were humming and buzzing near the porch lights, but Laura's cigarette smoke kept them from biting. "I'll invite them in for dinner. You can set the table."

"I'm in my sneakers," I said. "I should go out."

"You can't set the table in your sneakers? Come on," she said. "It's fine."

But I wouldn't be deterred, wouldn't wimp out. I jogged out to the porch, dodging mosquitoes, fake-jaunty, and smiled at the pair of them.

"So you still up for a game, you two? Let an old man kick your collective butt?"

"I thought you'd abandoned us," Laura said with a leisurely shake of her head. She let smoke stream through her nostrils. "Nice shorts."

I looked down at my baggy, stained self; in that split second I'd forgotten what I was wearing.

"Actually, we were thinking of going into the city, right?" Alec said, flicking his eyes from me to Laura. "Maybe something's playing at the Angelika?"

Laura shook her head. "You know what, I think I should probably head back. I don't want to offend Neal by missing his girlfriend's hospitality. This might be my last, best hope of getting on his good side."

"Steamed eggplant," I said.

"Exactly," Laura said.

"Well, what about the MOMA exhibit?" Alec said, doing his best not to sound crestfallen. "This weekend?"

"Now that," Laura said, "is a definite. We'll take the bus? Meet at my parents' house on Saturday?"

"You're going to MOMA?" I asked, as though this had not just been established.

"Yep." Laura grinned. "I haven't been there since the renovation, and Alec says there's a David Smith installation I've got to see. Plus the building itself is supposed to be a masterpiece, yeah? And there's a really great restaurant downstairs. Maybe we'll make reservations if we're feeling fancy."

My son, as a rule, rejected fancy restaurants as both boring and capitalist. "That sounds great."

"You know, I haven't been there either," I blurted. "To MOMA, I mean. Or the restaurant."

"Then you should come along."

Alec gave me a look of death, which I pretended not to see. "You sure I wouldn't be cramping your style?"

"Oh, no," Laura said. "It would be fun."

"Maybe your dad would like to join, too. It could be a family outing. A little Stern-Dizinoff togetherness, like the old days. Remember when we used to go to Delaware in the summer? Rehoboth Beach?"

"My dad's not much for art museums, Dr. Pete."

"Well, ask him. Ask your mother, too."

"You really want to go?" Laura said while Alec glared holes into the porch. "A field trip?"

"It's been a long time since I've done anything cultural," I said. "I've got to keep this old brain from rotting."

"It's not such an old brain, Dr. Pete," Laura said, standing up. She grabbed her purse, tousled Alec's hair. "So I'll see you Saturday, kid?"

Kid. Thank God.

"You want me to walk you home?"

"Your mom has dinner ready, Alec," I said. If he hated me already, I saw no reason not to push it.

"I'm okay," Laura said. "I'll catch up with you on Saturday."

"Sure," Alec said, and the two of us watched as she tossed her hips down the front path, pausing by the forsythia bush to light another cigarette.

"She smokes too much," I observed as soon as she ducked around the corner.

"You are such an asshole."

"An asshole? Isn't that a bit much? Want to shoot some hoops?" Ordinarily I took more umbrage to name-calling, but I was inexplicably giddy. She called him kid. She invited me along on their date. She wasn't out to seduce my son and loosen his already-tenuous hold on grown-up life.

"I was going to go out with Laura *alone* and you turned it into a fucking family reunion."

"Oh, relax, Alec. You'll get to spend lots of time with Laura, I'm sure."

"But what the fuck *was* that? Why would you *do* that?"

"Watch your language," I said, heading over to the driveway, where a couple of basketballs were piled against the garage. "If you're that mad at me, let's get it out on the court."

"Why?" He was whimpering like a toddler. "You know I want to spend time with her, and you just totally inserted yourself where you don't belong."

"Stop whining," I said. "You're either playing or you're not."

He stared at me for a minute, then shook his head with more disgust than the situation could possibly have warranted. He stomped inside and slammed the door in case I hadn't gotten the point.

"Suit yourself," I said out loud, and made thirteen free throws in a row before Elaine called me in for dinner.

IF ALEC WAS angry with me for the rest of the week, I was too busy to notice it. After a slow postholiday start to things, by Friday the New Year had reached normal levels of calamity, and that night I was in the hospital until just past ten. I came home and collapsed, balling my tie up in my fist and tossing it across the bedroom, then undoing all my buttons. The house was quiet, the rooms were dim, and I tilted my head up to the ceiling and thought about just passing out like that, still dressed, a Weejun dangling off my toe.

"You all right?"

"What?"

"You look like a corpse." Elaine must have been holed up somewhere downstairs; she came into the bedroom with a smear of chocolate on her chin and sat down next to me on the bed. I licked my finger and wiped it off.

"I just had a little," she said. "I shouldn't even keep it in the house."

"I didn't say anything."

"I know what you're thinking." But she didn't. The phone rang and I reached over her to pick it up. I was awake enough again. My wife's whole face smelled like chocolate.

"Dr. Dizinoff? Pete? It's Arnie Craig."

"Arnie," I said, wondering again what the point was of paying for an unlisted number. "How you doing?"

"I'm good, good," Arnie said, although the embarrassment in his voice told me otherwise. "I'm sorry to be bothering you at home, Doc. On a weekend." The necessary preamble; he wasn't sorry so much as ashamed.

"It's not the weekend yet, Arnie. What can I do for you?"

He let out his breath, relieved. When patients called me at home, I did my best to be cordial, knowing that their anxiety almost always outweighed the importance of whatever they were interrupting. Most of the time, there was at least a semijustifiable reason to worry, enough reason to call 911, in fact, but the home callers either had a pathological fear of ambulances or emergency rooms or were familiar enough with me to know that I'd treat them kindly. Spiking fevers, worrisome rashes, diarrhea, water in the ears.

"It's Roseanne," Arnie said. "She's locked herself in her room, sobbing. She's been sleeping all day—all week, actually. I don't know, it's not like her," he said. "She's just been so, so unlike herself lately. I'm worried," he said. "I didn't know who else to call."

This was a matter for a psychiatrist, and I told him so. I used to be wary of suggesting mental health treatment, especially to burly guys with Jersey accents, à la *Monsieur* Craig—whatever general distrust these types had of doctors usually went triple for shrinks. But it was going on eleven, and I wanted to take my socks off. "A good psychiatrist will sort this all out."

"There's other things, too, though, Doc." Arnie wouldn't let me off so easily. "She lost a little more weight. I noticed because she doesn't have much of an appetite—I was watching. I didn't mean to interfere with her privacy, but we even brought in lobsters the other night, from John's Fish, you know, and she wouldn't touch them. It was strange. My girl always liked to eat."

"Well, to be honest, it sounds like a bout of depression, Arnie," I said. "Loss of appetite, mood swings, it's all part of the game. But it's very easily treatable—there are all sorts of medicines. Very fixable. I really recommend that you see—"

"But what does she have to be depressed about? Is it still that boyfriend?"

"It doesn't necessarily have to be *about* anything, Arnie," I said, wondering how there could be anyone left in Bergen County who hadn't seen a Paxil commercial.

"I'm sorry?"

"Look, Roseanne's a young girl in a transitional time. She doesn't know what she wants to do with her life, just made a big move back to the East Coast when she thought she was going to build a career in California. She has a lot to worry about. It's a difficult adjustment for her. But I think, with some counseling, she'll really be fine. Call Round Hill Psychiatric in the morning. They're a wonderful practice, all of them. Owen Kennedy specializes in young adults—maybe Roseanne will want to see him."

"I thought about taking her to work with me," Arnie said. "To the lot in Paramus tomorrow. Rosie's good with business, you know, and I thought if I gave her something to do, something to focus on, but my wife said she wasn't sure if that was the best thing. But I think I need to keep her busy, don't you think so, Doc?"

"That could be good." I sighed. Keep her busy. Just try to relax. Put on the Barry White and let nature take its course. "But first she needs some mental health attention, she really does. It doesn't mean she's crazy if she goes to a psychiatrist," I said, doing my best to soothe without condescending. "It only means she needs a little bit of help."

Elaine gave me an "another crazy patient?" look; I shrugged at her and felt a surprising stab of sadness for spunky, miserable Roseanne and her confused galoot of a father.

"I don't know much about shrinks," Arnie confessed.

"They're nice guys, Arnie. They'll take great care of her."

"Okay," he said. "We'll call tomorrow."

Elaine was still looking at me. I looked away. "You take it easy, Arnie, okay? Roseanne's gonna be all right."

"Thanks, Doc. You, too." And we hung up, and I closed my eyes, and exhaustion washed back over me like a tide.

Elaine lay down next to me and I could feel her warm body along the length of mine, feel her gearing up to say something. Any chance I could pass out before she opened her mouth?

"The car's making funny noises."

"The car?" I kept my eyes closed. Elaine drove a three-year-old Saab 9000 for which she'd gamely learned to handle a clutch, but the thing was a sled, useless in snow, rain, even distant thunder.

"Like this sputtering noise all week. Like a sort of—" She pressed her lips together and made a floppy sound with her tongue.

"I just had Arnie Craig on the phone. I could have asked him about it."

"He's a mechanic?"

"A car dealer."

"So what does he know?"

"He knows cars."

"I'll take it in to the mechanic on Monday," Elaine said.

"Good idea." We were reconciled. I felt her remove my shoes, my socks, unbuckle my belt. We still hadn't made love in this New Year. Which was dangerous: ever since her illness, no matter the other distractions in my life, I'd tried to be as conscientious as a Boy Scout about having sex with my wife. I didn't want her to feel unattractive, in any way less than desirable, when she was so prone to feeling that way without any interference from me. If I told her I was really too tired to do it, I'd set off a night of recriminatory panic. Not worth it. But still, as she lifted my undershirt and rubbed her manicure up and down my chest, I couldn't imagine how I was going to gird myself.

"You wanna?" she whispered, easing me out of my boxer shorts.

"Elaine," I whispered back, noncommittal.

She kissed me. My wife approached sex with the same competence and enthusiasm with which she approached throwing dinner parties, as a taxing but ultimately pleasurable chore, and something that should be done regularly for the sake of a healthy marriage. "Is that a yes?"

"Sure," I said, mustering whatever energy I could dig.

"Have you been good?" she asked me.

I nodded. This would help. "I've been very good," I answered chastely.

She smiled and shrugged out of her utilitarian underwear. For some reason, when making love to my wife, I liked to retreat to a little boy persona and often came within ten seconds whenever she started cooing that I was a "good boy." "Good boy," she would whisper, as I thrust and pumped on top of her (or behind her, or underneath; Elaine was as cheerful as a cheerleader about assuming whatever position I wanted). "Good boy," she would murmur into my hair. "Good boy." And she would sigh and draw a finger down my back.

"I want to be a good boy, I want to be a good boy." Which was true, which was all I'd ever wanted.

"Help me be good," I would beg her. "Please, please, help me——"
And then blast, it was over.

But tonight, after she'd sat astride me for all of five minutes, I
considered attempting to fake it——did she really have to know?——and
then to my surprise I sputtered out a small orgasm; satisfied, my wife
climbed off me. She and I made love like the sexual revolution had
never happened; my satisfaction supported her sense of herself as a
woman, and even if only one of us came (that would be me), we could
usually both go to sleep content.

"I love you," she whispered, kissing my sandpapery neck.

"Me, too," I said, and I fell asleep, my clothing piled like sandbags
all around my spent body.

CHAPTER FIVE

IF YOU HAD asked me a week or two previous, I would have told you there were very few things I'd be less likely to do on a perfectly reasonable Saturday than shlep to Manhattan and spend twenty dollars on art, especially since (and whether I'm saying this out of fatherly pride or ignorance I'd rather not examine) I could see the same sort of stuff or better just by heading over to the studio above my very own garage.

"Twenty dollars," Iris marveled as we lined up behind a tour group of Swedes. "Is it just me, or does that take nerve?"

"What do they do about tourists who come from countries where twenty dollars is, like, a week's worth of wages?" The Red Menace, dressed entirely in camouflage, a flak jacket and a tight little mini-skirt, scowled at the entire lobby.

"Those kinds of tourists probably don't make it all the way to New York," said Laura gently. "Or if they do, they're not the ones who only make twenty dollars a week."

Amy turned her scowl to Laura, but she was already floating away to an art installation near the coat check. Thirty years old, but her father was going to pay her way—well, I suppose that was the family dynamic and I shouldn't notice, but . . . I watched her tilt her head, purse her lips at a canvas streaked with red, green, a constellation of sparkling gold bullets. Laura was dressed in dark cords and a dark, long-sleeved T-shirt, her hair back—again, she reminded me of a graduate student, astigmatic, poverty-stricken, pale from too much time in the stacks. I watched as she considered the bullet painting, and I wondered what she saw. I would have turned to ask my son, the expert, but he had already gone to stand next to her. Evidently I was buying his ticket, too.

"I think they like each other," Iris said to me as she pocketed her credit card.

I shrugged and turned to the lip-pierced kid behind the register. "Two, please."

The first few floors of MOMA—a building, by the way, designed to make the average shlub from New Jersey *feel* like the average shlub from New Jersey, all vertiginous white walls and odd angles and don't-even-think-about-it-buster guards idling along the doorways—were jammed with the sort of exhibits I would have made fun of if it had been just Joe and me, if everyone else had stayed home. A group of paintings called *The Four Seasons,* which looked, each of them, like the floor of a sloppy nursery school. Some kind of oil painting that turned out to be only partly an oil painting, and partly an octopus shape made out of—wait for it—elephant dung. A canoe hanging from the ceiling stuck with five thousand arrows.

"What do you think of *that?*" I whispered to Joe, pointing upward to the canoe. The seven of us were all still doing our best to stick together, moving as a slack cohesive unit from one baffling artwork to the next.

"I think it's—"

"Commentary," said Amy, who'd overheard.

"On?"

"Well, it's a canoe, right? Transportation for indigenous people from the Eskimos to the Polynesians."

"Yes," Joe agreed.

"But it's hanging above us. And it's pierced with arrows," she said. "What do you think all those arrows represent?" Ah, the Socratic method; I remembered it from medical school.

"Modernity?" Joe guessed.

"White people?" I asked.

"Colonialism." Amy triumphed, putting her left hand on her narrow hip. "The destruction of traditional cultures, cultures native to the ground they were found on, by mostly European forces bent on stealing wealth and kidnapping labor to promote their own imperial ends, and fill their war chests, too. So they could battle their European neighbors, you know? England versus Spain, the Dutch versus the English, the French versus the English. Did you ever really consider where the tools and the wealth to fight the Armada came from?"

"I guess I didn't," Joe said. He sounded guilty.

"Exactly," Amy said. We went quiet then, the three of us, staring at the canoe. I couldn't help thinking what it would feel like if one of those arrows dropped down and boinked me on the head. It would probably smart like nobody's business.

"I suppose now it would be a decent analogy for the war in Iraq," Amy reflected. "This canoe, I mean."

"Really? They use canoes in Iraq?"

She shook her head at me, but pityingly: I was only a shlub from New Jersey worried about being boinked on the head.

"Haven't you heard of the Iraqi marshes?" she asked. "One of the treasures of the Middle East? A nature preserve for dozens of types of fish, and birds, the sacred ibis, the African darter? The homeland of the Marsh Arab people? It was drained by Saddam during the war with Iran, and with the ongoing warfare there, efforts to restore the wetlands have proved totally unsuccessful."

"Right, right, right," I said, but Neal ushered her away before she could tell us anything else, leaving Joe and me to feel oddly delighted by her imperial little dressing-down. "That's one heck of a girl there, huh?"

"And have you noticed how short her skirt is?"

"Amazing."

"Truly."

We wandered over to the next piece of art.

Minutes later, as we moved into a room full of video screens and desecrated American flags, my twitchy eye found Alec and Laura. They were standing together as they moved from piece to piece, but they weren't really saying much, and I couldn't tell, from the respectful distance I tried to keep, whether their silence was awkward or familiar, a mutual understanding that in the presence of great art, it's better not to say a word, or a simple lack of any idea what to say to each other. Alec, every so often, would mutter something, and Laura would tilt her head at her grandfather's angle, but they really didn't seem to be sharing too much, and they certainly weren't touching, which seemed meaningful.

After forty minutes or so of pretending to understand the first-floor installations (at twenty bucks, we weren't about to dismiss a single exhibit), we meandered upstairs to the deco furniture and modernist housewares. In the front part of the first room, by the floor-to-ceiling windows overlooking Fifty-third Street, a Jaguar E-Type sat on a platform, shiny like glass and absolutely useless in the middle of all this wacky art. It was like seeing an embalmed thoroughbred. The four gentleman in our company stood in front of the car and mourned.

"One day," Neal said. "Seriously. One day I'm gonna have a car just like that. How much do you think that baby costs? Like, half a mil?"

Half a mil?

"What's the point?" Alec prickled. "It's not like there are any roads you can drive something like that on. That car's meant for speedways and the autobahn and that's it. If you can't drive it ninety, don't bother."

"Or," I suggested, "maybe you're supposed to drive it really slow, preferably somewhere like Rodeo Drive or Monte Carlo, so that everyone can admire it. Like James Bond."

"That's ridiculous. What's the horsepower on this thing?" Alec seemed to be getting mad; I patted his arm, but he shrugged me away. I supposed he was getting nowhere fast with Laura. "If you're gonna have a car like this, you should drive it like it's supposed to be driven," he said. "Otherwise you might as well stick it in a museum."

"I really am gonna have one of those things one day," Neal murmured.

"Will you take your old man for a ride?" Joe asked. "Especially if you're gonna go spinning through Monte Carlo like James Bond?"

"Sure," Neal said. The kid was impossible to tease. He wanted to touch the car, I could tell. He wanted to bend over and lick the glassy paint job.

"You'll never drive a car like that, no offense, Neal," Alec said. "I don't even think they make them anymore."

He shrugged. "So then I'll find one," he said, "on the Internet. On eBay."

"You've got to be fucking kidding me."

"Dude," Neal said. "They sell everything on eBay."

At this, Joe and I grinned at each other and left to turn one more 360 around the gallery. I didn't know how Joe could have spawned a kid quite as unlike himself as Neal—what odd coupling of helixes had produced such an equal and opposite reaction. And still, sometimes at my late-night darkest, I thought of Neal and Joe and felt a twinge of something like—well, something close enough to envy. To yearning. Neal Stern was brilliant, a good kid with a profitable career in front of him, and a foxy little girlfriend, and never once had he been busted for drugs, nor had his friends stolen a pair of opal brooches from his mother for no apparent reason. And even if he could be a little hard to take sometimes, I couldn't help admiring his drive, his preternatural assurance about what his life would bring him. But it's fine, it's fine, I told myself. Alec will be fine. Lavish a little more patience on him, a little more time, and soon enough he'll return to school, finish a degree, meet a nice girl, and forge a career, and by the time Elaine and I have traded in the Pearl Street Victorian for an expanded water-view bungalow on Lake George, Alec will be investing in a minivan to bring up the grandbabies for the summer.

(I shouldn't be so cavalier about it. This was—and is—my truest, most deeply longed-for fantasy. It's so simple. It shouldn't be so hard. It's what everyone we know wants, too.)

"So you liked that ride, huh, Dr. Pete?" said Laura, who caught me idling in front of a pod-shaped silver coffee table.

"Oh," I said. "Well, it was pretty, but cars, you know. They aren't really my thing. Just need 'em to get you from one place to another."

"I thought all men liked cars," she said.

"Not all men."

"Well." She took off her glasses and wiped them, casually, on the side of her T-shirt, lifting it just enough so that I could catch a glimpse of the white, white skin of her belly. Which could not have been her intention, and I shouldn't have been looking, but still I found myself all too quickly staring down at her shoes and then at my own.

"I grew up in a city, remember," I said. "So cars weren't a big deal for us. My dad didn't even buy one until I was seven or eight. We took public transportation. My mom never learned to drive. Not like you kids, cars for your seventeenth birthdays."

"I didn't get a car for my seventeenth birthday," she said. "And not for my eighteenth either. But that was okay. I wasn't really allowed to drive."

Were we really going to take the conversation in this particular direction? "Well, I guess you weren't—"

"I was too scared to get my license," she said. "I only got it when I started working at the goat farm, I guess five years ago now. I had to be able to drive a truck. But I remember starting at Country Day, watching all the seniors in their fancy cars, driving to school a whole five or six blocks from their houses. I remember thinking that it seemed so ridiculous. But of course, I was the only one still taking the bus."

"Well, neither did Alec," I said. "Get a car for his birthday."

"No?"

"He wanted one." And would have gotten one, too, had it not been for the Dan and Shmuley incident, and had he not been behaving like such a shit for most of his sixteenth year.

"That's funny," Laura said. "He seems like the kind of kid who's always had everything he ever wanted."

Now what did *that* mean? "He's been rewarded appropriately when he does well," I said, "and encouraged to behave differently when he doesn't."

"I remember him as such a sweet boy, you know?"

"He's still a sweet boy."

"He's changed, though."

"Of course he's changed." What was she getting at? "But he's still a wonderful kid. We've been very lucky."

"Yes?"

"Yes," I said. "Very."

"High school can be so hard," she said. "It kills me how little adults remember it, or how they try to glorify it. But everything that's happened to me in my life started from that place." She stuck her hands deep in her pockets and looked up at me with a bleak smile, and I surprised myself by smiling back. And by letting something loosen, quickly and surprisingly, like a can falling off a shelf.

"You've come so far since then," I said.

"I have and I haven't. I've certainly traveled a lot, learned how to do things. I have actual manual *skills,* which I'm proud of, certainly. I can reattach a muffler. I can pour rounds of goat cheese. But you know" — she kept looking straight at me — "no matter how far I go, no matter how much I do—"

"Well" — I cut her off — "that was a long time ago."

"It was," she said. "But I'm starting to be able to talk about it, which feels good. The weird thing is there's nobody who wants to talk about it with me. My parents certainly don't — why would they? And my siblings find the whole thing mortifying. They don't remember it, and they don't want to hear about it now. All this time later, I can at least — well, I don't have to pretend it never happened, but I guess everyone else still does."

She tilted her head, and in that moment I saw in her not the baby killer, not the older woman out to unravel my son's fragile grasp on maturity, but a girl who'd been through a nightmare and had come back to rejoin her society. I saw the girl I'd pretended to see all the time.

"How are you doing these days?" I asked her, letting my voice go a little softer. "Is everything all right?"

"It is," she said. "Most of the time."

"It's good to see you again," I said.

"Thanks." She smiled at me, slid her eyeglasses back on her face, and hung her head as though she were a little bit embarrassed, and I felt a little embarrassed, too. "It's really nice to see you, too, Dr. Pete." And then we smiled at each other once more, and she turned away, heading over to a big poster of a leopard standing in front of a panther, growling, and I myself turned to a strange sort of black wooden structure—maybe another representation of colonialism? I couldn't tell. A black sort of basin shape, protected by sinuous, infolded wings, and a tall post sprouting from the head of the basin, curving over as if to peer inside, and the whole thing rocked back and forth. I looked over at the sign to see what the hell it was. Oh, of course, I thought, taking an appreciative step back. I touched it, guards be damned, and admired its gentle back-and-forth. The protective, curvy wings. The post for a mobile to hang from. The irony wasn't lost on me: a cradle.

UPSTAIRS WERE ROOMFULS of Cézanne, van Gogh, Picasso, Matisse, and I exhaled with the dim-bulb relief of liking what I was supposed to like. Iris found me in front of one, a Rousseau, a Gypsy asleep in a desert night, a lion examining her, a lute and a jug of water in front of her, a dreamy smile on her face. None too realistic, but comforting in its way, like a nursery rhyme. The moon seemed to have a happy face painted on it. The lion seemed extraordinarily gentle.

"What do you think of it?"

"What do I think?"

"I mean, do you like it or what?"

Thirty-four years after I first saw Iris, long red hair swinging loose as she sat in front of me in calculus class, I still wanted to say something that would impress her.

"Sure, I like it," I said. "Even though it's not particularly realistic.

I mean, they probably don't have lions in the Kalahari." Which was the best I could come up with on such short notice.

"Who says that's the Kalahari?" She took a closer look at the painting, stepping a few feet in front of me. "Rousseau was never in a real desert, so there was no reason for him to base this painting on any particular place. I think he just had an idea of a desert. And an idea of a lion, and a Gypsy, too. He only saw taxidermied wild animals during his lifetime. Went to the botanical gardens to study the plants."

"Huh."

"The critics thought he was a joke. They thought he was as primitive as his paintings. He didn't get any recognition until after he died, when there was a real rewriting of his artistic legacy."

"How do you know that?"

"PBS special," Iris said.

She took a step back, stood next to me. Despite four pregnancies, Iris was still built almost like a teenager, slim and small-breasted. She wore dark jeans, a loose black blouse with the sleeves rolled up. Short heels. The two of us standing side by side like that, looking at a painting, someone might think she was my wife. Someone might imagine the nice life we'd built together, the happy, successful children we were raising, the romantic vacations we took together, leaving all those children with one set of parents or the other. The museums we frequented every Saturday.

Years ago, I'd watched her in freshman calculus, everyone else scribbling notes furiously except me and her — her because scribbling wasn't her style, me because I was too infatuated with Iris to hear a word the professor was saying, much less write it down.

"Too bad Elaine isn't here," she said.

"I know," I said.

"She would have loved this. Whose baby shower is it again?"

"Someone from the English department."

"But isn't she just an adjunct? She really has to go to these things?"

"Well, you know," I said. "She wants to be a good soldier."

"Elaine is so responsible," Iris said. "Especially as far as obligations are concerned. It's one of the things I admire about her."

"She's very admirable," I said.

"She is."

I never got up the nerve to approach Iris. We were assigned the same study section and she talked to me first. She wanted my notes. How to explain that I didn't have any?

Too smart for notes, you some kind of smart-ass? she demanded in her deep, grumbly voice. I'd never heard anything like it. She was from Allentown, the daughter of the city's last kosher butcher. She smoked marijuana. She went braless. She blew my virgin mind. There were other girls at Pitt, I knew that, but especially that first year I never even thought to look at any of them. What was there to look at? Blond girls with ponytails and convertibles, free-love guitar players, Afropower black chicks with muscle-bound boyfriends in dashikis. I wanted a science major. This science major. A redhead.

Well, why don't *you* have notes? I sputtered.

I was hoping you'd take them for me, she'd whispered.

But we've never talked before. How was I supposed to know you wanted me to take notes for you?

You can have my notes, said the scrawny crew cut who was listening in. I knew that crew cut—he always sat exactly three seats to my left and watched Iris with almost the same yearning I did. He had twitchy little shoulders and moles on the side of his neck, which I hoped were cancer. And how's this for hideous: Iris ended up dating crew cut for almost a year before I introduced her to her future husband. I couldn't believe it when she dumped him for Joe—I mean,

Joe was nice and all, but at least the crew cut had hair. (Why not me, Iris? Why not *me*?) And I also couldn't believe it when she told me that crew cut—they'd kept in touch for a long time after college, his real name was Ralph—died of aggressive melanoma right before we all turned forty.

Iris introduced me to her sorority sister Elaine Meers at a mixer during October of our sophomore year. She had yet to trade in Ralph, but still it seemed more and more clear to me that my chance with her was never. So then, Elaine: short and fair, a soft, girlish voice (especially compared to Iris's bottomed-out grumble), soft, skinny legs, and a heavy bosom, which I liked. And she liked me. She took me so seriously, listened to what I had to say about school, Nixon, Vietnam, all my half-informed or half-assed opinions. I decided to become more educated for her—smarter for her. And Elaine made me feel not only smart but necessary, gave me the courage to pursue being a grown-up. Her belief in me always outweighed my own.

I proposed to her exactly one month after we graduated. She was going to study English at City University, I was off to Mount Sinai, we were twenty-two, I loved her. But still, not until Iris was pregnant with Laura—and I mean visibly pregnant, I mean *waddling* pregnant— did it really sink into my thick dinosaur skull that Iris Berg would never, ever be mine.

(Why not me, Iris?)

But still. Somewhere underneath, deep, deep down in her cool, thin interior, I think Iris remembers kissing me at a just-before-spring-break party, 1973. Elaine wasn't feeling so well and Joe was already back in Philly helping his dad dry-clean. There was Curtis Mayfield on the stereo and thumb-sized joints passed around by other people and she tucked herself into my arms. And I didn't even have to prepare for it, steel myself. She tucked into me, and I just leaned down and kissed her. And didn't stop for hours. Every molecule of me more alive than it had ever been. I didn't think of Joe. I didn't think of Elaine. I didn't think at all.

We never mentioned it to each other again, to the point where, if I didn't have it written down—I used to keep a Pepysianly obsessive diary—I might not believe it had ever happened. But it happened. And when I'm feeling maudlin, or curious about what another life might have been like, I remind myself that Iris would never have loved me, trusted me, believed in me the way Elaine did. I remind myself that things turned out the only way they could have. Iris has teased me since the day we met, but Elaine has kept me upright.

And so now I can stand next to Iris with almost no residue of longing whatsoever, knowing that we've built such good, friendly, neighborly lives that to long for her even a little would ruin all this good life I've built. Iris Berg is not worth that. So I stand next to her at museums, sit next to her at dinner parties, and faithfully attend her New Year's brunch, and if I can remember what it felt like to let my fingers linger between the spaces of each pebble of her verte-brae, I have forced that memory as far away from me as it will agree to go.

"What else do you know about Rousseau?" I asked her, the Satur-day crowd around us beginning to swell.

"He was a customs inspector," she said. "Apollinaire wrote his epi-taph. *We will bring you brushes paints and canvas / That you may spend your sacred leisure in the light of truth.* I always liked that. The light of truth."

I pretended to have heard of Apollinaire, nodded appreciatively. We were still gazing at this painting, although I'd run out of things to see in it.

Iris wiped her hand along her cheek. It was getting warm in here, and she was starting to flush; her eyes were sparkling. Out of the corner of my eye, I saw Joe approach to put a protective arm around her hip. Self-consciously, I took a step backward.

"Whadyou two say, fifteen minutes we head down for lunch? I think the crowd's getting hungry."

"Our reservation isn't until one thirty," Iris murmured.

"So we'll sit at the bar," Joe said. "This joint's got to have a bar, right?" His shlemiel act. He rubbed Iris's hip.

"I'm sure it does," I said.

"Good. We'll round up the troops in fifteen minutes."

"Sounds great."

"You enjoying all this fancy-shmancy art?" he asked. "Your kid could be up here one day, maybe. You might be the father of a future famous artist."

"We should live to see the day," I said, which is something my mother liked to say.

"We certainly should," Iris murmured, and Joe gave her hip a quick slap.

"We certainly should."

And then Iris and Joe meandered Cézanneward, and I remained grounded in front of the Gypsy and the lion, thinking a little bit about Laura, but mostly about her mother.

LUNCH WAS EXPENSIVE and silly, all tiny portions and bizarre combinations, raspberry-flavored pork belly, but my son and I were the only two to notice. Laura rhapsodized about the combinations of key flavors and oozed over the wine list, and Joe and Iris, who have always been nuttily catholic about what they put in their mouths, seemed to enjoy trying everything. Even the Red Menace put away her concerns about twenty-dollar-a-month tourists to indulge in a thirty-five-dollar lamb shank, and Neal mentioned twice that he'd dined here several times before.

The waitress had seated us while Laura was in the bathroom, which meant that by no design of my own, Alec ended up sitting to my left and Laura to Joe's right, so Alec and I ended up in a private and funny discourse about whether to order eighteen-dollar veal kidneys (not when there was twelve-dollar liverwurst on offer!) while Laura and her father kidded each other privately, too. Everyone ordered meringues for dessert except the two of them, who went in for the double butterscotch sundae. I could tell from Joe's face he was delighted.

And then lunch was over. I handed over my AmEx without even looking at the bill, but Joe handed it back to me with a patrician shake of his head, and as we walked back to Iris's garage on Fifty-fifth Street, I felt both exhausted and thrilled with the way the day had gone. I'd seen some art. I'd learned a thing or two about Rousseau (and would Google Apollinaire as soon as I got home). I'd watched my twenty-year-old son and his thirty-year-old dream date get on like old neighbors (which of course they were) but nothing more than that, nothing to be suspicious of or concerned about.

"Thanks for lunch, Joe. I'll get you next time."

"Ah," he said, waving me away.

Elaine would be home by the time we got back and we could cook dinner together; I think I had some linguini in the freezer from the Italian store in Hopwood. The Nets were playing the Cavs tonight; maybe we could watch *en famille*. Alec and I could talk about art during the commercial breaks and he could explain that bullet painting to me. Or maybe—and here I was going a little overboard, I knew—but maybe, even though the Cavs were a big draw, I could get some still-decent seats to the game if we showed up at the

Meadowlands early. Maybe—how pie-in-the-sky—but maybe Alec would agree to a game with his old man.

"So I'll see you tonight then, huh?" Alec said to me as a pregnant attendant swooped around with Iris's car. I tore my eyes away from her plumlike figure—she was almost as round as she was high, sweaty, her skin oddly pale, making me wonder if she'd ever heard of gestational diabetes—and turned to my son, who was wearing a shit-eating grin as if he'd just won a call-in contest on the radio. Laura, who reeked of Marlboros, was standing next to him with both her hands in her back pockets.

"What are you talking about?" I asked as Iris took her car keys and Joe handed the attendant a fiver.

"We're going out," Laura said. "Just for a couple hours." She smiled and arched her back the tiniest bit, and her shirt rose up on her stomach, and I thought, You are a tricky, horrible woman, you really are, and I was immensely sorry that for a few minutes in a room full of art deco furniture I had given her any benefit of the doubt.

"Where are you going?"

"Out, I don't know. We're gonna see some more art, right, Alec?" And she ran a carcinogenic hand up and down my son's bare wrist.

"Haven't you guys seen enough art for one day?"

"C'mon, Pete." Iris grabbed my arm. "Let's leave these kids alone."

Oh, Iris, please: keep your basket case away from my son. He's only twenty; he still has time.

"Don't worry," Laura said, and she was laughing—I could see her smother a laugh. "I'll have him home by curfew." And Alec, who ordinarily would have grimaced over even a tiny reference to the C-word, just smiled.

"I was thinking, though, I was thinking"—everyone piling into the SUV—"I was thinking maybe of getting some Nets tickets. LeBron James is in town. Laura, you'd be welcome to come."

"Well, and that sounds great, Dad, but there's a gallery I want to show her, up in Harlem." At least he looked apologetic. "The one that does those nature paintings I told you about? The one with the owners from Piermont?"

Nature paintings? Piermont? I dimly remembered having this discussion when we were fighting over whether Alec could or would transfer to the New School with a little help from a patient of mine who sat on the board. Alec had said there was a gallery in Harlem that might be interested in his work and therefore he wasn't even going to think about school until he found out what was what on the professional front, didn't we understand that? By this point it was clear that we weren't going to pay for a sentimental education in Europe and so I steamed that I didn't want to hear about galleries until we'd figured out his college plans. Inside, I was raging like a lunatic, but outside, I was as calm as a man who'd recently gotten home from an hour's worth of psychotherapy with his wife could possibly pretend to be.

"We'll just take the bus home," Laura said. "You don't have to worry."

"Sounds great," Iris said. "C'mon, Pete. They'll be fine."

"But—," I said. "But—okay." I suppose I knew when I was defeated. I closed the door but powered down the window so I could continue talking at my son. "Listen, do you need some money?" I asked, which was code for, You're still just a child, you know, don't get ahead of yourself. Which was code for, Don't you forget you still live in my house.

"No, dad," Alec said. "I'm cool."

"You are? You're cool?"

But before he could say another word, Iris had jolted us out of the garage and onto Fifty-fifth Street, east toward the FDR, and because there was no traffic, because it was a balmy January Saturday, because there was nothing to keep us in New York City except my son wandering around with a white-bellied baby killer, within fifteen minutes we were on the Palisades.

"Pete, you want to go to the Meadowlands tonight?" Joe asked me, turning around to face me in the backseat. In the very rear of the car, Neal was nuzzling the Red Menace.

"Not really," I said.

"You sure?"

"I'm sure."

"But don't you want to see LeBron James? We could get some floor seats, that can't be too hard."

"Not tonight, Joe."

"But—"

"I said I don't want to see the goddamn game," I said, and I brooded the whole of the Palisades, down Maycrest Avenue, and all the way to our front door.

THE BIG YELLOW house on Pearl Street was always, if we dwelled on it, too big. Victorians were built for Victorians, which is to say people born into an age without either reliable birth control or a postwar infertility epidemic; we had four bedrooms. Each was small except for the master bedroom, which the previous owners had made by merging two of the larger bedrooms; they had also added on, at presumably great expense, a four-piece bath. But the rest were no larger than certain walk-in closets I had seen, and when I got home to an empty house, I peered into each of them, looking for who or what, of course, I had no idea. My son's bedroom had been stripped bare before he set off for college, stripped down to the duct tape he'd used to tape up his huge Escher poster and his Kandinsky prints, and now that he'd moved back home, the floor was cluttered with the Bed Bath and Beyond crap we'd bought him before his initial departure: cardboard dressers, toiletry caddies, a gorgeous Samsonite suitcase. His bed, an extralong double that took up three-quarters of the floor space, was sloppy and unmade, sheets crumpled back to reveal the stained white mattress we'd gotten him as a high school freshman, when he'd cracked six foot two. I surveyed the mess, then called Elaine's cell phone. She didn't pick up.

It was dimmer than it should have been; one of the lights in the overhead fixture had burned out. I took a step stool from the hall closet. I changed the lightbulb. How many internists does it take to change a lightbulb? Just one on this quiet January night. I screwed in the bulb and put back the step stool. We'd moved into this house from the two-bedroom in Morningside Heights that we'd rented for a song. I was a third-year resident, Elaine was working on her dissertation, and no babies, no babies—but we saw this house and it was too big and too expensive and we were well aware of all that. Yet the thought of all these rooms filled with our future family made us feel safe enough, I think, to try it anyway.

I pulled up the mattress cover, the dark blue sheets on my son's bed. I pulled back the curtains; 5 p.m. and dark out already like midnight, but the lamplights on Pearl Street were glowing. I wanted to clean up the rest of his room but I didn't know how. I didn't know where his stuff belonged, and I didn't want to open his closet and uncover whatever secret things he kept there. Instead, I sat down on his floor.

The Sterns had moved to Round Hill two years after we did, bought themselves a large, fancy house without worrying how they'd pay for it—Iris had just scored a job at Merrill—or how they'd fill it with children. A sprawling split-level, five bedrooms plus the rec room, and I remembered how Elaine and I oohed and aahed our way through it on our first tour, which Joe and Iris led hand in hand. Then we sat at their new kitchen table, glass and brass, and wolfed down pepperoni pizza.

"Iris isn't convinced we'll like it here," Joe said, perhaps less diplomatic than he should have been considering we were the ones who'd talked them into moving to Round Hill. But Joe was never particularly diplomatic on more than one beer.

"No, that's not what I said," Iris said. "I'm just still wondering if we should have bought in the city. Or just thinking about what it would have been like."

"Did you really want to live in the city?" Elaine asked. This was 1984, after all, when Columbus Avenue was still considered a frightening thoroughfare and only the suicidal strayed north of 125th.

"Well, I always thought it might be nice to have something in the Village. Maybe a little townhouse, I don't know."

"Not enough space," Joe said.

"I didn't want to live in New York City, anyway," said Laura, who appeared in the kitchen doorway with a book jammed under her arm. Her red hair was long and stringy, falling in front of her eyes. I guess she was eight then. "It's dirty there."

"It's not dirty, sweetie," said Iris. "It's interesting."

"There's garbage on the street."

Iris shot me a look, as though I was supposed to defend her. I rose to the occasion. "It might have been a decent investment. And a fun place for you, Laura."

"We wouldn't have had enough bedrooms," Joe said.

"It would *not* have been fun," Laura said.

"All right, all right," Iris said. "We were never going to live in the city, I get it."

"How many bedrooms does a family really need?" I asked.

"Five?" Joe shrugged. "Six?"

"Six?"

"It's hard to know," he said, passing Laura a slice of pizza, "but we might end up needing six."

My wife and I met each other's eyes, trying not to seem aghast. Six bedrooms. Five children. Here we were on year four of inexplicable infertility, and the idea of even one child seemed like such a miracle. Iris stood, grabbed two beers from the fridge, cracked them both, and handed one to me. Our fingers brushed against each other's.

"Well, you guys have a bunch of bedrooms, right?" she asked. "Six may sound like a lot, but, you know . . . these Round Hill houses are spacious."

Elaine and I looked at each other. What overkill, what narcissism, what stupid hopes we'd had. "Our bedrooms are small," I said. Joe and Iris knew we wanted children, but I don't think they ever realized just how much. This was not the sort of thing one talked about in those days, not even to one's closest friends. And I didn't want to embarrass my wife.

We were all quiet then as we watched Laura dissect her pizza, handing the pepperoni to Elaine, who quietly tucked it into a napkin. I remember thinking that Elaine would have such fun with a daughter. A long-haired, bookish daughter.

"You done with your pizza, sweetheart?"

"I'm not really hungry," Laura said. "I'm sorry."

"Not even one piece?" Joe asked.

Laura poked at her slice a bit sadly. "I'm sorry," she said again.

"You don't have to apologize," said Elaine, pushing the girl's stringy red hair softly out of her eyes.

"Thanks," Laura said, sliding out of her chair, giving Elaine a grateful smile. I watched my inexplicably infertile wife watch Laura leave the kitchen. That night I held her close to me and told her that I was so sorry.

IT'S ALMOST MIDNIGHT now and I watch the lights in the house snap off one by one. Kitchen, television, living room, hall. My son's room, the former master bedroom, where Elaine can no longer bear to sleep—those are the lights that go off last. I sit by the window and inspect the house for a while. It's time to repaint the siding, really, or even replace it, and even though it's ugly, we should probably go vinyl, for upkeep's sake. If Elaine really intends to kick me out, I'll make arrangements to do this before I leave. It's not the sort of thing she likes to deal with, hiring contractors, comparing estimates. There's a guy across the street from my office in Bergentown, he has a siding and trim business, and he'd probably do a decent job for not too much money. I'll call him Wednesday morning, after I know what's what. I wonder if they'll be able to side it this shade of green.

I'm interrupted in my musings by a knock on the door, and my heart flips for a minute. The Craig boy? Has he followed me here? No, even more unexpected: my wife, holding two travel mugs. "Tea," she says. She's wearing sweatpants, a denim jacket. In the months I've been living in the studio, the months of our marriage's strange illness, she's never visited me this late at night before.

"That's nice. Thanks."

"You're welcome."

Like everyone in Round Hill, Elaine's having a hard time putting aside the accusations against me. I think this hurts her even more than it hurts me.

"I put some honey in it," she says.

"That's great," I say. "Thank you."

My travel mug is a party favor from Janene Rothman's kid's bat mitzvah. Elaine watches me while I drink; she's still standing there on the rickety wood landing outside my door. "Do you want to come in?"

"Iris says Joe's trying to reach you."

"I know."

"She says you're not picking up your phone."

"I'm not."

"She wants to know why." Elaine and Iris, former sorority sisters and best of friends, have, of course, suffered a weakened bond in the aftermath of everything that happened, which I find sad. Iris is no longer prone to just stopping by our house during a jog around the neighborhood, as far as I can tell, nor do they go on joint shopping expeditions, nor do they meet at the Garland Chophouse for the occasional postwork drink. But it seems at least they still chat sometimes.

"I don't feel like talking to him, I guess."

"Do you know why he's calling?" She holds the travel mug to her chest, to the space between her breasts.

I haven't told anyone, not even her. But back when I was taking care of Roseanne Craig, I said to Joe, I have a patient who seems a little depressed, and ignoring medical ethics entirely, I even told him her name. Joe was my best friend, and sometimes we talked like that. We used to talk about everything. Joe said, You should check for several things besides depression. You shouldn't take it for granted that she's depressed. I ignored him. I had other things on my mind. And now there's the malpractice case, and all Joe has to say to her family's lawyer is, I told him so. I told him what to check for. If he'd listened to me, the outcome would have been fine. And then the judge would find me guilty, and I would have to pay up, big-time. I would have to pay for all these wrongs I've done to the Craigs, but also, and maybe more importantly, to Joe.

"What is it?" Elaine asks. "Maybe he's reaching out in friendship?"

It amazes me still, her tendency toward optimism.

"I doubt that."

"Well, Iris wanted me to let you know," she says. "Maybe you should change your mind and pick up the phone." Her tone is gentle, but she has an unsure look on her face. She's going to see the lawyer in two days. What will Alec think when I'm homeless, wifeless, jobless? Will he feel sorry for me then?

"Do you want to come in?" I ask again.

She shakes her head no, pushes a stray piece of blondish hair behind her ear, and retreats back down the steps. I watch her to make sure she gets back in safely, and then I sit down on the steps to consider re-siding the house and drink my tea.

CHAPTER SIX

My father died on a cloudy, windless Monday, Valentine's Day, 2005. His passing was more unexpected than Joe's father's, and less melodramatic—exactly how I'd like to go out sometime in the blurry future. He'd taken my mother for a romantic two-for-one lobster lunch at Geno's on the Hudson (damn the kashrut on a holiday named for a saint), come home, sat down in his old cracked chair in the foyer. When my mother came to bring him his ritual glass of ginger ale before the *Dr. Phil* show, she found him cold and pale, nose tipped up as if he was sleeping. If he hadn't been so cold, she said, she might not have known at first. Myocardial infarction.

My father was eighty-one years old, healthy as far as eighty-one-year-olds went, a cautious man, a gentleman. He was the person who taught me right from wrong, who took the jigsaw puzzle of the world and made it into a simple picture: work hard, stay safe, do better than your own dad. When the cold war ended and the Soviet Union finally fell, my father celebrated his vindication with a small glass of vodka, the only irony I'd ever known him to perform. My mother called me on my cell phone and said, "I think something's wrong with your father," not because she didn't know exactly what was wrong, but because she didn't want to upset me. I drove to Yonkers more slowly than I should have. Phil was already there when I arrived.

"He died forty minutes ago," my brother said at the door, his face maybe a bit more pale than usual, but calm. He was dressed in the callously expensive way of a partner at a Manhattan law firm: wide-wale corduroys, French-cuffed shirt, pale blue cashmere sweater. There was a trickle of something whitish, sputum, near his neat ivory collar. Phil had tried to give my father mouth-to-mouth. "Mom's with him at Montefiore."

"Excuse me?"

"A heart attack," Phil said. "The EMTs took him to Montefiore."

"And you think he's dead?" I said, because it was just like that for my brother to announce that our father was dead, and just like that for me to fight with him about what should have been indisputable fact. Because I was one year older, and I was the doctor, and I was the one who would have known whether my father was dead. Not Phil.

"As soon as he got to the hospital," my brother said. "They tried to revive him — they had defibrillators, but I guess it was too late. I was waiting for you to get here." He eyed me. "What took you so long, anyway? Was there traffic?"

"What do you mean, he's dead?" I was the doctor, but this made as much sense to me as it would have to a child. My father wasn't dead. In the past five years we'd gotten his LDL down to 130, his HDL elevated, his triglycerides stable. He had done a CT scan less than a year ago, showed a promising lack of calcium in the arteries, and had no C-reactive protein. He was on Sectral, a beta-blocker, and a low dosage of Lasix, a diuretic, so we'd managed to get his blood pressure down to 140/90, which wasn't too terrible, all things considered. And I was on him about his diet. I'd gotten him to cut out the occasional cigar. And therefore he was still alive.

"Right there," my brother said, pointing to the worn leather arm-chair, the television, muted but still turned on. Phil drew himself up to his full six foot three. "Let's get to the hospital."

"I don't—"

"He's dead, Pete," Phil said. "The EMTs couldn't resuscitate him. So let's get out of here, okay? I don't want to leave Mom by herself." He looked down at his sweater, caught sight of the sputum, wiped at it disgustedly with his sleeve.

My phone rang and it was Elaine. I told her what had happened, and she let out a yelp of surprise or anguish and burst into tears. She said she'd meet us at Montefiore, but for some reason I could not imagine making it to Montefiore. I sat down in my father's chair.

"So you're not gonna go?"

"Just give me a second, Phil, okay?"

He shook his head, paced around the small living room, breathing out his nose forcefully, like an animal. I pretended not to notice. I felt the smooth leather of the chair under my arms, imagined I could still feel the warmth of my father's body pressing down on the chair's coils and springs.

"You were stuck in traffic, Pete?"

"Phil, you're not blaming me for this."

"Let's just not make it any worse than it already is," he said. He wouldn't stop pacing around the room. He was leaving a trail in the deep burgundy pile. "Let's get to Mom."

He was blaming me for this. I guess I understood; I was blaming myself. I closed my eyes. I could not imagine making it to the hospital. I could not imagine leaving this chair, this carpet, this apartment where I'd grown up. It smelled like a million meals, pot roast, Sabbath candles, my childhood, defibrillators, EMTs.

"We've got to go, Pete," Phil said. "Or I'll just go without you, if you can't handle it."

At the hospital I held my mother and looked at my father's body, stroked his hand, saw the gray in his skin and his eyes, but it was only after I talked to the doctors in the ER—plaque rupture, arrhythmia, nothing anyone could prevent, just like half a million deaths a year in the United States—it was only after I'd absolved myself that I truly believed my dad was gone.

"There was nothing you could have done, Pete," my mother said as we drove back to the apartment. She was right. But still, another death on my watch.

AND SO, A year later, February 2006, we left Round Hill for the unveiling before 9 a.m., silently, Alec still half-asleep in the backseat. Elaine drove. Dizinoffs are buried at the Beth David cemetery out along the Queens-Nassau border, right near the Belmont Park racetrack. All four of my grandparents, Aunt Iz and Uncle Nate, my mother's cousin Louise, who died of diphtheria and whose case was used as a warning to all us kids to button up—they're all there facing east toward Jerusalem, and we've sprung for something called "perpetual care," which means their graves will never go dusty. We arrived first and tripped our way through other people's dead families. A crowd of Hasids were shraying near an open pit.

"You okay, Pete?" my wife asked me.

"Sure," I said. "I'm fine."

"You don't have to say that if you're not," Elaine said, putting a hand on my arm.

"I'm fine," I said again, and I shrugged her off.

"This weather," she said. "Strange, right?" Then she moved toward someone she used to go to grade school with, who by coincidence was buried right near my family.

"Is this where we'll end up, too?" Alec asked after we'd both placed stones on Uncle Nate and Aunt Iz's graves. "I never really liked Long Island."

I shrugged. Actually, Elaine's parents had given us—as an anniversary present seven years ago — two plots near the ones they'd picked out for themselves down in Florida. Elaine wrote them a florid thank-you note, knowing, since they were *her* parents and she'd spent a lifetime decoding their bizarre and unwelcome displays of affection, that they really had meant no harm. I was indignant, both at the timing of the event and at the thought of spending eternity at a guano-dusted memorial park near my wife's parents, but Elaine told me to cool it, we would deal with it later. So far we haven't.

Alec was kicking at a few dandelions sprouting near Walt, my second cousin once removed. "Because, no offense, this place is really depressing." Maybe twenty yards from Cousin Walt's feet, cars cut one another off as they raced toward the Belt Parkway.

"Can you imagine a cemetery that *isn't* really depressing?"

"No," Alec said. "It's not just the death. It's the whole idea of rotting, too. Your bones putrefying in a mahogany box." My son was wearing a pale blue shirt, a tie, and khaki pants just a bit too short for him, so I could see the socks he'd stolen from my drawer. His hair was slicked back with too much gel. Even at twenty, he didn't have much in the way of a beard, still a bit of crusted-over acne along the jawline where some spirals of beard were valiantly trying to push through, and I remembered him at his bar mitzvah, almost as self-assured back then, and almost as tall.

In the distance I saw my brother approach in a long black cashmere coat, Hasid-style, holding my mother's arm as though she were an invalid, helping her slowly navigate the pebbly path. "Alec."

"He looks like he's accompanying the queen," Alec said out of the side of his mouth. "Look how careful he's being."

"Well," I said mildly, "your uncle likes to be solicitous."

"That's because he's a solicitor." Alec grinned at his little pun. "But I think you're wrong. I don't think he really likes it."

"Then he's a good actor," I said.

"That's what I think, too."

"He's always been a good actor," I said.

"You either have it or you don't."

"Hey, Pete," Phil said, meeting us on the pebbly path. My mother looked drawn, trembly. She'd suffered her third ministroke two months before, and this one had left the right side of her face sagging.

"Phil," I said, reaching out to give my brother a hug, heartily false on both our ends.

"Peter," my mother said. "What a day this is. What a day." She touched my arm. "Although your father would have liked seeing everyone together."

"You doing okay, Mom?"

"It was good of Phil to pick me up," she said, and I pressed my lips together not to say anything. Phil lived fifteen minutes from Yonkers, right on the way to the cemetery. There was enough room in his Range Rover for his whole family plus my mother's cane, should she need it. Elaine approached, touched me gently on the back, and leaned forward.

"Ruth, hello."

"Hello, dear," my mother said, and she let Elaine reach up and press a cheek to hers. Then they stood back and examined each other for a moment the way they always did. Elaine, short and soft and appropriate in a loose, dark coat; my mother, tall and stiff and adamant in the stained, puffy hip-length jacket she'd worn without change or apology three seasons out of four since my father died. "What do I have to get dressed up for?" she'd ask, not looking for an answer.

Phil's wife and daughters soon appeared by the grave, followed by a small collection of surviving cousins and friends, balding women behind walkers, men stooped and deaf, each grabbing my mother and rocking back and forth, hugging me, hugging Phil. Then the Sterns approached with Laura, not a surprise. She had shown up again and again since our afternoon at MOMA, rarely going inside the house but sitting on the porch with Alec for hours, chatting about who knows what, me spying, a stooge, in the light of the lamps Elaine and I had found on that long-ago trip to Bedford. Elaine would bring me coffee as I sat stiffly on the couch by the window, holding the same copy of *JAMA*, my vigil stupidly disguised. They never touched, Laura and Alec—I should know, I was hawklike in my observations—and sometimes lapsed into long silences, and Laura always left before midnight. And I suppose I was starting to relax. Sometimes I managed to actually read an article. Sometimes I managed to finish it.

"Uncle Pete." Phil's younger daughter, Lindsey, whom I'd always liked the best of that whole bunch, came up to give me a hug. She'd inherited her father's bony height and her mother's dramatic French features, beaky nose, and blue black hair, which maybe had she grown up in Paris she could have pulled off, but which in Scarsdale ensured she'd go without a prom date. She was nineteen, studying modern dance at NYU, and Phil wondered openly and cruelly how she'd ever find a husband.

"A whole year without Grandpa," she said.

"I know, Linds. It's hard to imagine." My father had been so wholly charmed by both his granddaughters, but especially this one. I suppose he sensed she needed the greater part of his admiration. I remember, a few years ago, he treated Lindsey to a date at the Rainbow Room, the fanciest place he could think of, the night the rest of her class was jigging at the prom. They listened to Michael Feinstein croon standards and he let her drink as many champagne cocktails as she wanted at fifteen dollars a pop and then took her for a spin on the dance floor because that's the kind of guy he was.

"I want to call him all the time," she said. "I keep thinking he could come down to visit, we could go to the Second Avenue Deli or something, we could go to the movies. And then I remember he's gone."

"He would have loved that," I said. "He was an enormous fan of yours."

"He was an enormous fan of yours, too," she said. "He really was."

"Well," I said, and we reached for anything else to talk about, but of course there was nothing, and soon she, too, was engulfed by the small crowd of aunts, cousins, family friends who wanted to comfort themselves by reaching up to pinch her cheek. Near RIVKA DIZINOFF (1915–1989), Elaine and the Sterns were talking, and Laura had meandered to the gate by the roadside to try to light a cigarette. In the distance I could see Phil's diminutive rabbi making his way through the headstones, and I felt myself take several steps backward to distance myself from all of it. In the past year, I'd felt close to my father dozens of times: staring out the window of an Amtrak train, anticipating the first juicy bite of a hamburger, the lousy second half of a Nets game, a drive up the Saw Mill—but right now he was nowhere to me. Another step backward, and I bumped into my son, who was removing himself the same way.

"I've been thinking about something," Alec said, his voice tentative. He was still kicking at the nearest flowers. Ten yards away, Laura was staring past the gate, sucking down a Marlboro under a smoky halo.

"Yes?"

"Well, it's weird, but . . . but do you think Grandpa's already disintegrated?" he asked. "I was wondering, how long does it take for a human body to decompose? Is he still actually there? Or are we holding this ceremony for a bunch of bones?"

"Are you serious?"

"Yeah," he said, looked guilty, but I knew he wasn't being flip—he'd always had a taste for biology—and he stopped kicking at the dandelions and shrugged his hands deep into his pockets. The truth is this was something I, too, had reflected on throughout the year, and it would come to me at odd hours: falling asleep to Elaine's heavy breathing, waking up to find her already out of bed, that first draining piss of the day, catching my saggy jowls in the mirror over the sink. Age, age, death, and we're gone.

"Dad?"

I took a breath, and the cool air felt welcome. "I suppose that most of the flesh has disintegrated," I said. "But the bones are still there. The clothes. Some hair. We put him in an ebonized coffin, which means that it will take longer for his body to decay."

"Why'd you do that?"

"I don't remember," I said. "I believe it's what your grandmother wanted."

"Does it bother you to think of him under there?"

"No," I said, surprised. He rarely asked me about my feelings. "Does it bother you?"

"All the time," Alec said. "It really does," he said, "all the time." And then he wandered off toward the gate, to Laura.

A few feet away, near the crowd—I could see it, though I wasn't yet ready to visit—my father's headstone squatted fresh and shiny under its protective cheesecloth covering. I couldn't bear to look. My father, the same exact height as my mother, and as time passed, it shrank them in exactly the same way, and sometimes they would walk leaning on each other, their heads almost touching at the temple. I couldn't look at his grave. Bones, clothes, hair.

And then the tiny red-faced rabbi called us to order, and I no longer had a choice.

AFTER THE BRIEF, rote memorial service of Hebrew prayers, generic words of remembrance, my mother's dignified tears, removal of cheesecloth, mournful gazes, my brother holding tight to my mother, more Hebrew, we lunched at an Italian buffet across from the racetrack, in a private room bedecked with horseshoe-shaped bouquets of mums.

"This was the best they could find?" I heard Iris murmur to Elaine as we trooped in.

"Nobody wanted to shlep."

I sat near my mother, Elaine sat near the Sterns, and various cousins filled the spaces in between. Laura and Alec were wedged together in the middle of the table, across from Lindsey and Phil, and the four of them were gripped by conversation; they didn't pay attention to any of the rest of us and took forever to rise for the buffet. From the look on Phil's face I could see that he was delighted to have, after all these years, some close-up interaction with Laura, the baby killer in the flesh, and when Cousin Marvin's grandkid got passed Laura's way and she held it for a moment with a practiced gootchy-goo, my brother couldn't tear his eyes away.

"So how's medicine these days?" My cousin Norman, Aunt Iz's third and least obstreperous son, sat quietly to my right. Norm had taken up music composition and still lived, as far as I knew, in a Yonkers studio right down the street from where he grew up. Aunt Iz referred to him as the *durchfall,* the failure, right until the day she died, which was mean-spirited, I know. But there was something about short, runny-nosed Norm that begged for derision, even from his own mother.

"Medicine?" I said. "Not bad, thank God." A single morning with my family, and I had adopted the rhythms of their speech.

"You do heart surgery, right?" he asked in his dreamy way.

"No, just internal medicine."

"But some surgery?" He sounded hopeful. "Every once in a while?"

I shrugged, let him think what he wanted, took a sip of my pasta e fagioli. Out of the corner of my eye I saw my mother poke at her soup, and I wanted to go talk to her, check in.

"Hey, do you know any single ladies?" Norm asked after watching me take a big swallow.

"I'm sorry?"

Norm raised and then sank his shoulders dramatically. "I'm looking for a nice lady to take out, Peter. I'm turning fifty soon. I need a nice woman to take care of me, I've decided."

I blinked. I'd always just assumed Norm was gay, not that I'd considered the matter more than a handful of times in my life. "Jeez, Norm," I said. "I'm afraid I don't."

"Nobody?" He looked at me, dejected, with those round, rheumy eyes. "But you're a doctor, Peter. You meet new people all the time."

"Well, it doesn't exactly work that way when patients come into the office. I'm not really meeting them in a social way."

"But surely you know some nurses?"

"Norm, I don't—"

"What about her, over there?" Norman motioned past my shoulder with his spoon. "Who's that girl?"

Oh, give me a break. "Well, Norm, I think she's a little young for you, don't you?"

"But who *is* she?" he asked. "She's so *pretty*."

"Her name is Laura Stern. She's an old family friend. Remember my college buddy Joe? She's his daughter."

"Is she single?"

"Norm, she's not—"

"Do you think maybe you could introduce me to her?"

"I just don't think that would be appropriate, Norm. This isn't the right occasion for that sort of thing."

"But you said she's an old family friend."

"Norm, I know, it's —" And then so quickly we both could have missed it, Laura and Alec pressed their lips to one other's and then in an instant removed them. They did it right in front of Phil and Lindsey, right in front of all of us, and then, not two seconds later, they did it again. I felt my extremities turn to ice. They were kissing. My son and Joe's criminal daughter. And these were not the passionate kisses of people just falling in love with each other — worse, much worse, they were the kisses of familiars. Of people who had been kissing for ages already. How could I have missed this? How could they have escaped me?

"Well, Christ, Peter, she's Alec's *girlfriend?*" Norm said. "Why didn't you say she was his *girlfriend?*" And if the whole of my family hadn't been in the room, I would have quietly forced his face into my soup bowl and held it there until he drowned.

"Peter, if she's Alec's girlfriend you could have told me. It's not like I'm going to *say anything weird,* I just thought she's sort of *hot —*"

"She's not his girlfriend," I hissed. Then I pushed out of the way, making sure to give Norm's seat a nice jostle, and headed for the buffet.

"But *Pete!*" he called from his chair, aggrieved. "Why didn't you —"

Manicotti, rigatoni, chicken parmigiana — *chicken parmigiana?* My parents kept a kosher home for fifty-nine years! — and I squeezed my fists hard enough to hurt. I turned my head, accidentally caught Laura smoothing Alec's hair with her small fingers, her pearl ring, squeezed my hands harder in front of a tray of hardening garlic knots.

"You okay, honey?" Elaine, my soft, appropriate wife, with her arm around me.

"No," I said. "Not really."

"You want to go home? I think we can just leave if you want." She kept her arm around me. "Nobody will mind."

"I can't."

"Sure, you can."

"Elaine—"

"If you want to go, we'll go."

And look like a shmuck. And give Phil a golden opportunity at filial one-upmanship. And leave Alec in the suckery tentacles of his thirty-year-old paramour. And leave my paralytic mother to her unkosher meal.

"I want to go home," I said to my wife.

"So then," my wife said, "let's go."

Explaining to everyone that she wasn't feeling quite so well, a little tired, Elaine and I got into the Audi, and she took the wheel.

"What's wrong?" she asked as we eased out of the parking lot, but I was too disgusted to answer. We were quiet past the racetrack, the four-lane slog of diners and gas stations on the bumpy road toward the Belt Parkway. In the distance, the Manhattan skyline shimmered like an oasis, but I kept my gaze on my hands knotted together, my fingernails chewed down to the pink, veins lumping near my knuckles. Elaine turned on the radio, the classical station. I shot her a look. I wanted her to know I wanted quiet without having to say anything. But her eyes were on the road where they should have been, and so we listened to Ravel the rest of the way across Queens.

"Did you know Alec was seeing her?" I asked, two stoplights from the Triborough Bridge. I could hear the accusatory note in my voice, but Elaine missed it.

"Of course," she said. "They're together all the time."

"And you knew it was romantic?"

"I assumed," she said. "Why? Didn't you?"

"And you didn't say anything?"

"What should I have said?" She looked at me sideways. "I knew it would upset you."

"Of course it would upset me! She's endangering him! She's putting him in danger, Elaine. Of course it would upset me."

"Oh, don't be so melodramatic," she said. "She's not putting him in danger. This is just a little flirtation before he goes back to school."

"He's not going back," I said. "He's totally derailed. I can sense it. The more time he's with her, the more derailed he's going to be."

"What are you talking about?"

"She'll keep him stuck where he is," I said. "She has no sense of purpose, no goals, no nothing. Flits from jewelry to goats to God knows what. Spent the years she should have spent in college in a mental institution. A mental institution!" I felt my jaw tighten. "They were kissing at my own father's unveiling and you think this is just a little flirtation?"

"Peter, control yourself." We were approaching traffic on the Deegan, near Yankee Stadium and the grim shells of old warehouses, eighteen-wheelers in front of us and on every side.

"Why, Elaine?"

"Why what?"

"Why can't he just enroll in school, date someone his own age, get a goddamn degree, get a job, get a life? Is that so hard? What have we done wrong that he thinks the rules don't apply to him? That he thinks he can just swan around Round Hill with someone like Laura Stern and not go back to school and not get a real job and not get a life and that's okay?"

"What have we done wrong?" She sighed heavily. "Are you really asking me that?"

"Why is it that everyone else's kid goes to college and our kid is spending all his time with a baby murderer?"

"Peter, stop it!" We were at a complete standstill now, trucks walling us in. "Please, stop it. You're losing all perspective."

"What kind of perspective would you like me to have?"

"Peter," she said, reaching across the seat to take my left hand, unknot it gently from my right one. "Pete, come on," she said. "Laura is a distraction for Alec for the next few months. He's lonely. She's company for him. That's all. Stop overreacting, please."

"He wouldn't be lonely if he went back to school like a normal person."

"He is a normal person."

"He's at an age, Elaine—he's at an age where decisions he makes now impact the rest of his life. When I was his age, I was applying to medical school. You and I were engaged. I was building a life. I wasn't living like a teenager in my parents' garage."

"Your parents didn't have a garage."

I shot her a look.

"Honey, come on, try to relax." I shot her another look, but I was feeling an uncomfortable tightness in my chest, and my dad's MI came quickly to mind. I decided to try to listen to my wife; I took a deep breath, let it out through pursed lips. As we moved across the bridge, Manhattan receding behind us, the Ravel turned to Chopin. I tried to fill my head with the music, tried to drown out the image of the two of them kissing in the restaurant, kissing casually, as though they'd been kissing their entire lives. But it was useless.

"I just can't let him lose control of his life, Elaine. He's our only son. He's our only chance to . . ." The George Washington Bridge now, enormous gray twists of cable, a huge American flag hanging above us. Then the Palisades. Snow receding into the hawthorns.

"To what?"

Naked branches and dark green pines lining the sides of the road. Along the shoulder, a small female deer. Our only chance to ensure a legacy for ourselves. To ensure future happy generations. To make up for all the kids we didn't have.

"To what, Pete?" she asked again.

"To get it right."

"Oh, honey, I promise." She kept my left hand in her right one as she drove. "I promise you, we already got it right."

My wife had spent our marriage trusting in me; at that moment I should have trusted her. Instead, I stared out the window at the route I'd memorized years before, the deer, the trees, the school, the street signs, trying to figure out what would be required of me if I was going to rescue my son.

CHAPTER SEVEN

SIX YEARS AGO, a Tuesday morning, Elaine found a smallish lump on her left breast while she was trying on a new sports bra at Macy's. She let it sit for a week, hoping it would go away, and sometimes it did seem to disappear for a few hours, only to reemerge when her panicky fingers did a more invasive probe. The following Tuesday, a visit to Rhonda Nighly, a biopsy, and a diagnosis: stage 2 B invasive ductal carcinoma, unaffected lymph nodes. The prognosis, considering everything, wasn't terribly bad. Rhonda asked her to come in as soon as she got the test results, but Elaine had a class to teach at ten and was able, somehow, to expound upon the Wife of Bath at Bergen State while Rhonda Nighly's office manager logged her results into a patient database. I met her at the oncology office that afternoon, listened to the news, asked Rhonda everything I remembered about ductal carcinoma from medical school, and kept my arm tight around Elaine's shoulder.

"The prognosis?"

"We'll have surgery, chemo, probably six to eight rounds. The cancer is hormone-receptive, so we'll start her on Tamoxifen. Nothing too radical."

"And then?"

"We caught this relatively early, Pete." What was with all the "we"?

Elaine caught it, Elaine would have surgery, Elaine would suffer through chemo alone. The best we could do was to guide her and do our best to hide our superstitions or doubts. And perhaps it was this folksy "we" that did it, or perhaps it was just my own panic, but for all my pride in my collegial workplace, when it came time to schedule Elaine's surgery, without even blinking I asked Rhonda Nighly to send us to Columbia.

"Columbia?" she said. "But wouldn't you rather have her right here? Elaine, wouldn't you rather be here?"

Elaine looked at me as trustingly as a deer. "You'd rather have me at Columbia, Pete?"

There was no reason the more-than-competent surgeons at Round Hill couldn't have handled the job, but I explained to everyone that, if the ladies had no objections, I was more comfortable doing it somewhere less familiar, that if God forbid something went wrong . . . although, truth be told, that wasn't it. Like so many Round Hillers who needed nephrectomies or partial thyroidectomies or scheduled C-sections, I wanted the name-brand New York City Ivy League teaching hospital for my wife and her extremely routine surgery. I wanted docs I looked up to. I didn't want to feel like one of the smartest guys in the room.

"You know, Columbia has terrific outcomes."

Rhonda shrugged at me—I wasn't making any real sense—and said she'd refer us to an oncological surgeon across the river. Was I sure I didn't want to go with Charlie Joffe? She'd worked with Joffe for years, liked him, trusted him; he did beautiful reconstruction work. I'd seen Joffe get looped on Coke-and-whiskeys at the annual hospital holiday bash. No way were his bloated hands going to slice into my wife.

So Elaine and I checked into the massive surgical ward on 168th

Street on a gloomy Wednesday in May, 7 a.m. Just getting to the hospital was a nightmare, with traffic on the George Washington Bridge and double-parkers crowding my entire way to the garage. Dominican music blaring already on the street corners, kids dressed in Catholic school uniforms lining up at bus stops, and the demented partisans of the New York State Psychiatric Institute wandering the corner of Haven and 170th with their mouths wide open and their eyes half-closed. We were listening to the classical station and Elaine held her left hand against her right breast, the one they weren't going to touch. She hadn't eaten in twenty-four hours, as per Rhonda Nighly's instructions and her own nervous stomach. For some reason, I'd been ravenous and snuck two grilled cheese sandwiches and a leftover piece of brisket in the middle of the night, well after Elaine had fallen asleep.

My folks were staying with Alec, who was probably old enough to stay by himself and had in fact begged to do so, but we wouldn't hear of it. I'd be home again that night, but we wanted them to be there when he got back from school; we wanted them to make him dinner, to help him remember that today was like any other day. Or to drive him in after the surgery if he wanted to come and just be at the hospital. My father was still an able enough driver and, in light of the seriousness of the day's events, would even splurge on a parking garage. He'd been hospitalized himself twice for arthroscopies and cardiac stents, and was wonderfully optimistic about the whole thing.

"Don't worry, kid," he said to Alec on the phone. "Your mom will be wearing a bikini again by the summer."

"Grandpa, that's disgusting."

"Your mother in a bikini?" My father chuckled. "She's got a lovely figure, your mother. But don't tell your dad I noticed. He's likely to get jealous."

"Grandpa, seriously, that's gross."

As for Elaine's parents, we would tell them about the surgery when the whole thing was over. Everyone preferred it that way, especially Elaine.

So we checked into the hospital, which was both familiar to me, with its endless hallways and gurneys and smells of chlorine, and unfamiliar, too, so sprawling and busy. At Round Hill, medicine was practiced with a dignified hush; at Columbia Presbyterian, the Broadway hum swelled into the corridors, and the shouting and laughing and gossiping and beeping filled every corner until we were shown to Elaine's room, where everything was suddenly very quiet.

"Well," I said. I was carrying her overnight duffel. The day before, I'd gone out and bought her a new robe, the most expensive one I could find. I put the duffel down next to the bed and wondered where I could buy a dozen roses around here. "You'll be great, honey. And in a matter of hours this will all be over."

"I know," she said, still holding her right breast.

The tech who'd led us to the room slipped away. Soon we would meet various nurses and the surgeon, and Rhonda Nighly promised she'd stop by, but for now we were alone. Elaine was supposed to put on her backless, buttless hospital gown. She took her hand from her breast, slowly unbuttoned her nice white shirt.

"Do you want anything?"

"No," she said. "What would I want?"

"Really? Nothing?" (Although what could I get her? She was not allowed to eat or drink, we'd packed three weeks' worth of paperbacks and *People*s into her duffel.) She smiled wryly at me and finished unbuttoning her blouse.

"You know what I want? No cancer," she said. "That's what I want."

"And that's what you shall have, my dear."

She smiled weakly at my gallantry and folded her shirt neatly on top of the bed. She slid out of her pants, then unfastened her bra, and although I knew it wasn't possible, I could swear I could see it glowing right underneath her skin, the quarter-sized mass of rapidly dividing cells in the milk ducts underneath and just to the right of her left nipple.

"Here," I said. "Let's get you into that dress." I unfolded the paper gown and helped Elaine slide into it. "You look great."

"Don't be stupid."

"No, really," I said.

"Well, I won't look so great tomorrow."

"Of course you will," I said. I tied the ribbons on the back of her gown and then stood behind her and kept my arms around her, buried my head in her soft blondish hair, kissed her there.

"Pete, if anything happens—"

"Nothing will happen—"

"Just don't let Alec forget me, all right?"

"Elaine, this is routine surgery." We'd been so good this whole time. I couldn't let her descend into lachrymose panic now. I couldn't stand it. "The surgery can't kill you."

"You don't know what they'll find."

"They've done a million tests. They know exactly what they'll find." Which wasn't exactly true—even the most common cancers could be a festival of nasty surprises—but still, I'd seen the MRIs, seen the tumor in its three-dimensional glory, and agreed with Rhonda Nighly that the thing looked beautifully contained for the moment.

"Can you just let me say this, please? I know you don't want to hear it, but I need you to let me say it."

I tightened my arms around her. "Okay."

"Okay," she said, and for a second it felt as if she'd forgotten what she wanted to say, and the tension in the room disappeared, but then she spoke up again. "I want you to tell Alec all about me."

"Elaine—"

"I want him to remember who I am, the things about me that made me different. What made me special. Not just that I was his mother but also, you know, the person I was."

I let out my breath heavily. "Okay."

"What will you tell him?"

"What makes you special," I said. I refused to use the past tense.

"Like what?"

Did she really want to do this? I tightened my hold on her. "You're a wonderful mother. You love him. You're kind."

"Be more specific."

"You grew up in Squirrel Hill, Pittsburgh, Pennsylvania."

"What else?"

What else? "You know how to pronounce Middle English. You have a great sense of humor. You can do the Sunday crossword in pen. You don't like raisins." I put my chin on her head.

"Keep going."

"You always know where all the lost things are in the house. It's like you have radar. You have a beautiful singing voice."

"That's good," Elaine said. "Tell him all that stuff."

"He knows it already."

"But don't let him forget it," she said. "I wanted to . . . I was going to write him some letters—one of the chat rooms was talking about that, writing letters to your kids for each of the major events in their lives, graduations, weddings, birth of their own kids, you know." Her voice was even. I had squeezed my eyes shut. "But I couldn't do it. It just felt so stilted. And pessimistic. Because most of me is sure I'll make it—"

"Elaine, of course—"

"Pete, please," she said. She so rarely cut me off. I kept my eyes shut. "But just because you never know. Because surgery can be unpredictable, right? Because we don't know exactly what will happen. I need you to promise me you'll keep me alive for him. You'll remind him about the person I was."

"I will."

And I held her like that until Rhonda came into the room, with her firm handshake and her cheerful laugh, and we swept away the lachrymose mood with a reassuring mix of medical jargon and upbeat predictions, and then the gurney came and took Elaine away and I wandered up and down 168th Street, afraid to go too far away but also unable to stay too close to the operating room.

At 2:40, when my cell phone rang, she was still in surgery. "I want to come," Alec said. "Tell me how to find you guys."

"No, look, I don't know how long it will be, and when she comes out of surgery she'll be—"

"I want to come," he said. "Grandpa said he'd drive me. I'll be there when she gets out. It's right over the bridge, right? How do we get there?"

He was fifteen and full of conviction, and I was too exhausted to put up a decent fight. What were those good reasons to keep him away? I'd forgotten.

"Take the Hundred Seventy-eighth Street exit off the bridge and make a right onto Fort Washington. She's in the Milstein Pavilion. There are signs. Call me when you get to the lobby and I'll meet you there."

"Okay," Alec said, stoic, determined. "See you soon." And because he meant business, he clicked off without saying good-bye.

I met him and my folks twenty-two minutes later; my father must have done eighty on the Palisades.

"How is she?" my mother asked. She and Alec were about the same height back then and had the same dark brown eyes and pointy chins. They both wore their anxiety by turning fierce, aggressive. My father, on the other hand, liked to turn every worrisome event into a party and headed to the gift shop to buy balloons.

"I'm sure she's fine," I said. "The surgery takes a while because they're doing reconstruction at the same time."

"Should they be doing that?" my mother asked. "Maybe they could just take out the tumor, finish her up another time?"

"Mom."

"I'm just saying."

"If we can minimize the times she has to go under anesthesia, that's a good thing."

Alec was standing bug-eyed, straight-backed, his hands tight at his sides. I watched him clench and unclench his fists.

"But everything's looking really great. The doctor came out a while ago to let me know everything was great." This was untrue. I had yet to hear a peep from the surgical team, and about ten minutes before Alec arrived I'd almost grabbed some scrubs and wormed in there myself to find out what the fuck was going on. I figured out too late that the problem with doing this at Columbia was that nobody knew who I was. This should have been evident from the start, but I must not have been thinking.

"What about that doctor over there?" My mother pointed. "Maybe he can tell us something?"

"Do you even know who that doctor is, Ma? Do you even know what he does?"

"He can tell us who to ask."

"I know who to ask." We were still standing in the too-bright lobby of the Milstein Pavilion, wheelchairs derbying past us. "C'mon," I said. "Let's go up."

"We're not staying," my mother said. My father had just returned with the balloons. "C'mon, Hesh, give Pete the balloons. We're leaving."

"You sure?"

"We'll be at home, sweetheart, if you need us. Only a fifteen-minute drive away."

"I'll call you," I said, suddenly grateful. She knew I didn't want her around and spared me having to tell her so. "I'll let you know how it all turns out."

"Hug her for us," my mother said, and my father pressed his circus-colored balloon ribbons into Alec's hand and kissed us both, and then the two of them threaded their way out of the pavilion, my father with his arm around my mother's waist. If you'd asked me how much longer I thought he had to live, I would have told you twenty years.

"C'mon, Dad," Alec said, holding the balloons tightly. "Let's go up."

We loitered outside the surgical ward silently for another two hours, in a windowless waiting room littered with coffee cups, terrible magazines, a television whose channels were impossible to change blaring soap operas. Alec made a decent show of reading a three-month-old *U.S. News and World Report,* but I couldn't fake it and kept jumping up and down as though my springs were wound too tight, which they were. I knew the specifics of her surgery, though. I'd discussed them with Rhonda several times, once or twice meandering through oncology in the hospital at odd hours, knowing she'd be there, then cornering her to ask about Elaine's Bloom-Richardson score, her lymph nodes. I'd even plunked my cafeteria tray next to

Charlie Joffe's once—rejected Charlie Joffe, who was good enough not to question my decision to send Elaine to Columbia and instead overstayed his lunch break drawing me little diagrams on napkins. Elaine would be perfectly fine. If they couldn't handle the reconstruction postmastectomy, they'd simply put it aside for another day.

But even as I was reminding myself of this and a thousand other encouraging things, even as I was hypnotizing myself with words like *Tamoxifen, Herceptin, Femara,* I was up again, standing as close to the operating room as I could lawfully get.

"You want some coffee, Dad?" Alec asked me. I hadn't heard him follow me down the hall. "I was gonna go downstairs and find the cafeteria."

I shook my head at him. His mother and I—we had known each other since we were nineteen years old. We had grown up together. I had truly tried to do my best by her. There had been moments, of course—infertility and its attendant hysteria, building my practice, worrying about our money, my own occasional distractions, her own goals, and the fact that it's hard to live every day with another person and love her on a constant graph. Love, so the song goes, is a parabola. But right now, we were at the top of the parabola. This was, of course, because my wife might not live to see the downward slope.

"Well, would you mind if I left?" Alec asked. I didn't answer, and in a second or two I heard him pace backward down the green-tiled hall. From the other direction, a pair of men came marching purposefully. I envied them their swagger, their all-access pass to every corner of this swollen, hideous hospital. As they approached, they each looked more and more like doctors of the old school, sitcom doctors, with graying temples and white coats flying open and stethoscopes rounding their necks and shoes that managed to stay polished, never mind the 168th Street debris spotting the floors. They were the doctors I had always imagined I'd become someday, although of course I wasn't quite that self-delusional. But still. They probably kept pieds-à-terre in the city; at least one of them fucked his nurse regularly; both of them probably played golf.

And then I realized that the one on the left, slightly taller, patrician bump on his nose, heavy gold ring, had been my favorite professor at Sinai. Dr. John Falls. Falls was a legendary neurologist, specializing in paralyses, aphasias, dysphasias. Winner of so many awards and medals so early that it had seemed almost certain he'd flame out hard, but instead he published one more brilliant paper after another and landed a faculty position at Sinai by the time he was thirty-two. He'd been an Olympic pole-vaulter during college and right after and entertained us, during rounds, with tales of Mexico City '68. What the hell was he doing here?

I watched him speak with that old, familiar purpose with his colleague. Maybe he had a high-level consult, a big-name conference. Maybe he was working on some city or state policy matters that would years from now trickle down to docs like me.

"Dr. Falls," I muttered under my breath.

Falls had always gotten along well with his students. He wasn't so much older than us, after all, and I think he and I had maybe had something resembling a friendship. We'd joke around after class, or when we bumped into each other in the hospital. I remember he had a slightly filthy sense of humor. He was an amateur baker and would bring dozens of cookies, bashfully, to hand out on campus; baking was how he relaxed. Bitter rumors spread that he was gay. If I'd thought I could follow in his footsteps, even fifty steps behind, I would have maybe become a neurologist, too. But I knew my limitations then and now.

The men had stopped ten feet away from me to finish their conversation. I watched them but tried not to look as though I was eavesdropping. Something about a subdural hematoma. We were around the corner from the operating room. I knew Falls would know how to find out what was going on with my wife. If anyone could, it was him.

Five minutes, seven, the two were still talking. My voice burst from me and I couldn't stop it. "Dr. Falls," I said, this time loudly. The men didn't look up. I waited until the other one said his good-byes and headed in the opposite direction.

"Dr. Falls," I said for the third time as John Falls marched purposefully my way. As he came closer to my view, I saw that scar on his forehead—I'd forgotten about it—an angry slash from a pole-vaulting accident.

"Dr. Falls," I said. He didn't look up. His hearing must have diminished as he'd gotten older. Almost thirty years ago I'd been taking his class, up all night getting ready for boards, my wedding coming up, Elaine wanting me to visit the hall on Long Island with her, see if I had opinions on tablecloth colors, flower arrangements, me too overwhelmed with med school to give the tiniest shit. Dr. Falls and I got together for a beer one breezy afternoon in the back of the old Kinsale Tavern, and I told him all about my wife-to-be and her grumbles. He was just about to get married himself and we compared notes.

"Dr. Falls," I said again as he grew nearer. "John."

The neurologist looked up at me. There was sadness and distance in his eyes.

"Yes?"

"Pete Dizinoff," I said. "Um, I was—"

"I'm sorry?"

"I was your student at Sinai," I said. "Pete Dizinoff. My wife is in—"

"Oh," he said. He blinked. "Dizinoff, yes. Sure. Can I help you?"

"My wife is in the OR, ductal carc—"

And then his pager rang much too loudly. I took a step back. Doctors like Falls were never in the dark. They never had to stand outside an operating room, waiting for a merciful colleague to tell them what was happening inside.

He blinked again. "I'm sorry," he said. "I'm sorry, I really must—"

"Of course," I said, and I watched as Dr. Falls hurried down the hallway, his white coat flapping, his polished shoes tap-tap-tapping on the stained tile floor.

I put my hands in my pockets and let my chin fall toward my chest.

Then I felt a warm hand on my sweaty back. "It's okay, Dad," Alec said. I hadn't even known he was behind me. Together, we watched as Dr. Falls turned the corner and disappeared from view. We went back to our places, my son in the waiting room with his magazines, and me as close as I could dare to the operating room, knowing better than to try to open my mouth again. Whatever I could ask wouldn't change anything, anyway. A better doctor would have considered that.

BUT IT SEEMS to me now that even that sad moment was full of grace. For Elaine survived: six hours and forty minutes after she'd gone in for surgery, I watched the nurses and residents wheel her out to the recovery room, gray-faced, barely conscious, but indisputably alive. "We got the whole tumor," the surgeon said. "All of it." Alec was standing next to me. Without looking at each other, we squeezed hands. We were lucky then—I was so lucky then. That night I slept in the chair in her room the way I had the night Alec was born, my jacket rolled between my shoulder and the side of my face.

Now, today, six years later: no more son, no more best friend, no more sterling reputation. No more happy marriage. No longer, even, a practice in Round Hill, no more modern art on the walls or Aeron chairs in my office, since Vince and Janene suggested three months ago that perhaps the time had come for me to find solo digs.

These days, then, instead of a cool sweep down the hill to my familiar examining rooms, there is a clanky drive to Bergentown, my new two-room office partitioned like a private eye's. I park in the chain-link lot behind a movie theater. My examining room sits above a Filipino restaurant, and the smells of garlic and bananas waft up all afternoon. After work I eat dinner, sometimes with Mina, who has stood bravely by me for reasons I don't try to fathom. Then I go to the hospital for rounds every night. Home, up the staircase to the studio, a long time staring out the window, and then to bed. I see different patients these days—fewer well visits, frankly, and more blacks, who not only die at disproportionately higher rates than similarly aged whites but must suffer morally impeachable doctors as well.

I venture nowhere near the JCC.

Oh, my patients still love me. For the most part they never bought *New York* magazine's best-doctors issue and therefore have no idea how far down I've come in the world. And there are several stalwarts who've followed me from Round Hill to Bergentown, and I appreciate them all and treat their bladder infections and strep throats with the same patient attention I did up in my fancier digs. However, I no longer try to sleuth out good, juicy diagnoses. I refer patients to the specialists who are still willing to be referred to by me. My patients, holding their cracked Sunday purses, nod tightly at me and press onward.

But one of the strange blessings of this past year is that I've remembered how much I like practicing medicine. Insurance woes and paperwork and privacy policies—these are all worries of another class and place. I'm just glad to still be around. I give my patients free drug samples, they almost weep in gratitude, and I remember that even someone like me can still do good in this sad world.

When Elaine opened her eyes in the recovery room, the first thing she saw was my face, and the first words she heard were mine, me, telling her I loved her.

AS ALEC'S BEHAVIOR began to change in his senior year of high school, we started tracing his troubles to the cancer. Early trauma, according to the psychotherapist, could have long-term consequences for adolescent development, and both of us had been so concerned with Elaine during that time (which was as it should have been, right? Wasn't she the one who was sick?) that maybe we never spent enough time thinking about Alec's reaction to his mother's brush with death. We hadn't sent him to therapy. We hadn't taken him to any of the adolescent counseling groups Tuesday evenings at the JCC.

"You really should think about it, Pete," Phil had said to me in that tone he was so good at. Elaine had been home for a month, the summer had launched its first heat wave, but still she was going about chemo with diligent good humor, despite one insult to her body after another. Phil and Mimi had come by for a visit, bearing platters and coffee from Zabar's.

"How do you think this is affecting Alec, seeing his mother so sick? She's bald, for Christ's sake. That's got to be tough on a kid."

"How is it affecting *him*?" I asked. "The only person I'm worried about here is Elaine. I'm trusting Alec will get through this fine as long as she does."

We were in the kitchen, the one room in the house where Elaine couldn't bear to be. The smell of food, the very thought of it, made her heave. All she could tolerate was Cream of Wheat and McDonald's vanilla milkshakes, to which I added a cup of cold water as per her preference.

"You remember when Mimi's sister died?"

"A totally different situation, Phil." Mimi's beloved younger sister had done some sort of peacekeeping work for the UN and had died in a plane crash in Ghana the year before.

"We were all so focused on Mimi and her parents that we never really thought about how this might affect the girls. And then Lindsey starts having nightmares, she wets the bed, doesn't want to go to dance class anymore, we've got to put her on Prozac."

I wished he would respect his daughters' privacy just a little. "Well, this is a different situation," I said. "For one thing, Elaine didn't die in a plane crash—"

"Don't be sarcastic," Phil sniffed. "That was a tragedy."

"I recognize the tragedy, Phil," I said. "And as you know, I feel terrible about it. But all I mean is that this circumstance is completely different. Alec's been great. Completely supportive, wonderful to Elaine, helpful around the house. I'm not worried about him at all." This was true as far as those days went. He was only a sophomore in high school then, he still played JV soccer and painted all the backdrops for the high school musicals, and of course he had his art classes. He'd offered to give it all up if I needed him around the house more, or if his mother did, and we were both so touched by the gesture we almost teared up. Then we assured him that no, no, we wanted his life to go on as it was. So it did.

"Lindsey's shrink costs three hundred dollars an hour," Phil said. "But honestly we think it's worth it. Although there are cheaper options if you're not comfortable with that price bracket. I'm certain there are community therapy alternatives if you'd rather. Or perhaps you know some psychiatrists at the hospital who could refer—"

"Phil, if I thought Alec needed therapy, I'd pay for therapy."

"Sure," Phil said. "I know that. But I'm just saying sometimes there are hidden symptoms. It's not what kids tell you," he said. "It's what they *don't* tell you that counts."

I refused to take parenting advice from my brother and looked at the floor.

"Anyway," Phil said. "She looks great. They did a terrific job on the surgery. You'd never know she had a mastectomy. Really. A masterpiece."

"Were you checking out Elaine's breasts?"

"It wasn't out of prurience, Pete. She just had reconstructive surgery," he said. "I wanted to see how she looked."

"You were checking out my rack, Phil?" Elaine toddled into the kitchen for the first time in weeks, followed closely by a hovering, pinchy-faced Mimi. She'd pulled it together for their visit, was wearing a long cashmere sweater Iris had bought her as a you-go-girl present after the surgery. But she refused her itchy nylon wig and made do with a flowered scarf around her head. Not all of her hair had fallen out; she still had her eyebrows and eyelashes and an odd sort of tonsure.

"Checking out your rack?" Phil laughed. "I certainly was. And you've got a fine one, if I do say so. Your husband can confirm, in fact, that I referred to it as a masterpiece."

"Thank you very much." She grinned. She was in the best mood she'd been in since the surgery. "I've always thought so, too." She sat down at the table with us, and Mimi brought out a tray of soda water.

"Listen," Phil said, "I was just saying to Big Brother over here" — this was how he often referred to me in conversation, as Big Brother — "that you might want to think about a little therapy for Alec. Just to make sure he's processing everything okay, with your illness and all."

Like Elaine didn't have enough to think about? Why couldn't he just drop off his Zabar's and go away?

But Elaine was sanguine. "You know" —she took a moderate sip of her soda water— "I was thinking the same thing, but he's just been so mature about everything, so together. I even asked him at one point."

"You asked him?"

"Sure." She looked at me quizzically—had she done something wrong? "Just if he wanted to talk to someone about what was going on with my health. He was surprised I even suggested it."

"Of course he was surprised," I said. "Because he's completely fine."

"Your son is such a nice boy." Mimi sighed. She was perfectly fluent in English but still her sentences often sounded slightly off, as if they'd been poorly translated. "He wants to take care of his parents, so he does not want to ask for special treatment."

"You think that's what it is?" Elaine said. "He's afraid to trouble us with any demands?"

"I think the kid just doesn't need therapy."

"It's not a sign of weakness, Pete," Phil said. "I've seen a therapist. I'm not ashamed to admit it."

"Why did *you* see a therapist?"

"Is that really your business?"

"You brought it up."

"All his friends were doing it." Mimi smiled. "Phil could not resist."

"I'm a human being, Pete. We all have damage buried deep within our psyches that's worth uncovering, damage that's incurred from the simple act of growing up. But I thought maybe I had some specific psychic . . . ailments, I guess, is the word—ailments that were worth exploring. So I decided to try it."

"Psychic ailments."

"In fact I only went a few times," he said. "But I found it useful. I have to say if I'd had the time in my schedule, I might have pursued analysis—that might have really been something. My psychiatrist said I had some very interesting issues to explore, which might have been fully realized in an analytic setting. Of course," he said, "it would have been impossible to find that kind of time. Analysis is a five-day-a-week thing, an hour a day. I'm much too busy to make that kind of time in my week."

"Phil," Mimi said, "we are talking about Alec. And Pete says he does not need therapy. So it is likely that he does not. But still perhaps you should ask him?"

"Ask me what?" Alec said, marching into the room with his two cousins behind him. There were now seven of us in the kitchen and suddenly my thoughts ran to Elaine's depressed immune system.

"You want therapy, Alec?" Phil asked.

"Therapy? Why?"

"To deal with your mother's illness," he said.

I put my balled-up fist to my forehead.

"Oh," Alec said. He went to the refrigerator and pulled out three cans of Coke. "Nah," he said. "I mean, I get why you'd ask, but I think I'm okay."

"You sure?"

"I'm sure," he said, and he disappeared with his cousins out the back door, simple as that.

"Okay," Mimi said. "So it looks like he does not want therapy."

I was still sitting forehead-to-fist.

"Nevertheless, I'd keep an eye on him," Phil said. He stretched his arms above his head. "You're right, though. He's a well-adjusted kid." He slapped his hands on our table. "I'm gonna make myself a sandwich. Anyone else want?"

"You know," Elaine said, "maybe I feel like a little sandwich, too."

"You're kidding," I said.

"A little company's doing wonders for me, I guess." She smiled. "Given me my appetite back." Which was, of course, wonderful, but *this* company, Elaine? *This* company? Even with all this talk of therapy and the heavy, greasy platter of corned beef and pastrami, which they couldn't have thought not to bring? And plastic tubs of chicken soup, as though you have a cold and not cancer?

But suddenly she was standing at the marble breakfast bar, picking a slice of pastrami off the platter and eating it with her hands. "Yum," she said. "I don't know why, but it really does feel good to eat something solid."

"Well, that is wonderful, Elaine," Mimi said, rustling through our cabinets for plates, knives, mustard. "Every day will be a little bit better, I think."

"Until the next round." Elaine sighed and stuffed another piece of pastrami in her mouth. "You know what this nausea feels like today? A little like being pregnant. Like that weird kind of one-minute-you're-starving, the-next-you-want-to-puke pregnant thing."

"I remember that well," Mimi said.

"I wish I could still get pregnant," Elaine said. "Don't you, Pete? Wouldn't it be nice to have another baby? Maybe I still could. Maybe the chemo hasn't destroyed all my goods."

"Really?" Mimi said. "You would have another baby? I could not even imagine. I don't have the energy anymore. For me, I am just waiting for grandchildren."

"Oh, I don't know." Elaine smiled. "A baby in the house would be something to look forward to. Would make all this worth it."

Elaine was forty-seven and irradiated. She was having 50 milligrams of Cytoxan forced into her veins through a Hickman cath for the next six months. And even before all that, twenty years before all that, she hadn't been able to hold on to an embryo.

"A little brother for Alec," Mimi mused.

"What do you think, Pete?"

"Just look at his face," Phil chortled. "White as a ghost. He thinks he's gonna retire in fifteen years. Big Brother doesn't want to start paying for college when it's time for him to buy a nice pad in Florida and sail off into the senior citizen sunset."

What were we talking about here? Was everyone in this room out of his mind? I stood and walked over to the window that looked out onto the backyard. Alec and his cousins were sprawled on the brick patio. They looked as though they were talking about something important, nursing their Cokes and pursing their lips. Alec needs therapy? Alec needs intervention? Alec needs a brother or a sister?

"Don't worry, honey," Elaine called. "I'm probably only kidding."

But Elaine, even if you weren't, it would still be impossible.

"I'm just feeling some nostalgia for my feminine parts, is all. I don't really want a baby."

"Okay," I said, still looking out the window. All we'd wanted for so many years was a baby. Now here he was, long legs kicked behind him in our very own backyard.

"Pete, can I make you a sandwich?" she said.

"That would be great."

"Pastrami or corned beef?"

"You decide," I said, and I sat back down at the table to watch my flower-turbaned wife lick French's mustard off her fingers one by one. A few hours later, Phil and Mimi and the girls left, and Elaine disappeared into the bathroom, where she vomited up everything she'd eaten that day and let me sit with her on the cold bathroom floor and rub her back and wash her neck with cool, damp towels. I put her to bed around seven o'clock, and afterward Alec and I decided to rent a movie, something loud and stupid with lots of explosions, and he and I sat on the couch and munched on leftover deli meat and went to bed much later, Bruce Willis's cries for backup still ringing in our ears. If they wanted to try to pathologize our son, that was their prerogative. As far as I was concerned, he was about as perfect as a fifteen-year-old could get.

CHAPTER EIGHT

HAD ELAINE BEEN diagnosed in 1971, she would have had about a 30 percent chance of survival over the next five years. If she'd been diagnosed in 1981, the rates would have gone up by 15 percent. But she was diagnosed in April 2001, and therefore neither Rhonda Nighly nor anyone else on the cancer floor was terribly surprised when, just a few months after Elaine began chemotherapy, her estrogen concentrations were normal and she was as clean and cancer-free as she'd been ten years before. She'd lost weight. Her hair was growing back into a chic little pixie cut that she spiked up with her hands. She'd started wearing a bit more makeup to return the color to her cheeks and the sparkle to her eyes. She'd started wearing more jewelry, too.

This was the renaissance of our marriage, the very heart of the renaissance, and who can say if our rebirth was due to her survival, Elaine's new interest in herself and her own happiness, or my own deep gratitude that she'd made it through okay and still loved me, needed me? I started buying her little gifts I knew she'd like, a framed black-and-white photograph of Central Park, a big purple orchid in a little pot. And I planned weekend getaways to New England, bed-and-breakfasts, the sort of trip I'd always hated—show me a shared bathroom and I'll show you the door—but Elaine began to take for granted. She clipped travel articles out of the *Times* and left them for me in my study; dutifully I'd make reservations and check in with my folks to see if they'd come watch Alec for the weekend (Alec, who was more and more resistant to babysitting, who was now taking driver's ed, who'd grown two inches and dropped soccer and suddenly started hanging out with those idiots Shmuley and Dan).

Elaine and I had started doing something else together, too, during this time, something we were ashamed to even admit to Joe and Iris, much less to our kid or our folks. We went about it with unpracticed secrecy, and when people inquired where we were on Saturday mornings, we'd mumble nonsense about "alone time" or, say, "Just out shopping, you know . . ." But the truth was that Elaine had read an article about a synagogue in Park Slope, Brooklyn, and wanted to try it. The place was a good hour's drive from our house, a tricky-to-find neighborhood where neither one of us had ever been. But the appeal of this particular synagogue was that it was full of survivors and sufferers—as well as vegetarians, lesbians, Ethiopians, and hippies. The rabbi herself had lost a breast years ago. Elaine thought we could check the place out maybe one Saturday morning, if I didn't mind. In accordance with the renaissance, how could I mind? We hadn't been to services since Janene Rothman's kid's bat mitzvah two years before, but still, the morning after she'd read the article, we left the house at the crack of dawn to cross two bridges and several highways to reach the survivor's synagogue in Park Slope.

"Welcome, welcome," said the rabbi, a heavy woman in a tight T-shirt that revealed every fold of her flabby torso and the great gaping space where her right breast should have been. "It's wonderful to see you again," she said, even though we'd never seen her before in our lives.

"What have you gotten me into?" I whispered to my wife, who grinned sheepishly at me and spiked up her hair. There were Old Testaments on desks by the entrance, song sheets in a basket by the door, and a basket of ugly hand-knit yarmulkes right next to the song sheets. I plunked one on my head and followed Elaine to a seat. In fact, there were lots of healthy-looking seniors and beautiful young people and a healthy sprinkling of forty-somethings in ugly knit yarmulkes and hip Brooklyn shoes. Elaine was on my left; to my right sat a lovely brunet, maybe thirty-four or -five, who wore a loose linen dress cut low in the front and the back. As she squeezed in next to me, her leg pressed accidentally against mine, and I felt an appealing tingle.

When my grandfather was still alive, he and Phil and my dad and I attended the Orthodox shul down the street from our Yonkers apartment. Elaine attended her parents' Orthodox shul her entire childhood. For both of us, the Jewish liturgy brought to mind the mingled smells of ancient prayer shawls and arthritic old men, the sensation of standing for hours on our feet. A female rabbi? Mixed-gender seating? Brightly colored WEAR A CONDOM, SAVE A LIFE posters in the entrance hall? Every old Jew we'd ever known would have turned around and walked right out.

But lessons from the anatomy lab came to mind: disregard the color of the skin or the gender of the specimen; inside, the blood and guts all looked the same. Books, hymns, prayers—they were all the same. The cantor had a husky singing voice, the rabbi read Hebrew with an authoritative snap, and within minutes Elaine and I lost ourselves in the words of the songs we'd sung growing up.

Hear, O Israel, the Lord is our God, the Lord is One.

Blessed be his glorious kingdom for ever and ever.

Did we believe that once? I think we must have. It's possible I'd never stopped believing, actually; I'd just stopped thinking about it.

Remember these words which I command you this day, and bind them onto the doorpost of your house, and on your gates.

I watched Elaine's lips move as she repeated the prayer.

"Do we believe all this?" I asked her after the prayer.

"Of course we do," she said, and I was glad.

The Torah reading was about the rules for entering the land of Israel, and the pretty brunet next to me stood to receive an aliyah. She was introduced as the survivor of a car accident, and only then did I notice a long pink scar snaking down from her neck to some secret place underneath the linen shift. I crossed my legs. She read Hebrew poorly, and the rabbi leaned over to whisper the words in her ear. She giggled, embarrassed, and started over. Absentmindedly her fingertips traced the line of her scar. I crossed my legs again and looked down at my lap.

Afterward the rabbi invited anyone who'd been through a recent trial to stand up and introduce himself.

"Stand up," I said to Elaine.

"I don't need to," she said. She held my hand. "I'm here with you. That's enough."

"Come on," I said. "You've been through a trial. A big one."

"Maybe next week," she said. I hadn't considered that we'd be doing this again.

The woman with the scar had wedged herself back next to me. "Good job," I said to her.

"I was terrible," she said. "But I made a nice donation to the synagogue after the accident, so they have to let me up there to read. One of these days I'll get it right." And I was glad to see that in one more way, all these temples were exactly the same.

On the car ride home, we listened to a British man read boring short stories on NPR and pretended to find the short story experience meaningful. Elaine mused, "Maybe we should bring Alec next time."

"Alec would rather clean toilets than go to services."

"How do you know?"

"C'mon," I said, turning onto the FDR. "I can't even get the kid to apply to college."

"What does applying to college have to do with going to services?"

"They're just things obedient kids do. Alec hasn't been particularly obedient lately."

"I'll ask him," she said.

But upon our return, it was clear Alec was in no mood to discuss religion. "Where were you guys?" he asked suspiciously. "I wanted the car keys."

"You can't use the car if we're not here."

His feet were up on the table in the kitchen, and he smelled nastily of unwashed clothing and the hard detergent stink of Listerine.

"Alec, get your feet off the table," Elaine said. "I'll take you for a drive later if you want."

"I don't want to go for a drive with you," he sneered. "I needed the car."

"For what?"

"Nothing," he said. "Forget it."

"Well," she said. "Did you have any breakfast?"

"Not hungry," he said, keeping his feet right where they were. "Where were you guys, anyway?"

"Nowhere," I said, thinking it sort of sweet that he cared.

He sighed. He'd pierced both his ears and started wearing ugly little wooden plugs in each of them, the sort of thing you saw in *National Geographic,* what bushmen stuck in their lower lip. He'd also pierced one eyebrow with a tiny gold ring.

"You were at Shmuley's house last night?"

He sighed again, which I took as an assent. Elaine hung her shawl on the peg by the door and went upstairs to take a bath. As far as our son went, I was the chief interrogator.

"What did you kids do? Trigonometry homework? Discuss politics, maybe? Debate funding for the arts?"

He stood up and let out an enormous, revolted grunt. "Jesus Christ." He turned to leave the kitchen, stomp up the stairs to his bedroom. How was this the same kid who, just a single year ago, had attended to his mother's health concerns with the diligence and tenderness of a visiting nurse? He'd been smoking pot all night (forget his breath, it was right there on his clothes wafting toward me) and I felt my stomach clench a little before I reminded myself what the therapist had said—it wouldn't kill him.

"Alec, come back here."

"What do you *want?*"

"College visits," I said. "You still haven't made any decisions." It was now the August before his senior year, and we had yet to take the requisite trips to hilly Ithaca, depressed Poughkeepsie, the frosty climes of Bowdoin and Bates—while already, months ago, Joe had taken Neal to Cambridge, New Haven, and Hanover. I had secretly hoped to cut Elaine out of the fun and take Alec myself, load up the Audi with some music we could agree on and a handful of AAA maps and recommendations for out-of-the-way upstate jazz clubs or Vermont breweries or New Hampshire theaters. I thought maybe even Springfield, the Basketball Hall of Fame, if Alec was interested in any colleges up around Northampton. (In my imagination, of course, Alec was in an unusually compliant mood.) The kid's GPA was no better than average, but I was sure there'd be a handful of well-regarded liberal arts colleges with good painting programs that would be happy to accept our boy. We had, after all, no intention of applying for financial aid.

But Alec continued to stymie my road-trip plans. He couldn't have cared less about the little circle of higher education that I'd drawn in red ink on my newly purchased *AAA New England,* nor would he even agree to check out any university Web sites. Elaine was more relaxed than I was about these matters. "He'll figure it out when he figures it out," she'd say. But I knew what the deadlines were for early admission, and I knew most of the kids in his class had already written their essays.

"I'll get to it," he said.

"What about Rutgers?"

"What about it?"

"That's a no-brainer application," I said. "You could just fill that out so you have a backup."

"Fine."

"That's it?" I said. "You want to go to Rutgers?" Rutgers was the state university, a good deal as far as higher education went, but this was the one big-ticket item in my life for which I was willing to pay retail. I'd been adding to Alec's college fund since the day he started kindergarten, two grand every fiscal quarter, so that he could go somewhere leafy and expensive and I could spackle the school's sticker on the back of our cars and drink my morning coffee out of its mugs. It was my right, my reward for having paid Round Hill Country Day tuition all these years, for sitting in on all those college advisement meetings, for watching my colleagues jog lap after lap around the JCC track in their Stanford shorts and Columbia T-shirts.

"Alec, I'm not trying to nag you—"

"You're not?"

"But if you don't take this stuff seriously now, you might regret it later."

"Why don't you let me worry about what I'll regret later?"

"How about Massachusetts?" I asked. "We could visit some Boston schools, maybe head down through the Berkshires on our way home."

"Whatever."

"Is that a yes?"

"Aargh."

"Alec? Is that a yes?"

"Sure, fine," he said, in a tone of voice that let me know he was doing me a huge favor. "I don't know when I'm free, though. I've got a lot of things going on, not that it seems to matter to you."

"Next weekend? Wait, damn, I'm on call next weekend. The weekend after? What do you think? I'll book hotels."

Alec raised an eyebrow at me. "You're serious? You want to do this in two weekends?"

"Completely," I said.

"I'll see," he said.

"What do you have to see?"

"Dad," he said, "I'm pretty busy. You don't seem to respect that I have a life independent of your own."

"I'll make reservations," I said, and Alec rolled his eyes and went upstairs, which I decided was an assent.

I ended up picking seven schools to visit over three days, and despite himself, Alec seemed to have a decent time at some of them; the most expensive ones, of course, he liked the best. He especially admired Hampshire, appreciated the school's laid-back approach to required courses and felt the art studios passed muster. He also liked the student who led us on a tour, who sported the same hideous eyebrow piercing Alec did and spoke in serious tones about his research in comparative astrophysics. Neither of us were sure what comparative astrophysics entailed, but the kid seemed very authoritative and slightly condescending, so we didn't ask any questions on that topic.

Still, despite Alec's clear preferences, he didn't bother filling out the relatively simple Hampshire application online. I knew because I checked his personal computer, and though I felt a bit guilty, I reminded myself that parents have to monitor these things. When I asked him how his essay was progressing, he would snort at me and ask me to stop hovering for five seconds, please. We were still months away from the ecstasy bust or the opal brooch incident, and I tried to accede to his wishes. He wanted me to leave him alone; for entire days I'd leave him alone.

But then Neal Stern got into college early decision and I knew for a fact that the Hampshire application, and all the others, were still sitting on his computer undone, and I almost had a fit.

"Come on over this afternoon," Iris had said. She was on a Saturday jog through the neighborhood and had stopped in for a cup of coffee. "Turns out the kid wangled his way into MIT. Joe bought a cake."

"Iris, that's fantastic," Elaine said, stirring hazelnut Coffee-Mate into her mug. "You must be so proud."

"Not half as proud as Neal is." But she was smiling. Of course she was proud. Who wouldn't be? If it were me, I'd frame that first MIT bill and hang it on the wall. I'd turn out a replica of the acceptance letter in bronze.

"Well, I can't wait to say congrats. MIT," Elaine said, "is really something." However, my wife had continued to show an irritating lack of exasperation with her own son's laconic garbage vis-à-vis college. As far as she was concerned, he could enroll at Bergen State in the fall if he wanted, and he could just keep living at home and she could drive to work with him a few times a week and have a little company. I wasn't allowed to say that Bergen State was not exactly what I'd envisioned for our son without getting into nasty spats about elitism and my wife's workplace, so instead I grumbled and kept my mouth shut and begged Alec to please, please, please, just write his fucking essay. And then Iris left and I disappeared into my den with my laptop.

"Pete, what are you doing?"

"Nothing, just some reading. Leave me be."

"You want to head over to Joe and Iris's?"

"I need some time, Elaine. I've got some stuff to finish up."

"What are you working on?" What was her problem?

Part C: Describe the person I most admire.

It took three hours and a certain amount of self-admonition, but in the end I think I did a fairly reasonable job of explaining in the first person why my own father, Alec's grandpa Hesh, was a wonderful and admirable human being who had greatly impacted Alec's life and left him with a respect for hard work, family obligations, and dedication to his community. A few phone messages with the answering service at Round Hill Country Day, and Alec had his recommendation letters secured. All we needed now was a transcript, some short answers to questions re: awards, sports, and after-school activities, and a couple of lines about what Alec might major in and why. It hadn't been my intention to fill these out, too, but the truth was it was easier to hide in my study and fiddle with Alec's application than it was to go out and nag him. And it actually didn't take all that long. By four that afternoon, I was celebrating Neal's MIT acceptance in the Stern kitchen, helping demolish a chocolate cake. Iris had fired up the Crock-Pot full of cocoa.

"Neal," I said, shaking the kid's triumphant hand. "Job well done."

"Yes, it was," he said, chocolate on his lips, MIT on his sweatshirt. "Yes, indeed." And I caught Joe's eye, but he looked away, went to the cupboard to pull out some more mugs. I sat down then in the breakfast nook next to Pauline, who was fourteen, pimply, with a mouth full of braces, but still infinitely more graceful than her older brother. She handed me a plastic fork for my cake.

"My dad's so sad that Laura's not here," she sighed.

"I'm sorry?"

"That's why he has that face on," she said. "Like, Laura's his favorite. The precious. He's so bummed that she's not here to celebrate." She sliced off a neat square of cake. Her red hair fell lank down her back. "The precious," she said.

"What do you mean?"

"Like in *Lord of the Rings*?" I shrugged to show that I had no idea what she was talking about; she shrugged back. "His precious one," she said. "No matter what the rest of us do, you know, we won't live up to Laura."

"I doubt that's true, Pauline."

"Believe what you want," she said. "It's true, though." We regarded each other for a moment, me thinking that of all these wonderful kids, how unfair that Joe favored the criminal, and Pauline almost certainly thinking exactly the same thing. "I'm getting more cake," she said. "You want some?"

"Sure," I said. "Thanks." And I looked over again at Joe, who, sure enough, was gazing thoughtfully, a bit sadly, at his son's chocolate-stained grin.

ANYWAY, THREE MONTHS later, Alec was accepted to Hampshire. Because I could not help myself, I brought home, for celebration, a large chocolate cake. We were so thrilled to have a bit of good news after the night in jail and the brooches and etcetera that nobody bothered to ask Alec many details about his application, and he himself seemed not to want to press it but rather just to accept our congratulations graciously, as if this bit of good fortune had always been his due.

And then, after only three semesters in—well, there's nothing more to say about that, except that one evening after Alec had returned to live in our house for a year and a half to dedicate himself to painting deer and mooning over Laura Stern, I came home from work to find brochures from the New School, NYU, and the School of Visual Arts on the kitchen table.

"Elaine? Did you send away for these?"

"I'm sorry?" She was stirring soup. "Huh. I didn't even see those. I guess Alec must have gotten them."

I refused to acknowledge my heart's optimistic leap and ate my soup and chicken without saying another word about the brochures. The boy was nowhere to be found—the studio lights were out, his Civic had disappeared—and until I confirmed the mail with him, I could not hope for the best. Frankly, ever since I'd seen those kisses with Laura, I'd had less and less of an idea what to say to Alec or how to say it, and our relations risked hitting that awful low of his senior year in high school, the only other time in his life when we didn't say a word to each other for entire weeks. But of course this time I'd found myself avoiding him, not out of rage, but out of an odd sort of fear about what I might say if I opened my mouth. And he avoided me because it was easy.

Alec came home around midnight, smelling like secondhand smoke, and found me sitting at the breakfast bar pretending to read. I'd left the brochures on the table.

"Hey, Dad."

"Hey, Al," I said, flipping the pages of my *Cleveland Clinic Journal* as casually as I could. "Have fun tonight?"

"Uh-huh," he said, and he sidled his sneaky way to the refrigerator to glug soda straight from the two-liter.

"What did you do?"

"Hmmm?" He wiped his sticky mouth with his sleeve and put the bottle back in the fridge. "Nothing, really. Drove around with Laura."

"Really." I swallowed. "So you two are—"

"We're nothing, Dad." He laughed. "I mean, I don't know what we are."

I had to assume. "But you still like her."

"Of course." He sat down at the table with me. He'd long since removed the ring from his eyebrow, but he still wore those contemptible plugs in his earlobes and had kept the habit of fiddling with them when he had nothing else to do with his hands.

"And what about these?" I said, gesturing to the brochures. I'd been hoping he'd bring them up himself, but I couldn't wait all night. "They were just sitting here on the kitchen table when I came home."

"Oh, those came? I went online to check them out and they ended up asking me for my address so they could send me brochures. I don't know why they bother, why they've got to waste trees, when everything I need to know's right online."

"I see," I said.

"There are these pop-ups, they just demand your address before you can even think straight—"

"And you visited these school's sites to check out—"

"Their transfer programs," he said. He was still fiddling with his earlobe.

"The transfer programs?" I put my journal down and looked straight at my son. "You're really thinking of going back?" I did my best to keep my voice casual, but it probably betrayed me, because Alec smiled indulgently.

"It was Laura's idea, to be honest. She thinks I need some more instruction to really get my painting to where it should be. And also that I'd end up making important contacts if I stayed in school. In the art world it's so much about who you know, and she thinks it's easier to get the big galleries to pay attention if you come well recommended."

"Laura said that?"

"See, Dad?" Alec said. "She's not pure evil."

"Who said pure evil?"

He laughed, stood up. "Anyway, the applications are due in a couple of weeks, so I don't know. I can't make any promises. But I'm thinking about it. These are probably the three best programs in New York. The ones I can get into, anyway."

"Look," I said. "If you need anything, money for the applications, whatever, just let me know."

"I will."

"And if there are any other schools, anything else you want, maybe we could take a trip to Boston . . ." Why was I so intent on Boston?

"No, no matter what, I think I'm gonna stay in New York. It's where the art market is. And Laura's moving to the East Village at the end of the month, anyway."

"She is?"

"Yeah," he said. "She's losing her mind at her parents' crib."

"I see," I said. Well, New York was a big city.

"Anyway, good night." He headed upstairs.

"Good night," I said to his retreating back. And then I stayed awake another whole hour, reading the flimsy brochures, and reconciling myself to the fact that Laura's influence on my son was not only not as bad as I'd assumed it would be, but perhaps even better than my own.

NYU, the School of Visual Arts, and the New School. I had a patient who was on the board at the New School. I'd call him first thing Monday.

"THE SAAB," ELAINE said several mornings later before I'd completely opened my eyes. "It finally died."

There are dozens of conversations you don't want to have while you're still in your pajamas, dreaming cheerfully about a drive across Sonoma with the cute, slightly cross-eyed blond who serves you your daily coffee at Dunkin' Donuts. This was only one of them. "What do you mean, died?"

She was nudging me with her toes. "I mean I was driving to the gym and I barely made it down Pearl Street before the car shuddered like an epileptic and died. AAA towed it to Round Hill Collision, but I don't care what they do to it, I don't want to drive that thing anymore."

I rubbed my eyes. All I remembered was the happy dream in the vineyards of Sonoma. If I fell back asleep right this second, I'd still be there.

"Pete?"

"You want a new car?"

"We could probably trade the Saab in."

"How could we trade in a dead car?"

"It's still under warranty, isn't it? Or something?" My eyes finally focused; Elaine was in her yoga clothes, sitting cross-legged on the pillow next to my head.

"I suppose."

"But let's say I'm driving in Newark, Pete, and the whole thing dies again. It takes forever for a tow to come to Newark. I don't need that kind of stress."

"Fine," I said. "Let's go car shopping."

She clapped her hands once like an excited child. "And no more five-speeds. I was really done with that stick shift, to tell you the truth."

While Elaine was in the shower, I knocked on Alec's door to see if he wanted to come along—when he was a kid, he used to love to visit car lots, and my feelings toward him had been so warm in the weeks since I'd found those brochures that really I wanted his company all the time. But Alec wasn't in his room, and when I looked out the window I saw his Civic was gone, and I wondered where he could be at eight thirty on a Saturday and then realized he'd probably never come home last night in the first place. Had Laura moved to the East Village yet? Was it already the end of the month?

"You ready?" Elaine crept up behind me. She was wearing a navy suit, as though we were off to a business meeting and not a bunch of outdoor car lots on Route 17. "I think I want a Jeep this time."

"A Jeep?"

"Something powerful," she said. "Something kind of fierce."

"A Jeep is fierce?"

"Come on, Pete. I want a more powerful car than that dinky little Saab, you know what I mean."

"You mean you want to spend a lot of my money on a new car."

"Exactly," Elaine said. "Let's go."

The woman who greeted us at Craig Motors' front door was dark-haired, dark-eyed, with a lovely figure and a professional smile; I had expected a wiry, balding man in a collared sweater, or maybe hefty Arnie Craig himself. Instead, this lovely young thing, who was wearing a black suit more sharply cut than Elaine's navy one, hair pulled into a neat bun. She wore wire-rimmed glasses and pale pink lipstick and looked so much better than she had the last time I'd seen her that she recognized me first.

"Dr. Dizinoff! It's nice to see you."

"Roseanne, look at you," I said. "You look wonderful."

"Oh." She waved her hand in front of her face.

"How long have you been working here?" We shook hands, and I was glad to note that her color was good, her eyes were clear, her voice strong. She'd lost a bit more weight since I'd last seen her, but she still looked healthy—trim but not emaciated. I was glad to see she was working, and thought that in her professional getup, nobody would ever know half her torso was emblazoned with tattoos.

"I just started six weeks ago," she said. "But would you believe I actually like it? My whole life I wanted to run away from the car business, I wanted nothing to do with sales, but it turns out that I'm actually sort of good at it." She smiled bashfully. "We've got a new lineup of Jeeps that are just flying out the door, and as you probably know, American sales countrywide aren't what you'd hope for. But they're doing really well over here."

"Well, that's probably because you're the one selling them," I said. I really was delighted with how well she looked. Some patients just stay with you; for whatever reason, Roseanne Craig and her depression had stayed with me, but now (through no intervention of my own, I had to admit) she seemed so much better.

"I think we're in the market for an SUV or a Jeep, isn't that right? This is my wife, Elaine," I said. "The car's for her."

"Terrific," Roseanne said, shaking my wife's hand, too. "Why don't you tell me what you're looking for specifically and I can show you what we've got."

Roseanne turned out to be the sort of saleswoman who would do any car-dealing father proud; she was efficient, knowledgeable, precise, and no-bullshit. I knew the Craigs would offer us a modest deal simply because I took care of them healthwise, but I also knew that we'd spend a bit more money on options we didn't really need because Roseanne was closing the deal. She put us in a Jeep Commander and took us for a spin around the backstreets off Route 17, near the never-quite-finished Forrest Avenue overpass.

"Now, the nice thing about this car is that it has a much smoother ride and faster acceleration than you see in some competing models. Plus all the space you'd want in an SUV, but the mileage of a sedan."

"Which is?"

"Eighteen city, twenty highway," she said. She was sitting behind us on the center bump, leaning forward to facilitate conversation. The model we were driving had a GPS system, and Elaine kept checking it out even though she knew perfectly well where we were.

"You offer this thing in a hybrid?"

"Not yet," she said, "but GM is working on some terrific hybrid models for 2010. When it's time to trade this in, you'll have a variety of large hybrids and plug-ins to choose from."

"Come on," Elaine said. "Nobody's ever going to want to plug in a car."

"You'd be surprised, Mrs. Dizinoff," Roseanne said. "For over one hundred miles a gallon, people will change their behavior."

"One hundred miles a gallon?"

"That's just the beginning," Roseanne said. Her voice was cheerful, but she was rotating her wrists in their sockets, and I thought I saw her wince. "Make a left up at the gas station—that'll give us a shortcut to the office."

"You okay, Roseanne?"

"Okay?" She blinked, stopped working her wrists. "I'm great!" I wondered at her grin, whether she was hiding anything. "Really," she said. "I'm really great."

When we returned to the dealership, Arnie Craig emerged from some back room and gave us each an enormous, two-handed shake. "So what do you think of my little girl?" he asked. "Hell of a saleswoman, huh?" Craig was powerfully built, a few inches shorter than me but wide-shouldered and chunky-legged, and although he had a soft belly, there was something in his posture of the high school football player he'd certainly once been.

"Hell of a saleswoman indeed."

"She really is," Elaine concurred. Then she drifted off to take one more spin around the showroom and leave us to the details.

"They're interested in the Commander, Dad."

"Great choice." He slung an arm around his daughter. "You trading something in? Interested in financing?"

"My wife's Saab was just towed to Round Hill Collision."

Arnie gave me a knowing look and Roseanne smiled. "Well, if you choose to finance, we'll get you excellent terms," she said. "Unless you'd rather determine the financing yourself. I know the doctors' association sometimes helps with auto lending."

She dealt with enough doctors to do her homework, one more point for her.

"I'm gonna go tend the floor," Arnie said, giving his daughter's shoulder a rub before letting it go. "You're in good hands here."

She rolled her eyes at me, smiling the whole time, then led me to her desk, modestly appointed with a family photo and a brightly painted miniature of Saint Francis of Assisi and her Berkeley diploma hanging overhead. Roseanne was, I'm sure, the only salesperson in the room with a degree from Cal, but she seemed quite at home in this environment. She'd probably grown up in this very room.

"Can I get you something, by the way? We've got pretty good coffee in the back, and I was thinking of asking the receptionist to call in for some bagels."

"I'm okay," I said. "Elaine and I just had breakfast at the Old Lantern."

"Good omelets," she approved. Good salespeople approve of everything you choose as long as they're not selling it.

"Listen, Roseanne, we're gonna take the car."

"Don't you want to check with your wife first?"

I gave my head a nonchalant shake, but she raised an eyebrow at me, so I complied. "Well, but I have a feeling. And I want to tell you how great you look, generally speaking. You feeling okay? Everything going all right?" Maybe it was inappropriate to ask her about her health at this juncture, but what the hell, we were going to buy this car, and I wanted to know. "Your wrists hurt?"

"My wrists?"

"You keep rolling them around."

"I've been playing tennis," she said. "Working on my backhand."

"Well, that's good—tennis is good. And you're sleeping? Eating?" I wanted to ask if she'd gotten herself over to Owen Kennedy or anyone in his practice, but I stopped myself: this wasn't the right place. "Energy levels?"

"Same as always."

"Any particular changes you've noticed? Anything else?"

"Not really."

"Not really?"

"I mean, no, I don't feel that much different than I did before. Maybe a little tired sometimes, but it's just that I've been working so hard."

"Okay," I said. I realized I'd brought the conversation to awkward ground. We smiled at each other for a few seconds. "Well, I think you sold us a car. You're a heck of a saleswoman—your dad is right."

"It's in my blood." She smiled, rotating her wrists again. Tennis, she said. Fine, tennis. But the light from the window shifted, and I could see darkness under Roseanne's eyes and knew that at the very least this girl needed more sleep.

"Should I get out the paperwork?"

"Absolutely," I said. "Then afterward you should go home and take a nap."

After we'd picked up the certified check and signed the papers, Roseanne handed Elaine the keys, dangling from a bright silver Craig Motors keychain. We drove back toward home full of appreciation for the Craig family, cheap gas, good credit, no traffic, New Jersey and its inestimable plenty. And I didn't think about Roseanne Craig for a long time after that, my thoughts consumed, as they were, with my son and the direction in which his life was heading. But every so often, driving along Route 17, I would think about stopping in at Craig Motors and saying hello, maybe even taking a new Lincoln for a spin with Roseanne at my side. Making sure she was healthy—house calls, more or less. But I never did, and when the Forrest Avenue overpass was finally completed I rarely found myself on that part of Route 17.

SCARCELY TWENTY-FOUR HOURS after we brought home the Commander, I found Alec standing in the driveway, sniffing around his mother's new car, peering into the trunk as if he expected to find some treasure there. He picked up and dropped the netting that stretched across the trunk, which was supposed to hold our groceries or luggage in place, lifted it high enough to snap, dropped it again. He slammed the trunk door shut and bounced the bumper up and down with his hands.

"May I ask——"

"Oh," he said, turning around, a shy look on his face. He was wearing a filthy T-shirt and shredded jeans, and his entire person emitted the noxious smell of paint thinner. "I was just seeing what kind of load this Jeep can bear."

"A load of what, exactly?"

He blew out through his nose. "I have some new paintings that I was gonna bring to this place in Harlem, the one with the owners——"

"You told me."

"Right, well, the owner, the one I sort of know, she came to the Red Barn on Thursday and I showed her my slides."

"And?"

"And she thought I might bring some actual art over and see how it worked in the space. She said she doesn't really get what she needs from slides."

"Therefore you want to drive your mother's new car into Harlem."

His face hardened. "Look, I don't want to put you out or anything——"

Was it wrong for me to bristle at his sense of entitlement? Was it wrong for me to wonder why everything I had still belonged to my son? "Listen, it's just that we brought this car home yesterday, and today you want to drive it to a still-not-necessarily-one-hundred-percent-safe part of New York City."

I could see him ball his hands in his pockets. "Fine, forget it. I'll tell the gallery I don't have the transportation——"

But I hadn't meant to get there so fast. "No, Alec, no, look. You can drive the car to Harlem, of course. I just——" He was glaring at my feet. "Just let me see the paintings first."

"Why?"

"I'm curious." He raised an eyebrow. "I just want to see what you've been up to locked up in that studio, that's all."

"Why?"

"Can't I see my son's paintings? Aren't I allowed?"

He shrugged deeply. "Seems to me you're allowed to do whatever you want."

"Great," I said. "So show me your paintings."

He shrugged again and led me up those rickety wooden stairs to the studio above the garage. I hadn't stepped foot in it since the day we'd finished renovating; now it was covered in drop cloths, stinking of oil paint and spirit gum, crammed with easels, frames, canvases, and large paintings stacked up against the walls. I blinked. This was exactly how I'd imagined it to be, how I'd wanted it.

"So which ones are you bringing to show the gallery?"

"I'm still trying to figure it out," he said, gazing at his oeuvre and picking a scab on his chin.

"Did she ask for anything in particular?"

"Not really," he said. "I think I should only bring four or five, you know, since I don't want to look desperate, bring her everything I've ever painted. And in general she likes larger canvases, I know."

"How about this one?" There was a large oil in the southeast corner of the room, brightly colored, a herd of deer racing headlong down a suburban road, mangling all the street signs in their way.

"Really?" He looked as if he was about to laugh. "You like that?"

"Is that funny?"

"No," he said. "No, not at all. I'm just surprised we have the same taste. That's my favorite one, too."

For a moment I felt my chest fill. "It is?"

"Yeah," he said. "I've been working on it for half the summer, really trying to make it feel epic, kind of scary. Like the herd has been unleashed and is about to take over the whole world."

"It does feel that way. Like an emergency, somehow."

"It does? You think?"

I went closer to the painting. In the background, in muted tones, were the grim burning outlines of a city. The deer eyes glittered at me. "It feels like the Horsemen of the Apocalypse, almost. Except deer." I sounded idiotic. "What I mean is —"

"No, no, I get it. That's exactly what I was going for, a spirit of destruction, the feeling that we're on some sort of collision course with nature. Except in my paintings, nature wins. In the real world, I don't think it works out that way."

"You get their forms so well," I said. "How do you do that? You just see the deer in your head and are able to paint them?"

"From the back window," he said, "I can see deer all the time. It's almost a petting zoo out there these days, you know? I take pictures and bring up the images on my laptop, but half the time I don't even need to look. I just have these pictures in my brain, the pictures go straight to my hand and onto the canvas."

"That's pretty amazing, Al." The deer's coats looked satiny. Their hooves sparked against the asphalt like metal.

"You think so?"

"Well, I'm no expert —"

"I know," he said. "But you really like it?"

I turned to my son, surprised. He hadn't seemed to give a fig about my approval since he was fifteen years old, and now here we were almost six years later, and he had that same look I remembered from his childhood, prickled eyebrows, a sort of hopeful twist of the mouth. Eyes big. Except now, of course, I looked up at him, since he was a good two inches taller than his old man, and I felt pride gust up inside me.

"Alec, I think it's terrific. They'd be fools not to take it."

He shrugged again, turned back to the painting, hunched his shoulders, my big little boy.

"You'll get a lot of good instruction when you're back at school, right?"

He shot me a look, but I kept my posture nonchalant. "I guess. That's what I'm hoping."

"And there will be teachers, painters, instructors—they'll get you ready to be a practicing artist. Take you to galleries, meet agents, that kind of thing?"

He nodded, stuck his hands in his pockets.

"What are you thinking?"

"Nothing," he said.

"Nothing?"

"Would that be cool with you?"

"What?"

"If that's what I ended up doing. If I ended up being a practicing artist."

"I thought that was the whole idea."

"I might not make a lot of money, you know."

"I never thought you would," I said. Then I realized how that sounded. "What I mean is, money doesn't matter. Money will come, eventually, if you—"

"I know what you mean," he said. His hands were still in his pockets, he was hunched, but his lips were pressed into a nice little smile.

We were quiet for a few seconds. "You want me to drive with you?" I asked. "To the city?"

"You want to?"

"Sure," I said. "I've got nothing much going on today." This wasn't really true—I was supposed to make rounds, and then Joe and I had been talking about going to the driving range and hitting a few balls for the hell of it.

"Cool," he said. "That'd be great." And I could hear it in his voice: he meant it.

But in the end, Elaine went with him to the city—my pager went off and I couldn't escape rounds as I had thought. She called me at the hospital to let me know that the woman at the gallery had rejected our son's work. "She said it was, I don't know, too allegorical? That he should go more abstract. She did seem to like the painting of your father, though. But not enough to take it."

I was leaning against the nurses' station, and watched as the catering truck brushed against a rack of IVs. "Is he okay?"

"You know how he is," Elaine said. "Acting all tough about it. I think deep down he's pretty hurt, but I'm sure he'll get over it eventually."

"Why?"

"Why?"

"Why are you so sure?"

"You know," Elaine said cheerfully. "Rejection is part of the artist's life."

I hung up without saying good-bye. On my way to the driving range I stopped at home, went up to Alec's studio, and took another look at the deer paintings he'd left behind. Allegory my ass. There were deer chewing down fences, chewing up gardens as I breathed. There were gas leaks, carbon emissions, big new Jeeps driving two small people down smooth suburban roads. There was destruction upon us, Alec knew it, captured it, and fleshed it out brilliantly, and

I felt confident the Harlem gallerist would one day feel like a fool for not having paid attention.

IF YOU WERE CURIOUS, by the way, about the end of my marital renaissance, it happened four years before we bought the Jeep — that would be five years from where I sit tonight — on a cool October evening in 2002, the night Elaine got into a fender bender on the turnpike with her five-speed Saab and I came home late from the hospital to find Iris commiserating with her at our kitchen table.

"What happened?"

"Oh, some kid slammed into me," Elaine said. "Some asshole."

"What do you mean?"

"A nineteen-year-old. And it took forever for the cops to come, and he didn't want to give his insurance information and kept trying to write me a check to cover the damage so he could get the hell out of there."

"You didn't accept his check, did you?"

"Of course not, Pete!"

I went to the wine rack for some screw-top red we kept for occasions such as this.

"The kid was such a shmuck, really. One of those spoiled kids in a Beemer, but you could tell he was freaking out that his parents would find out he'd damaged the car. Chain-smoking. I wanted to tell him, Look, shithead, I've been cancer-free for eighteen months, I don't need your nasty little carcinogens blowing my way on top of whatever's rising off the turnpike."

"Nobody's hurt, right?"

She looked at me wryly. "Nobody's hurt."

"Where's Alec?" It was nine o'clock, and he was grounded. He'd been busted for hanging out near the elementary school with Shmuley and Dan only the week before. I had asked him repeatedly what he wanted with the elementary schoolers (the whole thing seemed much creepier to me than the bust with the ecstasy tablets; what teenager on earth wants to hang out near a K–8 unless he's a pervert?), and he kept saying he was just "chilling," they didn't even realize they were *near* the elementary school, he swore to God, until finally he told me to fuck off and slammed the door.

"Where's Alec?" I asked again.

"I don't know," Elaine said.

"What do you mean, you don't know?"

"Jesus, Pete, I've had a hell of a day, all right?"

I sighed heavily and opened the refrigerator. There was nothing to eat, a half-opened can of tuna, some take-out Chinese that had been congealing for weeks. I slammed the refrigerator door and opened the pantry. Maybe we had a can of soup.

"Pete, would you calm down?"

"The kid is *grounded,* Elaine, or have you forgotten?" I didn't want to raise my voice in front of company, but it was difficult to stop. "Elaine, the kid is *grounded.* He needs to start respecting some authority around here, okay? So that he doesn't get in trouble with the cops again, okay?"

"Why are you yelling at me?"

"Why don't you know where Alec is?"

She stood, and with a look on her face that reminded me of no one more than our son, she stomped out of the kitchen and up the stairs. I looked over at Iris.

"Where do you think he is?"

"Probably with his friends." She poured herself some of our screw-top red and sat down with me at the kitchen table. Iris had been part of our lives for so long that she didn't feel the need to leave when things got ugly between us; in fact, that's when she felt obliged to stay. "I'm sure he's okay, if that's what you're worried about."

"It's not really what I'm worried about," I said. "I'm sure he's fine."

"So then?"

"I want him to start taking us seriously. If we say he's grounded, he's grounded. But he's not going to take us seriously if Elaine keeps undermining us."

"She had a bad day, Pete."

"She had a fender bender."

"A fender bender can make for a bad day. Especially on the turnpike."

"Alec doesn't respect us," I said. "That's the thing, he really doesn't respect us at all. And we're his parents. He should respect us."

"And he will, when he's older."

"We love that little shit more than anyone else ever will."

"He loves you, too, Pete. Come on," she said. She sipped her red; it left a pale bluish stain on her teeth. "He's just seventeen. It's a horrible, horrible age."

I stood, found some crackers in the pantry, a corner of cheddar in the fridge. I made myself a sandwich. It tasted good with the red. "He wasn't like this two years ago."

"And he won't be like this two years from now either. But right now it's hormones and senior year of high school and everything else. He's a bastard right now, but it won't last forever."

"I wish he weren't a bastard." I sighed and refilled my glass. "Sometimes I actually hate him. You know what that feels like? To hate your own kid? But he talks to me with that mouth and I just . . ."

"I know," she said.

"I want to kill him."

"I know."

It was perversely easy to talk to Iris about problems with my kid; I suppose knowing she'd had it worse than we did made me less ashamed of talking about how bad we had it.

"It will go away eventually," Iris said.

"It will?"

"Or at least it will grow more dull, and there will be other feelings to mitigate it." Her graying red hair was pulled back in a ponytail, and she was wearing a blouse with the top few buttons sloppily undone. A pair of thin chains around her neck. The skin on her neck dusted with freckles. I poured some more wine in her glass.

"I don't hate Laura so much anymore. But I did for a long time."

"How'd you stop?"

"I just did," she said. "I'm not sure there's a terrific process I can recommend for learning to forgive your children. Time makes us forget, that's part of it. Time and age. And I didn't want to spend my whole life hating my oldest child, so another part of it was a choice. I just chose to forget what she'd done, or chose to work at forgetting, and time did the rest."

We were quiet for a while. I could hear the upstairs pipes start to gurgle; Elaine was running a resentful bath.

"The hardest thing for me was that I hated her even while I was helping her. I threw everything I had into protecting her, yet part of the time some secret part of me really just wanted to throw her to the wolves. To say, New Jersey, this is what she's done, she's ruined our lives, take her and do what you will."

"But of course you couldn't."

She laughed a short, barking laugh. "I tried to explain my feelings to Joe once and he slapped me."

"Joe?"

"The only time he's slapped me in our entire marriage. Twenty-seven years. I decided I deserved it. But it was pretty hard. I had a bruise on my cheekbone. And afterward there was none of that 'Oh baby, I'm so sorry,' buying me jewelry and shit. I could tell if I brought it up again, throwing Laura to the mercy of the courts, he would have slapped me again just as hard."

"Jesus."

"I know," she said, and I thought of Pauline at her kitchen table: *None of us can ever live up to Laura, his precious.* Not even Iris. What a fool.

We both polished off our glasses and refilled them, while upstairs the bath kept gurgling and I could hear the faint pulse of some kind of music Elaine liked, the Indigo Girls or Joni Mitchell.

"We'll look back at this and laugh," Iris said, the stain on her teeth growing darker. I imagined I had a matching one.

"He really hit you?"

She brushed her hand lightly across my cheek, high, where the cheekbone rises to meet the ocular depression. "Right there," she said. "I told everyone I fell, just like in the movies."

"It's almost impossible to bruise that part of your face." I reciprocated, reached out and touched her fragile cheekbone. "When you fall, instinctively you lean forward with your hands to catch yourself, even if you're pushed against a wall or something. That's why people break their wrists all the time; that's the usual injury from a fall."

"So then maybe my hands just weren't working right that day."

"Then you would have taken it on the chin," I said. "The other instinct we have is to turn our heads to protect the tops of our heads, our eyes, our braincases."

"So you're saying the only way for a person to bruise her cheekbone is to get slapped."

"Well, something could have fallen on you," I said. "Maybe a car accident."

"If Joe ever hits me again, I'll know what to say."

"I can't believe he hit you."

"I can't believe I told you." She shook her head, swirled her wine around in her glass. "That was one of those things I'd planned on taking to the grave."

Without thinking about it, planning on it, I put my hand on her back and rubbed it gently, the way I would if a woman I was friendly with was telling me her troubles; right now a woman I was friendly with was telling me her troubles. But still I ran my hand along the back of her bra strap for just a second, and it was deliberate. I know, I know, all this good, neighborly life we'd built up over the years—forget it. I didn't care. Iris kept her forehead in both her hands, looking down at our kitchen table. Or maybe her eyes were closed.

I ran my hand up and down her back, and who knows how much time passed. I only stopped when I heard the jostling at the door. Alec.

"I couldn't get a ride," he said, blind with his own self-regard, so that everything about the scene he confronted seemed normal, or invisible. "Before you fucking freak out."

"Get upstairs," I said. He marched past both of us. My hand had been back in my lap for whole seconds. I heard him stomp up the stairs two at a time.

Iris straightened up, then stood. "You should go have a talk with him." My hand still prickled from where it had been touching her. I wondered if her back was prickling, too.

"Thanks for coming over," I said.

"I came for Elaine."

"Well, still."

"Of course."

I leaned down and moved slowly to her mouth (screw Joe, he'd slapped her; screw Elaine, she didn't care about our kid), but at that millimoment where everything is decided, she turned her head. I like to think I did, too. I ended up brushing my lips just below the memory of her bruise.

"Good night, Pete."

"Good night," I said.

I stood by the doorway and watched her lights turn on, listened to her car start up, felt the pressure of her soft freckled skin against my lips. And that was the end of the renaissance. Everyone who's ever had intentions knows they mean much more than actions do.

CHAPTER NINE

I SLEPT WELL last night, a surprise considering everything I'm expecting in the next forty-eight hours, and the fact that I didn't get to bed until after one. Now it's seven on the dot and my blankets are twisted around me and the pillow is on the floor.

Next door the Kriegers are warming up, something about cereal and who's driving which kid to school. I look out from the west window; my house is still there and Alec's Civic is in the drive. Today is Monday, and I should be in my office by nine, a healthy day of work ahead of me. Sometime this afternoon my lawyers will hear from the judge about the Craigs' case. I wish I knew how to feel about this.

Just as I'm about to step in the shower, the Vivaldi pipes up again. Joe. Maybe I should pick it up. But I cannot think of what to say to him, and I still don't want to know what he has to say to me. It's cowardly, I know, and I've always hated cowards, but I just watch the phone until finally, after six rings, it switches over to voice mail. He's leaving me a voice mail as I watch. A voice mail, brightly blinking, which I delete without stopping to check.

THROUGHOUT HIS ADOLESCENCE, a time when hormones rage like the Mississippi after a storm, Alec seemed, as far as we could tell, as virginal as a churchly novice. Neither Elaine nor I had gotten enormous amounts of high school nooky, but still, there'd been enough to assure our parents and peers we were normal. For me it was Karen Brauner, who later became a New York State senator; for Elaine, it was a future rabbi named Israel, who tried to get lucky after the movies every Saturday night and only succeeded once, just before Elaine left for Pitt.

But as for Alec, throughout his senior year at Round Hill Country Day he belonged to an exclusive and entirely male set: Dan, Shmuley, and whatever ingrates they'd picked up from the public school gymnasium. Which was strange, since he was a good-looking kid, give or take a piercing, and because he'd always had female friends growing up. I could clearly remember him running around with Stacy and Liza Beckerman, who used to live across the street, and hanging out at the mall with a mixed-gender group of kids in the sixth and seventh grades. But by his senior year he'd started leading a monkish existence, and he announced six months in advance that he had no intention of attending the prom.

"But why?" Elaine asked. Round Hill outdid itself every year come prom time, renting out a Manhattan nightclub and chartering stretch Hummers to drive the kids in, twenty at a pop.

"You wouldn't understand." The three of us were hanging out on a Sunday evening completely incidentally; Elaine was fine-tuning a lecture, I was watching a Nets game, and Alec was grounded.

"Try me."

"Well, first of all I'm in prison, and who knows if my parole officers would let me go to a dance."

"Very funny."

"Second of all, I have no patience for that bourgeois bullshit. I need to ride a Hummer to the fucking Limelight to get wasted with a bunch of privileged assholes from Round Hill? I don't think so."

"Oh, come on," Elaine said. "Isn't that a little much?"

"Is it?" He had his long legs stretched out in front of the television, was doodling something on a sketch pad. We'd have him home for eight more months, and despite ourselves and how happy we told each other we'd be to get rid of him, secretly I missed him just a little already. Which was preposterous. The kid was a nightmare.

"But isn't there a nice girl you might like to ask?" Elaine said.

"Mom."

"It's your *prom,* Alec. I want to take pictures of you all dressed up in a tuxedo. It's my right as a mother."

"Elaine, I don't think that's his thing."

"It's not my thing, Mom."

"I think that's really too bad," she said. "You guys can make fun all you want, but I think that's just too bad. You only get one high school prom, you know."

"One is more than enough."

"I went to my prom," she said, as if it mattered. "Your father went to his."

"I wore a pink ruffled shirt," I offered.

Alec gave me one of his rare smiles. "Pink ruffles?"

"I looked damn good."

"I wore a blue taffeta dress," Elaine reminisced. "Which I made myself on my mother's sewing machine. We went to a fabric store downtown, which was a very big deal. And my date picked me up in his father's Buick and I felt like Cinderella, I really did."

"Well, look, if it makes you feel better, Mom, I promise to go to every dance they have at Hampshire."

"There probably aren't any dances at Hampshire," she said. "That's why you like that school. It's a no-school-dances kind of school."

"But if there are, I'll go. And bring a nice young lady and send you lots of pictures."

She tossed a cushion at him. "Stop teasing me."

He laughed. So did I.

"So what is it, Al?" I was pushing my luck, but I wanted to know. "What do you have against the girls at Round Hill? You used to like them, didn't you?"

"Ah," he sighed. "It's just hard for me to relate to them, I guess. Their priorities are so fucked up. Clothes and parties and image. It's such adolescent bullshit."

Elaine and I both quashed our smiles.

"Maybe it'll be better in college," she said mildly.

"It has to be."

"Fingers crossed," I said.

"Don't be a dick," Alec said.

But despite our son's predictions, Hampshire, as far as we could tell, harbored few women of acceptable gravity. Most of the coeds we met when we visited seemed deliberately flaky, and their unwashed hair and unshaven legs didn't suggest substance as much as a snotty lack of hygiene. During one particular drive back, Elaine mused, with a certain amount of bravado, that Alec might be gay, but I told her that it was unlikely, that in his early teens he'd carved so many huge palm-wood breasts.

"Would it bother you?" she'd asked.

"Bother me?"

"If he were, you know." I gave her a long look. She was behind the wheel, and I was picking out a book on CD—either a biography of Napoleon or one of Robert Moses. She finished her thought loudly. "If Alec were gay."

"Of course not." But I was lying, and she could tell, and she rolled her eyes at me. I stuck the Napoleon in the stereo and listened to the opening credits. If Alec were gay, if my son were gay—I shuddered and then stopped myself from shuddering, started over. If Alec were gay—well, sure, so what? The life I wanted for him was a career that gave him pleasure, a family, some material comfort—despite the lump in my throat, I knew that being gay wouldn't necessarily prohibit any of that, although it would make it indisputably harder. And he'd be an outcast in so many communities. Professionally, socially, religiously. What did Jews think of homosexuality? Was there a specific doctrine? Were we as ugly about it as the Catholics?

"It wouldn't bother me either," Elaine said, and I couldn't tell if she was serious. "It might take some adjusting to, but it would be okay."

"You don't really mean that."

"Sure I do," she said, unwrapping a PowerBar with one hand. "If he's happy, I'm happy."

"You're being a little glib, aren't you?"

"Glib?"

"Don't you want grandchildren?"

"We could still have grandchildren," she said. "They let gays adopt."

"But your own grandchildren—"

"What, you mean biologically?"

"Yes," I said. "Biologically." Throughout all our conception troubles, we'd never spoken about adoption; it was a given that we wanted to raise our own child, our own genetic expression. No way were our ancestral evolutions going to end with us when we had so much to give.

Elaine seemed to give it some thought. "It doesn't matter to me, really," she finally said. "There are lots of babies in the world who need good homes. If Alec decides to adopt one day, or not have kids at all, well, it's his life, isn't it?"

I couldn't believe that Elaine didn't want to have grandchildren

with me. How could she not want our grandchildren? She was lying.
She was being contrary.

"All I'm saying is I want Alec to be happy. If he were gay, it would
be—well, it would be an interesting thing to adjust to. And of course
if it were up to me, I'd like to see him happily married with a family
of his own. That's my idea of happiness. But it might not be *his* idea
of happiness. So what do you want me to say?"

"I want you to say you want grandchildren."

"Of course I want grandchildren," she said. "Didn't I say that?"

"No."

"Okay, fine. I want grandchildren. But I can't control whether I
have any, so I'm not going to worry about it."

I turned the Napoleon back up. A mother in Corsica went into
labor on a sweltering August day in 1769 as orchestral music swelled
around us.

"What's that look?"

"I think you're full of crap, Elaine. I think if twenty years from
now we don't have any grandchildren, it's going to break your as-long-
as-he's-happy heart."

She shrugged, signaled a lane change—she always signaled a good
minute before she actually shifted—then checked her rearview and
blind spot.

"Pete, would you want Alec married and miserable for your sake
or happy and alone for his?"

"Married and miserable," I said, "as long as there were grandchildren."

"You're turning into a crazy old man before my eyes."

"I want grandchildren. I don't think there's anything crazy about
that. Every parent wants grandchildren. You can laugh all you want,
but I refuse to bend my position even two inches."

"Oh, Pete," she said. We drove into Hartford, that miserable city with all those half-empty skyscrapers and nowhere to stop for a decent bite. She chewed on her PowerBar. "I guess you win."

"Good." This was, of course, my favorite way for our arguments to end.

"But you've got to tell me something," she said. "Promise me that even if Alec *is* gay, or if he decides he doesn't want to get married, or if he doesn't want children, you'll still accept him because he's your son. And love him just the same."

"Accept him or be happy about it?"

"I know you won't be happy," Elaine said. "But just tell me you won't be ridiculous, won't sever all ties or something nutty like that."

"He's my only child," I said. "I would never sever all ties."

"Good," she said, and we kept driving. In Corsica, the land was rugged, damp, and thorny. The young Napoleon grew up surrounded by rocky cliffs and turbulent seas. Even as a small child, he was rambunctious, tenacious, a conqueror. It wasn't until we passed the last exit for Hartford that it occurred to me that Elaine had actually won the argument.

So with all this anxiety about Alec's sexuality and his dating life and my perhaps premature fixation about whether he would gift us with any grandchildren, you'd think that on a particular Sunday morning ten months ago today I would have been happy to hear some odd bumping, murmuring sounds coming from his room when I got up very early to head to the courts. An odd sort of bumping, a fumbling, muttering sound, and for a second before it hit me, I thought there was a raccoon trapped in the walls.

Thump. Thump. Laughter.

And then I got it, and I stood in the hallway listening to my son make love as quietly as he could and felt a hideous, terrifying chill all over my body.

There was more laughter. More thumping.

In our house? He had to do this in our house? I stood frozen, listening. I was in my gym shoes, my shorts. I felt like a fool, that's what it was—as if he was making a fool of me right there in my own house, making love to Laura Stern, our best friends' oldest daughter, a murderer, making love to her in the bed we'd bought him under the roof we'd bought for him in the home we'd made for him, which he'd lived in all his life. How little respect he had for us—how little respect any of them had for us! We were foolish, idiotic, the relics of another age. Obsolete. He was the future. And this was what he was doing with himself.

I stood there until the noises stopped. Then I bolted down the stairs and out of the house, slammed the car shut, and got to the JCC courts early enough to have them to myself. I lost myself in the pulsing sound of it, ball against hardwood, ball against backboard, ball swishing through net and bouncing down again. I dribbled furiously, laying up shot after shot. I was sweating through my T-shirt, so I took it off and threw it to the bleachers on the side of the room. I made eight, nine, ten layups in a row. I jumped up and dunked the ball into the basket. It felt great, so I did it again.

But sometimes it happens when a person loses himself in physical exercise—he doesn't want it to happen, but it does—that images or feelings he's tried to suppress for hours or even days come rushing into his head amid all that sweat and adrenaline. My guard was down. I couldn't help it. As I dribbled the ball up and down the empty court, the Round Hill Municipal Library bathroom swam in front of my eyes, and it was my own granddaughter in the sink, three months premature, eyes still blind, desperately waving her arms, waiting for someone to save her. But nobody knew she was there. And in the corner of my vision, a flash of Laura Stern's red hair gleamed as she approached with a hammer, to smash in my desperate, wailing granddaughter's skull. I tried to put myself in the picture. I tried to take the baby out of the sink. I cradled the basketball in my arms, but I couldn't change the way I saw what happened in my mind. In the Round Hill Municipal Library bathroom, I was nowhere to be found.

STILL, HE'D GOTTEN into the New School. I kept reminding myself of that as I showered, dressed, drove across the bridge for no particular reason, found myself at the Fairway grocery store, throwing strange items into my shopping cart to keep myself distracted. Miniature blinis. French beets. He'd gotten into the New School. And not once did I make any jokes about the tuition prices, not once did I say anything about how he'd better not mess up this time. He'd gotten into the New School, I'd sent my patient on the board a bottle of very good cabernet, and I kept my fingers crossed and my mouth shut and knew that in just one month he'd be back in classes, and in a mere two years (we should live to see the day) his mother and I would stand up at graduation and cheer as he threw his mortarboard in the air.

"You bought groceries?" Elaine asked as I unloaded the Fairway bags onto the breakfast bar. "I thought we were ordering Chinese. What's this—smoked sturgeon?"

"We're ordering in?"

She gave me a curious look. "It's Sunday," she said. In the years since her cancer, Elaine had gotten into the habit of marking the weekend with a regular delivery from China Lou's and saving the fortune cookies for midweek necromancy. She examined my jar of pickled radishes. "What do you propose we do with these?"

"Snack on them?" I didn't even remember putting the radishes in my cart. "Martinis?"

"We don't make our own martinis," she said.

"Couldn't we?"

She sighed, leaned up to kiss me on the cheek. "I guess so," she said. I wanted to say something to her, mention the hideous noises from Alec's bedroom, but I didn't know how to bring them up without also starting an argument about whether I was being too dictatorial about our son's social life, and I didn't feel like fighting. What to say? How to begin? While I was thinking, she left the kitchen. I sat down on a stool behind the breakfast bar and assessed the cornucopia of packages I'd left strewn across the marble. I scratched the stubble on my cheek. Pickled radishes. Scottish shortbread.

"I see you went to the grocery store." I turned around, both surprised and not even slightly to find Laura Stern in my kitchen. She was dressed in jeans and one of Alec's T-shirts, oversized and paint-stained. I guessed she'd been in our house all day.

"What are you doing here?"

She poked through my haul. "Some interesting stuff you brought home."

"You've been here all day?" She picked up the package of beets, then looked at me. Was I supposed to offer her food now, too?

"I was in Alec's studio," she said. "Reading. It's hard for me to find a quiet place at my parents' house."

"Aren't you living in the city?"

"I'm here half the time," she said. "Alec just left for the Red Barn, wanted me to tell you he'll be home late. He's teaching a night class."

"If you're living in the city, why would you spend half your time here?"

"This is where my family is." She put down the beets. "Why?"

"I just . . . I guess if I had an apartment in the city, I would stay there."

She gave me a half-cocked smile, took the barstool next to me. I felt chilly. "It's nice to get a change of scenery," she said. "I like to keep moving. And I like how quiet it is in Round Hill. I only really appreciate this place when I leave."

"Maybe you should . . . leave more often?"

She smiled as if I'd said something funny. Either she or Alec had cut the neck out of the T-shirt she was wearing, so that, sitting next to her, I could see her thin clavicle and the two thin chains she wore around her neck the way her mother did. She smelled flagrantly of soap. We both leaned our elbows on the bar, and I wondered what I was supposed to say or do next. I thought maybe I could put away groceries.

"What's that?" she asked, pointing at a small yellowish bruise on the inside of my forearm.

"It's a bruise," I said.

"How'd you get it?"

"I don't remember."

"Why don't you remember?" She put her slim index finger, beige nail polish, just above my bruise, on the part of the forearm that tickles when you touch it. Why was she touching me?

"It didn't hurt that much," I said. I wanted to stand and put away the groceries, but her finger was like a concrete block.

"But it looks like it hurt."

I sat there and felt her finger tickle my forearm. Her neck was freckled like her mother's. I thought about the noises in the upstairs bedroom, the giggling and whispering, raccoons behind the wall. "No," I said. "It doesn't." Her hair was thick and red the way her mother's used to be, before her mother's hair had started to gray. I wondered when Laura's hair would start to gray. I wondered what my son would think of her then, if she would be just as appealing as ever, or even more so, with silver threaded through her hair. Or if she would suddenly just seem old.

"You look a lot like Alec," she said. "It surprised me when I first saw him again, how much he'd started looking like you."

"He's my son," I said gruffly. "Who else should he look like?"

"Is Elaine home?"

"She's upstairs," I said.

"I see." What exactly did she see? Why was her finger still on my arm? Iris used to be this way, a toucher, a flirt. She used to give me hugs and kisses on the cheek when we'd meet casually on the quad at Pitt. I was eighteen, nineteen. No woman who wasn't my mother had ever kissed me so casually before.

"I should put away the groceries," I said, but still I didn't move.

"I'll help you," she said, but she didn't move either. And we stayed like that, her finger on my arm, my brain weaving and remembering, my forearm prickling, her red hair waving down past her shoulders.

She moved her finger back and forth just slightly, tracing a vein. "Laura?" I asked.

"You don't like me much, do you, Dr. Pete?" she asked.

I said nothing. She kept tracing the vein on my arm. Finally, after who knows how long, Elaine yelled downstairs to see if I wanted to call China Lou's for delivery or if she should do it herself.

"I guess I should go," Laura said.

"I guess you should," I said. She moved her hand, and my arm tensed for a minute.

"Alec will be home late," she said.

"Thanks for the message," I said.

"I'm really not so bad, Dr. Pete," she said. "You ought to give me a chance." I didn't say anything back and didn't wait for her to leave before I started to put the groceries away, pickled radishes, Scottish shortbread, fancy French beets. As Elaine came down the stairs to order dinner, the bruise on my forearm started to throb.

THE SUMMER WAS ending. The hospital was quieter, the patient stream began trickling a little slower, and our office was perfectly empty when Roseanne Craig came in at the tail end of a Friday afternoon. Janene Rothman was in Nantucket with Bill and the kids, Vince Dirks had long since disappeared—he stopped seeing patients at three o'clock—and by the time five thirty rolled around I'd started to feel like a stooge all cooped up on a beautiful afternoon. Also, it was Elaine's birthday, and we were having dinner tonight as a family, and I had yet to buy her a present. I was supposed to grill tuna.

Tonight would be the first time I'd seen my son since the previous Sunday, when I'd heard him and Laura. It had been easy enough to avoid him; he'd doubled his hours at Utrecht, since he wanted to pay for his own books and supplies, and then, at night, half the time he didn't come home at all but instead "crashed in the city," which was code for staying at Laura's place in the East Village. Which I tried to just forget about, and which I was able to forget about most of the time if I directed my mind to other things. He was starting school in three weeks. When the New School catalog came in the mail, I made Alec sit down next to me and go over it page by page; we perused Russian History after the Cold War, Italian Art of the Renaissance, Advanced Molecular Biology, Astronomy for Poets. It was a beautiful thing, the two of us in my study, perusing that thick, shiny catalog, and I was filled with that too-rare feeling that my son and I were on a joint mission, and that he understood what his responsibilities were in getting that mission fulfilled. Alec picked out four classes: Pottery I, Studio Painting, American Lit, Anthropology. We never mentioned Laura.

"Dr. Dizinoff?" Roseanne said. "Do you have a second? I don't have an appointment, but your office manager said . . ."

I was surprised; Mina was usually severe about letting patients in without appointments, especially at the end of a Friday. But I was glad she'd let Roseanne in. The girl's ponytail had come loose and her color was high. She'd never gone to a psychiatrist, I could tell. I wondered if her father had talked her out of it.

"Come on in, Roseanne, sit down," I said. "What can I do for you? The Jeep's holding up well, if this is a business call."

She twisted the pearls around her neck and gave me a half smile. "That's good," she said. "It's one of our best-rated models."

"You're not here to talk about the car, huh?"

"Not really," she said, sitting down. "I don't know," she mumbled. "It's sort of embarrassing." I remembered the tough, tattooed girl I'd met in my office not so long before, and wondered again what had brought all this heartache on. She'd told me a few loose details all those months ago, the boyfriend who left her for a man, the bookstore they were going to open together in San Francisco. She'd been so full of bravado before. My heart went out to her.

"Tell me."

"It's just, I don't know, my mood keeps swinging in this weird way," she said. "Sometimes I'm really angry for no reason, and then sometimes I just want to cry. Yesterday I sold an Escalade—do you know how much the commission is on one of those things? But my brother yelled at me, he said that I should have turned the sale over, since he's the one that does the Escalades, and I locked myself in the bathroom and cried."

"That's rough."

"The funny thing is that my dad brought me to work to cheer me up, and in general it *does* cheer me up! I like doing it! I can't frankly believe it, since never in a million years did I think I'd like being on the floor. But I do! But then sometimes I just . . . my stomach starts to hurt and I just have to go lie down somewhere. I can't take it."

"Roseanne, how old are you?"

"I turned twenty-three last month."

Twenty-three. How hard it had become to navigate this age. Only thirty years ago, all you had to do was finish school, marry your college sweetheart, pick a job, and stick with it. Now these wonderful kids were breaking down all around us.

"Is anything else bothering you? Physically? Emotionally?"

"Not really," she said. "All I want to eat are Doritos. Sometimes sushi. My period was late a couple of times, a little spotty. I know what it sounds like, but I'm not pregnant."

"Are you sure?"

She rolled her eyes at me. "Unless it's a virgin birth."

"Maybe I should give you a pregnancy test just to double-check."

"Dr. Dizinoff, I promise you—"

It was irresponsible of me, but I trusted her. "Okay," I said. "Anything else?"

"I don't know," she said. "Any one of these things, it's not like any of them is such a big deal, but I just don't feel like myself, and I don't know what to do about it. I feel like my body wants to rebel against me and is just waiting for the right moment."

"How long have you noticed these symptoms, Roseanne?"

"On and off," she said. "Maybe a year and a half. Maybe since I first came in and saw you."

"And did you ever pursue any psychiatric care?"

"But if it were all in my head, why does my stomach hurt all the time?"

"You know, depression isn't all in your head, necessarily. It's a problem that starts in your brain, specifically that you're not making enough serotonin, which is an important chemical in mood regulation. Serotonin deficiency can cause a whole spectrum of effects, including, sometimes, an upset stomach or strange food cravings, alongside sadness or emotional swings. Which is why I'm curious about whether you ever visited a psychiatrist. He or she could make a proper diagnosis and would be better equipped than I am to give you the right medication."

"I just don't think I'm depressed like that."

"Crying in the bathroom, Roseanne?" I said gently.

She sighed. "I don't know, I guess it's not the sort of person I thought of myself as, you know? A depressed person. At Cal, every other moron saw a shrink. It was like a badge of honor. They were all bragging about their Prozac or their lithium or their Ritalin. I always thought it was such crap."

"It's an illness, Roseanne. If I told you I suspected you had diabetes, would you tell me you thought insulin was crap?" This was a cliché, but it usually worked.

She sighed, was quiet for a long moment. I let the quiet linger. "What did you say the name of that doctor you like is?"

"There's Owen Kennedy at Round Hill Psychiatric. It's right down the street. He's the one that specializes in young adults, and you'll like him. He's an incredibly nice guy."

"Actually, maybe I'd like to speak to a woman?" That was good, since it meant she'd thought about the therapeutic process, could envision herself taking part in it.

"There are two women over there," I said. "April Frank is the one I know better. She's terrific—I think she's from California herself."

Roseanne allowed herself a little nod.

"I'll call the office on Monday and see if I can get you an appointment."

"Thanks, Dr. Dizinoff," she said. "I appreciate it." She adjusted her pearl necklace so that the clasp hung behind her neck. "I don't mean to be such a skeptic about psychiatry—"

"You don't have to explain."

"No, really, I'd like to, if you have a second—"

"Of course."

She took a breath, let it out in a sort of bitter little bark. "When my boyfriend—I mean secretly, you want to know the truth, he was my *fiancé,* we were going to get married. He'd proposed. I hadn't had the guts yet to tell my dad—I think my dad always smelled the truth about Frogger. About Chris, that was his real name. Chris. We fought about it. He thought he wasn't man enough for me—"

"Ah." So I wasn't the only Round Hill father who objected to his child's romantic objectives, despite the lenient and liberal times we lived in. I felt a burst of solidarity with lumbering Arnie Craig.

"It was a problem, of course. That my dad didn't like him, because my dad and I have always been super close, and—"

"I can imagine."

"Anyway, we were going to get married. He'd secretly proposed over Christmas, a little ruby ring, I still have it. And then he comes out with this affair. He's having an affair. With a man! And instead of being rational about it, I tell him—I mean instead of just leaving him in the dust, I tell him, Don't worry, it's just a phase, let's go to couples therapy and work it out."

"Couples therapy," I said.

"Can you believe it? Like I can *therapize* him out of being gay? But I do, I take him to student services, they have every kind of therapy, and for an entire year we try to work out whether or not Frogger is gay. And he's supposed to be honestly thinking about it. Keeps telling the therapist he loves me, wants to be with me, it was just that one month when it happened, it won't happen again. I believe him! The therapist believes him! And the entire time he's sleeping with that guy from Stanford."

Oh, dear. "Roseanne, did you ever take a—"

"I took an HIV test right away and then another one at a clinic six months ago. I'm negative."

How could I not have thought of that sooner? I hung my head. It was always a surprise when I let my assumptions get in the way of good medicine.

"I'm sorry all this happened to you, Roseanne. I really am."

"Yeah, well—" She looked down at her hands for a moment, picked at a cuticle. "It feels good to talk about it with someone who's not one of my friends. I can't tell my parents the whole truth. And my brother would probably go find Frogger and kill him. Literally."

"Well, listen, anytime you want to talk and you don't feel like going to your psychiatrist, you can always stop by and talk to me," I said. And I meant it.

She stopped picking her cuticle. She had a small, lovely smile.

"Do you have any plans the rest of the summer?" I asked. "Any vacations to look forward to?"

"Actually, some friends from high school have a place on a lake in the Adirondacks. Saranac Lake. We're going canoeing next weekend."

"Well, that sounds like fun. Something to take your mind off things."

"Oh, please." She laughed. "I've never canoed in my life. They told me we were going to have to catch our own dinner, and that's where I drew the line. No way am I gutting a fish. It's not like we're on *Survivor* or something."

"Research before you go," I said. "Tell them there's a good steak house somewhere in the area and gutting fish might lose its appeal."

"Good idea."

"Or just order in pizza."

"I don't think you can order in pizza in the woods."

"You'd be surprised," I said. "I once had pizza delivered to a campsite in Yosemite."

"You like to rough it, too, huh, Dr. Dizinoff?"

I grinned at her. In my heart, I knew she'd be fine. "I'll check in with you on Monday, okay? Let you know how soon I can get you in to see April."

"Thanks," she said, and we stood and shook hands. If I'd had no sense at all of professional protocol, I might have drawn her in for a hug. I liked her for a million reasons. She was smart, pretty, tough, showed initiative in her work and her love life and her health. If Alec would only date a girl like her — maybe there was some way to introduce them? It was a shame we weren't in the market for another car.

"Doc?" Mina stuck her head into my office as soon as Roseanne disappeared. "Let's get out of here before anyone else shows up."

"Good idea," I said. "Have yourself a great weekend, Mina. I'll lock up."

"*I'll* lock up," she said. "You still haven't bought Elaine a birthday present."

"Aah!"

She laughed her snaggletoothed Lithuanian laugh. "There's a sale on at the Gilded Lily downtown," she said. "They close at seven. Hurry up." Mina. My shining light.

I found a parking spot right in front of the store and left fifteen minutes later with a healthy-sized hole in my wallet and a nice, sparkling evening bag, a silk scarf, and a pair of earrings made from Venetian glass, which looked like psychedelic bottle caps but which the saleslady promised me my wife would love. She could tell I was running late and was just going to take her word for it. I handed over my AmEx without even checking the price tag. When I signed the receipt, I gasped.

But my generosity was rewarded by some joint miracle of stoplights and traffic, and I beat Elaine home with time to spare. I rolled up my sleeves, arranged the presents on the kitchen table, got to work mixing a marinade for the tuna steaks in the fridge. We'd have tuna, grilled vegetables, and mashed potatoes swirled with the wasabi I'd found at Fairway (a neat little trick I picked up from the Food Channel), and Alec was supposed to pick up a cake for dessert. I called his cell.

"You're checking to see if I forgot the cake."

"Did you forget the cake?"

"I'm at the bakery right now."

"Good," I said. It was good to hear him. "Use my charge card."

"I wouldn't do it any other way."

So that by the time Elaine was home, the tuna was resting in the marinade, the potatoes were bubbling, the vegetables had been sliced and washed, I'd set out a little tray of olives and cheese, pulled two brunellos from the basement and a nice pink champagne, and even managed to change out of my shirt and jacket into a clean white T-shirt with LIPITOR scrawled across the back.

"Happy birthday, Lainie," I said when she came in, hauling an overstuffed briefcase and a fifty-four-year-old smile. Elaine was seven months older than I was. Back when that was more of a laughing matter, I used to tease her.

"What are these? Presents!" My wife loved presents; she dropped her briefcase and grabbed the first little package, the one with the earrings.

"Did you go to the Gilded Lily? Oh, you shouldn't have!" And she tore into her packages and gushed over each of them and treated me to a long, grateful smooch right there in the kitchen. Then she stuck the earrings in her ears—they still looked like bottle caps to me—and tossed her hair this way and that. "What do you think?"

"You look beautiful."

"But do I look old?"

"Not a day over thirty."

"You lie, you lie, you lie," she said, and she wrapped me up in another big smooch. It was amazing what earrings and a handbag and a scarf could do. "I'm just going to run these upstairs. Pour me something to drink, will you?"

I turned on the stereo, opened the doors to the patio, dragged out a bucket of ice, and wiped the dust and cicada shells off the outdoor furniture. Just as I was about to pop the pink champagne, Iris and Joe appeared in the backyard, carrying a much better bottle, some frosty Krug.

"Where's the birthday girl?"

"Krug?" I asked as Joe handed me the bottle. "Why are you two such show-offs?"

Joe shrugged and Iris pecked me on the cheek and then we went inside to pour five glasses and wait for the rest of my family to join us.

"What'd you get her, Pete?"

"A handbag, a scarf. Some earrings. I don't know. I'm so bad at that stuff."

"Iris? Is that you?" Elaine called from upstairs. "Come up and see my presents! Bring me some champagne!" It was her birthday and she was treating herself to a little girls-only.

"Sounds like you made her happy," Joe said.

"Ladies love me," I acknowledged. I took the plate of sliced vegetables outdoors to the grill and got started.

It was a nice August evening; the whole summer, in fact, had been reassuringly temperate after a few short-lived June heat waves. The hundred-year-old maples that shaded our backyard shook with squirrels climbing up, up, up and chipmunks scattering along their trunks. We used to keep a bird feeder out here for the robins and jays, the occasional oriole, but the raccoons kept figuring out how to swipe the feed and we didn't like having them so close to the house. We still got raccoons back here sometimes, though. Raccoons, rabbits, skunks, all those deer.

Joe sipped his Krug appreciatively. "Say what you will about the suburbs," he said, as the grill flamed beneath us.

"I was thinking the same exact thing."

Alec came walking up the path from the driveway, an enormous cake box balanced precariously in his arms.

"There's some champagne for you in the kitchen." I wanted all of us to be festive.

"Great," he said as he backed his way into the house. "The cake cost seventy dollars."

"You're kidding."

"Doesn't it feel like money actually doesn't mean a thing anymore?" Joe asked. "Like money has been separated from all sense of value?"

I looked at my old friend, whose wife cleared a million dollars a year. "Sometimes."

"It does to me all the time," he said, and Alec came back out with his glass of champagne.

"So how's it going, kid?" Joe asked. "Getting ready to start school?"

Alec shrugged, glugged his Krug like it was soda pop.

"Slow down," I said. "That's no way to enjoy a good champagne."

He rolled his eyes and took a prissy, delicate sip. "I've been trying to finish up these small oils before I go," he said. "But I've been working overtime at the store."

"Well, you'll be able to keep working on them at school, won't you? Taking some studio classes?"

Alec shrugged, then glugged the rest of his champagne. "I guess."

"What will you be taking?"

"Just, I don't know, some painting, an English class."

"Anthropology," I said. "Studio pottery."

"The potatoes are boiling over, Dad."

"Shit," I said. "Here, you watch the vegetables. I'll go—"

"No, it's okay, you guys hang out," he said. "I'll make the potatoes."

"No, but there's a secret—"

"You want me to do that wasabi thing, right?" he said. "I'm on it."

"You know how to do the wasabi thing?"

"You stir wasabi into mashed potatoes," he said. "It's no big deal."

Why did he have to deflate my wasabi thing? It *was* a big deal, completely wonderful, an unexpected, hard-to-place spicy kick in a bowl of fatty off-white potatoes. Jerk.

"He looks good, Alec," Joe said, a bit generously, after Alec disappeared.

"Yeah, well." I spiked some zucchini on my fork to flip them over.

"No, really," Joe said. "He looks happy. He's gonna have a great time at school."

"To be honest, I think he looks so damn happy because he's spending too much time with your daughter."

The thing with Laura and Alec had been going on for months now, but Joe and I almost never talked about it. We were each embarrassed, I guess, of our own disapproval. I didn't want Joe to think I didn't *like* Laura (although I probably didn't), only that I didn't like her for my son, but this was a finer point than I felt comfortable making. I expected Joe felt similarly about Alec.

"So what do you think of that?"

"The truth?" I said, poking the eggplant. We were two middle-aged men standing over a grill; we could have been talking about anything, sports, the weather, our wives.

"Of course."

"I don't like it," I said. "The age difference, everything. And Alec's at such a vulnerable point right now. I wish he'd just concentrate on his schoolwork and not be involved romantically. Especially with a much older person."

"I don't like it either," Joe said. "I'm not sure it's the best thing for her to be dating a kid."

"When she moved to the East Village, I thought—"

"So did I," Joe said. "In fact, that's part of the reason I thought she was going so abruptly. So she could sort of cool it with Alec without having to have a difficult conversation. But evidently he spends a couple nights a week there—"

"He does," I said.

"It's funny, if he'd wanted to date Pauline, I would have been thrilled. I used to think about that, actually, how nice it would be if those two somehow—"

"But it's Laura."

"I know."

"Do you think it's like—" and I wanted to be delicate, but at the same time I really wanted to know what Joe thought. "Is it like arrested development on her part? Or something? I mean, Alec, God bless him, is not necessarily the most mature kid, and you'd think Laura would get a little bored."

"Could be," he said. "I'm not sure how much she's really dated in her life. She might feel comfortable with a younger person. It could be a power thing."

"Does it . . . does it bother you to think about—"

"I don't," Joe said.

"Me neither," I said. Which was a lie. Sometimes, just as I was falling asleep, I heard those bumping, murmuring sounds in my head and wanted to die.

"Ah." Joe shuddered (he thought of it, too) and changed the subject. "Anything interesting in the office lately?"

"Let's talk about anything else, huh?"

"Don't you think?" He looked down into his flute.

"Let's see . . . the office. The office. A girl I like came in today, Roseanne Craig—you know her? Arnie Craig's kid? I've been seeing her periodically, complaining of malaise, some weight fluctuation, amenorrhea, food cravings—"

"She pregnant?"

"Swears to God she isn't, although I probably should have made her take a test."

"She's pregnant."

"She said it would have to be a virgin birth, and I imagine she knows the last time she had sex."

"She's pregnant."

"Okay, well, let's just say for a second she isn't, for the purposes of this conversation. We bought a car from her six weeks ago, Elaine's Jeep. She didn't seem pregnant then, at least."

"She's a car dealer?"

"Works for her father," I said. "Comes in about a year ago, complaining of depression, some weight loss—clearly she doesn't really know why she's there except her dad wanted her to come."

"Okay."

"Then she tells me this story. Seems her boyfriend left her and she's stuck back in New Jersey when she thought she'd spend her life in California running a bookstore."

"Tough break."

"I tell her she needs a shrink, she says she's seeing a reflexologist." We shook our heads at each other. "Then we buy the Jeep from her and she looks great. But then she comes in today again and is absolutely depressed. I like this kid, too. There's something winning about her."

"Will she see someone?"

"I told her to go to April Frank at Round Hill."

"Could it be something else?" he asked. "Not depression? Maybe autoimmune? Endocrinologic?"

"What, like a thyroid thing?"

"I don't know," he mused. "You see Hashimoto's every so often, it can present like that. And I had a woman with Addison's a few years ago. Mood swings, weird food cravings, nausea."

"Joe, I've seen maybe two cases of Addison's since I started practicing. Nobody has Addison's. And she hasn't mentioned any dizziness, no joint swelling."

"Well, it can't hurt to check." Joe, God bless him, was a terrific doctor, but one of those docs who ordered every test for every possibility, even if its statistical likelihood was negligible; he'd consider tropical wasting diseases for women who'd never left Bergen County. It was one of the reasons I only rarely talked shop with him: I preferred a different type of induction and chose to use reason and observation instead of expensive and unnecessary testing.

"I told her I'd try and get her an appointment with April on Monday," I said. "I'll see what April thinks, if she thinks it's depression or something else."

"Fair enough," Joe said. "But still, maybe you should call her, bring her in for some blood work. Or maybe send her to an endocrinologist." Then he went into the kitchen to get the bottle of champagne. I wondered what his patients thought when he automatically went to the worst-case scenario (pregnant, thyroid, Addison's). Joe was a high-risk OB, a fraught subspecialty that required infinite diligence; for some reason he'd always found delivering babies who might die more rewarding than delivering babies who were sure to live. He got off on brutal cases: the worse the chances, the more invested he became.

We resumed our position by the grill and stared down at the vegetables, letting the flame warm our faces. The vegetables were turning nice and glossy, their edges just starting to char.

"You ever want to hunt, Pete?"

"Huh?"

"Like go hunting for a deer or something, then skin it and age it and cook it."

I thought of Roseanne gutting a fish on Saranac Lake. "Never once in my entire life, Joe."

"I've been thinking about that lately," he said. "With all the deer on the side of the highway, a person gets ideas. What he needs to do to survive. Or what he's capable of. I'm full of soft skills, Pete, but I've been thinking I need to sharpen up a few of my hard ones."

"You're serious?"

"Totally serious," he said. "I've been daydreaming of packing up Neal and Adam and driving up to Maine or somewhere, stopping at L.L. Bean, bagging us a deer."

"That's rather rugged of you, Joe." I started forking up the finished vegetables and dropping them on the plate.

"I'm not explaining it well," he said. "It's just, I want to actually do something physical, self-reliant. Depend on myself for an entire meal, for more than that. Prove that if it were just me and the woods, I could survive."

"You and the woods and L.L. Bean."

"I probably won't do it," he said.

"No, no, it sounds . . . well, it sounds like a midlife something or other, to tell you the truth."

"I know." He chuckled. "Most guys just buy a Corvette, right? Or sleep with a twenty-five-year-old?"

"Now that's the spirit."

Iris came out onto the patio.

"Joe, come on, we've got to get to the airport." Pauline was arriving home from a six-week idyll in Tuscany, learning Italian and writing poetry before beginning her career at MIT.

"I guess it's that time," Joe said, turning to shake my hand. "Don't mention I said anything about the twenty-five-year-old."

"Wouldn't think of it," I said. I waved at Iris and watched the two of them descend step-by-step down the lawn to their car, holding hands the way they did at the most casual moments.

If I had known that it would be the last—no, no, I won't do that. There's nothing to gain by doing that. I'll leave it there: I watched the two of them descend step-by-step down the lawn to their car, holding hands they way they did at the most casual moments, and then turned to bring the vegetables in, to bring out the tuna, to serve my wife her birthday meal. We gathered around the table together. It was a beautiful evening.

ALEC HAD DONE a pretty good job with the wasabi potatoes, which were maybe a bit kickier than I would have done them but were nevertheless a strong showing. He'd painted Elaine a tiny miniature of the George Washington Bridge at sunrise and had it mounted in a quirky copper frame. She squealed over it even more than she'd squealed over the earrings I'd brought her, which was fine. We put down the two brunellos with impressive ease and sat out in the backyard, the cake plates still cluttering the table, the three of us just enjoying the hum of the night, the buzz of the mosquito zapper, the faint swoon of Lionel Hampton from inside the house.

"I was thinking of heading to the Bergen bookstore next Friday," Elaine said. "If there's any way to see what books you need, we could probably get them through the school, use my employee discount."

Alec shrugged. The idea was that he'd spend the first semester at home, where after all he had a fine studio, since the New School didn't guarantee housing for transfers. After the first semester, if all was going well, we'd look into something for him in the city. He hadn't mentioned moving in with Laura in the East Village, which was good because then we didn't have to fight about it.

"Fifty-four," Elaine mused. "Can you believe your wife is fifty-four? I'm an old lady, Pete."

"You're nothing of the sort."

"I think I saw in one of your magazines, Mom, that fifty is the new thirty. Which means actually you just turned thirty-four."

"Trust me when I tell you fifty-four is *not* the new thirty-four," she said. "But don't I wish it were."

We were quiet then. I wondered about Elaine's wish to return to thirty-four. Those were nice times, I know. We were new parents, just moved to Round Hill; I was building up my reputation at the hospital and Elaine was making friends in the neighborhood. But it was before she'd gone back to teaching, which gave her so much satisfaction, before I'd really established myself, before we'd gotten to know Alec as a person. In many ways, I was a happier man now than I was at thirty-four. In many ways, that particular evening, I was as happy as I'd ever been.

"What are you thinking about, Pete?"

"Musing," I said. "A bit drunkenly."

"What about you, Al?"

"The same." He reached out with his fingers and stole a chunk of cake, just like his mother did when she wasn't worried about her figure. Then he licked it off his fingers one by one. Just like her.

In the back of the yard, on the southwestern corner of the property line we shared with the Kriegers, two small deer pushed their tentative way out of a clump of lilac bushes. They were adolescent, probably female, since they were undersized and still spotted. Usually deer like that presented in much bigger groups. I wondered if their mother had been hit by a car.

"Get your canvas, Al," Elaine whispered, as if human voices still had the power to scare suburban deer away.

"If Joe were here, he'd shoot them."

"What are you talking about?"

"He told me today," I said, "he's had a notion to take Neal and Adam up to Maine and go deer hunting. Stop at L.L. Bean first."

"You're kidding," Alec said, shaking his head. "Laura would just love that." I couldn't tell if he was being sarcastic.

"Joe wants to go shoot deer?"

Suddenly I was embarrassed for my friend. Round Hill obstetricians, especially of the Jewish persuasion, did not frequently admit to red-state bloodlust. I shrugged and watched the deer watch us, their huge black eyes hopeful and slightly dazed in the last light of the day.

From the Kriegers' side of the lawn, maybe ten feet in front of the deer, Kylie Krieger emerged in mustard-splattered overalls with half a hot dog in her hand. Kylie was probably five or six, a freckle-faced urchin who waved maniacally at me when I passed her in the street.

"I want to feed them!" she squealed. Then she looked at us guiltily.

"Hi, sweetheart," Elaine called.

"I want to feed them!" she said again, and she thrust the hot dog in her palm out toward the deer, who looked at her curiously.

"Well, why don't you, then?" Elaine said.

"Kylie! Kylie!" Mark Krieger, who back then I had no idea could throw a coffee mug as hard as I now know he can, came running into our yard after his daughter. "Kylie, what did I tell you about coming onto the other people's lawns—"

"It's okay," Elaine called. "We're happy to have her."

Mark looked up at us gratefully. "We're trying to get her to stand still for, I don't know, more than five seconds at a time."

"But Daddy, *I want to feed the deer!*" And then she threw the hot dog with all the might in her five-year-old body, and the deer backed into the lilac bush and hustled away, immune to the charms of our tiny neighbor.

"Nooo!" she shrieked as the deer scuttled into the darkness of the tree line.

"Oh, Kylie. You scared them."

"Where'd they go, Daddy? *Where did they go?*"

"Honey, deer don't like hot dogs. That's what I was telling you—"

But it was too late. She flung herself into her father's arms and began to weep uncontrollably, hitting her palms against her father's chest again and again. *I want to feed the deer. I want to feed the deer.* Mark shot us an apologetic look and we shook our heads in sympathy. Maybe later I'd knock on their door, see if they wanted to come over for a glass of cognac. He looked like a man who could use a drink. He retreated back to their side of the lawn, and I could hear his wife start to panic. "Jesus, Mark, what happened to her? She's hysterical!"

"God, you couldn't take me back there for all the world," Elaine said. "Temper tantrums and crying jags? No way."

"But I thought you said you wanted to be thirty-four again."

"I guess I forgot."

"Come on." Alec laughed. "I wasn't really like that, was I?"

"You?" Elaine grinned. "Oh, no, you were a perfect angel all the time. You have frosting on your nose."

He wiped his nose with his thumb, then licked the frosting off his thumb. "I was an angel, wasn't I?"

"From the day you were born," Elaine said, and then we were all quiet again for a while, the throb of Kylie's hysterics still thumping in our ears.

"I have to tell you guys something," Alec said.

This should have served as a warning for us to jump to our guards immediately, but the night was so languorous, our sense of peace so palpable, that our guards were impossible to find.

"Laura and I are moving to Paris."

It didn't even register. Not as a joke, not as a threat, not as a sentence. I reached out and cut myself another tiny sliver of cake.

"I'm sorry, Alec," Elaine said. She waved away my offer of half the slice. "You want to what?"

"I don't *want* to anything," he said. "I'm doing it. Laura and I are moving to Paris in two weeks. She knows some people there, some guys from Tunisia, actually, who she harvested grapes with last spring. They're opening up an art gallery-slash-clothing store, and they need someone to manage it, and they'll pay her off the books."

"That's great for Laura," Elaine said, "but what on earth does that have to do with you?"

"I'm going with her," he said.

"But you're not," I said. Only slowly were any of the words he was saying even making sense in my brain. "You're starting school next week."

"No," Alec said. "That's what I'm trying to tell you. I'm not going to school. I'm moving to Paris. With Laura."

"But that's impossible," I said. "You already registered. You picked your classes."

"I'm going to withdraw," he said. "I'm moving to Paris."

"Alec—"

"Don't be ridiculous," I said. "You're starting school. Next week. You picked your classes. We put down the deposit. You're starting school."

"Actually, I'm going to withdraw," he repeated. "Look, I'm sorry, I know you're disappointed, but I still feel that my education would be better served if I went to Europe and—"

"Alec, I don't think you're hearing me. You are starting school. Next week." I couldn't even pronounce the word "Paris."

"Dad, I'm sorry, but I'm not."

"Listen to me," I said. "I know you like Laura a lot. I know she seems like a very mature, interesting older woman. I know it seems like she's had a lot of life experience—"

"Dad, this isn't about—"

"Let him finish, Alec."

"Laura Stern is not going to take you *anywhere*. You are not withdrawing from school. You are not moving to Paris. You understand me?"

"Dad, unfortunately you can't really tell me what to do anymore," he said. "I turned twenty-one in July. I'm an adult."

"You are hardly an adult, and I absolutely can tell you what to do. We've indulged your bullshit long enough, and you are going to start classes next week like we agreed on."

"Pete, lower your voice." I hadn't even realized I was yelling.

"Dad, look, I'll refund you the money—"

"*Do you honestly think this is about money?*"

"Yes," he said. "Of course it's about money."

"You are out of your mind, you know that? This isn't about *money*. This is about you. You and your life. We have been, in my opinion, way too indulgent with you as you've dicked around for the past couple of years, but *no more*. You are going to school, you are *graduating* from school, and after that, if you want to move to Paris with some slut with a criminal record—"

He stood. "What did you call her?"

"Alec, sit down."

"No, I won't. What did you call her?"

"Alec, sit."

"A slut with a criminal record? Is that what you think of her? She's only your best friend's daughter, Dad. She's only someone you've known all her life."

"Exactly," I said. "I've known her all her life. And if you think for one second you are getting on a plane to go to Paris with her, you are so out of your mind you should be committed like she was."

"Fuck you, Dad."

"Alec, you will not talk to me that way."

"Fuck you—"

We only stopped when we heard the soft bubble of Elaine crying. "Please," she whispered. "Please. It's my birthday. Please can we not fight today?"

Alec sat back down, but his arms were crossed over his chest and he was glaring at me. I would have switched places with Mark Krieger in an instant, if only I could pick the kid up in my arms and tell him he'd been a bad boy and lock him up in his room for the rest of the week.

"Could we not talk about this right now?" Elaine said. "Please?"

"I'm sorry, Mom."

I just continued to glare at him.

"Next week," Elaine said. "For me, okay? Do me a favor, just cool it for one week. You can talk about this again, but in the meantime, don't withdraw yet, okay, Alec? Okay? And we'll talk about this more on Friday."

"But—"

"Please," Elaine said. She wiped her nose with her wrist. "Friday night, you two can get together and talk about all of this. But not until then. Give it a week. Please."

"Fine," Alec said. He was chastened.

I stood, stormed into the kitchen, slammed the door, slammed some dishes in the sink. I wiped the champagne flutes off the counter in one furious gesture and let them smash on the floor.

Elaine had had fifty-three happy birthdays before this one. God knows you can't win them all.

I WENT TO work Monday morning determined not to let Alec's temporary insanity disrupt my entire week. Between appointments, on the exam room phone, I called the New School registrar to make sure the kid hadn't withdrawn; he hadn't. I asked them, if he called, not to let him, but they said that wasn't really in their power. I begged. They said no. I hung up.

I had a packed day at the office, which was terrific as far as keeping me distracted went; if I was lucky, there'd be some huge crisis right around seven o'clock, which would keep me in the hospital until I was too exhausted to think straight. Elaine and I hadn't talked about Alec the whole weekend. We went about our separate lives and were cordial with each other even as we chose to dine separately—our heads, such as they were, buried in work. As for Alec, he was doing triple shifts at Utrecht and, of course, crashing in the city. I'd had a passing idea to call Joe and talk to him about this, but as I picked up the phone my hand froze and suddenly I couldn't talk to him, knowing what I might say. It occurred to me that part of me—most of me—blamed him for this. Which was unreasonable, of course. But if children are the sum of their parents, what the hell did Laura say about him?

So Monday I showed up at the office with no small relief and was soon crushed with patients. An arthritic hairdresser I'd been watching for years, two new diabetics, a few squeezed-in semiemergencies, a hypochondriacal magazine editor with chest pains who thought she was having a heart attack but had actually just strained a muscle in Pilates. A teacher with pretty bad bronchitis. And then a round of college students in for their physicals, armed with somber-looking sheets I had to sign off on.

During lunch, I asked Mina to put in a call to April Frank's office to see if she could squeeze Roseanne in. That evening, luckily for me,

but of course not for them, two of my patients were admitted to the
ER with various middling-to-serious complaints, so I stuck around
to hold their hands as specialists came by and did the voodoo that
they did so well. I made rounds. I grabbed a dinner at the hospital
cafeteria: chicken piccata, raspberry Jell-O. I thought about going to
the JCC, but when I looked at my watch I saw it was almost ten. I
drove home, making up a long route, onto the Palisades for no particular reason, and by the time I got home, the lights were out as I'd
suspected they'd be.

The week progressed in this same busy fashion: Janene came back
from Nantucket midweek with a box of homemade caramels for the
office—this is what she did when she went on vacation, sat around
with her kids and went swimming and made candy. It was a distinctly
female thing, I thought, to bring presents for the office; never once
when I'd gone away had it occurred to me to bring anything back for
anyone other than myself, and when Vince Dirks traveled—usually
to some godforsaken place to shoot long-range photographs of squa-
lor—all he brought back was some kind of stomach bug or strange
rash or both. Elaine started classes. I got Roseanne an appointment
in two weeks' time to see April, who was apologetic but overwhelmed
by the number of patients she had clamoring at her door.

But still, my stomach rumbled with the thought of my oncoming
conflagration with Alec on Friday night. Of course there was some
kind of chance he would return to reason, decide to go to the New
School as we'd agreed, and put thoughts of Paris and Laura out of
his head. There was even some small chance that Laura herself had
come to her senses and decided that Paris would be a lot more interesting without a twenty-one-year-old who didn't speak a word of the
language tugging at her sleeve the whole time. True, my hopes were
dampened a little by a Wednesday afternoon call from my brother,

who told me that Alec had asked his cousin Lindsey for some last-minute French lessons. "What the hell is with that kid this time?"

I could feel the heat start to rise in my chest. "He's thinking of studying abroad," I said.

"Don't you need to actually be studying something to study abroad?" I could imagine Phil leaning forward on his ebony desk in his office on the forty-fifth floor. Calling me in between five-hundred-dollar billable hours just to bust my ass.

"He's starting the New School in the fall," I said, heat rising faster now, up my neck, my cheeks. Phil was silent. "Did someone tell you otherwise?"

"French isn't such a useful language, Pete. Someone should mention to him, if he really wants to find himself a constructive pursuit, many of the gardeners and restaurant workers in the New York area rely on Spanish."

"Fuck off, Phil."

"Just trying to be helpful, Pete."

I don't know which one of us hung up first.

But it did occur to me that week, when I was at my most exhausted, that maybe the proper tactic to take here would just be to relent. Alec would go to Paris, run out of money or patience, yearn for home. Or he and Laura would start to grow apart, and then, alone and unable to find work in a town notoriously unfriendly to outsiders, he'd bide his time for a while before returning to our doorstep, cap in hand, as they say. Or he'd go, they'd have a big fight, and he'd come right home in time to get to school with only a week's worth of missed classes and very little schoolwork to make up. No matter what, he'd be back at school eventually, which was the important thing.

But it wasn't lost on me that this was his senior year, or rather it was supposed to have been his senior year, and that next May there'd be a round of graduation parties for the likes of Neal Stern among others, and we would have to answer endless questions about what Alec was up to — or worse, our neighbors and associates would know better than to ask. Sure, it might sound grand to say, Oh, he's living in Paris now. But I would know what was at the rotten heart of that: our son working at some Tunisian-owned clothing store and serving as the plaything of a woman half again his age. And I wouldn't be able to look any of my neighbors or associates in the eye, because it would be likely I wouldn't have spoken to my son in months or even a whole year.

And this was what was on my mind when I bumped into Joe in the hospital cafeteria.

"Where've you been?" he asked casually. Joe tended not to eat in the hospital cafeteria unless he'd just gotten off a delivery and was starving; otherwise, his practice liked to order in.

I shrugged and loaded up my tray with baked chicken, salad, and a Coke and watched as Joe assessed the steam-table options with a finicky glint in his eye. Oh, for Christ's sake, take the chicken, it won't kill you.

"Just trying to figure out how to get my kid not to ruin his life."

"Sorry?"

"Just trying to get Alec not to—" And then it occurred to me. "Joe, you know, right?"

"Know what?"

"That they're moving?"

"Who's moving?" he asked. "Moving where?"

Oh, Joe, my ignorant brother. We paid up and found an empty table in the corner of the room. "Joe, this will probably sound as insane to you as it did to me, but you should know that our children are planning to move to Paris together in a week and a half."

"Paris? Paris, France?"

"I thought you knew."

"How would I know?"

At least our own kid had the courtesy to give us some warning. "Evidently Laura knows some Tunisians with a clothing business in Paris," I said. "Alec thinks he'll get a better education in the arts if he just, I don't know, hangs out with her and absorbs the fumes."

"She's leaving?" He looked down at his plate, arranged his fork on his melamine tray. "Already?"

"Joe, you didn't talk to her about this? She hasn't said anything?"

"I thought she liked it in the East Village," he said. "I mean, her roommate's been a little difficult, but she was supposed to get a job, she was looking into it. There's a yoga studio downstairs from her, Avenue A Yoga. She thought maybe she could get certified to teach."

"I guess there's been a change of plans."

"I guess so." He sighed. He rubbed his bald spot.

"Any chance you could maybe, I don't know, say something to her? Tell her this is—"

"You know, I really enjoyed having her around," Joe said, picking at his chicken. "It's been so long since we got to spend time with each other, got to know each other a little," he said. "It's been so long."

So this was where we were. My son's future was in the toilet and Joe was strumming his sad guitar. "Look, I don't think—"

"Remember that day we all went to the museum? Wasn't that a great day?" Christ. "I thought to myself, at the end of that day, that this was the sort of thing I'd been missing, the company of my oldest daughter alongside the company of my oldest friend. We were driving home, and I was thinking about how many good times we'd missed over the years because Laura hadn't been there."

"That's what you were thinking about?"

"Yeah," he said, a little abashed. "I know, I know, but I've always had a soft spot for that girl, Pete."

"I'm not sure you have to write her requiem just yet."

"It's just with Pauline leaving for college, I consoled myself that at least Laura was back in town. That even though my youngest was leaving, my oldest was back in my life."

I let my breath out heavily. "Maybe you can talk to her?"

His head drooped. "There's never any talking to her. Once she gets it in her head to go somewhere, she goes. She was at her aunt Annie's house, I remember, until she just decided one day to pack up and leave. Annie was frantic. Turns out she'd left a note. Same, really, with the goat farm. She could have stayed, even though the place got sold, but she decided she wanted to go pick grapes or something. So she left."

"Well, maybe this time you could ask her to stay." I didn't know how to explain my position delicately. "It would be helpful to me, Joe, if you asked her to stay."

"Why do you think she'd listen to me?"

"Because she's your daughter?"

"So?" He laughed. "Look, ever since Laura's trial, her time at Gateway, she's—well, she hasn't really been compliant, to say the least. I could get on my knees and beg her to stay, tell her how much it would mean to me, to you, but she'd just give me that sad, condescending look she has and tell me that the spirits are calling her, whatever, she has to go. How could I stop her?"

"You could tell her she's forbidden."

He laughed out loud. "Pete, you can't forbid a thirty-year-old woman to do what she wants to do. No matter how much you'd like to."

"Alec was supposed to enroll in college," I said bitterly.

"And Laura was supposed to get a job." But Laura wasn't the tragedy here. Laura wasn't the colossal tragedy. Or maybe she was once, but that was a long time ago.

"Listen, I've got to go," I said. I'd eaten three bites of my chicken. I stood. "So what are you going to say to her?"

"What can I say?" He shrugged. "I'll tell her I love her. Maybe Iris and I will make plans to visit. You and Elaine could come. We could all go to the Louvre together. Another museum trip."

"Are you serious?"

"Sure," he said. Innocent as a lamb. I shook my head at him and stormed out of the cafeteria, into my car, and back to the office, where unfortunately I was too early for my next patient and had to stare out the window for nine infuriating minutes, biting my nails and doing everything in my power not to pick up the phone, call Iris, and tell her to put her fucking foot down right this instant, since her husband was too much of a pussy to get the job done.

FRIDAY NIGHT ARRIVED full of dreadful expectation. I had assumed that Alec would meet me at the house by dinnertime for our scheduled parley. Our man-to-man. But when I got home at six, he was nowhere to be found. Nor at seven, nor at eight, nor at nine or nine thirty. "Where is he?"

Elaine shook her head. "Did you try his cell?"

I tried his cell. No answer.

"I thought we had an appointment to talk about Paris tonight," I said. "To explain to him our point of view."

"He knows our point of view," she said.

I didn't want to lose my temper. "To make him *acknowledge* it. To make him understand."

"I'm sure he's coming home," Elaine said. She'd been on the treadmill in the living room until my pacing became intolerable. She and I had done a terrific job of not talking about this, and we weren't going to start now. I tried to watch some of her television program, some kind of cop show, but I couldn't concentrate on the imbecile plot; I kept listening for Alec on the front steps, trying his cell phone every ten minutes.

"Where is he?"

"I guess at Laura's? Or at the store?"

I tried the store. He wasn't there.

"Do you have Laura's number?"

"You could call Joe." I couldn't call Joe. I bit off the last remaining corner of my thumbnail and stormed upstairs.

"Where are you going?" I didn't answer. Alec's room was a mess— Coke cans, art supplies, and, God help me, a few torn condom wrappers—but there, on the floor, was his Samsonite, the suitcase we'd bought him to take to college. I opened the thing up. Neatly packed, all ready to go. I thought perhaps if his passport was in there, I could just take it. I could just take his passport and destroy it and then he wouldn't be able to go anywhere, much less Paris. I went through his clothing, layer by layer, the side pockets, the zipped outside pocket. No passport.

No passport, and the packed luggage: he'd never meant to talk to us again about school. He'd never meant to talk to us about anything. I picked up the phone next to his bed and started calling airlines—Air France, American, Continental—but none of them would release passenger information to me, much less tell me if they had an Alec Dizinoff and a Laura Stern booked on some future flight, exact date and time unknown. On his desk sat the shiny New School catalog. Had he *ever* intended to go? Was the whole thing a gigantic setup? When I came home four months ago and found those brochures—did he intend to go *then*? Or was he just looking to make a fool of me? Did he have some sort of perverse agenda against me even then?

I looked at his suitcase, his gorgeous, beautiful Samsonite suitcase, which he was supposed to take to college and keep there for four whole years. I opened up the window—it was stiff, it stuck, but I did it—and then I picked the thing up in both my hands. I threw it as hard as I could into the New Jersey night, into the yard and the property we'd bought and paid for all those years ago, we'd bought and paid for all for him, we'd picked this life out all for him.

And then I went to bed.

I heard Alec creep up the stairs at two in the morning. If he noticed his suitcase was gone or his window was open or his garbage was newly scattered all about his room, I suppose this is just one more thing I will never know.

CHAPTER TEN

IT WAS STILL dark out when I woke up, but there was no falling back asleep, and I didn't want to. I threw on my clothes, kissed Elaine on the forehead, and crept out of the house. No pager, no cell phone—I wasn't sure where the day would take me, but I knew I didn't want to be tracked. I was surprised at how many Round Hill lights were on this early on a Saturday, and people on the streets—dog walkers, a pair of intrepid joggers, a mother pushing a stroller around the block, still in her robe.

It was six thirty. I took myself to the Old Lantern to suck down coffee and a western omelet. I felt a heightened sense of myself, my pulse in my wrists and my temples; if I were another sort of man, I might have been on the fringe of an anxiety attack. But I took deep breaths and forced my breath to steady, and it did. Despite my best efforts, my mind pushed back fifteen years ago to that morning Joe Stern asked me for help spiriting his daughter away to Mexico. Her trial was still six months in the future and nobody knew what that future would bring. If only we had managed to get that girl to Mexico, everything would be different now, my whole story would be different, but it's hard to know fifteen years in advance what you'll hope for so long down the line.

Through the plate glass window, scratched with late-night teenage graffiti, the sun came up. The bleary-eyed waitress refilled my coffee mug and the diner scene sprang alive: seniors, postal clerks, public-course golfers, a few cops sleepy from a night patrolling downtown Round Hill. Crime figures were up this quarter, and I knew more than a few Manor and School District ladies who now bought their groceries exclusively in Hopwood rather than risk a parking lot mugging in our own downtown Grand Union. There'd been a reported rape near the John F. Kennedy Gardens two months earlier. Two of our Round Hill public school kids, eighteen-year-olds, acquaintances—the details were blurry, but still, a rape. For people who noticed or cared about these things, Round Hill property values had suddenly ticked downward.

I poured ketchup on my hash browns. I watched the television play silently above the counter. ESPN. A few feet in front of me, sitting right up at the counter, but I hadn't even noticed until now, was Officer Barnes, the nice old cop who'd done us a favor and kept Alec in the clink that night five years ago, after the elementary school bust. He'd done as decent a scared-straight job as a twinkly-eyed old geezer could do, spent the whole night reminding Alec about every subcode in the New Jersey drug enforcement act. It did the trick back then, and Alec seemed relatively reformed when we picked him up at six in the morning. Never again, guys, he swore. I mean it. I'm so sorry. Never again.

From the counter up front, Officer Barnes waved at me and smiled. He was tucking into an enormous plate of the Saturday special, steak and eggs. Did he remember me or did he think I was someone else? And how were we supposed to fight serious Round Hill crime with the jolliest police force this side of the Mississippi? I took a sip of my coffee and waved back. My heart, which I'd propped up with grease and caffeine, was sinking fast. I left a twenty on the counter and disappeared out to the parking lot, where morning's first dewy light was still shining on the cracked concrete.

I put on my sunglasses and headed up toward the Palisades. I can't honestly say that a plan was forming in my mind, that I had any particular course of action. If I knew anything, it was that Laura Stern was my last hope, and only by talking to her might I possibly get some understanding of what she and Alec were up to. If nothing else, their plan sounded so ridiculously vague—I knew that Alec would do nothing to clear those plans up for me. At the very least I had to know what they were thinking they were going to do. Didn't I deserve at least that? Maybe Laura would be able to inform me of pertinent information like *where* in Paris (even foreign cities have neighborhoods) and *how* they were going to get housing and *when* they planned on returning and of course, most important, *why, why, why, why, why.*

Why, Laura?

This should have been his senior year. If he wanted to go to Paris that badly, I would have taken him.

The Palisades to the George Washington Bridge. Six-dollar toll. Traffic on the FDR. Construction at seven thirty on a Saturday morning, and I was stuck at a full stop in that hideous, half-crumbling underpass. I watched the sunlight shine down on Queens, a tugboat slog its way up the East River. Above me the lovelies of Sutton Place were just rising from their featherbeds. I tapped my fingers on the steering wheel. I turned the radio on, listened to sports radio for the asinine repetitiveness of it. This is Mike from Massapequa Steve from Seaford Bernie from Bay Ridge Richie from Rockland I want to talk about Jeter Randolph Matsui Rodriguez Reyes the Giants the Knicks the Rangers but nobody had a word to say about my poor Nets, who'd made it to the playoffs once again this year and collapsed, once again,

in the second round. The traffic started to move. I turned off the
radio.

It didn't take much cruising off the Houston exit to find Avenue A
Yoga, nor did it take much detective work to find the button marked
CHANG/STERN in the retrofitted brownstone right above it. I had been
fortunate enough to find a parking spot right across the street and
watched my car as I buzzed up.

And buzzed up.

And buzzed up.

If she thought she was getting away from me this easily, she was a
fool; I would sit on the stoop and wait all day. What did I care? I had
nothing else to do.

I buzzed up.

"*What is it?*" Through the exhausted fury of the voice, it was hard
to tell if this was Stern or this was Chang.

"Laura?"

"Yes? Who is this?"

"It's Pete Dizinoff. Dr. Pete. I want to talk to you."

She was quiet on the other end for many seconds. This was rude;
simple manners said that she should greet me and inquire about how I
was doing or, more courteously, let me in. I was an old family friend.

"What do you want?"

"I need to talk to you."

"About?"

"Laura, can you please just let me in?" I made no promises, like I
won't take up too much of your time, or I just need to ask you about
a few things. I had no idea how much time I would take and I had no
sense of what we would, in the end, really get down to talking about. I
still had a baby picture of Alec in my wallet. If I had to, I would force
her to stare at it to get her to understand.

She buzzed me up, and I took the stairs up two floors in a clean, renovated, wallpapered hallway. There was only one apartment per floor, which meant the apartments were nice-sized, which meant that Joe and Iris had set Laura up well, since how on earth would that girl be able to afford Manhattan rent on her own?

"Dr. Pete?" She was still in her nightclothes. Short silk shorts, a lacy blue top, a fluttery little blue robe. As if she'd posed for a Victoria's Secret campaign before getting out of bed. I thought of her sitting in my kitchen a few weeks ago, her finger on my forearm. I thought of Iris in her white bikini all those previous summers, idly eating breakfast in a kitchen in Rehoboth.

"Dr. Pete?" Laura said again.

"I'm sorry to barge in this early," I said, embarrassed, suddenly, for both of us.

"That's okay," she said. "I understand." She did? "Want some coffee?"

"Sure." So we were going to be cordial about this. Good. She led me into the kitchen and sat me down at a little wooden table that got perfect eastern light.

"My roommate's not in. Otherwise she would have freaked out when you buzzed. Wendy really needs her beauty sleep. A person is not allowed to make any noise before eight a.m. weekdays, ten a.m. on the weekends, and if you do, you have to bear terrible consequences."

"That sounds burdensome," I said. I watched her slim back as she took coffee out of the freezer, measured it into the filter. Her red hair was piled on top of her head. In another life, another kitchen, this was Iris.

She said, "I'm pretty good at keeping quiet."

So we were quiet while she made the coffee, and listened together to the pot burble and steam. I understood then at least part of what was so seductive about Laura—any woman who can make strong coffee in lingerie in a Manhattan apartment can look like a miracle to a middle-aged suburban guy—but I still didn't understand what a woman like this could possibly want with my poor, addled son.

"So you want to talk about Paris, right?" she said when the mugs were in front of us, sugared and creamed.

"I just need you to help me understand what this is about."

"There's not much to it, Dr. Pete," she said. "I have some friends in Paris that I met during the *vendange* last fall. Some really nice guys with connections in the fashion business. They're opening up a clothing store near Les Halles—it used to be the main food market for Paris, but then it got demolished and they built this mall and these parks instead. It's a touristy part of the city," she said, "and they need someone to help them with the English-speaking customers. Hence, *moi*."

"Fine," I said. "But what about Alec?"

"He wants to come."

"And what will he do when he gets there?"

She tipped a little more sugar into her coffee. "I really have no idea," she said. "Help out around the store, I guess, although I told him I couldn't be sure there'd be enough work. Maybe he could sell his paintings on the street. People do that, you know, in that neighborhood."

"You want him to sell his paintings on the street."

"Why not?" She sipped her coffee, and it suddenly occurred to me that it was quite possible she didn't care about my son at all.

"Laura, if I ask you something, will you answer honestly?"

"I'll do my best." She scratched at a pale reddish eyebrow.

"Why do you want my son with you in the first place?"

She laughed. "Why wouldn't I?"

"Do you know what it will mean to have a twenty-one-year-old tagging along with you in Paris? A kid who's never been there before? Who doesn't have a job? Who doesn't speak French?"

"You make him sound so *helpless*," she said. "He'll be selling his paintings. And he wants to go to all the big museums, see the major art."

"And then what?"

"Then what?"

"Where do you plan on living?"

"My friends have an extra room to start," she said. "And then I'm sure we'll find a place of our own."

"Ah." We said nothing else for a minute. I watched a pigeon perch on the fire escape outside her window, cooing nervously. I tried to see Laura as a little girl again, the daughter of my oldest, dearest friends. I looked at her, looked through her, saw her in her baby carriage, Elaine and me walking her through Fairmount Park, along the Schuylkill River, Boathouse Row. I remembered her toddling around, jelly on her T-shirt, a cup of apple juice in her hand. I remembered her carrying books under her arms, oversleeping all those mornings in Rehoboth. I refused to think about the handicapped bathroom in the Round Hill Municipal Library and all that had transpired after.

"What about visa issues?" I finally asked.

She laughed again. "We'll be paid off the books, Dr. Pete."

"I see."

"It's no big deal."

"Of course not." Somehow, oddly, I was heartened at how half-assed this all sounded. If they'd had a plan, an excellent plan, I would have been more alarmed. "Laura, you can understand why I'm not thrilled at the idea of Alec going off to Paris with you."

"I know," she said. "Of course I know." And she actually reached out and patted my arm as if I were the child here and she were the one explaining certain hard truths. "But the thing is, Alec really wants this. He really wants to go. So who am I to tell him he shouldn't?"

"Laura, you care about Alec, don't you?"

She laughed again, a condescending, infuriating laugh. "Alec is one of the most incredible people I've ever met, Dr. Pete. He's smart and dedicated to his art and to what he believes in—"

"He's a kid."

She waved her hand across her face. "Listen, I've explained it to him that Paris will be hard, that we won't have a lot of money, that we won't know a lot of people. And for a guy like him, who's grown up with every comfort, it could be tough. But he doesn't mind. He says he doesn't need a lot of money, a lot of community."

"Laura, he's saying that because he's an infatuated kid. A kid! As long as he's with you, he doesn't care about anything else."

She stood to refill our coffee mugs. "It's sweet, isn't it?"

"Sweet? Are you joking?"

Something occurred to me: her roommate was gone, she was wearing this sexy lingerie, but still Alec had come home in the middle of the night. "Why isn't he here?"

"Oh, he wanted to stay," she said. "But sometimes I have to send him home, you know? I think it's better for us if we don't spend every single second together."

"What do you think it will be like in Paris?"

"Alec understands me, Dr. Pete. He knows I can't be around other people all the time. Sometimes I just need my space. Alec gets it. He understands."

"Laura, if you told Alec to dress up in a clown costume and climb the Empire State Building, he'd pretend to understand. That's how infatuated twenty-one-year-olds behave."

"I think he deserves more credit than that," she said.

"You do, huh?"

She sat back down again with our mugs, then reached to a drawer behind her for her cigarettes, her lighter, and her ashtray. "Sure," she said. "My question is, why don't you?"

It was galling to be told how little credit I was giving my son, but still I was impressed with my own fortitude, my ability to sit in that lovely, sun-filled kitchen with Laura Stern in her underwear and not get loopy with rage. Her voice was grumbly in the morning, even before her first cigarette of the day, but as she lit up and blew smoke in my eyes, I was still thinking as clearly as I ever had.

"Look," I said. "I have enormous respect for my son. I think he's a terrific person, a talented person, a kind and generous person. If I thought less of him, I wouldn't be quite so bothered by his desire to run off to Paris with you. Perhaps you can understand that."

"Have you ever even been to Paris?"

"Does it matter?" In fact I had been there once, on a vacation ten years ago, part of a four-stop European tour. We'd spent the whole time shopping for an umbrella except for one day at the Louvre, which I'd surprised myself by enjoying. I remembered the big painting of Napoleon crowning himself in front of a disgruntled Pope. I remembered Elaine getting lost in the rooms full of tiny Greek figurines.

And then I remembered Laura in the Museum of Modern Art, and the curvy black wings of the bassinet.

"I think it matters," she said. She took a deep drag of her cigarette. "I think every experience matters. There's no one way to live a life, Dr. Pete. There are just a million different possibilities."

"Forgive me for disagreeing," I said. "There are only the possibilities you make for yourself, and if you make stupid decisions when you're young, you're cutting off those possibilities, one by one. Right is right and wrong is wrong, and that goes for plans about your future as much as it does for anything else."

"Right is right and wrong is wrong?"

"Almost always," I said, the "almost" a defense against sounding inflexible.

"I guess I just don't understand what wrong decision you're talking about. The decision to go to Paris with me? Is that really cutting off all his future possibilities?"

"His decision not to finish college, Laura. His decision to run off after a pipe dream, a woman he barely knows. A country he's never been to."

"Alec and I know each other, Dr. Pete."

"I want my son to have every opportunity," I said. "Surely you can understand—"

"There is no one right way to live a life," she said.

"Laura—" I cut myself off, startled to find I wanted a cigarette of my own.

"Look, I get that you want what's best for Alec, and I get that you think college is the best thing possible, but the truth is, lots of people are very successful without four-year degrees, and lots of people travel the world when they're young, and it's not like we're talking about Alec going to darkest Nigeria or something with a total stranger. It's Paris, Dr. Pete. With me. And I know what I'm doing. And he's allowed to make his own choices, whether you think those choices are right or wrong."

She stubbed out her cigarette, unpinned her hair, let it fall loose and wavy over her shoulders. Then she pinned it up again, carefully, into a knot on top of her head. She was breathing sharply through her mouth. She got mad the same way Iris did, in long, ranting passages and heavy breathing. I didn't say a word.

"Dr. Pete, Alec doesn't want to disappoint you. But he also can't disappoint himself. He's not going to Paris because he wants to be with me. He's going to Paris because he wants to be himself."

For Christ's sake. I sighed and shook a cigarette out of Laura's pack, cancer be damned. "Do you mind?" She shook her head. I hadn't smoked a cigarette in thirty years or more, and the gesture put me in mind of my psychiatric rotation all those years ago, when even medical students smoked happily.

"Laura, we seem to be at an impasse," I said, inhaling. I had forgotten how wonderful that first inhale can be. The bronchi in your lungs expand, your blood vessels constrict, the nicotine reaches the brain within ten seconds. Euphoria, especially if you're not used to it.

"We do?"

"What I mean is that although it's interesting, this conversation really isn't going anywhere. I came here to ask you to let Alec loose. To let him live the best life he can. If you care about him, surely you'll do that."

She stood to look out the window, at the cooing pigeon, which had been joined by a comrade. She shook her head a little. The cigarette smoke plumed around her head and out the window, toward the birds. "If I care about him," she said, turning around, tapping on her cigarette, a melodramatic flourish. I took another drag on my own smoke. Her thin limbs glowed in the sunlight behind her. It seemed suddenly that I'd already been here longer than I'd planned.

"Why don't you put on some clothes, Laura."

"I'm perfectly comfortable."

"It would be easier to have this conversation, I think, if you were dressed." It was incredible to me that my son had ever had access to this woman.

"*You're* the one who barged in here, Dr. Pete. You are not an invited guest, and I was perfectly comfortable before you arrived, so—"

"It would be easier, though, if you—"

"What are you really doing here, Dr. Pete?"

I smoked my cigarette to the filter. She remained standing. The kitchen was filling with our smoke, and I wondered what the beauty-sleep roommate would think of that. It was ten fifteen already; Elaine was long up, and she'd probably already tried my cell phone and heard it ringing in my study. She was probably worried about me.

I stubbed out my cigarette. After a moment's hesitation, I lit another one. My brain was buzzing.

"You want to slay the scary dragon who's threatening your son?"

"Don't be ridiculous."

"I don't think I am." She sat back down finally. "And I wish you had the balls to come out and say it. You don't think I'm good enough for him. You hold my past against me."

"Laura"—I didn't like her referring to my balls—"that has nothing to do with—"

"You think that something that happened to me when I was seventeen years old has tarnished me forever and that you can't let your son near me for fear of what I'll do—"

"Something that *happened* to you?"

"Yes—"

"You take no responsibility for what happened? You think it happened *to* you?"

"So you do want to talk about it, then."

Oh, for God's sake. "Look, Laura, this isn't about you. This is about my son, and what's best for him, and if you would just—"

"If I would just?"

"Let him *go*—"

"You can't forgive what happened to me when I was a kid. You want me to suffer for it, even now."

"Cut it out."

"Fine," she said. And then we were both quiet again, and I listened to the click of the metal clock above the window. The room was cool—the kitchen breeze was keeping things temperate—but still I was starting to sweat and feel a little nauseated. All that nicotine and coffee, and the aftereffects of the Old Lantern's western. And the fact that this conversation was simply pointless but that I had nowhere else to go, nowhere else to be. If Laura couldn't help me, nobody could. I stood, poured some tap water into my empty coffee mug, and drank it down quickly, standing at the sink. I did it again.

"If you wanted, you could have asked me for a glass of water."

"This is fine," I said.

"It is?" She arched her voice, her eyebrow.

"It's fine," I said.

"I wish you'd just be honest with me, Dr. Pete. If you're going to interrupt my morning, drink my coffee, the least you could do is honor me with a little honesty."

I sighed, felt the breeze from the window against my neck. "This tap water is just fine, Laura. That's the God's honest truth."

"I was sixteen," she said. "My period was late."

"I told you, that's not what I'm here to talk about."

"I prayed every day that it would come, even after five, six, seven weeks had passed. My body started changing. I was putting on weight, so I started wearing bigger shirts. I volunteered more in gym class—I thought exercise might help. I started running in the mornings before anyone woke up. "

"Laura, this is not what I'm here for."

"I had horrible cramping. I was always nauseous. Always tired. I pretended to have some kind of gastrointestinal something, my dad prescribed me drugs. I took all of them, too many of them, but nothing happened."

"I said this is not what I came here for." I didn't want to go through all this again, I honestly didn't. I just wanted her to leave Alec alone.

"Do you know what it's like to be an outcast in your own home, Dr. Pete? Do you have any idea what it was like for me after everything happened? My own mother unable to look at me? And when I dared to go out on the street—people staring, whispering, laughing at me? Yelling at me? They called me the baby killer. Neighbors, people I thought were friends. It got to the point where I basically couldn't leave the house. People called up my parents, left the most horrible things on their answering machine. Someone mailed a bloody knife to the house. Someone else mailed a decomposing kitten. They had to change their number again and again, but people kept finding out. People kept condemning them, like it was their fault. People pointed at me on the street and yelled that I was a baby killer, without having any idea what happened or why it happened or . . ."

I remembered that time, that moment, the way I, too, engaged in whispers in parking lots, synagogue functions, steak house dinners. The way I wasn't there for my old friend Joe. We'd never talked about any of this. He'd never told me about the things in the mail.

"It's the hardest thing to escape from, being lonely."

I looked at her.

"You want to know what I need from your son? I just need him to be near me," she said. "It's the hardest thing to escape from, being lonely, but Alec saves me from that."

"That's not his job," I said. "You need to let him go."

"I can't."

Afternoons, I would leave the ramshackle beach house in Rehoboth and watch the old men dig for clams. Usually I went alone, but sometimes my son, five, six, seven, came with me, bent down in the sand, and raked through it with his fingers. Occasionally he'd come up with clams of his own, immature and bubbling in his hands, tiny, the size of babies' thumbnails. He'd show them to me, palms up in front of his nose. Come here, Dad. Check this out. What do you think those are? Baby clams, they're just babies. What should we do with them? Put them back and let them grow. That's right.

I missed that kid; I missed my son.

"Nobody's ever wanted to take care of me the way Alec does," Laura said.

And then 1991: the Soviet Union fell, and there was no more good versus evil. There was no more compass. Or maybe I lost my compass later. Maybe the magnet went screwy right in that kitchen above a yoga studio; I don't know.

"Why can't you just leave him be?"

"The thing about it is that with Alec, I'm never lonely," she said. "He loves me completely. He keeps me safe."

"Safe," I muttered hoarsely. Did that word mean to her what it meant to me?

"Did it ever bother you that nobody wanted to know how I ended up pregnant? There wasn't even a peep about finding out who the father was?"

"As far as I remember, Laura, there was a lot of consternation. People wanted to know, your father wanted to know—"

"My father *knew,*" she said. "He was the only one who did know. I told him finally when I couldn't stand him begging anymore."

"He didn't know, I asked him—"

"Trust me," she said. "He knew. Or rather, he knew I didn't know. Which was of course much worse."

"Jesus," I said. "Laura, did something happen to you back then?" It was like a lightbulb. She was a teenager. She said it herself: she was lonely. She was always alone. Maybe even in the John F. Kennedy Gardens, reading a book, finding some peace late at night in a public place—

"Did something *happen?* A lot of things *happened,* Dr. Pcte."

"I mean—"

"What happened was that I used to go to the Grand Union late at night and let the public school boys who worked there have sex with me right next to the Dumpster," she said. "Sometimes the smell of rotting food still reminds me of sex."

I blinked.

"I said—"

"I heard what you said." Well, this was just wonderful. And what was the point of telling me this, exactly? What was the point of filling me in on this sordid bit of history? She was trying to shock me, trying to let me know I shouldn't mess with her. Fine. I didn't want to mess with her. I just wanted my son to go back to school, get a life, not end up on some godforsaken island making cowrie-shell jewelry.

"When I got pregnant, I knew I had to get rid of it, but I didn't know how. Isn't that ridiculous? I knew anything you wanted about the Brontë sisters but I had no idea how to get an abortion. I didn't drive, I didn't know where an abortion clinic was, and I knew that if I told my parents, they'd find out what I was doing when I said I was at the library. And I couldn't do that to them."

"So instead you—but why would you do that?" I was still stuck on where we'd just been. I thought about Joe dropping her off at the library. I thought about him going back two hours later to pick her up. Acne-scarred Laura. Face-in-a-book Laura. Her father thinking, My teenage daughter at the library, poor girl, no social life—well, at least she's safe. "Why would you go to the Grand Union and do that?"

"I told you, I was lonely. Alienated youth, high school outcast looking for affection, a little attention from the opposite sex, whatever. And I liked having sex."

"Laura, no sixteen-year-old girl goes behind the Grand Union to have sex because she likes it."

She dismissed me, shook her head. "You probably don't remember what I was like back then, but I was . . ." She started again. "Back then, every day was torture, Dr. Pete." She lit another cigarette. "I would do whatever I could to hide, not go to school, but of course eventually I'd have to go. I had no friends. Zero. I was tortured from the sixth grade on. Every day. It got worse as I got older."

"But I still don't understand why you would—"

"Sixth, seventh grade, they called me Yeti. They called me fire-crotch, and for the longest time I didn't even know what that meant. When I was in the eighth grade, they passed around a hate petition that the whole school had signed: I hate Laura Stern. They gave it to me in homeroom." She took a breath. "In high school they started leaving tampons in my locker, sometimes covered in ketchup, sometimes real blood. Some frozen fish once, in a Baggie with dead leaves. They called me fishybush. If I had to go to the bathroom during school, they'd follow me in and stand in the stalls over me and watch me. I stopped going to the bathroom. They'd take my clothing from my gym locker. I stopped going to gym."

So kids were cruel. I knew kids could be cruel. "Is this supposed to be some sort of justification, Laura?"

"Justification?" She gave me a look, sadness and disdain. "They would follow me home. They threw used condoms at my bedroom window."

"Why didn't you tell your parents?"

"What could they have done about it?"

"Told somebody? Transferred you?"

"Where, to the public school? Are you kidding? Besides, if I told them, it would have broken their hearts. I wasn't about to do that to them."

"Your parents would have protected you."

"Nobody could have protected me."

Her explanation made no sense at all. Getting a little roughed up in high school gave her the right to do what she'd done? "So instead you went to the Grand Union—"

"Jesus, I don't know why I'm bothering to explain this." She stood up with such force that her chair rocked backward, but she didn't stop talking. "The boys were nice to me there, that's all. I liked going there. They were nice. It didn't start out as sex—it was just, I don't know, it was just a weird kind of companionship at first. Friendship. I was a loser, they were losers, it was almost like we had a little club." She ran a hand through her hair. "And then I got pregnant, and I panicked."

"But surely you knew you could see a doctor."

"What doctor? Who? My *father*? For him to find out? The whole world to find out?"

"The whole world wouldn't have—"

"I didn't have the courage to inject myself with bleach, do any of the things I'd read about in books. So I beat myself. On my belly. Beating myself with my fists, running into corners. I threw myself down the stairs a couple of times. Whatever I could to miscarry."

"Laura, you don't have to tell me this."

"My stomach was covered in bruises. So were my thighs, from bumping into things. Totally discolored. And I kept going to the Grand Union, too. Thinking maybe that would somehow dislodge the baby."

"Laura," I said. In my head I saw my old best friend Joe. And I saw his wife, Laura's mother, Iris.

"Finally I started contracting at around six months. I went to the library. It was the first place I could think of. I was sure that I would deliver a dead baby, that nobody would ever have to know. I could pretend the whole thing never even happened. I couldn't believe the thing started crying when it came out of me."

"Laura, please. Please," I said. I felt desperate. How could I have ever thought she was a reasonable woman? "Please stop."

"Don't worry, Dr. Pete. I'm not trying to *justify* anything. I'm just telling you what happened."

"I came to talk about Alec."

"Bullshit. You came to talk about this. Because this is what you're afraid of—that someone who could do what I did isn't fit to be seen with your son."

"That's not what I—Laura, I told you, I just want Alec to have a future."

"You just want Alec to have the future you've already chosen for him."

There was no point to this conversation. I thought about picking up my jacket and leaving, but I did not. "The first time I slammed its head, it was still crying," she said. "I didn't know I had it in me. I was panicking, freaking out. I couldn't believe it."

"Oh, God," I said.

"I had to do it a second time to get it to stop."

And again, for long minutes, we just sat there. I should have picked myself up, picked up my jacket. I should have taken myself to the door. But I didn't know how at that very moment. I swear to you I didn't know how.

"If you want to know the truth," she finally said, "about why I like your son so much, it's that he keeps me from the worst part of myself. From my own worst instincts. The truth is, as you seem to have figured out, I don't really *want* him following me halfway around the world. Of course it would be easier, it would be better for a million reasons, if I could go by myself. But Alec keeps me from hurting myself. He keeps me from panicking. I can just lose myself in that devotion, you know? I can just swim in it. I'm scared to be without it."

"You can't use my son as your lifesaver," I said. "He's worth more than that."

"Before I knew how much Alec loved me, I was so lonely," she said. "My life was going nowhere. I was back here with my parents, out of options. My siblings couldn't stand me. My own mother couldn't stand me. I even went down to the Grand Union," she said. "It's amazing the way places like Round Hill don't change. The Dumpster's the same, the rotting food smell is the same. And there's still a group of teenage boys back there who are more than happy to do whatever they want to you, who actually can't believe their luck. I walked behind the store and saw them and I thought, I could do this. I'm still so lonely. I still need to feel something close to human connection." She paused. "Until Alec came into my life and loved me enough to stop me from needing to feel that."

"You cannot use my son that way," I said again. "It's not right."

"I need him in Paris with me," she said. "He protects me from myself."

"You cannot use—"

"It's not really using him." She went to the window again, opened it up a little higher to let out our smoke. Then she just stood there in her little underwear in the halo of the sunlight, looking at me with her arms crossed, as if she was challenging me. But why my son, Laura? Why can't you just leave us all out of your sad story? "Or if it is," she said, "then clearly your son likes being used."

"Laura—"

"In fact, I think he loves it." She laughed again, her grumbly, condescending Iris laugh. "You should see him," she said. "He loves it. He really does. Just like at the Grand Union but a million times better, a million times more grateful. Thank you, Laura, this feels so good, Laura, you're the only one who gets me, Laura, thank you, thank you. You're not like my fucking parents, they think they get me but they don't, I fucking hate them."

"Stop it. Stop."

"My father, especially, he's such a pompous bastard, I can't wait till I never have to listen to his pompous bullshit again—"

"Stop it, Laura."

"Your son really hates you, you know that?" she said. "It takes everything in his power to hide it from you."

"That's not true, Laura."

"Sorry, Dr. Pete, but you judge him and me, we're gonna judge you right back. That's the way it goes."

"Laura," I said. I saw my son, six years old, his palm full of tiny clams. I saw Iris in the kitchen, in a white bikini. I saw my son, a grown man, in bed with this woman. Noises like raccoons trapped behind a wall. I heard Laura and my son laughing at me when they thought I wasn't listening.

"Assholes like you," she said, still laughing, "you think you know everything, but you don't know a goddamn thing."

And it sprang out of me. I don't know what it was, or where it came from, but it sprang out of me like a wild animal: I hit her so hard across the face that I heard something crack.

Something cracked. Something broke.

But she didn't cry out, only breathed heavily. How could she not have cried out? What was the matter with this woman? Because when I looked up at her finally, blood was pouring from her nose, trickling from the corner of her mouth. Her nose was askew at the cartilage bridge. Her lips were already puffy. She was quiet.

The memory of Iris's bruise.

"Jesus, I'm sorry—"

"You hit me," Laura said thickly, dumbly, holding up a wrist to her bloody face.

"Laura, let me—"

"You hit me," she said again.

"Look, I . . ." Had I broken her cheekbone? Her jaw? Did I have that kind of strength? But no, she was talking clearly, her jaw was clearly intact. Her teeth were in her mouth.

I went to the freezer, looked for some ice, frozen vegetables.

"Get out," she said. I turned to face her, her nose still pouring blood, and it had gotten on her wrist, her lacy top. God, noses bleed so much more than they really ought to. I pulled some paper towel from the counter.

"You should put some ice . . . ," I said, but then I faltered.

"If you don't leave right now, I'm calling the police." The police, Jesus. The police—I've always been such a coward. I tried to force the paper towel into her hand, but she wouldn't take it, so it dropped to the floor. She needed ice.

"Laura, I'm really sorry," I said. "I didn't . . . I didn't mean . . ."

But I had meant it, and it could not be undone, and maybe there was some tiny part of me that was glad to see the way her nose gushed. Maybe. For this is what she said to me when I opened the door.

"I used my knee."

This is what she said. I was opening the door to leave.

"Not a hammer," she said. "Not a baseball bat. My knee. Just slammed the baby down twice, hard. Didn't even have to think about it," she said. "I'm surprised my father never told you."

LIKE A CRIMINAL, Lady Macbeth, I washed the drops of blood off my hands in a McDonald's bathroom on First Avenue. How had I gotten blood on my own hands? I still had nowhere to go, no good plan of action. So I decided to walk south to Chinatown, to take some comfort in the cacophony there, and then I kept walking, farther south, and then east, over the Manhattan Bridge, which I didn't even know a person could walk over. It did not occur to me to go anywhere in particular, only to keep walking, walking, walking, to walk farther and farther away from Laura Stern.

Brooklyn felt like another world. I pushed through the parks near the bridge, along the busy shopping streets, the cobblestoned passageways leading out to the waterfront. I kept walking, my feet starting to hurt in my shoddy sneakers, the crack of my hand against the side of Laura's face playing and replaying itself in my memory. I made a right and found myself in a district of warehouses, slowly being turned into condominiums and lofts. I kept walking until I found the water. That terrible soundtrack—crack, crack, crack.

My body still seemed odd to me, and I was nauseated. My hand pulsed where it had made contact with Laura's cheek. But I felt, oddly, more righteous than ever in my determination to keep Alec home. Everything about Laura proved that he should stay home, that I was right. The problem was how to tell him. The problem was how to return to myself. I had never hit a woman before. I had never broken anyone's bones. I was a doctor, after all. I had taken the Hippocratic oath.

My mind was sufficiently with me that when I passed a bank with a clock on its sign and saw that it was almost three, I knew I should call my wife. I found a pay phone and my credit card and dialed.

"Where are you? I've been so worried. You left your phone."

"I know," I said. "I'm in the city. I just . . . I needed to walk around."

"Are you all right?"

"More or less."

"You threw Alec's suitcase out the window last night."

"I know," I said. "I'm sorry."

We were both quiet for a moment.

"Pete, if he goes to Paris, it's not like we'll never see him again—"

"Not now, Elaine, okay?"

More quiet.

"When are you coming home?"

"Soon."

"By dinnertime?"

"I'm not sure."

"I think maybe I'll go have dinner with someone," she said. "Alec's working and I could use the company."

"Great," I said.

"Pete, I need you to take care of yourself, okay? Whatever happens with Alec—I just need you to take care of yourself. This isn't good for you, the way you've been acting. This isn't . . . healthy."

I hung up the phone and kept walking. Was I okay? Was I healthy? Why wouldn't I be? What was unhealthy about wanting to protect my only child? What was wrong with me that I would do whatever it took to keep him safe? I kept walking, Laura's choked voice still in my ears, the baby, her knee, and people wanted to know what was wrong with *me*.

It only occurred to me where I was going when I got there. Morning services were long over, and this wasn't the sort of institution that was religious enough for afternoon minhah, but still, it was a comfort just to see the building in front of me. I thought of my grandfather in his old black coat. The dozens of relatives in their black-and-white glory on my parents' foyer wall. I thought of my dead father, ushering Phil and me into our pressed black pants, walking with us hand in hand to synagogue every week. We were six years old, seven years old. I had never been on an airplane been to a baseball game been ice skating seen a mountainside but I knew the warm firm feeling of my father's hand in mine, the musty smell of that synagogue, my grandfather kissing me and my brother on our heads and slipping us each a quarter because we'd been such good boys. It's for us, Phil once told me decades ago in the Yonkers bedroom we reluctantly shared. They did this all for us. We might not like it, but we know why they did it.

And God strike me down if he wasn't right.

I GOT HOME just past nine o'clock. The house was empty. I went outside, shot basket after basket. A good, heavy sweat to wipe off the lingering residue of a horrible day. I'd sweat it off and then I'd shower it off and then I'd figure out what to do next, what to say to my son. I wondered if Laura had gone to the emergency room, if she'd told them what happened. Probably not. Nosebleeds cleared up, broken noses generally healed by themselves, and she seemed like a tough enough cookie. She'd wait it out. She'd hold some ice to her face. I made a jump shot, and then another one.

Inside, my cell phone started to wail. A few seconds after it stopped, I heard the house phone go. I made another ten free throws. I heard my cell phone start up again, and then the house phone. Christ, *had* Laura gone to the police? Already? My hand started tingling again. I made another fifteen free throws. The air was wonderful, cool and brisk, but the crack, crack, crack was playing in my head. A week before Labor Day, the dying embers of the summer. The house phone started going again, and I finally went in to catch it, but I was too late. I looked at my cell phone.

I had missed thirty-nine calls.

It was tough to piece together exactly what had happened from the fragmented messages, but the last thirty-five of them were all from Arnie Craig. He wanted one thing from me, and then another. And then another.

Could I get to Saranac Lake?

I pressed replay on that first message, and then on the second. It was only a five-hour drive from Round Hill, straight up I-87. Could I get there? Did I know anything about the hospital there?

Where are you, Doc?

Sorry to keep calling, Doc, but—

What was Addison's disease?

What was an Addisonian crisis?

And then the messages changed. A heavy, choking-off voice.

It was too late. Why didn't you tell us she had this disease? A disease of the adrenal cortex? Which is right above the kidney? Which you can test for?

She had all the symptoms, Doc, I know she did. An endocrine

problem? She had an endocrine problem? My little girl wasn't depressed at all, not like you said she was.

You did this. You did this, you fucking bastard. This is your fault.

I know she saw you. I know she saw you last week. You told her she was depressed. But she had Addison's disease. I'm gonna get you, you bastard. You killed my little girl.

ROSEANNE CRAIG HAD been diving off a rope swing on an island in a too-shallow finger off Saranac Lake. She'd hit her shoulder hard on a rock, started to thrash and drown. A friend pulled her out of the water in plenty of time and got her up onto the bank of the lake. She sputtered, sat up, nursed her shoulder. But then, a few minutes later, everything changed. The shock of the event sent Roseanne into an Addisonian crisis. She screamed from the pain in her legs. She vomited. Her blood pressure dropped. She lost consciousness. The group of friends — Roseanne and two other girls — were on an island in a deserted part of the lake. They had to load Roseanne into a canoe. No cell phone service, no ambulance access. They paddled alongshore and found a deserted summerhouse with a telephone. They broke in through the porch and called an ambulance. But by the time they got Roseanne to a hospital, by the time the doctors assessed the problem, by the time hydrocortisone and saline and dextrose were administered, the only thing left to do was ask the Craigs whether the doctors could offer Roseanne's corneas for donation.

The hospital put the time of death at five fifteen that afternoon. I'd been watching the light shift in the synagogue.

My cell phone started ringing again.

"Oh, Arnie," I said when I answered. "Oh, Arnie."

"I'm gonna get you for this, you fucking bastard. You killed my little girl."

"Oh, Arnie," I said again. "I'm so sorry. I'm so sorry."

"I'm gonna—"

"Arnie," I said, maybe moaned. "Oh, Jesus, Arnie."

Roseanne Craig with the frog tattoo that stared up at me as I palpated. Roseanne Craig with the black suit and the pearl necklace. Roseanne Craig with the Marxist bookstore. Roseanne Craig, salesperson of the year, an Escalade under her belt already. I was crying, but this was not an admission of guilt. "I'm so sorry," I said.

"I'm gonna get you, you bastard." And Arnie was crying, too. "I'm gonna fucking get you for this." And the two of us held the phones to our ears and cried at each other and stayed like that for quite some time until our wives arrived and gently put each of us to bed.

CHAPTER ELEVEN

THE NEXT MORNING was the eye of the hurricane, but I didn't know that yet. In years past, before Doppler radar and twenty-four-hour weather channels, when the eye was still not necessarily a familiar part of the hurricane phenomenon, Florida fathers would check on their garages, Georgia farmers would check on their fruit trees, and the second half of the hurricane would arrive as fast and fierce and angry as a Roman god and sweep everything away: father, garages, farmers, and fruit trees. The storm would dump all of them miles away from where they'd started, twisted and mangled and dead as leather. I had a second or so of peace before it hit me that Roseanne Craig was dead of an Addisonian crisis that I had failed to diagnose. Then the entirety of the previous day hit me, too, and I didn't want to get out of bed. I took Elaine's hand. It was not yet six in the morning.

"Pete," she mumbled. "Come here." I let myself curl up against my wife, felt the thick, reconstructed flesh of her left breast against my fingertips. I smelled her hair. But I was not lulled back to sleep by this comfort, because I was suffering the first horrible inkling that all this might be denied to me in the not-too-distant future. The satiny luxury of lying in bed with my wife and holding her close. I knew even then, maybe not that I was in the hurricane's eye, but that the angry gods were not done with me. I pulled her closer to me. I ran my hand down the folds of flesh along her side. The padding over her hip bone. She murmured something in her sleep—Mmm, Pete—and turned to face me. She kissed me groggily, then turned around again and spooned up into me and fell back asleep.

Two hours later, she woke up and we got out of bed. The morning felt ludicrously quiet. I decided to go down to the study with a sheaf of deckle-edged writing paper from the spindly ornamental desk in the corner of our bedroom, Elaine's little piece of Victoriana for our Victorian.

"What are you doing?" she asked. She was making the bed.

"I'm going to write a letter to Arnie Craig and his wife."

"You are?"

I looked stupidly at the paper in my hand.

"Pete, honey, you said yourself that Addison's is incredibly rare, that it almost always presents like something else. What did you call it? A wolf in sheep's clothing."

"I know," I said, "but Joe—" I stopped, felt the writing paper in my hand crumple. This was the first time I consciously stopped myself from admitting what Joe had suggested I check for, saying out loud that Joe Stern had put me on notice.

"Joe what?" She finished straightening our pillows. "Joe would have checked for Addison's?" She sighed. "Honey, Joe Stern is a lunatic. You've said so yourself a million times, a wonderful doctor but a lunatic as far as second-guessing himself goes. He'll give a pregnancy test to an eighty-five-year-old woman."

I cleared my throat, dropped the paper back down on the Victorian desk. "Joe's practice doesn't get eighty-five-year-old women."

"You know what I mean. You can't compare what you should have done to what Joe would have done."

But Joe Stern had told me to check for Addison's. He'd put me

on notice. But I was too . . . sure of myself, full of myself. And my
mind was on other things: my son, his daughter. I was too terminally
distracted to be my old sleuthy self. And now Roseanne Craig was
dead.

I picked the paper back up off the desk. "I still think I'd like to
write him a letter," I said. "He was almost a family friend."

"He sold us a car."

"Elaine—"

"I just don't want you to take this too hard," she said. "But go. I'll
make some coffee."

I spent the next three hours bent over the letter in my study. I
wasn't used to writing longhand, and I wasn't used to writing personal
letters either. The words didn't come. And after a while, when they
still wouldn't come, I started going through my journals, through my
Physician's Desk Reference, Medline, to read everything I could about
Addison's disease. My reading told me nothing I didn't know. Addison's, a failure of the adrenal glands to produce adequate amounts
of cortisol, is distributed equally among the old and young, men and
women. The disease can cause depression, irritability, cravings for
salty food, some nausea, some skin discoloration. However, in 25
percent of cases, symptoms do not appear until an Addisonian crisis.
And even if symptoms do appear, they are usually the same as those
present in much more common ailments. Thus Addison's can be quite
tough to diagnose.

Outside my study, I heard footsteps and some murmuring. Alec
was checking to see if I was home. Perhaps he was preparing for a
showdown. Perhaps he would come storming into my study, demand-
ing to know why I'd gone through his bag, why I'd tossed his bag
out of the house, and what would I say? He'd want to know why I
wouldn't let him live his own life. Why I thought I could still control

him. I closed my eyes and listened to my son interrogate my wife. *Is he home? Is he planning on staying here? I don't know. Did you ask him?* He'd storm into my room, want to know what I had against Laura Stern and his future happiness. I would say to him, Laura Stern? At least she's still alive, idiot. Other people's daughters are dead this morning.

But instead my son, like a coward, slipped away out of the house—I heard the door open and gently close—so I turned back to my letter.

"Dear Arnie, I inadequately managed your daughter Roseanne's care during the past twelve months. I wish I knew how to tell you how much I admired your daughter, how well I thought of her. How dear she seemed, and how I wish I could, how if only I had another chance I would . . ."

"Dear Mr. Craig, it is hard to know how to sufficiently express how bad I feel. Losing a patient is never easy, but to lose a patient so young, and so full of life . . ."

"The truth is, Mr. Craig, an old friend of mine *told me* to check for Addison's disease, along with other autoimmune or endocrinologic concerns, but instead I ignored his good advice and then went out and bashed his daughter's face in."

I tore that last piece of paper into tiny shreds and buried them in the bottom of my wastepaper basket.

"Dear Mr. Craig . . ."

I went upstairs, took a long, hot shower, and tried to scald the previous day off me like a fungus. I scrubbed hard inside my ears, under my fingernails; I got soap in my eyes and in my mouth. When I emerged, I sat in a towel on the bed for no particular reason and watched the street below our window. After all that activity yesterday, every phone in the house was silent. The street below was silent, too, for a long time. Then Mark and Kylie Krieger walked down the street, hand in hand, Kylie talking animatedly about—a deer she saw? a puppy? a squirrel? And then nothing again for the next eight minutes. And then a car. And then another car. But as far as I could tell, it was nobody I knew.

"Pete? You up there?"

Elaine was making egg salad for lunch. I got dressed, threw my dirty towel in the hamper, smelled the lingering scent of Ivory soap all over me, and went downstairs. Elaine had made me a sandwich with watercress in between the egg salad and the bread. She was going out to do some errands.

"Listen," she said. "I want you to be a bit nicer to yourself, okay? You can't sit around blaming yourself for what happened to Roseanne."

"Okay," I said.

"Really, Pete. This isn't good for you. I know you liked that girl, but—"

"Just let me grieve a little, Elaine."

"Pete—"

"Please let me be."

She put plastic wrap over the egg salad bowl, wiped the crumbs off the petri-patterned marble breakfast bar. She took a sponge to our counters. Her hair was in a maternal strawberry-blond cut just below her ears, she wore khaki pants and a blue polo shirt, and she looked more like an old hausfrau to me than any woman I ever thought would be my wife. Yet we had such a loving, such a tender relationship. Real tenderness. Elaine and I had suffered our trials, our infertility, her illness, my weakness, but still we'd built this life together. She was as much a part of me as my own skin after all these years. What will I tell the world about you, Elaine? You have a beautiful singing voice. You can pronounce Middle English. You are as rare and magnificent as a condor.

If I had tried to make a life with anyone else, I would have failed. But she held on to me after all these many failures, after I had not been grateful enough to her, time and time again.

"I'll be home in a little while," she said. She straightened her polo shirt. "You want anything at the grocery store?"

"No."

"You sure?" I nodded. "Okay, then." She came over to my perch and kissed me on the temple. "I love you, Pete."

"I love you, too." And then I watched her walk out of the kitchen. I will not let myself start with those "if only's" here, because I have been good about not indulging myself yet and I'd like to maintain my strength on that lonely front. So instead I will only say that the eye of my hurricane lasted perhaps seven hours, which is long by meteorologic standards, but which barely gave me time to catch my breath. I finished my sandwich. I stared out the window. I still don't know what I was hoping to see. I remembered Roseanne Craig leaving my office and how I'd wanted to give her a hug.

I WAS BACK in my study when the doorbell rang. My first thought was of Girl Scout cookies and Jehovah's Witnesses, neither one of which was worth getting up for.

"Pete!"

"Pete, are you there?"

Iris and Joe were at the front door. They almost always just came up through the back. I saw them through the window before I opened the door: they both looked worn out for some reason, both slightly stooped. The gray was shining through Iris's hair, and Joe's forehead looked red, as though he'd been rubbing it all morning. I was clutching the draft of another letter and it did not occur to me yet to worry.

"What's going on?"

"Laura's gone, Pete," Joe said.

"Gone?" I opened the door wide to let them in. We sat down together in the living room, which we rarely did, in general preferring the friendlier precinct of the kitchen, close to the food and the booze. "I don't get you."

"She's gone," Iris said. "She took her passport, her clothes, her medicine. She's gone. Her roommate said she just packed up and left the apartment."

"Does the roommate know where she went?"

"Did you rape her, Pete?"

"Did I . . . I'm sorry?" Did I *rape* her? Rape her?

"Wendy said her face was bruised, she was wearing bloody pajamas."

"I'm sorry . . . did I what?"

"Were you in her apartment, Pete?" Iris asked.

No, Iris—you couldn't believe this, Iris. Come on. *Rape?* Yes, I did hit her, and yes, I did make her bleed. I probably broke her nose. I might have given her whiplash, even. And these are sins, I know, and I felt terrible about them, but—but I didn't *rape* anyone. And a broken nose isn't insurmountable. It isn't septicemia, myocardial infarction. It isn't Addison's disease.

"Pete, why don't you tell us what happened," Joe said. He was trying to sound reasonable, but there was panic in his voice.

"Wendy showed us what she'd been wearing," Iris said.

"I didn't rape your daughter." What a ridiculous, gruesome thing to say.

"Peter, Laura is many things, but she is not a liar." Iris held Joe's hand, clutched it. "There were big drops of blood—"

"But I didn't—" I was proving a negative here, which was, of course, impossible. There was no way to win a fight with a missing woman. I felt the place where she'd touched my forearm start to throb. "Look, I don't know how to prove that I didn't do something I didn't do. But I did not—*I did not* rape your daughter. I have no idea why she would accuse me of something like that. I have no idea—"

"She left the city, Pete, she fled."

"—except to say that she's unstable. She's unstable."

"She didn't leave any information. We have no idea how to find her. And Wendy said her face was puffy, bruised—and her pajamas."

I wouldn't even respond to Iris; I looked directly at Joe. "You've known it for years," I said. "She makes things up, Joe, come on. You know that." My voice was betraying me; I was starting to sound nervous. Probably even guilty.

"Tell me what happened, Pete," Joe said.

I looked at each of them, their familiar, beloved faces. The light poured into the living room, making the gray in Iris's hair glint. How little she knew about her own daughter—what secrets Laura had kept from her her entire life. She'd wanted to protect her parents, she said. But what exactly did these people need protection from? Joe, with his successful OB practice? Iris, with her million-dollar salary? The two of them with their three kids graduating from MIT? "I went to her apartment, that's true," I said. "I went to her apartment."

"And then?"

"I just wanted her to see—I wanted her to see what she was doing, okay? I went to her apartment to have a conversation with her. I wanted to talk to her about her future plans with Alec."

We were all silent. Iris cleared her throat. "What next?"

"We talked," I said. I felt my skin turn clammy. "And then I left."

"Nothing else happened?" Joe asked.

How could I not admit it? But I couldn't. I was a clammy-skinned coward. I hadn't raped her, no, but I could not tell the truth about what I had done. I was protecting them, too, and myself. I hit your daughter, Joe. Your precious one, Laura, whom you love best.

"So then why was she bleeding when Wendy saw her?"

"I don't know," I said.

"Why did she say you raped her?" Iris asked. "I know Laura," she said. "She wouldn't just make something up, she wouldn't just lie like this."

"You think she's some sort of angel?"

"Excuse me?"

The saddest defense of the guilty coward, to go on the offense when the defense holds no water. "Your daughter Laura, she's perfect? You believe everything she says?"

"Peter, I just cannot bring myself to believe that she would lie about this," Iris said. "And the horrible thing is, I almost don't know what's worse—to think that she would, or to think that you could actually do this."

"She's lying, Iris. There's no way for me to prove it, but she's lying—"

"No," Iris said. "I saw her pajamas."

As though Laura were nunlike, squeaky clean. As though getting blood on her clothing was beyond her. As though she hadn't done the things she'd done behind the Dumpster at the Grand Union. As though she hadn't clubbed her own baby with her knee. And as though she hadn't blamed it all on a difficult childhood.

"Iris, I don't know how I can prove to you that it's not true, but you're going to have to believe me."

"Then why did she run away, Peter? Why is she gone?"

"Did something happen to Laura?" Elaine came into the living room, trailed by Alec. They were casual, happy, wearing sweatshirts. The untainted witnesses. My jury pool.

"She's missing," Iris said.

"What do you mean she's missing?" Elaine asked.

"She took her suitcase last night and her passport and disappeared."

"She's *missing?*" Alec's voice went high.

"Alec, I thought you were with her last night." He was the first person Elaine would think to accuse.

"No!" he said. "No, after work I went out with some of the people from work, we went to Film Forum, had a couple of beers. I called Laura's cell phone to see if she wanted to come along, but she didn't answer. Do you know where she went?"

"She's missing, Alec," Iris said. "That's what we're saying. We have no idea."

"What about Wendy? What did Wendy say?"

They were both quiet. They didn't want to accuse me in front of my family. But they looked at me.

"Dad?" Alec was sitting on the upholstered chair opposite me. He had his big hands on his knees. His voice was tentative. "Dad, do you know where she went?"

"I have no idea." I turned to Joe and Iris. They were expectant. They expected me to confess. "But I did see her yesterday," I said. I would explain myself as best I could.

"You saw her?" Alec's voice grew stronger. "Why would you see her? What business did you have with her?"

"Why did you see her?"

"Pete?" Elaine said. "Is that why you went to the city?"

"I saw Laura," I said, a bit stupidly. "I saw her yesterday morning."

"You did?"

"I just wanted to talk to her." Elaine was sitting next to me on the couch; Joe and Iris were on the sofa opposite. Alec was in the upholstered chair. We were a suburban set piece, a drawing room comedy.

"What did you say to her, Dad?" My son was boring holes into me. "What did you say?"

"I just wanted to talk to her about why she wanted to take you to Paris. I wanted to know what her thinking was. What her plan was."

"You had no right to—"

"Let him finish, Alec."

"She told me about the clothing store," I said. "And that you were going to sell paintings in the street." I looked at my son. "I asked her why she wanted you to come with her."

"I could have told you that, Dad," he spat. "It's because she loves me. Which I know you might find hard to believe, but—"

"No," I said. I couldn't let him continue to think that way. "I'm sorry, but no, that's not what she said."

He stood, started to come toward me.

"Alec!" Elaine shouted. "Let your father finish."

"You don't know a fucking—"

"Pete," Iris said, "what did she say?"

"She loves me. You have no idea about fucking anything, you know that? *She loves me.* Which is impossible for you to understand, I know, but someone else can love me besides you, you know that? You are not the only person in the world *entitled to me*—"

"She said Alec helps her feel safe." I didn't like interrupting my son, but I felt I had no choice. "She's using you, Alec. That's all."

"Fuck you, Dad. You don't know a fucking thing. You don't know a fucking—" He was standing now. He was ready to let me have everything he could give me, tall and powerful and impotent, too, because he didn't know what to do. What could he do but stand there and listen?

"So what did you do next?" Iris said dully from across the room.

"Iris." Joe put his hand on her arm. "We don't need to—"

"No," she said. "No. I want to hear him say it."

"Iris, we really don't—"

"Shut up, Joe. Just shut up. Yes, we do. We do need to. Pete, tell us what you did."

"I won't admit to something I didn't do, Iris."

"I still don't know why my daughter ran away, Pete. I still have no idea why she got hysterical and ran away. I don't know why her pajamas were bloody. I don't know why she would accuse you of—what she accused you of. My daughter is not a liar."

"Her pajamas were *bloody*?" Alec asked.

"Pete?" said my wife.

Yesterday morning. Laura Stern in her flimsy nightclothes, her flimsy little robe. Underdressed in a kitchen. In Saranac Lake, Roseanne Craig was still alive.

I said nothing. I looked at my locked-together hands.

"Well?"

Outrageous. She was the murderer, she was the one who had dumped her own daughter's body into a Dumpster outside the Round Hill Municipal Library, and yet she was accusing *me* of unspeakable crimes. Letting her roommate think she'd been raped. Letting her parents believe her roommate.

"Pete, if you have something to say—"

"Do you know what she used to do, your daughter?" I wasn't going to protect them anymore. "Back when she was in high school?

Back when she got pregnant?" I would no longer spare these people the truth. I was right and she was wrong. I didn't rape her. I was in the right.

"Pete?"

"She used to fuck half of Round Hill Public behind the Dumpster at the Grand Union. That's how she got pregnant, Iris. Ask Joe, he knows. That's how she got knocked up. Couldn't keep her goddamn legs crossed." I was amazed at this anger inside me, how it kept my mouth moving, moving, moving. Suddenly I couldn't have stopped talking no matter what. "That's how she got herself pregnant, your precious daughter who would never lie about anything. That's what she used to—"

"Pete?" said my old best friend. He wanted to protect his daughter, his wife—well, I wanted to protect my son. By telling the truth. Finally. "Pete, please?"

I was welling with it, I couldn't stop: "And here's another thing. The baby was alive," I said. "It was born alive. She smashed in its skull on her own knee. So you tell me that she's stable, okay? You tell me that whatever she says is worth hearing. That her accusations are worth hearing. Your own daughter is a murderer, okay?"

"Peter!" Elaine said.

"So don't you dare come in here with your accusations and your bullshit and your daughter's lies. She's a *murderer*."

"Peter!" Elaine said again.

"Get out of my house," I said. "Get out of my fucking house."

"Pete?" My old best friend Joe.

"What accusations, Pete?" asked my wife.

"That's not true," Iris said. "What you just said, it's not true." I think she might have been crying.

"Fuck you it's not true," I said, standing up. "Don't you come in here with your accusations, tell me what's true and what's not true. I know what's true. Your husband knows what's true. Your daughter's a murderer, that's what's true."

My son was standing over me, my son's fist had been balled and I hadn't even seen it. It slammed across my jaw with just enough force to send me back into the sofa.

"Alec!" Elaine screamed. The rest of the room was studiously quiet. "Jesus, Alec! Pete, are you okay?" She flew to my side. "Are you okay?"

Joe and Iris just sat there on the couch opposite. Iris was certainly crying now; tears coursed down her cheeks. Alec stood in the corner and nursed his fist. I worked my jaw up and down for a second. He had a nice, strong fist, Alec did. A nice, solid swing. Just like his old man.

"Leave this house."

"Pete?" My old best friend Joe.

"Leave my house."

I couldn't say anything else. My mouth tasted as if it was full of blood. I closed my eyes and waited for them all to leave, and after a few more minutes, they did.

I MOVED INTO Alec's studio that evening. It was only meant to be a temporary solution, somewhere for me to stay until we figured out what to do next. Alec didn't want the studio anymore—he didn't want anything from me—and so there was a place for me to stay. Elaine wasn't sure what to think (rape, murder, a Sunday afternoon), but it seemed necessary for me to leave the house. Something was very wrong there.

And as for me, what did I want? I wanted to stay close to home, although I didn't feel, necessarily, that I deserved to be at home. In my house. Right is right and wrong is wrong, and I knew what I had done.

And then there was the lawsuit. The papers arrived six weeks later, at my office in the middle of a busy day. There was not enough evidence for wrongful death, even though Arnie Craig, I knew, desperately wanted that, as did his son. (Roseanne's brute of a brother showed up at my office for the first time a month after the death and barged into the examining room, where I was listening to the lungs of an asthmatic elderly gentleman, screaming, That was my innocent sister! Wrongful death, motherfucker! We're going to haul your ass away for a thousand years!)

But I wasn't hiding from malpractice. That wasn't my real crime. Anyway, the entire Round Hill community knew about the lawsuit — you know how suburbs are — knew who was suing me, knew why he was suing, knew about the tragic loss of Roseanne Craig, one of Round Hill Country Day's finest, a promising young lady with a promising future. Still, we were a community of doctors. Doctors tremble at the tremor of a misdiagnosis. Should I have done more? Could I have done more?

Only one particular physician knew for sure. I had ripped the scab off Joe's family's pain. Would he do the same to me?

MY LAWYER CALLED today just as the last patient was clearing out. Mina knocked on my door, mouthed, "It's him."

"Him?"

She rolled her heavy-lidded eyes at me. "*Your lawyer.*"

I thanked her, took a breath. What would it matter, really? What would any of it matter?

"Nick?"

A sharp intake of breath. "Great news, Pete. The judge threw out the case."

I said nothing.

"Pete, you there?"

Good news. It's been, basically, the story of my life. But still sometimes it's hard to hear. "Yes," I said.

"I told you not to worry. I told you this was baseless. Judge reviewed the literature on Addison's. April Frank came through, told her about the referral. So she threw it out."

"Thanks, Nick." I had never told him, either, about Joe Stern's warning. "That's really great."

"Phew, right, Doc?"

"Yeah," I said. "Phew."

"I'll send you a bill." He laughed and hung up the phone.

Well then.

Well.

Mina poked her head in. I gave her a thumbs-up. Mina, wonderful, recalcitrant Mina, threw her arms around me and gave me a kiss on the cheek before shuttling, abashed, back to her cell.

I sat down behind my desk, fingered the smooth edges, the endless paper. I straightened a pile of journal articles. So this was Joe's game. He'd been calling to tell me that he hadn't told. To remind me that despite everything I'd done to him, done to his daughter, his precious one, done to his wife's peace of mind and the secrets he'd held so close—well, I needed to know that he was still a kind and decent human being. He thought I'd suffered enough, here in my Bergentown office, above a Filipino restaurant, no more fancy Round Hill office for me, no, sir. Living above a garage. My marriage in perverse limbo. Roseanne Craig's death on my watch. Joe Stern, my jury and executioner, had decided I'd been punished already. He wasn't going to make it any worse.

And so now what? What was there to do now?

I sat in my office for the rest of the afternoon, no more patients, no rounds until tomorrow. I just sat there, watched the asteroid screensaver jet across my computer screen, knew that tomorrow I would be here again. I clicked on my schedule program. My life would go on as it was. And why I had this instinct I still cannot explain, but it took everything I had not to pick up the phone and call Joe and tell him that his martyrdom was his own goddamn business, it meant nothing to me.

Mina poked her head in once or twice. I nodded at her, pretended to look busy. Monday afternoons I usually went over my files, returned phone calls, did insurance paperwork. I picked up the phone and listened to it hum in my hand.

I wondered how I would explain this to my son. I knew he'd expected me to lose the lawsuit. Elaine had told me so. I'd lose, and then we'd both have lost something and maybe he'd feel the connection? But now his old man was off the hook again. What would he think? He would have preferred it if I'd suffered. Maybe he would have forgiven me if I had truly suffered.

Vivaldi. My cell phone. I looked down, prepared to tell Joe this and more: I could have taken it, whatever he'd dished out.

"Pete? So what happened?"

I took a breath. "Elaine."

"What happened, Pete?"

"She threw it out."

"Oh, Jesus, Pete. Pete! Thank God!"

"I know."

"Why don't you sound happy?"

"I don't know." Why didn't I sound happy? "I guess I'm still taking it in."

"You coming home now? Will you come into the house?"

"Sure," I said. We still had to talk about logistics, procedures. She still had an appointment with the lawyer tomorrow. Well, good. Even Joe Stern couldn't stand in the way of that.

When I pulled up to the studio, I saw a U-Haul parked in the curve of the circular drive right in front of the house, Elaine standing on the porch.

"You're moving out?" I asked. "Or just getting rid of some of my extra stuff?"

"Oh," she said. "Well."

We sat down on the porch steps together. It seemed easier than going inside, and it was nice out again, warmish, not muggy the way it had been over the weekend. Crocuses, rabbits, magnolias. The deer had returned to the lilac patch in the back of the yard.

I didn't know what Elaine was doing with that U-Haul, but I guessed she was taking some of my stuff away, out of the house, finally. Banged-up office furniture. Piles of old magazines. Clothing I hadn't worn in years, or maybe even clothing I still wore. She had the right to get rid of what she wanted, it was her house now, and she could choose what to keep inside it. But I wondered how she'd load up the stuff herself. I wondered if I should help her.

"How do you feel?" she asked me.

"How do you feel?" I returned.

"Relieved, I suppose," she said. "Phil told me that a malpractice case like this could lead to wrongful death if things went astray. Years more legal horrors. More bills."

"I'd cover the bills," I said. "He told you that?"

"You know how your brother can be," she said. "Dramatic. I didn't really think you'd be arrested for wrongful death."

"Me neither," I said. "Although that would have really been the icing."

"It would have." She smiled, and we were quiet for a minute. If she was getting rid of my stuff, then it was probably time for me to find a new place to live, to get out of the studio and find an apartment. There were places in Bergentown for rent all the time, in the second stories of the commercial buildings, above the grocery stores and H&R Blocks. Or now, with the case thrown out, maybe I could even afford a little house, my own little backyard.

"You still look put-upon," my wife said.

"I do?"

"Like you're not happy."

"It doesn't seem right to be particularly happy, even with all this—even with things turning out the way they did."

"You just caught a break," Elaine said.

"I'm not so sure I did." What would a lost lawsuit have meant after everything else that I'd lost? I thought about Roseanne Craig and the smile on her face when she sold us a new car.

"I decided to cancel the appointment tomorrow with the lawyer."

"You canceled it?" I looked at her and saw she looked embarrassed.

"I'm almost fifty-five years old, Pete. I just . . . you know, I just want to stand still for a while. I can't stand any more of this you leaving or I'm leaving or we're selling the house or you're not here anymore and I have to drive somewhere to find you to talk about the things we need to talk about. I don't want to plan for my own retirement," she said.

"Your own retirement?"

"I'm really exhausted, Pete."

Two joggers put-putted up Pearl Street, a man and a woman, and he was pushing a jogging stroller. There must have been a baby asleep inside the jogging stroller. I didn't know these people, but I remembered Alec as an infant and the way, when he couldn't sleep, I would stand up and rock him in my arms, take him outside, walk up and down the street, rocking him.

After a while I said, "I would never make you drive to find me."

She didn't answer.

"I would always take care of you."

"That's not really true, is it?" she said, but then she waved her hand, waved away an argument she didn't feel like having.

"I did not rape Laura," I whispered.

"I know." But she didn't know. And that's why she kept me in the studio: even my own wife couldn't quite believe me. Even after a lifetime of believing in me—there was doubt in our marriage now. There was fear. There was a rumor that had spread as quickly and thickly as lava, smothering our little town of Round Hill, that I had raped Laura Stern. I was an outcast, not because I'd lost Roseanne Craig, but because there were whispers of what I had done to my best friend's daughter, and I could not prove I hadn't done it. There was no lawyer in the world, no matter how much I paid, who could win my trial by rumor. So I'd been kicked out of my office. I lived in a studio above the garage. For months my marriage had gasped for breath. This was punishment for something I did not do, but this was also punishment for letting Roseanne Craig die on my watch. Right is right, and it was true that I'd been very wrong.

Elaine wiped a finger under her eye, but she wasn't crying. Not really. Through all this, I don't think my wife ever cried very much.

"Elaine—"

"Why would Laura lie, Pete?"

"I don't know." I would go through this a million more times if I had to.

"Why were there bloody pajamas?"

"I told you—I told you. We fought. I hit her."

"I know," she said. "You told me." But she would never truly believe me, and she would have to live with that.

"I wish I knew how to feel," she said. "I have no idea how to feel.

All I know is that I'm not . . . I'm not brave enough to start out on my own—"

"It's not about bravery, Lainie—"

"I don't feel like being alone," she said. "That's all."

So tomorrow we would tick on, and tick on, and tick on. The forsythia by the driveway were blooming. The rabbits had eaten the heads off the daffodils.

I looked again at the U-Haul and caught on. "Alec's leaving because you decided not to go to the lawyer."

"Well," she said, "no matter what, he was going to have to leave sometime."

I tucked an errant piece of hair behind her ear, then moved my hand back to my lap. "I suppose he was."

"You were always going to have to let him go eventually."

"He's already gone."

"He might come back someday," she said.

I looked again at the U-Haul, SEE COLORADO in red along its broad white side. My son and all his things. I took a breath; then I put my arm around my wife. We hadn't touched like this in many months.

"I could change my mind one day, you know."

"I know," I said. "That's okay."

We sat like that, my arm around her, feeling her soft, warm skin under her flowered blouse. My wife, my porch, my forsythia by the driveway. I had done enough to lose them all, and yet here they were.

"I'm going to go in," she said. "I'm making stir-fry for dinner."

"Okay."

"There's some white wine in the fridge. One of the bottles from downstairs. I could open it if you want."

"That sounds great," I said. I listened to her walk up the creaky old porch steps, wonderful, wonderful wife, and open the door and close it behind her, and my eye caught the U-Haul again, SEE COLORADO, and again I was so lost.

So NOW I sit on the porch of this old Victorian house we bought twenty-five years ago with dreams of our children and our lives bursting from us, ambition and hope bursting from us. My wife is inside making dinner. There's a bottle of white in the fridge. I close my eyes and lean my head back against the wooden banister that leads from the stairs to our front door. Will I sleep in my old bed this evening? Will Elaine want to join me in the studio? Will she want to make love to me? Will I still have even that?

There's a stomp stomp stomp behind me. A young man with a heavy box.

"Alec," I offer. Of all the undeserved good things that have happened to me today, this is the one I want the most.

"Alec," I say again, getting up and walking toward him. He ignores me, balances the box on one knee while he opens the back of the U-Haul. I am standing next to my son. I haven't stood this close to him in a long time. I watch him heave the box into the back of the truck. The truck is filled with his things—canvases and clothing and palettes and easels. His stereo. His Samsonite. If he holds on a minute, I'll get him the books from the studio. There's that pile of magazines. The short stories his friend left him. If he only hangs on a minute, I'll help him—

"Alec—" I say as he slams the back of the truck shut again. He climbs into the front seat. He's so tall, my son. He's so sure of where he's going.

"Alec—" But it's too late. I watch him turn the engine on and drive away down Pearl Street. He makes a left at the end of the street.

He's heading north, up toward the Palisades. From there, he might be going anywhere. The U-Haul has left a trail of blackish oil on our drive and down our street, and it could lead him back like Hansel if he needs to come back home.

Although right now, at least, he's not going to come back home.

But I cannot, I will not, despair. One day, God willing, my son will understand. He'll have children of his own and then he'll understand. There's nothing a father won't do for his children. He will steal, he will plunder, he will desecrate himself. It doesn't matter, as long as the child is safe. One day, I know, my son will understand this: everything I've ever done in my life—I've done it for him.

ACKNOWLEDGMENTS

I'D LIKE TO first thank the physicians in my life: Dr. Brust, for the fact checking, Dr. Erlebacher, for the great idea, Dr. Gross, for showing me the funny side of obstetrics, and Dr. Grodstein, for being such a terrific father. Thanks, too, to Elliot Grodstein, almost a doctor, every bit my shoulder to lean on. Thanks to the Kennedys, especially Jessie, for her perfect title, spot-on editing, and invaluable friendship. Thanks to my writers and readers: Kelly Braffet, Gordon Haber, Hannah Harlow, Val Kiesig, Binnie Kirshenbaum, Adam Mansbach, and Lisa Zeidner, who not only read my drafts but also made sure I ate dinner. My beloved grandmother, the late Carolyn Edelstein, read an early draft and gave me ceaseless encouragement. Adele Grodstein proved it's possible to be both a wonderful mother and a practicing artist. The Paris American Academy gave me space and time to write, and the faculty at Rutgers-Camden provided sustaining collegiality, especially my friends in the English Department. Dr. Jon'a Meyer shared her illuminating research into neonaticide. Kate Elton and Georgina Hawtrey-Woore showed me how to make a good story better, while Kathy Pories worked brilliantly and tirelessly on this book's behalf. Rachel Careau provided exceptional copyediting, and William Boggess made me smile every time he picked up the phone.

Thanks always to Julie Barer, for every single thing, every single day.

Finally, and especially, thanks to Ben and Natey, for filling my life with love and joy.